THE
BELOVED

By J. R. Ward

THE BLACK DAGGER BROTHERHOOD SERIES

Dark Lover
Lover Eternal
Lover Awakened
Lover Revealed
Lover Unbound
Lover Enshrined
The Black Dagger Brotherhood:
An Insider's Guide
Lover Avenged
Lover Mine
Lover Unleashed
Lover Reborn
Lover at Last

The King
The Shadows
The Beast
The Chosen
The Thief
The Savior
The Sinner
Lover Unveiled
Lover Arisen
Lassiter
Darius
The Beloved

THE BLACK DAGGER LEGACY SERIES

Blood Kiss
Blood Vow

Blood Fury
Blood Truth

THE BLACK DAGGER BROTHERHOOD: PRISON CAMP

The Jackal
The Wolf

The Viper

THE BLACK DAGGER BROTHERHOOD WORLD

Dearest Ivie
Prisoner of Night

Where Winter Finds You
A Warm Heart in Winter

THE LAIR OF THE WOLVEN

Claimed
Forever

Mine

FIREFIGHTERS SERIES

Consumed

NOVELS OF THE FALLEN ANGELS

Covet
Crave
Envy

Rapture
Possession
Immortal

THE BOURBON KINGS

The Bourbon Kings
The Angels' Share

Devil's Cut

J.R. WARD

THE

BELOVED

•THE BLACK DAGGER•
BROTHERHOOD SERIES

GALLERY BOOKS
New York   London   Toronto   Sydney   New Delhi

Gallery Books
An Imprint of Simon & Schuster, LLC
1230 Avenue of the Americas
New York, NY 10020

First Gallery Books hardcover edition April 2024

GALLERY BOOKS and colophon are registered trademarks of Simon & Schuster, LLC

Simon & Schuster: Celebrating 100 Years of Publishing in 2024

For information about special discounts for bulk purchases, please contact Simon & Schuster Special Sales at 1-866-506-1949 or business@simonandschuster.com.

The Simon & Schuster Speakers Bureau can bring authors to your live event. For more information or to book an event, contact the Simon & Schuster Speakers Bureau at 1-866-248-3049 or visit our website at www.simonspeakers.com.

Interior design by Davina Mock-Maniscalco

Manufactured in the United States of America

10 9 8 7 6 5 4 3 2 1

Library of Congress Cataloging-in-Publication Data is available.

ISBN 978-1-9821-8008-9
ISBN 978-1-9821-8010-2 (ebook)

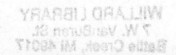

Dedicated to:
You,
an immortal who needed to be brought to life.
She's always going to be a better shot, though.

Glossary of Terms and Proper Nouns

abstrux nohtrum (n.) Private guard with license to kill who is granted his or her position by the King.

ahvenge (v.) Act of mortal retribution, carried out typically by a male loved one.

Black Dagger Brotherhood (pr. n.) Highly trained vampire warriors who protect their species against the Lessening Society. As a result of selective breeding within the race, Brothers possess immense physical and mental strength, as well as rapid healing capabilities. They are not siblings for the most part, and are inducted into the Brotherhood upon nomination by the Brothers. Aggressive, self-reliant, and secretive by nature, they are the subjects of legend and objects of reverence within the vampire world. They may be killed only by the most serious of wounds, e.g., a gunshot or stab to the heart, etc.

blood slave (n.) Male or female vampire who has been subjugated to serve the blood needs of another. The practice of keeping blood slaves has been outlawed.

the Chosen (pr. n.) Female vampires who had been bred to serve the Scribe Virgin. In the past, they were spiritually rather than temporally focused, but that changed with the ascendance of the final Primale, who freed them from the Sanctuary. With the Scribe Virgin removing herself from her role, they are completely autonomous and learning to live on earth. They do continue to meet the blood needs of unmated members of the Brotherhood, as well as Brothers who cannot feed from their *shellans* or injured fighters.

chrih (n.) Symbol of honorable death in the Old Language.

cohntehst (n.) Conflict between two males competing for the right to be a female's mate.

Dhunhd (pr. n.) Hell.

doggen (n.) Member of the servant class within the vampire world. *Doggen* have old, conservative traditions about service to their superiors, following a formal code of dress and behavior. They are able to go out during the day, but they age relatively quickly. Life expectancy is approximately five hundred years.

ehros (n.) A Chosen trained in the matter of sexual arts.

exhile dhoble (n.) The evil or cursed twin, the one born second.

the Fade (pr. n.) Non-temporal realm where the dead reunite with their loved ones and pass eternity.

First Family (pr. n.) The King and Queen of the vampires, and any children they may have.

ghardian (n.) Custodian of an individual. There are varying degrees of *ghardians*, with the most powerful being that of a *sehcluded* female.

glymera (n.) The social core of the aristocracy, roughly equivalent to Regency England's *ton*.

hellren (n.) Male vampire who has been mated to a female. Males may take more than one female as mate.

hyslop (n. or v.) Term referring to a lapse in judgment, typically resulting in the compromise of the mechanical operations of a vehicle or otherwise motorized conveyance of some kind. For example, leaving one's keys in one's car as it is parked outside the family home overnight, whereupon said vehicle is stolen.

leahdyre (n.) A person of power and influence.

leelan (adj. or n.) A term of endearment loosely translated as "dearest one."

Lessening Society (pr. n.) Order of slayers convened first by the Omega, and now by his son, for the purpose of eradicating the vampire species.

lesser (n.) De-souled human who targets vampires for extermination as a member of the Lessening Society. *Lessers* must be stabbed through the chest in order to be killed; otherwise they are ageless. They do not eat or drink and are impotent. Over time, their hair, skin, and irises lose pigmentation until they are blond, blushless, and pale eyed. They smell like baby powder. Now inducted into the society by the Omega's son, they no longer keep jars for their hearts, as they did in the past. Women now may be inducted.

lewlhen (n.) Gift.

lheage (n.) A term of respect used by a sexual submissive to refer to their dominant.

Lhenihan (pr. n.) A mythic beast renowned for its sexual prowess. In modern slang, refers to a male of preternatural size and sexual stamina.

lys (n.) Torture tool used to remove the eyes.

mahmen (n.) Mother. Used both as an identifier and a term of affection.

mhis (n.) The masking of a given physical environment; the creation of a field of illusion.

nalla (n., f.) or *nallum* (n., m.) Beloved.

needing period (n.) Female vampire's time of fertility, generally lasting for two days and accompanied by intense sexual cravings. Occurs approximately five years after a female's transition and then once a decade thereafter. All males respond to some degree if they are around a female in her need. It can be a dangerous time, with conflicts and fights breaking out between competing males, particularly if the female is not mated.

newling (n.) A virgin.

the Omega (pr. n.) Malevolent, mystical figure who previously targeted the vampires for extinction out of resentment directed toward the Scribe Virgin. Existed in a non-temporal realm and had extensive powers, though not the power of creation. Now eradicated, and replaced by his son, Lash.

phearsom (adj.) Term referring to the potency of a male's sexual organs. Literal translation something close to "worthy of entering a female."

Princeps (pr. n.) Highest level of the vampire aristocracy, second only to members of the First Family or the Scribe Virgin's Chosen. Must be born to the title; it may not be conferred. Have been outlawed by royal decree, but underground factions do exist.

pyrocant (n.) Refers to a critical weakness in an individual. The weakness can be internal, such as an addiction, or external, such as a lover.

rahlman (n.) Savior.

rythe (n.) Ritual manner of asserting honor granted by one who has offended another. If accepted, the offended chooses a weapon and strikes the offender, who presents him- or herself without defenses.

the Scribe Virgin (pr. n.) Mystical force who previously was counselor to the King as well as the keeper of vampire archives and the dispenser of privileges. Existed in a non-temporal realm and had extensive powers, but stepped down and gave her station to another. Capable of a single act of creation, which she expended to bring the vampires into existence.

sehclusion (n.) Status conferred by the King upon a female of the aristocracy as a result of a petition by the female's family. Places the female under the sole direction of her *ghardian*, typically the eldest male in her household. Her *ghardian* then has the legal right to determine all manner of her life, restricting at will any and all interactions she has with the world.

shellan (n.) Female vampire who has been mated to a male. Females generally do not take more than one mate due to the highly territorial nature of bonded males.

symphath (n.) Subspecies within the vampire race characterized by the ability and desire to manipulate emotions in others (for the purposes of an energy exchange), among other traits. Historically, they have been discriminated against and, during certain eras, hunted by vampires.

talhman (n.) The evil side of an individual. A dark stain on the soul that requires expression if it is not properly expunged.

the Tomb (pr. n.) Sacred vault of the Black Dagger Brotherhood. Used as a ceremonial site and, previously, the storage facility for the jars of *lessers*. Ceremonies performed there include inductions, funerals, and disciplinary actions against Brothers. No one may enter except for members of the Brotherhood, the Scribe Virgin's successor, or candidates for induction.

trahyner (n.) Word used between males of mutual respect and affection. Translated loosely as "beloved friend."

transition (n.) Critical moment in a vampire's life when he or she transforms into an adult. Thereafter, he or she must drink the blood of the opposite sex to survive and is unable to withstand sunlight. Occurs generally in the mid-twenties. Some vampires do not survive their transitions, males in particular. Prior to their transitions, vampires are physically weak, sexually unaware and unresponsive, and unable to dematerialize.

vampire (n.) Member of a species separate from that of *Homo sapiens*. Vampires must drink the blood of the opposite sex to survive. Human blood will keep them alive, though the strength does not last long. Following their transitions, which occur in their mid-twenties, they are unable to go out into sunlight and must feed from the vein regularly. Vampires cannot "convert" humans through a bite or transfer of blood, though they are in rare cases able to breed with the other species. Vampires can dematerialize at will, though they must be able to calm themselves and concentrate to do so and may not carry anything heavy with them. They are able to strip the memories of humans, provided such memories are short-term. Some vampires are able to read minds. Life expectancy is upward of a thousand years, or in some cases, even longer.

wahlker (n.) An individual who has died and returned to the living from the Fade. They are accorded great respect and are revered for their travails.

whard (n.) Equivalent of a godfather or godmother to an individual.

THE
BELOVED

CHAPTER ONE

Rural Route 149
Caldwell, New York

I gotta bad feeling about this."

As Mickey Trix's cousin spoke, he wanted to beat on the fucker, but it was his own damned fault. Why had he thought bringing the deadweight on a hit was gonna help anything?

"Mickey, you hear what I say—"

Overhead, lightning rippled across the night sky and the snowy forest came alive, the bare branches of the trees turning into arms that reached forward to grab, the knee-deep drifts reflecting the all-wrong flash back to the freaky storm. When everything went darker again, Mickey had a split second of double-thinking himself. It was fucking January. You didn't get thunderstorms in—

"Shut up." He searched those trees, which seemed to stalk instead of stand still on their root systems. "Fuck, why you always talking—"

"Where are we—"

Mickey turned on the dumbass as thunder rumbled. All the fucking snow made the landscape glow so he could see too much of his cousin's weak-dick chin and beady little paranoid peepers. The ski mask he'd given the fool was wedged up over a set of thin eyebrows, the layers of black wool a crown of bad intent that on anyone else would've been a warning that shit was about to go down. On Evan? It just covered up all the premature balding.

Even his fucking hair didn't want to be around him.

And who the *fuck* couldn't grow eyebrows. Even cue-ball-bald SOBs had eyebrows—except for when they had that shit, what was it called?

Alpaca.

"Mickey, we gotta turn back. I gotta bad—"

Mickey slapped that crap into silence, hard enough that his palm vibrated inside his glove. "I got business here, and you want to get into business, so we're coming to take care of business, you fuckin' *asshole.*"

As snowflakes swirled, Evan put his bare hand on the side of his face. "Why you gotta do that shit?"

"'Cuz you're doing *this* shit." He motioned back and forth between them, the sleeve on his parka flapping. "Now, come the fuck on. *Fuck.*"

Stomping off through the snow, he was not about to tell an adult male that he needed to put his goddamn mittens on. Besides, if Evan got frostbite, he probably wouldn't even know what it was.

Ten fucking years, Mickey thought. Ten years and he was getting nowhere in the organization or with their uncle. He was twenty-nine years old, still roughing up idiots who didn't pay when they lost at the book, still pushing small bags on the street. His pops had run the family at this age, and had been in charge right up until the old man had been shot twelve times on 19th Street.

Mickey was the fucking son of a legend, and there was a birthright to that. If his pops hadn't been murdered over that territory dispute with the Southend gangs, Uncle wouldn't be more'n a second-in-command of some crew on the secondhand side of the river—

Snap.

Mickey froze and scanned the woods.

"WhatwasthatohmyGod—"

"I stepped on something." If he hit the guy again, Evan was likely to start crying. "Fuck, relax."

As another lick of lightning flickered down, Mickey searched for true movement in the forest, not the shit that was an illusion. It was hard to tell, so he was going to stay where he was . . . until he was sure what was around them was safe. Well, safe-ish. Who the fuck knew what kind of booby-traps could be out here?

"Mickey, I know what you're doing—and we don't want to mess with him."

Scanning. More scanning. "I'm just gonna pay the guy a little visit. Talk to him."

"You're not here for conversation." When Mickey glanced over his shoulder, Evan's eyes narrowed like he wasn't completely stupid. "I'm not completely stupid."

Time to get moving again. "Whatever."

"Why don't I get to have a gun? You never let me carry a gun." Evan tapped him on the shoulder. "C'mon. Let's not do this—"

"You know what—just fuckin' go." Mickey took out the key remote to the car they'd left up on the county road. "Wait for me like a pussy, while I do the work."

"I'm not leaving you." Evan shook his head. "I know nobody thinks nothin' of me, but this guy, he's dangerous. There's something wrong with him."

"He's just another one of Uncle's enforcers."

"No, he's not. And you brought me 'cuz you know nobody else would come with you."

No, Mickey thought. He'd brought Evan because nobody else listened to the guy. But trading that kind of go-nowhere-gossip for what was supposed to be halfway decent backup wasn't working too good.

Punching the remote into his cousin's chest and holding it there, Mickey leaned in. "I'll handle this. Like a man. You go wait in the fucking car. Like a goddamn child."

Lightning fanned out across the base of the cloud cover again, and in the icy blue reflection, the fear on Evan's face was like a third person standing between them.

"Go on," Mickey ordered as his own resolve wobbled. "You're so fucking *weak*."

"I had a dream last night—"

"I hope she was good-looking." Mickey pushed the car fob into the front pocket of his cousin's parka. "In real life, you're only pulling shit."

"You're gonna die, Mickey."

"Great. At least then, I'm not dealing with you."

"You don't have to prove yourself to Uncle, you know. You're enough as you are—"

Mickey shoved at his cousin's shoulders, knocking him backwards into the snow. "Fucking *asshole*. I don't have to prove myself to nobody."

It was a goddamn relief to turn away—until he realized he was making a lot of noise with his heavy breathing, and that wasn't the smartest move. He was also letting the pissed-off get the best of him, and that was not only dangerous, it put him on Evan's basement-level, low-fi operating mentals. He was better than that.

He was the son of the rightful head of the family—

As movement registered in his peripheral vision, he glanced over his shoulder again. Evan was up on his feet, snowpack falling from his ass in clumps like he was taking a shit and it was coming out in black and white. With his hands tucked under his chin like he'd seen the boogeyman and his eyes all anime-tragic, Mickey was reminded that just because you were related to someone didn't mean you had nothing in common with them.

Leaving his cousin, he needed to keep his focus where it had to stay so he put his hand into the front pocket of his snow pants. The USB drive was right where he'd stashed it, ready to be used in the second half of this operation. A gun to the head of some techie had gotten the job done, a fake data trail created on the blockchain making it look like bitcoin had been stolen on a large scale from the family's digital wallets. He didn't need to understand how or what was being typed on that fucking keyboard or scrolled on that monitor. All that mattered was that his instructions as to the outcome were followed, and he knew they had been: He had the IT guy's wife tied up in his secret apartment on 21st Avenue—and hey, he was gonna let the Mrs. go, as long as his uncle came to the right conclusions when Mickey "found" the drive and turned it in—

A shot of paranoia had him glancing around, and he expected to see Evan trailing after him like a beat-down dog.

Nothing. Other than the gnarled trees, looking like they were an unholy army sprung from contaminated ground.

Fine, at least he didn't have to worry about the dummy.

With the storm's light show and grumbling guiding him, he kept going, pushing branches out of his way. When one snapped back and caught him in the ass, he wondered why the bastard he was going to kill tonight wanted to live out here in the fucking sticks. Then again, "Nathaniel"—chrissakes, what a street name to pick—was fucking weird. Never said much. Didn't mix with nobody. Didn't fight for the good jobs. Youda think he wouldn't be no problem, but Uncle liked the guy too much for his being an outsider. Hell, for being anybody. Natty-whatever-the-fuck was getting assigned the eliminations, the real work, not the banging-on-doors, nickel-and-dime runs.

Mickey hated to admit it, but the slick SOB knocked people off and got away with it like nothing no one'd seen. Last seven years or so? There was no counting the bodies, and there were ones who hadn't been found, no doubt. Most of the wet work had been done in Caldwell, but there had been some in NYC and Boston. Rumor had it that Uncle had asked him to go down to Florida and South America, but he'd nope'd the out-of-town trips. It was like he didn't want to get too far away from the core of the business, and sure, it could be 'cuz he had the Caldie cops in his pocket and that was how he'd evaded complications for so long.

Except it was more than that. Mickey could sense something just wasn't right, and he was done fucking worrying about it. Time to solve this problem and look like a hero to Uncle—

Up ahead, a ratty old log house appeared in a clearing, and talk about dumps. The place needed to be condemned, the roofline bumpy, one of the chimneys collapsed, shutters with evergreen cutouts hanging like bad teeth in the mouth of a suck-ass MMA fighter. The windows were boarded up, there was no car in the shallow drive, and the barn out back wasn't in any better shape.

If Mickey hadn't been one hundred percent sure of his intel, he wouldn't have believed anybody lived here, much less a hired killer. Then again, keeping a low profile was something Uncle appreciated in his contractors.

"But this shit is frontier land," Mickey muttered, his breath drifting off like he was vaping.

Fucking. Weird.

And not something he needed to think about. At the moment, Nathaniel was downtown with Uncle. Mickey was sure because he himself wasn't invited to the Thursday-night hangouts. So he was going to get in this crappy cabin, wait for good ol' Natty to get home, and then one bullet later, he was going to take the USB drive to Uncle and provide proof that the golden boy wasn't so golden, and Mickey was a fucking family hero who deserved respect—

His body stopped on its own, no conscious thought involved in the lockdown, every survival instinct he had starting to scream.

Someone was behind him.

And it was not Evan.

Trying to stay cool, he snuck his hand to the gun holstered just inside the hem of his parka. "You're not supposed to be here right now."

As he turned around, he brought the . . . weapon . . . out . . .

Tattoos. All over a bare torso that had more muscle in its pecs and arms than Mickey did in his entire body. With a freshly shaved head, a face that made women double-take and drop digits, and a six-inch wound that had been stitched closed by an amateur on his shoulder, Nathaniel was like a lifer in a prison yard. Or someone who should have been kept behind barbed wire for public safety.

"Where are your clothes," Mickey mumbled as his head started to hurt.

Another round of lightning burst free of the storm, and if he'd lived, he never would have forgotten what those eyes looked like as they met his own: Dead. Nothing behind them. The blue so dark it was like staring into black glass, and in the reflection? Mickey's own horrified face.

In that moment, he knew he should have listened. Not to idiot Evan, but to his own instincts, back when he'd gotten out of the car, up on Rte. 149—

"Uncle sent me," he mumbled, trying to course correct. "He tried to reach you. When he couldn't get through, he sent me. You want we go into your place while I tell you what's goin' on?"

Nathaniel lowered his head, those dangerous, gleaming eyes staring out from under the kind of brows real men grew, the kind that were a warning well-heeded on their own, no ski mask required.

"You're lying to me, Mickey," came the low voice.

"No, I ain't." Wincing, he tried to get his thoughts to pull together. "Sorry, I'll lower my weapon. We family, right."

"I hate liars."

"Me, too."

More lightning flashed—no, wait. It was a car, coming down the lane, the headlights making noon out of midnight, the log cabin worse for wear in the glare. When Mickey looked back to his uncle's favorite assassin, something swept by, close to his face. Jerking away, he went to slap off that which had already moved past him—

The gurgling was like someone draining an oil pan in an old-fashioned, gas-powered car, and he had no idea where the hell the sound was coming from. Until he tried to breathe.

Dropping his gun into the snow, he clapped his hands across his throat and felt a flow of warmth, smooth and thick as hot chocolate. "Wha . . ."

Nathaniel held a blade up and regarded the bright red blood on the stainless steel. Then he extended his tongue, stared across the cold glow into Mickey's eyes . . . and licked up the blade.

No, no, nonononono—

"Tastes like a liar. What's in your pocket, Mickey."

Mickey stumbled backwards—but he didn't fall back into the snow-pack like Evan, dumb, dipshit Evan, who had been so much smarter than him. Instead, he was caught by a grip on his shoulder, and then he and his killer were face to face—

The pain in his gut came quick and he looked down, wondering numbly how the lightning had found his stomach. But it wasn't the storm. A fist was pressed right against his abdomen, his parka puffing up around where he'd been stabbed so deep, the blade that had been stroked by his killer's tongue inside of him to the hilt.

The gurgling got worse, as there was a sudden pressure on his shoulder, a pushing down, after which the sawing started: in and out, in and out, the knife working upward through his internal organs, heading for his sternum. Mickey tried to scream, but with his windpipe sliced open, he couldn't call for whoever had just parked at the cabin and gotten out from behind the wheel.

Help . . . me . . . Mickey reached toward the person in the darkness, the blood on his glove dripping into the virgin snow. *Help . . .*

"Nate!" The man with the car strode up to the rickety front door and banged on it. "Where you at?"

Mickey's vision dimmed, like a veil had been pulled over his face. *Help me . . .*

He mouthed the words because there was no talking for him. No air in his lungs, no vocal cords. No . . . anything.

"Nate, we're late," the guy at the door hollered. "Come on, it's time to go."

Mickey Trix's last thought was that he wished he had turned around when he'd had the chance.

His stupid cousin, for once, had been too right.

CHAPTER TWO

The BDB Underground Housing Complex, a.k.a. The Wheel
Suburbs of Caldwell, New York

The Black Dagger Brother Zsadist, son of Ahgony, mated of the beloved Bella, sire of Nalla, fucking hated cell phones. He didn't like all the notifications, the vibrating, the *bing'*ing, the ringing. Also, they were breakable, and every two weeks, you had to charge them. Worst, he was required to carry one.

He hated being forced to do anything, especially when the albatross came with a marching band of irritations.

But there was another reason he despised the Samsung. As it went off with a text, he finished holstering his black daggers on his chest, picked up the unit from the midst of his weapons, and cursed at the images that had been sent to members of the Brotherhood and the fighters who stalked the night along with them.

Annnnd there it was: Never good news.

Another murder scene with contractor buckets from Home Depot, puddles of black oil on a concrete floor, and no bodies—because everything that had been killed had been reanimated and walked the fuck back out onto the streets of Caldwell. To hunt vampires.

He checked his old Timex—

"I thought you were off tonight."

He glanced across from the display of gunmetal on the kitchen counter-top. Over in the living area, standing beside his baby grand Steinway, Bella was in her favorite robe. No fussy silk for his *shellan*. She was in the flannel one that she'd given him last year when they'd all celebrated the humans' Christmas. He never wore it, but not because he didn't like the gift.

All that Black Watch tartan had better things to cover than him.

Pulling his leather jacket over what was on his pecs, he regretted arming himself here. He didn't like his female anywhere near his SIG Sauers, his explosive packs, the length of chain he wore around his shoulder when he was in the field.

"I love the way you look in that robe," he said as he stepped around the center island and blocked her view with his body.

His mate pushed some of her gleaming brown hair back and fiddled with the tie at her waist. "It was supposed to be a gift for you."

"Everything I have is yours."

Bella smiled, her blue eyes warming. For a moment, he went back, way back, to the first time he'd seen her down in the gym at the training center under the mountain. He'd been alone with just a punching bag and his inner demons. She'd stepped through the door . . . and brought the world to him.

Then again, she *was* his world.

Even now, after decades, he still felt like the luckiest male on the planet, in spite of what he'd been through back in the Old Country, and the triggers that still stalked him, and the separation from people that, no matter how many times he talked things through with Mary, he couldn't quite shake.

"Why are you looking at me like that," Bella murmured.

"You're unforgettable."

His mate laughed. "Shouldn't that mean you don't have to stare?"

"On the contrary, you always catch my eye."

Bella leaned to the side to see around him. "Your phone is ringing."

"Is it."

He walked over to her, a predator brought to heel by the female who could overrule even his kill instinct with just a whisper. Brushing his dagger hand over her hair, he followed a strand down onto the robe's collar, which she'd turned up against her throat. Peeling back the soft flannel, he inspected the bite mark over her jugular.

And felt a familiar shaft of self-hatred puncture his lungs.

She kissed his hand, sending a shot of pure lust into his gut. "I'm perfectly fine, and you know it."

"I should have been more gentle when I mounted you."

"I would have been disappointed," she shot back in a guttural voice. "You were hungry and I wanted to feed you. That is not the time to be gentle."

Between one blink and the next, he saw her sprawled out on their bed, her breasts rosy-tipped from his mouth working them, her legs spread, her sex swollen, glistening. He'd loomed over her, his arousal in his hand, his fangs descended, his hunger sharp as a blade. Even though he'd been dizzy with the need for her blood, he'd slid into her first, before he'd taken her vein. He hadn't wanted her to feel even a pinch.

"Your phone is—"

"Always ringing," he cut in. "The war can wait."

Z followed the lapel down to the tie that circled her waist. Under the folds of flannel, which were rough compared to the feel of her satin skin, his *shellan* was gloriously naked, and every time he breathed in through his nose, he smelled his own bonding scent on her body—which was the purpose of it. She was marked as his, and other males of the species would recognize instantly that she was claimed. It didn't mean she wasn't her own person, with her own choices and life. It did mean that if you fucked with her? You were going to know who was coming after you with their bare hands.

Oh, and even though he'd had her just twenty minutes ago, his sex thickened behind the button fly of his leathers.

"I want to be in you again," he said softly. "I like it when you come and I can feel it."

Lowering his head, his upper lip curled off his fangs in a way that pulled at the scar that curved from the bridge of his nose, onto his cheek, and down to the corner of his mouth. Even though he knew he was ugly, even though he was marked with the tattooed bands of a blood slave at his wrists and his throat, even though his back was roped with the whippings his mistress had given him . . . somehow Bella always saw beneath his surface, to that place that no one else, even his brothers or his own daughter, got to go inside.

His mate could have been his *pyrocant*.

Instead, she was his savior. His *rahlman*.

With a graceful arch, Bella rose up onto her toes and pressed her lips to his. "I like when I smell of your dark spices. When you go, you're still on me—"

His phone interrupted again and he squeezed his eyes shut. "I swear to *fucking* God, I am going to stab that thing."

"I think you have to answer it." She lowered herself down, her hands resting lightly on his leather jacket. "Someone needs you."

"Do you really want to ruin this moment."

"No, but I want to know what's going on that they're calling you so much."

"You and Nalla are safe here."

"Yeah, and you and the Brothers are always out in the field, and our daughter leaves this house every weeknight to go to work. You know how much I worry about her, even if she hates it—and don't get me started on you out fighting those undead monsters."

Z repositioned the collar back where his mate had it, then tucked the robe's folds tighter over her sternum.

"Tell me," she ordered.

He hated the war even more than he hated phones. Then again, the two were intertwined. No matter how much privacy he and his mate had here in the quarters they shared with their daughter, there was always an interruption looming, and again, never for a happy reason. Always death and pain and fighting and the reality that some night, he might never come home—some night, that bed they shared might become only hers, his scent on the sheets and her skin nothing but lingering proof that yes, he had lived imperfectly, but he had loved her to perfection, and their daughter was an echo of him to haunt her and keep her going by turns.

Wrath's death had shattered the illusion that dice could be endlessly rolled, and thirty-three years later, they were all still grieving in the aftermath.

"Don't hide the truth from me, Zsadist. That's not fair."

As he thought about responses, he decided that in his next life, he was coming back as an accountant. So when his mate asked how hard his work was, all he had to report was that his calculator broke and someone reheated cod in the break room's microwave.

"We've found another induction site." *Fucking Lash. Just like his father, capable of turning humans by the dozens.* "And it's a big one."

"Where."

"Downtown. So nowhere near here or Luchas House. Don't worry, no one is getting anywhere near Nalla's work."

She closed her eyes for a heartbeat. "Who are you going out with?"

No one. "Tohr will meet me there." *Eventually.* "Even with the trainees and the soldiers, we're stretched thin, so I have to go."

"You'll be careful?"

"Always." He kissed her forehead, pressing his lips just below the off-center part her dark hair always seemed to find. "I'll be home before dawn."

She stared into his eyes, into him, like she was trying to see the future. Or maybe influence it. "The war is heating up again. And I . . ."

It wasn't hard to read her mind. "Nalla will be okay. I promise."

"Even when she's out there, in the night?"

With a low, vicious tone, he vowed to his mate, "I will destroy anything that hurts her. Or you. Never doubt that."

As he pulled his *shellan* into his chest, he felt the shudder that went through her body just as his phone started ringing some more, and so help him Lassiter, he wanted to scream. *One night.* All he'd wanted was one full night off from the nasty business he did to protect the species.

"I try to talk to Nalla, but she won't listen to me," his *shellan* said against his pec. "I don't think she even likes me, at this point."

That makes two of us, he thought.

Easing back, he hated the way his *shellan's* eyes were watery, her fear just under the composure she was fighting to keep in place, her sadness like a gray veil draping her beautiful face.

"I'll sit her down," he said. "Again."

"She's at Auntie Beth's—"

He bared his fangs and hissed at the phone.

Breaking away, he went back to the table. "God*damn* it."

Shoving one of his two autoloaders aside, he grabbed the fucking thing and swiped right on the screen. "*What.*"

I-87, a.k.a. the Northway, southbound
3.4 miles from downtown Caldwell

"You gonna tell me why you were half naked in your side yard?"

As Shuli tossed the question out, he glanced across the interior of his newest Tesla. The stiff sitting on the passenger side of things was looking like he'd been taxidermied before getting strapped into the shotgun position. But the male was breathing.

Okay, he was pretty sure Nate was breathing.

"Well, at least you're in my car. When was the last time we went out?"

Although given how much fun this trip in from the sticks had been? He was wondering why he bothered.

When he only got more silence and the angular profile of what had once been his best friend, Shuli refocused on the three lanes of the

Northway up ahead. Traffic was light, and the auto-driving feature handled easily what was mostly eighteen-wheelers running the route from the Canadian ports to New York City.

"I'm not sure you living out there alone is doing you any good. You've turned into a recluse."

He looked over again, and remembered when the guy hadn't insisted on shaving his head. Not that the bald was a bad vibe. Then again, nothing short of a paper bag over those cruel, handsome features would fuck up the ten out of ten. Too bad the personality was what it was.

"It's a public service."

Oh, look. It talks, Shuli thought.

"You don't care about the public."

Nate shrugged, his thick shoulder shifting under the seat belt. "I'm not saying I care one way or the other. It's a statement of fact."

Thank Lassiter the downtown Caldwell exits started appearing, and Shuli debated which one to take. The first couple dumped out onto a bunch of one-ways, and he wasn't interested in fighting the surface road traffic lights for two miles. The next grouping funneled into the Financial District. Bathe, the club they were going to, was down on 16th on the far side of the skyscraper forest—

Fuck it. He disengaged the auto-driving and got off early because hitting the turn signal and playing with the steering wheel would distract him. From the silence.

Why was he wasting his time with this?

When the traffic signal at the bottom of the exit ramp was red, he drummed his fingers on the windowsill and wished he were still going seventy miles an hour.

"If you're this bitched," Nate remarked, "you coulda just left me where you found me—"

"Do you have *any* idea what tonight is?"

"Thursday. We're both off rotation—"

"It's my fucking birthday."

He didn't bother looking over because he knew when he saw all the no-reaction, it was going to make him feel like even more of a pussy, and that was not the kind of present he was interested in. Nice bottle of wine? A blow job—not from Nate. Some cake and coke? Great.

This bullshit? Hard pass.

"You were my best friend for a long time." Or more like, a long time ago, he amended. "People go out for birthdays. Their buddies come and people drink. There doesn't necessarily have to be presents or balloons. Just a good time."

The light turned green, and as he pressed down on the pedal, their acceleration was smooth and quiet, the headlights illuminating the double-laned one-way. Two blocks up, he hung a right onto a both-way four-laner. Like the highway, traffic was spotty, only the occasional car pulling out of a parking garage, most of the vehicles flowing with him on a thirty-mile-an-hour tide in between sixty-floor-tall glass spears. The sidewalks were empty because of the midnight and the cold—

A lone pedestrian approaching on the left-hand side of the road got his attention, and not because of the solitary thing. The figure was dressed in black, and it wasn't so much their size, it was the way they walked, with head lowered, shoulders forward on their hips, each footfall a punch through concrete into the earth itself: An animal, on the hunt, not a human out for a walk.

Shuli frowned as he recognized the scarred face in his headlights. The Black Dagger Brother Zsadist.

A frontline fighter, who was so much more than just one of the soldiers in the war like Nate and Shuli. The Brotherhood's training program was great and all; it taught you to shoot with accurate aim, stab with good follow-through, and know your way around bombs, poisons, and basic IT shit. But all that, even with the continuing education and performance reviews, couldn't take the place of the superior blood in that kind of male's veins.

Well, and then there was the Brother's personality disorder. He made Nate look like a fucking game show host. There were rumors about what Z had been like before he'd been mated and become a sire to his daughter, Nalla: murdering prostitutes for sport, killing vampires and *lessers* indiscriminately, living on the fringes because he was off the chain, to use an old expression. Sure, all of the Brothers had darkness in them—Rhage had that dragon with the pica problem, and Vishous had a glare that was like an ice spear, and you really didn't want to get Butch teed up—but Shuli had always worried about Zsadist the most.

Something about the way the male was always off in a corner, watching, made a guy feel hunted even though they were on the same team.

On that note, Shuli's eyes drifted over to Nate's hands. They were resting on the guy's thighs, the long fingers splayed out like he was about to palm up a basketball. Or someone's head before he popped it off the spine like a dandelion. Under the nails? Blood that, going by the subtle copper scent that lingered, was drying slowly.

When Nate had finally come around the side of that crappy log cabin, he'd been wiping his hands off on a whole-ass bath towel, the folds of the terrycloth waving in the flurries and the flashes of lightning. Shuli had smelled the soap, but underneath the Dial, the fresh blood had been obvious.

As it was from a human, he hadn't felt like he had the right to pry, and he'd thought of the rumors he'd heard about Nate working some kind of side hustle with Caldwell's black market. No doubt a reminder that vampires shouldn't be fucking with those rats without tails wouldn't have been appreciated.

So he'd made a joke about running water outside in the dead of winter. Nate hadn't laughed. But when did he ever?

Shuli thought of when he'd first met the guy. They'd both been doing construction on Luchas House, getting it ready for the initial group of residents to move in. Nate had been just out of his transition, and earnest as a goddamn Boy Scout. Now? He was bulked up with muscle, covered in iridescent tattoos, and had last cracked a smile back when AI had been considered a technological advance and paper money had still been a thing.

There had been a time Shuli could have asked the male anything—and only one reason for why everything was different.

"Christ, Nate. Hasn't it been long enough."

"This car ride? Yeah, it has. It's probably the only thing you and I are gonna agree on tonight—"

Shuli slammed on the brakes. As traffic skidded around him and blew their horns, he strangled the steering wheel and stared out over the hood. "Enough."

"I thought you liked this car—"

"Get out." He released the locks and glared across the seats. "I'm done with this tortured loner bullshit of yours. Rahvyn is not coming back to you. She was mated thirty fucking years ago, okay? And she was never yours to begin with. Grow up and get over it."

The change in the other male's stare was split-second, and Shuli couldn't believe the depth of hatred shooting out of his best friend's eyes.

Not that they had been friends for years. Jesus, and he was accusing the guy of not getting over something? He needed to take his own fucking advice.

With profound, but stupid, sadness, Shuli said roughly, "You've lost the plot, man. And I'm done trying to keep you tethered to the planet—"

Flashing blue lights strobed the interior, picking out the hard angles of Nate's face. He was leaned out on account of refusing to feed from anything but the artificial stuff his adoptive human mother had engineered in that lab of hers—and also maybe because he didn't want to concede to anything soft at all.

Probably shit barbed bricks into the toilet bowl.

"Fucking wonderful," Shuli muttered as he looked into the rear view mirror.

"You were the one who decided to park in the middle of the road."

"Fuck you."

In the side view mirror, the cop-bot striding down the flank of the Tesla was one of the new models with the animatronic faces. Shuli didn't know enough about computers to begin to guess at the technology required to project expressions that were non-threatening through plastic skin and a composite metal skull. What he was clear on was that he missed the good ol' days when patrol officers had minds you could manipulate at will.

He put his window down. "Sorry, Officer, my car lost power. It's back on now—"

"Greetings. I am Officer 9017 of the Caldwell Police Department. May I please see your—"

"The car just malfunctioned." Shuli pointed to the screen. "But the glitch in the system's fixed itself, so I'll be on my way—"

"Your license and registration, please."

Even though it was January, the thing was in a navy blue, all-season uniform, with long sleeves but no jacket. They even put wigs on the fuckers, some curly black hair buffering around the base of the CPD-branded cap.

"I'm telling you, Officer, it's cool. I'm just minding my business here."

"I am programmed to remind you that under the Civil Law Code, section one-four-nine-five, paragraphs one and two, all drivers operating a vehicle within the Caldwell city limits are required—"

The gun entered the periphery of Shuli's vision from over on his right—and the muzzle was pointed at him, at the meat of his pecs. Not the nuts-and-bolts of law enforcement.

"What the fuck are you doing," he said in a low voice to Nate.

As their eyes met, he held his breath as he recognized nothing of the male he had once known in the face and stare of the guy sitting in his passenger seat. Then the muzzle shifted a quarter of an inch to the right. The trigger was pulled, and a bullet narrowly passed by his sternum and plowed into the cop-bot officer, blowing him off of his boots.

"Oh, fucking *hell*," Shuli spat. "Are you even kidding me!"

As the patrol car's alarm started blaring, he punched the accelerator, and the Tesla went plaid and then some toward the next intersection. Plowing south through a red light, he played dodge 'em car with the traffic flowing east to west, his ten-and-two death grips wrenching the steering wheel hard left, harder right, less left, *really* right—

It dawned on him that, with Nate still sitting like a fucking statue in his goddamn passenger seat, he was taking the problem with him.

And that was his last thought before he overcorrected, hit a curb, and flipped his fucking car over.

CHAPTER THREE

N o. Just *no*. I mean, really?"

Nalla, blooded daughter of the Black Dagger Brother Zsadist, son of Ahgony, hated to draw the hard line, especially with someone like her best friend. But as she shifted her eyes to the mirror over her bathroom sink, she was too tired to argue while she wiped the condensation off with the heel of her hand. It had been draining to sneak in and avoid her *mahmen*. But what choice did she have? The subterfuge was better than having one of their usual stilted conversations.

Out in her bedroom proper, Bitty, adopted daughter of the Brother Rhage, lost her hey-I've-got-an-idea optimism. The female was sitting on the messy bed, leaning back against the padded headboard, her vintage Baskin-Robbins sweatshirt and well-washed jeans the sartorial opposite of what she was proposing.

"But it could be fun," she said.

Yeah, sure. If they were two different people. Or going to a different place. With different people.

Nalla tightened the tuck on the towel she'd wrapped herself in.

Then she turned around and frowned through the open doorway. "Hey, did you color your hair?"

"Oh, I did, yes." Bitty yanked out the tie and fluffed the lengths around, the reds that had been streaked through the darkness gleaming copper and pink. "Just some highlights. Sabine did it. What do you think?"

The shy pride in the female's heart-shaped face was a reminder that they were not the same.

"I think it's beautiful," Nalla answered gently. Which would have been her reply even if the dye job had been god-awful.

It wasn't, but Bitty didn't need the tinting. With all her dark hair, and a face that didn't need makeup, she had a natural glow to her that was worth so much more than the glamour shit the pick-me females and women plastered on themselves.

"Is that why you want to go out tonight?" Nalla grabbed her brush and started yanking it through her own wet tangles. "There are so many better places to go than Bathe."

Industrial accidents. Active volcanos.

Driver's license renewal lines.

Bitty regathered the waves and twisted the band back on. "That club is where everyone else goes, though."

"Popularity with the group you're talking about is not necessarily a great endorsement, in my opinion."

Ducking her eyes, Bitty focused on her phone. "I don't know why you dislike them so much. We've known them all our lives."

Yeah, well, we didn't choose "them," she wanted to say. The young of the other Brothers and fighters were family, sure. But any human movie about the holidays proved that just because someone was part of your origin story, it didn't mean you wanted them in your happily-ever-after epilogue.

"How 'bout we have a coffee somewhere together?" Nalla suggested. "Or we could go to a movie? *Spider-Man 15* is out."

The female shook her head and turned her phone forward. "We

need to do better than that. It's in the Tenets of Self-Discovery. *Seek the world around us.*"

Nalla gritted her teeth. "You're not still listening to that influencer."

"Influencer? She's a trained life coach, and she's teaching me so much. She isn't some, like, Instagram model. This is a real program for self-improvement."

On the Samsung's little screen, a woman was striding across a purple-lit stage, a mic up to her red-lipped mouth, her free hand waving around like she was trying to catch a bus. The volume was turned down, but it wasn't hard to imagine the message: *Love yourself. Give me $199 a month for this online course. Love yourself even more. Give me $599 a month for personal coaching sessions. Love yourself to the max. Give me $1,999 for this three-day conference.*

Life coach, my ass, Nalla thought.

The idea that some human was parading in Prada, shouting into a low-esteem void and monetizing the mental gymnastics, was offensive. The fact that Bitty, of all people, was falling for it? Ridiculous. The female had a saint's kindness paired with the intelligence of a military analyst. There was nothing she needed to learn from some snake oil salesman in stilettos.

"You could use her help, too, Nalla."

"Excuse me?"

Although maybe she didn't have a right to get so defensive. She'd just come back from Auntie Beth's—and although she'd been urged to try a fresh start with old conflicts on the parental front, the closest she could get to any cleanup was the hot shower she'd just had.

And no amount of loofah had scrubbed off her father's stranglehold on her life.

"I do *not* need that bullshit," she said as she switched her brush to her other hand. "And neither do you. It's nothing more than a cash grab. For godsakes, you're a trained social worker, just like I am. How are you not seeing this more clearly?"

"My background in therapy is how I know she's right about so much." Bitty put the phone aside on the duvet—but face up, so she could glance down like the woman was part of their conversation and Bitty wanted to make sure the Prada-chologist's POV was included. "You talk all the time about change. How you need things to be different in your life."

"The kind of different I'm looking for is *not* going to be at Bathe."

"How do you know? When was the last time you were there? We're both off from work tonight, and for the last whatever, what do we do when that happens? Sit here on our phones—" A *bing!* went off, and that cell was raised again. "Lyric's texted. She's there right now—oh. And so's Mharta. I guess they're all meeting up."

Nalla pivoted back to the mirror, put the hairbrush down on the sink, and went for her Secret deodorant. "There's nothing wrong with a little downtime, especially after the nights we put in with the residents and our clients. Besides, you don't like Mharta."

"Of course I like her, and downtime is all we have."

Pumping out some Clinique moisturizer, Nalla rubbed her palms together and then smoothed the yellow cream over her cheeks and forehead. "You need to stop listening to—"

"And I think you need to start. Resolve to Evolve is a movement. It's helped that many people."

"Is that the best they could do with the tagline?" Nalla looked over her shoulder. "Get real."

"There's a conference coming to Caldwell soon and I'm thinking of going to it. Well, the evening sessions, at least."

Nalla walked out into her bedroom and tried to keep her voice level. "I can't believe I need to tell you this, but personal growth isn't something you can pay for and it doesn't come from YouTube videos you sit back and watch. You need to do the work yourself—and conference? Come on, you're not going to find your life path at some Hyatt Regency ballroom surrounded by humans eating rubber-chicken entrées and taking selfies with that woman. You're also not going to find it at a club downtown where the IQ per square inch is lower than the body count

at the bar, and the people you're going there to meet are a bunch of pretentious, dagger-sniffing partiers."

Bitty frowned. "Do you know how negative you sound?"

"I'm not negative, I'm honest." She went over to her closet and
opened the double doors. "I'm just telling the truth here. I'm not saying
you shouldn't go anywhere or do anything. Even if it's to that club tonight. Just don't hide behind a talking head's prepared speech or think
they're going to make everything a-okay. Go because you want to see the
circus, and then be done with it when you're reminded of how much not
fun you have around half-naked drunk people."

From the built-in drawers, she took out some underwear and put
them on under the towel. Then she bra'd up and tossed on a t-shirt and
leggings. Even though the central heating was on, she added a black sweatshirt for insulation because there was something about January in upstate
New York that made the indoors cold. Even the subterranean indoors.

"I say we hit the Spider-Man movie. There's nothing at that club for
us—" Nalla stopped as she pivoted around. "Why are you putting your
coat on?"

"I'm going to leave."

"You just got here."

"I'll see you tomorrow on shift—"

"Bitty." Nalla put her palms forward, all hold-up. "Wait, you're offended? Seriously."

"I'm not sure what to say to that."

The other female's eyes roamed around the photographs of nature
scenes that Nalla had hung on the walls: A waterfall in the rain forest.
An island in the Pacific. A beach in Spain with the sun at the horizon.

Bitty shook her head. "I just know I'm not happy and I am going to
do something about it."

"Does this have to do with L.W.?"

That stare whipped over faster than a gunshot. "God, no. Why
would you say that?"

Well, reasons. "Fine, since when are you not happy?"

"Awhile now."

Nalla nodded at the phone held so tightly in her friend's hand. "When did you start listening to that woman?"

"You think because I'm interested in waking up within my own life, I'm getting corrupted by her or something?"

"This is just really out of nowhere. You love your job at Safe Place, working with the residents—"

"This isn't about what I do, it's about who I am." She motioned around the room. "This can't be all there is to life. I highly recommend you listen to her—"

"I am *not* about to be preached at by the interpersonal equivalent of an MLM, who's packaged like a savior. I'll take the real thing, not the marketing gimmick, thank you very much."

Bitty looked away. Looked back. "No, you're just going to keep being angry at your father, and stay here all night, stewing in frustration and staring at pictures you lifted off the Internet of places you will never go."

Nalla felt her mouth fall open. "I'm sorry, what did you just say."

"You can't have it both ways. Either you're not meeting someone because the great Zsadist will fucking kill anybody who dates you, or you're too scared to put yourself out there and try to make a life with a partner of your own. But if the latter's where it's at, don't talk to me anymore about how you're on lockdown and you hate it, and don't belittle me for trying to do something for myself."

"I do *not* need a male, thank you very much. And if I did, the kind of mate I would want wouldn't be hanging out down at Bathe with that bunch of hard-drinking assholes."

"They're more than that—"

Nalla pointed to the phone. "Is this what evolving means? You contort yourself and take up alcohol so you can find a mate? Great message—and you have to pay for it, I'm sure. If you want to rethink anything in your life, it's what you're watching on that fucking screen."

Bitty shook her head. "The fact that you're reducing and closing mind to the group of males and females you and I grew up with shows how much *you* need help."

Reducing? Closing mind to . . . "What the hell has that guru put in your head?"

Bitty zipped up her parka. "Like I said, if you're choosing this isolation, fine. I'm just not buying into the idea that martyrdom to your dad's shadow ban on dating is superior to any other form of delusion. At least I'm prepared to leave the house."

As the door banged shut, Nalla glanced around at the pictures that had always made her so happy.

"What just happened here?"

CHAPTER FOUR

T hirty-three years," the great Blind King said softly. "Thirty-three fucking years . . ."

Several underground living units over from where Nalla was standing barefoot in numb shock, Elizabeth, née Randall, mated of Wrath, son of Wrath, sire of Wrath, turned the light off in her own bathroom and leaned against the jamb. Across the shallow space of her little subterranean suite, her *hellren* was naked and stretched out on the twin bed she always slept on . . . and in spite of the way they'd spent the last hour, the sight of his heavily muscled, still semi-erect body was the kind of thing that she kept expecting to wake up from.

How is this not a dream, she thought for the hundredth time as she searched his aristocratic face.

Licking her lips, she could still taste the dark wine of her mate's pure blood, and the burn in her belly was the sustaining kind, something she had not known for—

"Thirty-three years, nine months, and three days," she corrected him. "Not that I was counting."

Wrath's pale green eyes, with their pinpoint pupils, narrowed on the glowing fixture overhead, as if he could actually see the dimmed light. "I was gone *that* long."

"You didn't . . . know?"

He shook his head and appeared to focus on her. "When the explosion went off, I felt the heat and the blast, and thought I was dead." He snapped his fingers. "The next thing I knew, I was walking in snow, up on the mountain at the mansion."

Beth could only shake her head at what Rahvyn had managed to pull off. Then she revisited the past that had, for her, seemed like a lifetime ago. "You saved Fritz's life that night. How did you know to go down to the Audience House?"

Those dark brows tightened. "Boo led me to where a couple of *doggen* were talking. They said he'd gone there even though I'd told everyone that Lash had discovered the location and it was no longer secure. I had this fucking awful feeling something was going to happen. Thank God I got there in time to push him out of the way. And Rahvyn never told you? What she did?"

"She just said I had to trust her." Tears flooded her eyes. "When you walked through my door tonight, with L.W. at your side, it all came together. But it's been . . . thirty-three years and an eternity for me."

"I can't fucking imagine what you've been through. And now that I'm here"—he gestured around the stark bedroom, the expression on that beautiful, harsh face turning tentative in a way she'd only seen once before, when he'd held his infant son for the first time—"I can sense all the years in the change of environment. Everything smells different . . . sounds different. I used to know where I was when we were in the mansion. Here? I'm lost in a forest of doorjambs and furniture, and the passage of time is in each step I blindly take and everything I bump into."

She remembered moving into these underground living quarters, along with the rest of the Brotherhood. There had been a sense of relief that she didn't need to sleep in the bejeweled First Family's quarters anymore, in that king-sized bed they'd shared . . . and also a total despair and ice-cold loneliness that first day when she'd put her head down on the pillow. Thank God George had been with her. Wrath's golden and she had curled up and she had stared at the ceiling for eight hours straight, Beth holding the dog as they'd both remembered the master they had loved so much.

God, that was forever ago, she thought.

At least L.W. had been able to sleep in his crib right beside them, but that was an infant for you. Their needs were fundamental, their awareness basic, and there had been such a kindness to all he hadn't been conscious of back then.

Not that things hadn't caught up to him later, sadly.

"Hidden in . . . time," she murmured. "Like it's something physical you can take cover behind. I'm never going to think of minutes and hours the same again."

"And I'm sure as shit not going to argue with how everything turned out."

Instantly, Wrath's harsh face was transformed by the love he'd always felt for her. Though his fangs were like a saber-toothed tiger's even when sheathed, and in spite of the fact that his black hair falling from that widow's peak was right out of the Dracula catalogue, he looked almost approachable . . .

Okay, fine, her *hellren* didn't appear at all approachable.

He was still an animal underneath a thin, civilized veneer that could be shed like a suit of clothes in a moment's notice. And screw the passage of three decades. He remained the male who had ushered her into who she really was all those years ago, a divine mystery who had done more to define the joy in her life than anybody else, and whose loss had taken all the color from her world. His "death" had destroyed her from the inside out, even as she had continued breathing, and his shocking return was inflating all those places that had suffocated.

How long until I can trust this, she wondered.

"Why are you so far away from me, *leelan*."

As he reached out to her, lifting one of his massive arms, the black diamond in the King's ring flashed, and the tattoos that ran up the inside of his forearm, the ones that detailed his purebred lineage in the Old Language, rippled.

"I'm just enjoying the view," she purred.

And what a view it was.

His waist-length black hair flowed over the pillow she'd laid her own head on, the ends dropping off into thin air and nearly touching the carpet. She thought about what the straight, silken lengths had felt like, draping all around as he'd mounted her, that which had faded from well-worn memories happening in real time, no distillation from recollections required anymore.

That warrior body of his was just the same as well, the muscles that padded his heavy bones marked with veins, his contours so different from her own. When he'd taken her, his weight had pressed her down into the mattress, and as he'd surged on top of her, penetrating her sex, marking her with his bonding scent . . . it had been like the first time.

Better than the first time—

A pain she didn't understand lit up behind her sternum, and she rubbed the spot that hurt. The sensation was familiar, the infection of grief and mourning like a pneumonia that refused to be cured and required her to make effort out of breathing. But if there was any moment she needed to be overjoyed, it was here, it was now. Her nightmare was over.

And yet the sense that this was all a cruel trick of her subconscious nagged at her.

Wrath lowered his thick arm, his pec bunching up from the movement. "I'm sorry. I should have been there for you. For L.W."

With a swipe of her hand, she wiped tears from both eyes. "How are you apologizing for your own death?"

"I can feel your pain like it's my own, and I don't know what the fuck else to do."

Her feet started moving before she even thought about going back over to him. "I'm not hurting. How could I be?"

"You're lying, but I don't blame you for the denial. Here, let me make room for you—"

"I'll just sit down here—"

They both laughed, and she lowered herself into the space he made as he shifted onto his side. Reaching out, she hovered her hand over the curve of his hip.

"Why do you hesitate to touch me?"

She smiled through her tension. "How do you know that when you can't..."

"See?" His black brows tightened over the bridge of his aquiline nose. "You can say it. I'm still as blind as ever. That hasn't changed."

Lowering her hand to his skin, she felt the warmth and smoothness of his flesh, and underneath, the ropes of power that wrapped around the curving bone of his pelvis. Her eyes shifted to his sex as it twitched, even though he had come five times in a row, deep inside of her.

"I just can't believe it's you," she whispered. "After all these years."

He brushed her cheek with his forefinger and rubbed the wetness away with his thumb. "It's a good thing, right? That I'm back."

Beth closed her eyes and turned her face into his palm. "Of course. God, why would you question that—"

"It's okay."

"What is."

"If something . . . if you found someone. You know. Thirty years is a long time."

Beth stiffened. "What the—"

"I mean, I'm trying to imagine what it was like for you. Moving out of the mansion, raising L.W. all by yourself, years going by, then decades. After a while, I wouldn't blame you for looking for some companionship—"

She put her forefinger on his lips. "Shh."

His sensuous mouth moved under the soft pressure she put on it. "I'm just saying. Thirty-three years is a long, long time."

Shaking her head, she went back to the worst scene of her entire life, the one that, in spite of all the grief that had followed, had been the source of her deepest pain: the moment she had been told he was gone. She'd been with L.W. in the young's playroom, their son working with his blocks, stacking them high as he had always done, the one-on-top-of-the-other like a compulsion for him. The door to the bright, cheerful room had opened, and she had known even before the Brotherhood had walked in wearing the black leather of war, and smelling of fresh blood, gunpowder, and *lessers*. But worse? When Tohr had come through them with George. The sight of Wrath's service dog, at the side of anybody other than his master, had destroyed her.

She had screamed until she had lost her voice, and for years afterward, she'd been woken up in the middle of the day by the image burned into her mind of Tohr's dagger hand locked on the grip of George's harness.

No one else had ever touched that except Wrath.

"There was *never* anyone else," she said roughly. "You were never far from me, whether it was in my memory or because I was looking at our son . . . or because I was watching Rahvyn be you in front of all the civilians, keeping the ruse up so that we could hold on to power until L.W. was old enough to rule. And then on top of that I had our son to raise on my own—and he was a handful, trust me. Plus I was ultimately responsible for the species. They all deferred to me—the Brotherhood, the fighters, Rahvyn. The last thing on my mind was sex, especially because it couldn't possibly compare to—"

A masculine chuckle came from deep in her mate's throat. "You say the sweetest things."

"Well, you are very good . . . at what you do," she said with a smile.

But then she thought back to the special kind of hell it had been to watch a three-dimensional, totally corporeal image of her *hellren* take those audiences with the civilians, speaking, blinking, breathing. The decisions had all been hers, whether it was making laws or ruling on cases or setting up precedents, but the mouthpiece had been Rahvyn's.

Or the image Rahvyn had projected.

The two of them had held the throne together, canceling the democratically elected provision for royal appointment that Wrath had put in place, making sure that the birthright was protected as L.W. had matured and gone through his transition.

Except the son hadn't wanted his sire's job.

"I never should have left you that night." Wrath drew his dagger hand down his face. "I shouldn't have gone out."

"Like I said, you saved Fritz's life."

"And ruined yours. L.W.'s."

She shrugged. "Our lives were gone anyway. The instant Lash set that explosive charge on the Audience House's back door, everything changed. If Fritz had died when he'd opened it? What if it had been Tohr? V? Any one of the Brotherhood? You never would have gotten over that. You would have been a different male for the rest of your nights and that would have affected me and L.W. One way or the other, someone's life would have been lost and none of us would have come out unclaimed by grief."

Abruptly, she pictured the Omega's son, the leader of the Lessening Society. Blond-haired, blue-eyed, skin the color of a porcelain sink. She was not one to hate easily, but after what he'd done to her? To all of them?

"Lash is fucking evil," she said. "He was the one who took you from us, who cheated you out of seeing your son grow up—"

As her voice cut out, the shift in Wrath's mood was obvious, even as his expression didn't change: The temperature in the bedroom dropped fifteen or twenty degrees, her body shivering as her breath came out in a cloud.

He hadn't considered that loss yet, she thought. Of L.W.'s childhood. Of the years with her, with his Brothers. He'd been so focused on the impact of it all on her and his son, that he hadn't done the math on everything that had been stolen from him.

And she knew her mate, knew him like the back of her hand.

"No," she started. "Please do *not* try to settle that score."

"It's all right—"

"Don't lie to me now." A claw of pure terror sliced through her heart. "Wrath, I have just gone through three decades of torture. Do *not* make me dread another time lapse like that. I don't have it in me. Especially now that L.W. doesn't need me anymore."

Her *hellren* put his palm out, patting at the air until he connected with her shoulder. Following the line of her neck up, he cupped her face.

"Don't say it," she begged. "Don't . . . do it."

"I cannot let this go. I am the King, and the species is my responsibility. How can I look anyone in the eye if I run from our enemy?"

Breaking away from him, she got up and paced around, noticing for the first time that the white walls were all blank, and there were no knickknacks or personal anything, anywhere. There was only a bureau, a bedside table with her contraband iPad on it, and a set of louver doors into her tiny closet. There wasn't even a dog bed for George, because he always slept with her.

When a light switch and the moldings around doorways were the extent of your decorative art, you knew you didn't care about where you stayed. This suite was like a dorm room before the student moved in. Or right after they moved out.

It was a metaphor for what her life without him had been like.

And now that the color had come back, he wanted to take it away from her by doing something fucking stupid to get back at Lash?

If Wrath hadn't already been dead for three centuries—okay, fine, *decades*—she'd be inclined to kill him all over again.

"You can lead in different ways," she pointed out as she stared at the bedroom door. On the far side of it? The hell of the war. "You don't have to be on the front lines."

"I was a killer before I was a King."

"What about L.W." *What about me?* "You know nothing of him, and maybe he's just needed you all this time."

There was a long pause. "The Scribe Virgin let me see him," Wrath said softly.

Beth pivoted back toward the bed. "What?"

"She met me at the front doors of the mansion. As I went inside, I could . . . see it all. The empty rooms, the furniture covered with sheets . . . the fact that there was no dust on anything even though it was uninhabited."

"Fritz goes back there. To clean."

"Of course he does." Wrath's smile was brief. His frown stuck around. "There was a glow up on the second-floor landing—and that's where I found L.W. in my study. He was sitting on one of the sofas, facing the throne. He was looking at that old carved wood like he hated it. He was not . . . what I expected."

"He's a lot like you used to be," she said sadly.

"That is *not* what I want to hear."

"We used to be so close, he and I. But after his transition . . . the anger came, and I lost him."

"We'll fix that."

"Not easily. I've tried with him, I really have. But kids are not like cars, Wrath. You don't give 'em a tune-up, and send them back out onto the road. Especially if they're nearly seven feet tall and fighting in the field every night."

Her *hellren* let out a soft growl, like he was facing off at someone in his head—whether it was L.W. or a *lesser*? No way of knowing, and neither was good news.

"Wrath." She waited until his eyes swung back in her direction, even though he could not see her. "Do you know why Fritz goes back to the mansion?"

"Because that *doggen* has a cleaning compulsion that probably needs to be medicated?"

"He goes there because he blames himself for your death and it has nearly destroyed him. He cleans those floors and polishes those bannisters and wipes off all the crystal fixtures with tears rolling down his face, until his fingers bleed and his palms are like leather, because he cannot bear what he believes he did to all of us." As her *hellren* squeezed his lids shut, she spoke with an anger that shocked herself. "Do *not* make us go through what we have barely survived. If you love me, if you love your Brothers and the family here, you will not turn a tragedy into a personal vendetta that gets you fucking killed again. You were saved by a stroke of luck. You're not goddamn immortal. And next time, Rahvyn may not be there with her magic."

The deflation in her mate was immediate, his chest seeming to cave in, and she told herself she'd been unfair.

But the war was unfair. Life was unfair.

And reality was ignored at everyone's peril—

Knock-knock-knock.

The sharp impact of knuckles on the locked door made her jump and whirl around.

"Beth," came a familiar voice. "We've got a problem—"

"Tohr?" Wrath said as he sat up in a rush.

As she glanced back at her mate, he was fixated on what was only twelve feet away, the star scar on his left pectoral going up and down as he started to breathe heavily.

"There's nothing in between you and the door," she whispered. "It's a clear shot. And George is still in the bathroom, asleep by the shower."

"Wrap yourself up."

"I already am," she said as she reached for a throw blanket.

Her *hellren* moved with banked power, his thighs contracting in ropes of muscle as he jumped up with a bounce that was all about his coordination—and then extended an arm out in front of himself. The way he walked across the shallow space, so strong and yet so vulnerable, made her feel protective.

As well as furious at him.

"Beth?" came the deep voice on the far side of the entry. "I've been trying to call you—I think your phone's on silent—"

Wrath opened the door. Standing on the threshold, Tohrment, son of Hharm, went silent as his navy blue eyes focused on what was before him—and then that stare shifted over to Beth. As all the color drained out of his face, she nodded once: *Yes, it's really him.*

Like George wanted to make the point as well, he trotted out of the bathroom and went to sit at the dagger hand of his master, leaning into Wrath's thigh.

Time seemed to stand still. Then again, the two warriors had shared too many experiences to count—and they appeared to be reliving each and every one of them as they faced each other.

Tohr cleared his throat. Then croaked, "My Lord . . ."

The two words came out on a strangled breath. And though the syllables of respect, which acknowledged the difference in station between a ruler and a member of the King's private guard, were what was spoken, they were not what was meant.

What they really said was: *My friend . . . my old, dear friend . . .*

Wrath held his arms out and Tohr fell into him like an oak tree whose roots had been severed.

Watching from behind, she rubbed the sting out of her eyes as the two males held on tight to each other. But the emotion wasn't just about the happy reunion. She was going to need Tohr in the coming weeks. Months.

He was the most level-headed of all the Black Dagger Brotherhood, and when push came to shove, he had a way of making enraged, off-the-chain fighters listen to common sense, even when the knuckleheaded, dagger-handed f-idiots were on the verge of a colossal killing spree—

Jesus, she thought with grim humor. If she was thinking like this? Her mate really was back.

"It's good to see you after all this time," Wrath said hoarsely. "Brother mine."

CHAPTER FIVE

Bathe Nightclub
16th and Market Street

Well, at least they got the memo on the water theme.

As Nalla took another step forward in the wait line, she made it to the start of the LCD screen that ran across the front of the single-story building. Pixels of blue and green undulated through a descent, creating a neon glow that from a distance spelled out B-A-T-H-E. Up close, it was a migraine aura on steroids.

Another step forward.

Blowing out her breath in a cloud, she stamped her cold feet and zipped her parka up a little higher. Ahead of her were three women who had on less clothing than you'd wear to a beach. Behind her, more of the same. Interspersed among all the *Bathe*-ing beauties—har, har—were lean men in snazzy suits that looked like knockoff repros of what Uncle Rehv and Uncle Butch wore on the regular.

With a tilt out of the lineup, she tried to gauge how much farther she had to go. Thirty yards? Maybe more. At least the two muscle mountains at the entrance seemed to be fairly efficient out-and-safe'ing prospective drinkers. They were choosy, though. More were sent packing than got in, and she glanced down at her blue jeans. If she was allowed to pass, it would be because they decided she was part of the after-hours cleaning crew.

Just as she eased back, a strange sensation went up her spine. Part warning, part . . . something else.

She twisted her head around. Nothing but human cattle in front of a trough that thumped with music and served up amnesia in a glass with a fruit garnish. Across the street, a Thai restaurant and the cafés on either side of it were closed for the night, so nothing there. Traffic was just a pickup truck and a sedan coming down the—

Her eyes narrowed. From out of the shadows, two men jaywalked right across the intersection, ignoring the traffic light, paying no attention to the vehicles that swerved around them and blew horns. Then again, they weren't men, they were vampires—and the pair were in an argument with each other, the beautifully dressed one on the left slashing his hand through the air as his mouth spit some obviously choice words, the one on the right ignoring the theatrics.

Shuli. And . . . Nate.

It was easy to ignore the former. The latter? Harder. Much harder—and she told herself the way she measured the male was because she so rarely saw him out. Even back about ten years ago, when she'd been making more of an effort to socialize, Nate hadn't made many appearances—and when he had shown up, he'd always stood back from everyone like he was a judge at the asshole Olympics and it was hard for him to decide who was taking home the gold.

He was doing that now. Even as his buddy ranted and raved next to him, Nate's stare was straight ahead, his stride thrown out as if he had somewhere better to be and all that noise directed at him wasn't going to slow him down in the slightest.

Her eyes dipped to his shitkickers. And took their time going up his leather-clad legs and his leather-jacketed torso. He was built like all the fighters were, with heavy shoulders triangled onto a lower body that was also thick with muscles, and try as she might, she couldn't ignore the way he moved.

There were a lot of things he could do with all that weight, and killing was only one of them. With the shaved head, and that hard, hawk-like face? He looked like an assassin closing in on his next target . . .

But maybe he was also a male ready for some rough sex with a partner who liked it that way—

Without warning, Nate stopped in the street and looked down the line at her.

As she sucked in a breath, the quiet sound was like the blare of a car horn—

Oh, wait. That was a car almost mowing him over. Not that he gave a shit. As the front grill of an EV stopped a foot from him, and the driver leaned out of his window to start shouting, all Nate did was meet Nalla's stare.

Not that he seemed any more happy to see her. Did he ever smile?

And now that she could see him like he was on center stage, he was bruised and battered as if he'd already been fighting—Shuli, too. The other male had blood on his fancy suit.

Somewhere, off in the very far distance, she heard the women directly in front of her laugh at some joke, and behind her, there was a whispered curse that may have been a shout. But her ears weren't working right as her eyes took up all of the bandwidth of her consciousness—

Shuli stepped in to the pissed-off driver, all kinds of calm-down motions making the male look like he was trying to fan out a fire with his palms. Which she supposed he was. And then he hooked an arm through Nate's and dragged him away.

With the departure, she felt as though something vital in her had been unplugged, and as a sagging occurred, she realized . . . that she didn't like the guy.

Because she didn't like how she felt when she was around him.

Rubbing her face and trying to convince herself that nothing had just happened, she hated the way she had to recalibrate back to normal and resented the hell out of the male—and herself. Who was he to her? Nobody. And she sure as shit wasn't the kind of female who lost her mind and her own life at the foot of some black-leather'd fighter she didn't know and didn't give a crap about.

She was better than that.

As she dropped her hands from her face, her eyes immediately went back to where he'd stopped in traffic. He and his well-dressed mouth-flapper were nowhere in sight, probably because Shuli had dragged their argument into that alley at the other side of the club.

"God*damn* it," she muttered.

Fucking biology. What the *hell* was she doing even thinking like—

"What the *hell* are you doing?"

As she jumped and looked toward the sharp, disapproving voice, she wondered if the Scribe Virgin had decided to come back to Caldwell and deliver some destiny to her for all the rose-colored glasses her libido kept forcing on her face. Or maybe it was a time-out for getting bitchy with Bitty earlier.

Oh. Great. The night was getting even better. It was not the *mahmen* of the species. It was a six-foot-tall female in a black bodysuit and thigh-high boots, whose sheen of straight blond hair fell to the contours of her absolutely perfect ass, and whose face sucked up all the attention of the men and women around them.

Okay, some of the would-ya-look-at-*that* was no doubt also her spectacular, gravity-defying tits that clearly were not bra'd.

Nalla couldn't even fake a smile. If she was deflated before, she felt positively run over by a sexy semi. "Hey, Mharta."

"Why are you waiting here?" The female sported the expression of someone presented with a particle physics equation and no scratch paper. "We don't wait."

She didn't wait. Mharta could probably get paid to go into the club.

"Come in with me."

Nalla shook her head as so many humans continued to look over. "No, it's okay. If they can wait, I can, too."

"But you don't have to. And if they didn't have to, they wouldn't, either."

"Will you keep your voice down," Nalla hissed. "And you don't know that."

"Are we talking about the same crowd of people here?" Mharta kept her volume right where it was, unyielding in the way the beautiful were—thoughtlessly because they didn't have to be thoughtful. "There are no altruists in this line. Or they wouldn't be trying to get into a club. Now, come on—or are you going to insist I smudge their memories so their fee-fees don't get hurt?"

When her arm was taken and she was pulled out onto the sidewalk, Nalla went along because it was better than continuing the argument in front of the very bunch of frozen-Popsicle Bathe-ers who were being run down. And the fact that both she and Nate were being piloted by someone with a mouth going was the only thing they were ever going to have in common.

So let her little heart cozy up to all *that* romance.

"I don't agree with manipulating their minds," Nalla muttered as they skated down the line.

"Well, aren't you a purist."

"It's an issue of consent."

The female paused and looked over her shoulder, her breath leaving her red lips in clouds that disappeared over her head. "What a human doesn't know—"

"They can't agree to. Just because we can get into their memories, doesn't mean we should."

Mharta laughed. "Well, at least we won't have to worry about the bouncers. You can take that right off your conscience."

As the female resumed her march of superiority, her stride became more exaggerated, all watch-this—and sure enough, as she approached the two big men, they strong-armed others out of the way like they were parting a crowd of concertgoers for the rock star everybody had been waiting for.

"She's with me," Mharta tossed over her shoulder.

All sorts of yes-ma'am spun around like flurries falling from the winter sky, so pleasing—and neither of the men spared even a glance at Nalla's parka or her jeans. And they weren't wincing like their heads hurt, or rubbing their temples, either. So no mental manipulation.

Then again, Lycra over a body like that was its own form of mind control. Especially with men who thought with their little heads as opposed to their big ones.

Inside, Mharta's reception was the same. People got out of the way, and not because they were scared. They were in awe, and even the music seemed to change its bass beat to match tempo with that toe-heel strut.

Must be nice, Nalla thought as she glanced around the dim interior. To dictate the world around you, instead of the other way around—

A human man bumped into her, part of whatever was in the six glasses he had corralled between his hands splashing onto her sleeve. With her super-sensitive nose, it was like taking an inhale directly through the neck of a gin bottle, and as a chaser, he shot her a glare, even though he'd been the one with the swerve.

"Sorry," she muttered because she didn't want trouble. When he kept on going, she rolled her eyes. "And Bitty thinks this is evolving?"

"What was that?" Mharta said while ignoring all the men around her.

Then again, maybe she was blinded by the blue and purple laser beams that shot through the music, ocular superheroes with nothing to save—or how about the floor that glowed, all blue lava without the heat. More likely, she was so used to the attention, it was like the air she breathed, something that was taken for granted even though it was necessary.

One thing about being a social worker? You learned a lot about how people operated, and the Mhartas of the world had a tendency to feed off the adoration they ignored, their boredom with it a calculated shield so nobody knew how much the ones they shunned mattered. Nalla had to try to fix a lot of the problems created by folks with that kind of attitude. In young. In partners who had been mistreated. In parents who were at the ends of their ropes. She did her best not to become jaded, but as somebody who connected deeply with her clients, it was hard not to be.

"Where are we going?" she asked because she didn't like the generalizations she was making in her head. However true they might be.

"You don't know?" The female glanced over, her hair shifting like a silk scarf down her back. "We're behind the velvet rope."

Some distance later, which probably wasn't all that far but felt like a mile or two, Mharta stopped in front of an archway guarded by another pair of bouncers. Unlike at the front entrance, these guys were in black suits and thin ties, and instead of seventy-five pounds of extra muscle and a matched set of don't-fuck-with-me frowns, this twosome looked like they used the pen, rather than the sword, to make their cuts.

And once again the unclipping of the velvet rope—yes, it truly was velvet, and blue—and the brisk nods through were too immediate to have been a mental trick on Mharta's part.

Things were no quieter in the VIP section, but they were certainly less crowded. Instead of all kinds of humans milling around a dance floor where people with little rhythm were having sex with their clothes on, sunken seating areas that could hold a dozen or so I'm-cooler-than-you's populated the floor plan like separate and distinct rooms: Each sectional was bathed—natch—in a different shade of blue. There was robin's egg Tiffany, middle-of-the-road sapphire, a bright teal, a lavender-ish periwinkle.

She didn't need her tour guide's direction to know which one their group had claimed. In the far corner by the emergency exit, there was a black-light glow, the midnight color falling from the ceiling so dense and dark, it was as if a void had opened up to claim the weak of mind and heart.

Nalla's eyes adjusted quick as she focused on the darkness, and she recognized some of the faces: Ahgony and his best friend, Bedlam. Rhamp and his fraternal twin, Lyric. And laying back in a sprawl, yet somehow still taller than the others, L.W., the heir to the throne. There were also others who ran with the pack who she didn't know, even though she'd seen them once or twice before.

No Bitty, though. Christ, if this turned out to be a wild-goose chase . . .

Also no Shuli, who was the leader of the pack, or Nate. Then again, they were probably still going at it out in the alley.

There was a cheer as Mharta's presence registered, and the female went right down into the sunken pit with a round of greeting, hugging and clapping palms, walking that line between it-girl-the-guys-want-to-sleep-with and everyone's-little-sister. Even Lyric looked glad to see the female, the two embracing and then putting their heads side by side so they could talk over the music into each other's ears.

Standing on the top step, Nalla fussed with the zipper on her parka. As the males looked over at her, she reminded herself that she had known most of them her whole life, but as none raised a hand in greeting or smiled, she felt that a door had been shut. Then dead-bolted. Then had a piano pushed against the panels.

Her fucking father. She was so sick of him—

Lyric jumped in front of her. "I'm so glad you're here!"

The female was wearing a floor-length silver dress that swirled around her body, and with her flaxen hair flowing in glossy waves like a shawl, and her heterochromatic blue-and-green eyes, she was like something out of a medieval fairy tale, ethereal and mysterious. As Nalla was hit with a full-contact embrace, her nose was filled with the scent of spring flowers and fresh night rain.

"Come sit down with me."

As her hand was grabbed, there was no saying no, and a seat was prepared when Rhamp was given the boot by his sister. After which . . .

Nalla glanced over at the males who were across a low table. They were staring at her like she was on some kind of criminal watch list.

"I'm here to see Bitty."

She said the words to Lyric. But she was talking at her audience of you're-not-welcome-here—

The emergency fire door behind the seating area flew open, and two people slipped into the club. The entry was so quick, the steel panel under the red EXIT sign closing so fast, that no alarm went off and no one seemed to notice.

"What the *hell* happened to you guys," someone barked.

"The birthday boy's already fighting," came another shout-out. "Let's goooo!"

Yup, Shuli definitely had a gash on his forehead that was leaking, but again, she hadn't been looking closely at him in front of the club.

No, she'd been too busy checking out who he'd been with—and enough with that. There was no reason to fall back into the staring thing. Like Nate was any different up closer?

"I need a drink," Shuli muttered as he limped over, sat down next to Rhamp, and put a stray napkin up to his temple. "It's been a long night even though the bitch just got started."

Nate did not follow his lead. As always he hung back, and in all his black leather, he nearly faded into nonexistence in the deep-blue lighting. Flaring her nostrils, she breathed in, and somehow, even through the smells of the alcohol, the aroused humans, and Lyric's perfume, the scent of the male's own fresh blood registered—

Great. She was looking at him again. But he really was wounded. His palms were scratched raw, and there was something wrong with his shoulder, his left arm sitting lower than his right . . . except suddenly she wasn't cataloging his contusions anymore. In the black light, his neck glowed with iridescent tattoos, and not for the first time, she wondered how far down his body they went. She suspected he had two full sleeves, but whenever she'd seen him, he'd always been in long-sleeved shirts, so she'd never seen more than his inked-up wrists.

Is there ink on his pecs? she wondered. *Covering his chest muscles, fanning out to his powerful arms?*

What about . . . lower.

Even though she didn't want to, she imagined him stretched out on a table, the Black Dagger Brother Vishous leaning over his abdominals, the high-pitched whirring of a tattoo gun—

Nalla stiffened as she met his eyes for a second time, and when his dark brows lowered, she stood her ground and refused to look away. He was just like Mharta, living in his own world, expecting everyone to fit into it on his terms. But screw him. She had every right to be at this godforsaken club—

"Bitty should be here soon."

Nalla forced herself to focus on Lyric. "Yes. Please."

What the hell was she saying.

A drink was offered to her by a human waitress in a white towel and a pair of high heels, and she took it because it gave her something to do with her hands. A sniff told her there was vodka involved and some kind of fruit. She took a test sip and grimaced.

When she glanced back to the fire exit, Nate was looking out over the crowd, his eyes narrowed as if he were searching for something, but his expression disinterested like he didn't expect to find it. Which was a contradiction. Then again, that was him. A quiet male whose every move screamed aggression. A loner who fought for the species, even though he didn't seem connected to anybody or anything. A deadly warrior who trained like he still had things to learn.

His lean face was interesting rather than handsome, the hollows of his cheeks making his jaw seem extra prominent, those brows slashing across the tops of his deep eye sockets, his lips tight with the kind of disapproval that suggested at least he agreed with her opinion on Bathe.

And even as Shuli ordered a round for everyone, Nate stayed where he was on the outside of the sunken area, a watcher, not a participant.

Or more like a disapprovi-ant.

"I'm really glad you came out, Nalla. We never see you anymore."

Lyric sat forward, so earnest, so lovely. And all Nalla could do was smile and nod as the music droned on.

Goddamn, she never should have come.

CHAPTER SIX

N ot with a ten-foot pole. Nope. I like my balls where they are,
thank you very much."

In spite of the thump-bump-pump of the music, Nate
overheard the pronouncement, but he didn't bother deciphering which
of the males seated on the couches below him was doing the talking.
Standing over the sunken sectionals, draped in the dense black-blue
lighting, his eyes were fixed across the VIP room to the opposite corner.

For one, because it was better than noticing that female—what the
hell was she doing here, anyway? For another, the group of humans who
were seated to the immediate right of the velvet-roped entrance was the
reason he'd come.

Fun fact? He really didn't want Nalla anywhere near them. Not that
she was his business.

"You're saying she's not hot," someone else said.

"Oh, she's hot. Like, the slow-burn hot, the one you don't notice
first, but that's got hidden talents, if you know what I mean."

He continued to ignore the conversation, his focus locked and loaded on the silk-suited men who were lounging back like they owned Caldwell. No women with them, but that was a "yet" kind of thing. They were here for sex, scanning the room with restless, slicing stares, their bodies staying on those white leather sofas while their libidos roamed what he'd heard them call the buffet of bitches.

Classy. Real fucking classy.

Nate knew the men by name. Knew also that the one in the middle, who was too old to be in a place like this, surrounded by men fifteen years younger than him, was the one in charge.

It might be Shuli's birthday, but Nate was here because he knew that every Thursday night, Mickey Trix's uncle was in residence at this club: This was where Uncle, as everybody called him whether they were relatives or not, preemptively started the weekends, running his empire while he caught blow jobs from women half his age, his ego pretending like his biological clock wasn't ticking—

"I'd do her."

"Ha! You want to be on the run for the rest of your life? Her fucking father will kill you. Do you know who her—"

"Yeah, I know. And what if I was interested in mating?"

Chuckling followed, the we-share-a-secret kind. "You're a slut. If you ever get mated, the world comes to an end."

Nate glanced down. The three males in front of him were Shuli's buddies, all aristocrats who had that same kind of money, those same kind of clothes, and those flashy watches and exotic cars. They were the set of partiers who referred to sunglasses as sunnies, who drank the liquor that was above the top shelf, and who dated human models before they mated the females their sires picked out just so they could stay in the will.

"You wouldn't have the balls to try her."

"I sure as shit would—"

"I would."

One of the males turned around and looked up at Nate. "How 'bout you? You in?" Then the guy slapped the thigh of the high roller next to him. "He's in. So come on, let's see who has the cajones to ask her out."

"What do we win?"

"What do you think," the aristocrat drawled as he looked Nalla up and down. "If she dressed right, she'd be a bitcoin. *She's* the prize."

Nate's molars gritted as he shifted his attention back to the "prize." Nalla was sitting next to Rhamp's sister, a total mismatch in those jeans and that parka. Then again, she never went to places like Bathe. And no, he didn't agree with how she was being discussed, but he'd heard it before. Everybody had heard it before: Zsadist was going to kill anyone who got too close to his little girl.

So leave her the fuck alone.

It was good advice. And something he didn't need to be reminded of.

Lowering his lids, he tried to make like he wasn't staring. She'd already caught him twice—both out in front and in here—and given the way she'd just glared back at him, he had to approve of how much she obviously didn't like him.

He so approved of her opinion.

So no, he absolutely wasn't rememorizing everything about her, from the way her hair was pulled back into a ponytail, the blond, red, and auburn ends disappearing over her shoulder, a halo of loose curls framing her face . . . to how her features were strong ones, just like her father's, especially her mouth. Her coloring was all Z's, too, those yellow eyes like a cat's in sunlight, her skin smooth and unmarked by freckles or moles.

She was going to leave in a matter of moments, he decided. Bolt the fuck out of here like she was being chased: Her hands alternated between being locked on her knees and rubbing up and down her thighs like she was having to force herself to stay in place. As she checked her watch again, he wondered what she was waiting for.

Except again that, like whatever dumbass dick-posturing was going on in front of him, was not his business.

Taking out his burner phone, he fired up a photograph he'd snapped earlier, and—

"Yeah, I'm totally in," one of the males said. Then he motioned at Nate. "Tall, dark, and tatted is in. You're up for it, too? Good. Let's settle this, boys."

Nate looked up from his cell and frowned at all the high-fiving.

Then he leaned down and clamped a hold on the shoulder pad of the loose-lipped jack-off who'd volunteered him for whatever game they were playing. The guy jumped like he'd been goosed in the ass, and as a set of pale eyes met Nate's, he bared his fangs at the aristocrat.

"Don't you *ever* speak for me again. Are we clear."

With a shift of his torso, he made it so that his leather jacket fell open and the forty he had holstered under his arm caught the black light. The second the message was received was obvious as those *glymera* peepers peeled wide.

"Um, yeah. Cool—"

Shuli cut through the apology, raising up from his seat across the way like he wanted a fistfight. "Will you *fucking* relax, and stop waving that *fucking* gun around."

"That's up to him, not me," Nate shot back.

The aristocrat between them put both hands in the air, stickup style. "No, no, it's good, Shuli. It was my bad. I'm sorry."

Nate straightened and went back to his burner phone, following through with a text under the image of Mickey Trix, who he'd gutted like a deer and left for dead in the ring of trees by his log cabin.

Then he hit send and stared across the VIP section.

Over by the entrance, the receiving cell was obviously on vibrate, as Uncle abruptly dipped a hand into his slick suit jacket and took out a device. He was talking to somebody as he glanced at the screen, and his mouth immediately stopped moving as he checked what had been sent.

The mobster stiffened, his hand whipping out in an STFU to the guy next to him. Then came the rager. Richard Montiere started yelling at everyone sitting around him, jabbing his finger into the men's faces, snarling so that his bulldog-ugly face got even uglier. And just like the aristocrat's submission, all kinds of palms went up with wasn't-me, nope, nuttin'-boss.

Interesting. Unless all those wise guys, including Uncle, had Oscar-worthy acting skills, Mickey hadn't been sent by the bosses.

That was all he needed to know.

With one last look at the female he never, ever wanted to see again, Nate turned to the fire door—

Rahvyn is not coming back to you. She was mated thirty fucking years ago, okay? And she was never yours to begin with.

"Fuck you, Shuli," he muttered.

Punching the release bar, he was slapped in the face with the cold, but he liked the sizzle in his pores and the fresh-ish air: However bad Caldwell's back alleys smelled, it was better than the human sweat stew in the club, and God, he hated the stink of alcohol in his nose.

As the steel panel slammed shut behind him and cut off most of the music, he sent his instincts down both directions of the alley, even though he didn't expect to catch the sweet roadkill bouquet of the enemy. The address at Bathe was a little too good for *lessers*. The field of combat had always been farther west, where the buildings were shitty and empty, the humans less likely to have cell phones, and the city's monitoring project, with all those fucking cameras, had long ago petered out.

The door opened behind him. "Where the *hell* are you going."

He glanced over his shoulder at the non-question. Shuli was leaning out of the club, and the male's expression was as dirty as his white suit, stains of disgust, anger, and frustration marking up all that handsome.

"I told the Brothers we'd be down here." Shuli pointed to his loafers. "They're gonna want to talk to you after that shit you pulled in the middle of Market Street."

Later, Nate would wonder why he went back over to the guy.

Searching his friend's face, he remembered where they had started. He didn't often go into his memory banks as there was nothing good in them, and sure enough, mental images of those early nights after his transition, hammering nails and painting the garage at Luchas House with Shuli, made his chest feel tight.

Especially when he thought about what had happened to make him never, ever go back to that farmhouse again.

"Let me go, Shuli," he said softly. "Just stop trying, okay? Consider it a birthday present to yourself."

For the briefest of moments, Shuli's face changed, the young male he had once been returning. Gone was the Chad-about-town with the swagger and the bitches and the money. In his place? The kid who had just made it through his own change, and was fumbling his way through all kinds of firsts with the kind of discombobulation that made you look for friends. Even in places you shouldn't.

"Yeah," came the rough reply. "I'll do that."

Nate nodded once. "Happy birthday."

He did not look back as he strode off, the sense that he was jettisoning a weight long held making him feel buoyant to the point of being too light in his boots—

He forgot all that emotional bullshit as Evan Montiere, the other nephew who'd trespassed onto his property, stumbled across the head of the alley like he'd been punched in the gut.

Or had maybe witnessed something that had made him sick to his fucking stomach.

CHAPTER SEVEN

Back out in the suburbs, underground, Wrath had something he needed to do before he left, and it was a solo mission. Trying to focus on Beth's directions, stressed like he always got when the war and all the shit that came with it crept into his private time with his Queen, he'd left her bedroom—*their* bedroom—and thought he knew where he was going. It shouldn't have been that hard. The layout of the Brotherhood's private quarters was just like an old-fashioned wagon wheel, spokes of corridors fanning out from a common area in the center to each of the satellite groups of a family's rooms, the whole also connected by a long, circular track that formed an outer rim.

Fucking simple. Except somehow, he got turned around and ended up in the central open area.

It was the first time he had become disorientated in his blindness in forever, and even with George at his side, and the handle of the harness squarely against his dagger palm, he was suddenly floating untethered through the galaxy . . . and never shall return.

"Fuck," he whispered.

Back before he'd gone completely blind, he'd had a little sight: Hazy, blurry, indistinct, foggy, furry, only blinks. But at least he'd had some shapes and shadows, could tell the difference between a hallway and a corner, could watch out for stairs and obstacles in his way.

Could fight the enemy downtown in the field.

By the time the blindness had come fully, all those places, like the mansion, the Audience House, and the Tomb, had been committed to a permanent visual map in his mind, one so carefully rendered by repetition and the accuracy of a powerful memory that the information his eyes fed him and what he recalled melded together, becoming a kind of sight. And as maps required a compass for orientation, so he'd had his four points: his hearing, his sense of smell, the sensations of his body's movement . . . and what became his one true north.

That precise recollection of his.

It had all been such a seamless integration into function that, with his characteristic arrogance, he'd assumed the competence was as innate to him as the genetic weakness in his retinas, a compensation for what he'd lost unfairly. Now he saw it for what it really was.

Just a familiar landscape.

And at the moment, he was lost in a future that to everybody else was just the present.

As his shoulder banged into something—doorjamb? whatever it was, it had no give and was next to a hole—he threw out a hand. Investigating with his fingertips, he found that yup, it was the molding around a door, and as he measured all kinds of depth and contours, shit was not like what it had been at the mansion, nothing ornate and hand-carved, curving or decorative. This was simple, machine-wrought, commercial-grade pine, a basic highlighter around a rectangle worthy only of a hasty step-through.

But it was home. Because this was where his Beth lived.

"We're going to figure this out," he said to George.

The golden snuffled, and waited for Wrath to step forward again. So he did. Nasty business, learning a space the hard way, bumping into things, terrified to trip, tentative, shuffling steps with his free hand out in front of him. He went around the circular space three or four times, and then he got it. The chair, the sofas, the table, the chairs, the food service area.

And when the layout was set in his mind, his awareness had extra bandwidth—and there it was. A scent he remembered.

By a doorway.

Like he could forget how rocky road smelled?

"This way," he said.

He knew he was back in one of the spokes by the metallic echo of his footfalls, and the confirmation on direction he needed was the next scent that reached his nostrils.

Silver polish paste.

Wrath followed the sweet chemical smell to a steel door, and he punched in a code with his left hand. As soon as he opened the heavy weight, he heard the rush of running water, and felt his boots step onto some kind of tile.

When George stopped, Wrath trusted the dog and went no farther.

"Fritz," he said as he caught the scent of his dear butler in and among the polish.

There was a rustle and the water was cut off, and Wrath imagined the ancient *doggen* turning around from whatever sink he was standing at, his black uniform—with its starched white shirt and bow tie perfectly centered at the popped collar—like something out of *The Windsor Family Cookbook*.

"Miss Rahvyn!" came the cheerful reply. "Whate'er may I . . . do . . . for . . ."

As that familiar voice drifted into silence, the faithful butler's lined face came to mind: Fritz's precisely coiffed white hair with its side part, and the wrinkles that gathered around his mouth because he smiled so much, and his expression of worried servitude, were as clear as if Wrath could see—

The sound of something clanging loudly on the floor rang out between them.

"Sire . . . ?" came the choked question. "Is it truly you."

Wrath held his free arm out wide. "It's me." The scent of the butler's tears was like spring rain on asphalt. "It's okay, Fritz."

"I do not understand," was the rough reply. "How are you here the now?"

In the silence that swelled as Wrath tried to think of an answer, he thought of Rahvyn. She reminded him of the Scribe Virgin, in the sense that that female tapped into energies that were so ancient, so powerful, they transcended definition or even description. So unfortunately he couldn't explain anything to his most faithful servant.

"I don't think the whys matter. It's all about where we've ended up. Back together . . . at last."

He tacked on that final part for the both of them.

The lesson in his "death" was becoming clear. Love, like time, was tangible. You could feel both in your bones, in your soul. And the latter was a thief if you were lucky enough to have the former.

"I'm glad to see you," Wrath heard himself say.

There was a muffled sniffle, and then a scrape across the floor, as if a chair were being pushed out of the way.

"My Lord. Please . . . forgive me, oh, please . . . my Lord, forgive me."

The *doggen's* voice came from a lower point now, as if Fritz was on his knees.

"There is nothing to forgive." Wrath shook his head. "Not a damned thing."

"It is all . . . my fault."

The scent of the elderly *doggen's* tears filled Wrath's nose, as he breathed in the sorrow and regret of a male of worth.

And felt an anger he knew could destroy him.

Releasing his hold on George's harness grip, he extended his dagger hand and moved forward until he made contact with a thin shoulder. The weight of the King's ring, the one that had been worn by his father, and his father's father, and all the Wraths who had come before—back to the first one whose skull was on that altar in the Tomb—was innate, the kind of thing he usually didn't notice because he'd worn it for so long.

Except he felt the heaviness now, especially as Fritz grabbed on to what had been laid upon him. The *doggen* kissed the black diamond and then pressed the ring and the back of his ruler and master's hand to his forehead.

While he wept.

Wrath lowered his own head and closed his eyes, even though that didn't change his vision. As he felt the moment wrap around the two of them, he was reminded of the way paths crossed, of how two strangers could become family, and how differences in station could dissolve when devotion to a job, and loyalty to an employee, transcended the work and became . . . love on both sides.

"It was my fault, sire," Fritz mumbled. "I defied your orders. I went out when I should have stayed in—"

"I know why you left. My Beth told me. You were helping Karolyn and her young. He needed his blanket, and you went to get it for him."

"I killed you—"

"You did *not*." He placed his palm on the *doggen*'s head. "You have to release that burden."

"But I robbed your son of his sire, your *shellan* of her mate, you from the both of them. I took from the species its rightful leader—"

"*Stop*. Right now."

In the quiet that followed, the butler sniffled and attempted to compose himself—and Wrath swallowed a growl. As the Creator was his witness, thirty-three years of pain was going to be taken out of Lash's fucking hide for so many reasons.

"I need you, Fritz," he said in a commanding voice. "Your King requires your service."

A shuddering breath rippled through the torrent of tears. "Y-y-you do?"

He wanted to hug the male and do the love-you thing. He wanted to share an awkward laugh after a dark-humor joke. He wanted to leave the past in the history books and never fucking think about that night Fritz had gone to help a subordinate—and they had all lost so much collectively.

But he had to communicate the layers in a way the butler would accept.

Hugs were out. Expressions of love were out.

"I've always needed you, and I always will. Who else could take care of my family and my home better than you? Rise, and resume your duties, secure in the knowledge that your services are required now . . ." Wrath cleared his throat. ". . . and forever more, Fritzgelder Perlmutter."

Good thing there was no better love language for a *doggen* than to tell them their job was secure, and they were so valuable they were required at their station to serve their King.

There was a sharp sniffle, and then Fritz gathered himself up off the tile in a shuffle that was as surprisingly sprightful as always. Wrath could just picture him tugging his sleeves down with a sharp snap, and then double-checking that his jacket was buttoned properly—no, he probably had on an apron as he polished the silver.

So he'd be making sure its tie was in place.

"It is my honor to serve you, my Lord," the butler stated with dignity.

Screw it.

"I love you, too, Fritz." Wrath held up his dagger hand. "And you're just going to have to suck that statement up, my man. I'm the King, and I can say whatever the *fuck* I want."

There was a soft chuckle, and then a shifting as the butler bowed once again. "As you wish, my Lord . . . as you wish—"

"Holy. Fucking. *Shit.*"

As a second clattering sounded out, Wrath turned toward the sound and smelled that rocky road ice cream.

"Rhage." He started to smile. "Some things never change. And thank God for it."

CHAPTER EIGHT

N o, thanks, I'm good," Nalla said over the music.

As she issued the shutdown, she glanced away from Nate's general direction to the aristocrat who was standing in front of her with a cocktail in his hand. The male had brought something pink and fruity over, and not only did she hate the supersweet smell, the little wedge of pineapple sticking out of the top was exactly the kind of unnecessary floofy stuff she despised.

Like adding flavoring to coffee. Coffee was coffee, for godsakes. It didn't need caramel or hazelnut or—

"You sure?" he prompted as he sat down next to her. "I think you'll like it."

She focused on him properly. In the dark-blue lighting, his black, slicked-back hair gleamed like he'd put a helmet on, and his pale suit shimmered, like it was made out of real gold thread. His face was attractive enough, in that it had no major flaws or blemishes, but the symmetry of his features was sort of relentless, as if he had been extruded out of a *glymera* sausage machine rather than birthed the old-fashioned way.

"What was your name again?" she asked.

He shuffled closer, put the drink down on the low table, and motioned to the glass. Like she'd forgotten that it was for her. "Toddhome the Younger. Todd, to you and my close friends. We've actually met before."

"I've certainly seen you around, Todd."

The smile that came back at her was slow and sexual. "So you've been watching me, huh."

"Yeah, tonight, actually."

"I'm complimented." His eyes dropped to her mouth. "I just threw this suit on, you know. It's no biggie."

"I've been watching your friends, too."

"I wouldn't bother with them. They're boring."

"Why are you wasting your time, then." She put up her hand. "Never mind. That's none of my business."

"That's right. Let's just keep this about you and me."

"I'm sorry. I'm not really interested in just us."

His brows popped up. Then he tilted his head to the side and seemed to look at her for the first time. "Aren't you a surprise. And if a ménage is what you're after, my boys and I can work something out. For sure."

Threesome? Golly gee, didn't she just win the fuck lottery. And holy crap, only a guy like him could turn a rejection into a bright idea.

"Well, see, I think you've already done that."

Now he frowned. "I'm not following?"

"Like I said, I've been watching you and your 'boys.'" She added air quotes because two could play at the douche game. "I saw the way you all checked me out when I got here, and then as you put your heads together and yucked it the fuck up. Next, you come over with a drink that is the last thing I'd volunteer for if I were stuck in the middle of a desert for a week." She put her arm across his shoulders and indicated the group of males across from them. "Let's give them a wave, shall we? 'Cuz your buddies are staring at us like they're watching a horse race they've bet on."

The male blinked. "Huh?"

She gave the peanut gallery a little hi-how're-ya with her free hand. "Would you like to know what I think is going on, or are you going to be a male about this and tell me yourself."

"Um . . . what?"

"So you're going to make me do the PowerPoint presentation. That's fine." Nalla gave him a pat. "I think you guys have struck up a competition to see who can get me to go into the private bathrooms with them first. It's a gentlemale's bet, of course. I have to be willing, and none of you are sure you're going to be successful. But it's a fun way of passing time on another otherwise slow Thursday night, m'I right?"

The flush that started at the aristocrat's starched collar and rode up his throat to his cheeks was the affirmation she didn't require.

"Am I missing anything?" She took her arm back. "I don't think I am. So how about you take your pink drink back there to your boys, tell them the game's done before it began, and console yourself with that piece of pineapple."

She left out what she wanted to tell him about the swizzle stick— and where to put it.

The male cleared his throat. "I don't know what to say."

Tilting her head to the side, she murmured, "Can I ask you something?"

"Yes." He sat up straighter. "But of course."

"What do you put in your coffee?"

He pulled a double take. "Ah. Well, I prefer crème de menthe."

"That so checks out. And yes, you should feel like an asshole right now. Because you're behaving like one."

"Yes . . . you're right. I'm—" He shook his head as he got to his feet. "I'm sorry."

He inclined himself into a bow, picked up the cocktail by its fragile stem, and went back to where he'd come from. As he parked it on the sofa across the table, there was some chatter from his "boys," but he shut that down quick as he saluted her with the pineapple on that swizzle stick—and then downed the drink on a oner.

"This was such a mistake," she muttered as she stood.

"You're leaving?" Lyric said. "Oh, wait—it's Bitty."

As the female waved over her head, Nalla glanced across the VIP section—

Okay, *wow*.

Down at the velvet ropes, Bitty stepped to the tuxedo'd guards, and talk about your glow-ups. No more jeans and a sweatshirt. She was dressed in a short black sheath that showed off what Nalla had certainly never guessed she had—and with her newly highlighted hair all loose and gleaming around her shoulders, and that lipstick, and the . . .

Were those false eyelashes? Nalla wondered.

Maybe it was just some really good mascara, but whether it was Maybelline or not, if it hadn't been for that familiar face, the female was almost unrecognizable.

And what do you know, the tuxedos gave her the Mharta treatment. As she was sent through with deference, Bitty only wobbled once on her high heels. The rest of the way to the couches where her fellow vampires were was smooth. Well, smooth-ish. She kept trying to keep the hem of her dress from rising, the tug-tug-tug doing little to increase leg coverage. Meanwhile, the female seemed to not notice the attention she was getting, all kinds of eyes going wide and staying put as she passed down the aisle between the sunken areas.

On the approach, there were a couple of low whistles from the "boys" on the couch across the way, and words spoken too softly to carry over the din of the music—and then those greedy, bored, conspiring heads were put together for a second time.

Nalla moved without thinking. She put her foot up on that low table in the center of the pit, and the next thing she knew, she was marching across the damn thing, knocking over glasses, breaking things. There was instant commotion, the males and females jumping back onto the cushions so their club clothes didn't get splashed.

She stayed standing on the table when she got to Mr. Crème de

Menthe, and she looked him right in the eye as she jabbed her forefinger down into his face.

Keeping her voice low, she said, "You and your boys leave her alone. If you don't, I will find out and I will make it right. Do we understand each other."

She didn't wait for an answer. Any reply from him was unnecessary: Consequential learning did not require consent. It was a law of the universe.

As she turned around, she got a gander at the ring of people staring up at her. Mharta was laughing and clapping with approval. L.W. was looking bored. Shuli was brushing at the dirt on his slacks like he was noticing it for the first time. And Lyric had both hands up to her cheeks, all *Home Alone*, that ancient Christmas classic.

For reasons she refused to acknowledge, Nalla was compelled to glance back at Nate—

He was gone.

Ignoring that stupid sinking feeling, she focused on Bitty. The female was standing on the steps of the seating area in her sexy dress and her high heels and her long lashes . . . with an expression of total shock on her face. As their stares met, Bitty dropped her eyes and shook her head with embarrassment.

Yup, so that just happened, Nalla thought.

Stepping through the debris field of broken glass and puddled-up liquor, she hopped back to the floor next to her old friend.

"Be careful in your new world," she said. "Not everyone's looking to help you evolve."

Walking off, she moused down the aisle that Mharta and Bitty had turned into a runway, and tried to fight the feeling that she was skulking away. She'd come to make an apology, and ended up issuing a smackdown, a threat, and a warning.

Not how she'd expected the night to go when she'd been brushing out her wet hair, being all judgey about that self-esteem peddler Bitty was obsessed with. The only solace she had was that she'd been right. She shouldn't have come out—

Up ahead at the archway into the VIP section, some kind of commotion was simmering up, a balding guy in jeans and a ski jacket flapping his arms at the tuxedos like he was trying to fly over them. But that wasn't what held Nalla's attention. Through the shades of blue lighting and the chaos of the club, a face stood out on the far side of the velvet rope.

Nate was off to the right, camo'd by the crowd as if he were deliberately hiding among humans—and his hooded eyes were locked on the out-of-place with the let-me-in's at the VIP entrance.

As she came up to the tuxedos, some guy in a double-breasted suit cut in front of her, barked at the black-and-white border guards, and grabbed the young guy, all but throwing him toward a sitting area filled with men in suits who looked like they should have aged out of the club.

Talk about getting fed to the sharks.

And hey, at least someone else was disturbing the peace.

Stepping outside the velvet rope, the music was louder and the people more tightly packed, and instead of heading for the exit, which would have been smart, she found herself searching for Nate's shaved head—

Through the faces and the milling bodies, she caught sight of the back of it, and before she could think straighter, she started off in his wake.

The blue lasers piercing through the crowd gave her a headache. Or maybe it was all the perfumes and clothes—wait, where was he? Standing up on her tiptoes, she hopped to get a look over the dancers and then tilted to the side—

"Excuse you," some man snapped as he jerked a martini out of her way.

"Sorry—damn it," she muttered as she put her forearm up over her eyes.

If one more frickin' laser beam fired into her retinas, she was going to—well, she didn't know what. But it was going to make her stunt with that table and the drinks look like amateur night.

By the time she got to the front of the club, she knew she'd lost the male she shouldn't have been going after in the crowd, and the fact that this was a disappointment as always made no sense. Not that anything about Nate had ever made sense.

Again, she didn't even like him.

As she turned in a slow circle and faced where she'd come from, she was struck by how many people were out living their lives, on a random Thursday in January. And it wasn't just in this club. It was all over Caldwell. All over the country, the globe. Every Thursday. All weekend long.

While she was working. Or staring at pictures of places she would never go.

She reminded herself that the things she did at Luchas House were important and that was why she took so little time off. That her father was a nightmare about her safety. That this club stuff was all bullshit because pink drinks and party dresses were a waste of time.

Staring at the sea of humans, she knew all of that was true, and yet a loneliness surprised her. How could you be locked out of something you didn't want to be a part of?

With an ache at her sternum, she turned her back on the scene. Unlike the entrance, there was no one holding up people from getting their exit on, and she stepped past two security guards with no problem.

Out on the street, she glanced at the Bathe sign with its streaking lights and flowing blues. The wait line was even longer, dispelling the old wives' tale that the dark hours belonged only to vampires—and the people were exactly like the ones she'd been standing with earlier, beautiful, barely clothed for cold, impatient for what was inside.

Zipping her parka back up to her chin, she tucked her hands into the pockets of the Patagonia and started walking in the opposite direction. She just needed an out-of-the-way corner so she could dematerialize without anyone seeing her disappear into thin air.

Then she could spend the rest of the night back in her room.

As she pictured Bitty all dressed up in the VIP section, FOMO wound up its Ferragamo and kicked her in the ass, and as she slowed down, she knew she had to shit or get off the pot, as the saying went. And of course she had to leave. Like heading back in and sitting with those people was a better option now than it'd been before she'd gone pro-wrestler on the drink service?

As she restarted with the walking, she didn't track the direction she went in. Not that it mattered. She just ducked her head against the wind, and avoided getting in the way of even more humans who were heading toward that wait line—

Five blocks down from the club, well away from the illumination of Bathe's front facade, a figure stepped out of an alley into her path.

In the darkness, she could see the flash of platinum hair and very white skin, and she recognized what it was even before the stink of baby powder and roadkill reached her nostrils.

In the *lesser*'s hand . . . a knife gleamed.

CHAPTER NINE

In the wake of Nalla's departure, Bitty, beloved daughter of the Black Dagger Brother Rhage, stared down at the table in the center of the sunken area. What a mess—and her first instinct was to ask for a bucket, a roll of paper towels, and some rubber gloves so she didn't get any glass splinters.

If only friendships were so easy to clean up—

"Now, *that* is how you make an exit."

Bitty glanced over to the sound of laughter. Mharta had thrown her head back, her hand resting at the base of her throat, her red nails like spots of blood dotting her jugular. The female was spectacular in her own LB without the D, and Bitty had to envy all that confidence as she didn't seem to worry about how much cleavage she was showing or how her body looked in that catsuit.

Then again, if you shrink-wrapped a Michelangelo, it wasn't going to look like a sack of potatoes.

"We'll take care of this right away," someone said.

"Here, we should let the staff get by. Bitty? Come over with me."

Shaking herself to attention, she nodded at Lyric. "Oh, right. Yes."

Actually, no. Not right. The humans, two women and a man dressed in blue uniforms, were on the approach with buckets, mops, and a rolling blue trash bin to take care of a mess they hadn't created. The fact that there seemed to be a team for these kinds of things didn't matter.

We should clean up after ourselves, she thought.

"Hey, Bitty, how you doing?"

As Rhamp stepped in front of her, she turned to him in a daze. The male was so similar to his father, Qhuinn, tall and broad of shoulder, with black hair that was pulled back by a headband and bright green eyes. He was good-looking for sure, and clearly an aristocrat, especially with the diamonds in his earlobes and the swagger that was as much a part of him as his impeccable bloodline. But he'd always been kind to her, as if he understood the reasons she was prone to being anxious.

Maybe one of his two sets of parents had told him about her history. She wasn't going to ask for details, though.

"Hi," she said to him, flushing.

"It's good to see you."

"I, ah . . . I got a new dress."

"You sure did. C'mere and hug me."

As they embraced, she glanced over his shoulder and stiffened at the sight of the male whose warrior body was sprawled on the sofa, his knees wide apart as if he were daring anybody to challenge how big his balls were: L.W. was the only one who hadn't jumped up when the drinks had gone flying.

His eyes were on Bitty. And he didn't look away from her.

He never did, and she'd never understood it. And for someone who flustered easily, the last thing she needed was to feel criticized for breathing.

Especially by someone like him.

"You good?" Rhamp asked as he eased back.

"I'm *so* glad you're here," Lyric announced, her warm, easy smile a relief. "I'd ask you if you want a drink—"

"But we know how the first round went," her brother finished for her.

Bitty laughed a little. Tugged some more at her hem.

"Don't you look great." Mharta's eyes narrowed. "Fab dress."

"Thanks."

"You're welcome." That calculating stare went up and down. "It's not your usual thing."

"No, it's not."

Other people came over and said hello. She recognized Shuli, of course. And there were some more males she'd seen around from time to time—not that they were in all that big a hurry to get too close. Like L.W., they hung back, giving her a nod or maybe a raised hand, but otherwise refusing to get involved.

Looked as if the window dressing wasn't fooling everybody.

What followed was a loitering that felt interminable, all of them standing around—except for the future King—as the cleanup happened. Which really didn't feel right. And then there were drinks to replace the ones Nalla had trashed.

As her head started to pound, Bitty sat down carefully on the sofa, keeping her skirt in place as best she could, and she was just as cautious with the test sip she took of the pink drink that had been bought on a round. As she grimaced, someone made a joke—not directed at her—and she didn't get the punch line. After that, there was more laughter—and an inside reference to a movie she hadn't seen.

She pinned a smile on her face, under the fake-it-'til-you-make-it doctrine, and then remembered that faking it was not part of the Resolve2Evolve list of progressions.

Not honest enough.

Trying the drink again, she coughed as it stung the back of her throat, and God, she just couldn't manage another try. As she leaned forward to set the glass on the low table, she closed her eyes. Which made both the sounds and the smells louder—

Everything suddenly retreated.

All her life she had been able to sense things, as if the center of her chest were some kind of tuning fork. The strange incidents were so much a part of her that she couldn't have isolated when she had first noticed them, but what she was clear on was that sometimes, she knew that things were going to happen . . . or needed to.

And she was feeling that right now.

The truth that she hadn't been able to tell Nalla earlier, that she had hidden behind the argument about R2E, was that something had told her to come here tonight, to this club, to these people.

She just had no idea why—

From out of the corner of her eye, she caught sight of Mharta going over to L.W. The way the female walked, with her hips rolling at the base of her spine, and her long legs extending out like she was taking a piece of the club and pocketing it with every step, was like, enough already. And then Mharta put her hand on the back of the sofa, leaned into it, and whispered into the male's ear.

Her cascade of straight blond hair swooped off her shoulder and went right between L.W.'s legs, the strands clinging to the black leather that covered his heavy thighs and his . . .

Well, *that* part of him, too.

Bitty looked away sharply. Then she reached out for that cocktail and took as much of a drink as she could. As she coughed and sputtered, she had one and only one thought:

Man, she really didn't like that female for some reason.

◆   ◆   ◆

Across the VIP section, in a whole different world, Evan Montiere didn't dare sit down as he was presented to his uncle like something that had been found out in the street. He really wanted to take a load off. His body was weak inside his bones and his head was light as a balloon, and seeing the man he dreaded more than anything in life made all of that worse: Richard Montiere was leaning back on a white leather sofa, one of his usual black three-piece suits open at the jacket, buttoned up tight with the vest and the shirt. The white tie was knotted precisely at his throat, and his shoes were so shiny, they glowed in the turquoise light that bathed him.

The red handkerchief in the breast pocket made it look like he'd been shot through the heart—and was such a tough guy, he refused to give in to his own death.

The lieutenant who'd brought Evan into the sit pit wouldn't let him go any farther. No hugging. No reassurance as he fought not to break down. Not even a handshake you might give a stranger. But he'd never had much in common with his family, and they'd never really liked him.

True to form, Uncle stayed silent in the awkward pause that followed, although his narrowed, cold eyes sure as hell were talking. And when Evan glanced around at the men seated on the couches, all of whom were extended cousins, he got nothing better. They all just stared back like they were picking out his coffin in their heads. He hadn't expected them to be helpful.

But he would have liked . . . something, from somebody, in his family, though.

"Mickey is dead," he croaked loud enough to carry over the music. "He's . . . gone. And I know who did it."

The lieutenant standing next to him, his third cousin once removed, drawled, "Yeah. Who."

You don't even care, he thought as he didn't look away from his uncle's face.

"It's that enforcer you've been using. Nathaniel."

Uncle finally moved, holding up his hand to silence his lieutenant's muttering. Then he pointed to the floor in front of him.

Evan had to sidestep around his escort, then squeeze through the runway between the coffee table and all the shoes of the other men so he could front-and-center.

"How do you know this," Uncle said.

"I saw it happen." Evan sniffled and rubbed his nose. "It was out on the guy's property. In the sticks."

"What were you doing there."

"Mickey wanted to go see him." Evan wiped his eyes. "He said he had business with him. I told Mickey we needed to leave. He didn't listen—and I saw it happen."

"You saw it."

"Mickey got . . . stabbed."

Well, there was the throat slashing first. But did that really matter?

Uncle looked to his left. Looked to his right. "My nephew got stabbed."

"In the stomach," Evan tacked on.

"And you're coming here to tell me this." Uncle pointed to the floor at his feet again. "To this club."

Evan glanced around at all the other strangers in the VIP section. The fact that they were drinking and laughing and sexing it up in the loud music was a kind of privacy veil. But his uncle would have found a way to humiliate him even if they'd been on family turf.

"Huh?" Uncle said as he cupped his ear and leaned forward. "I didn't hear you."

"'Course I'm here to tell you. You're gonna wanna do something about it. I mean, he's . . . your nephew."

"This guy." Uncle shook his head at the other cousins. "Can you believe my nephew."

There was some kind of grumble in response from all the man's people. And then . . . nothing. No one, even Uncle, said nothing.

"I don't understand." Evan swiped his hand across his eyes again. "You're not gonna let that guy get away with it. Are you?"

Uncle rose to his feet, pulling the two halves of his finely tailored jacket together without buttoning them. "You dumb sonofabitch. You come here, expecting me to pat your fucking ass. You want a fucking reward? For watching my nephew die? Get the fuck outta here." Uncle jabbed two fingers into the meat of Evan's pec. "You saw it? Why didn't *you* take care of the problem. Where's the head of the asshole who took one of us, huh?"

Each demand was punctuated with another punch of those fingers.

As his eyes stung, Evan mumbled, "I don't . . . understand."

"You're a fucking pussy. You shoulda done something when it happened, but you ran, didn't you, you little fuck. You saw the blood and wet your fucking pants. Jesus Christ, my sister should be alive to see this. Her fucking baby boy, looking for a pat on his back and a goddamn jerk-off 'cuz he saw his cousin get dead and did nothin' about it." Uncle thrust his jaw forward. "Get the fuck outta my sight. Before I decide to do something about *you*."

Evan stumbled away, tripping over the feet of the lieutenants, hearing the curses of the other men, the real men, who had his uncle's respect. As he scrambled up the little set of stairs to get out of the pit, he caught the toe of his snow boot, fell to the hard carpet, and heard laughter.

Pulling himself off the floor, he elbowed his way forward with that mocking sound in his ear, so loud that it drowned out the music, so loud that he was blinded by humiliation . . . and the next thing he knew, he was back on the sidewalk in front of the club. Shuddering in the cold, he looked up to the sky. He couldn't see any stars. Whether that was because there were still clouds from the storm or because of all the lights from the streets and the buildings, he wasn't sure.

More likely, his vision was all fucked up because he was crying.

With a hand that shook, he touched the cheek Mickey had slapped. Then he pictured his mother, withered in her bed, her lips the color of the pale blue light that had fallen from that ceiling onto those couches his uncle and cousins were on, all those men so far above him, even though they had been sitting down.

Finally . . . he remembered Mickey jerking as that knife had been driven into him—

Evan clapped a hand over his mouth to keep from throwing up.

Laughter brought his head around. A group of men his age were striding toward him, and they were dressed in club clothes, their suits not as slick as his family's, but way better than the jeans and ski jacket he was wearing. The fact that they had deliberately groomed their beards into shadows on their jaws and had the same longish hair made it seem like they were a branded set, something off the shelf that came in a charismatic six-pack, regardless of their differences in ethnicities.

A family by choice.

He didn't even have that.

As they passed him, the decision he had been putting off gelled inside his queasy gut, and he took out his phone. Going into his DMs, he scrolled up and reread the conversation he had been rereading for two weeks, at least. And with every line that he'd already memorized, he realized a precipice had been built. Word by word, the cliff had been constructed, and now, it appeared, he was standing on the lip of the great drop-off, staring into an abyss, the mysteries of which seemed safer and more comforting than the world he was living in. The world . . . he had been born into.

He knew he'd decided to jump when the shaking stopped: His hands were perfectly steady as he composed a text, and he didn't read it through twice, which was what he usually did when something mattered.

The response was immediate.

Evan put his phone back in his pocket and wiped his eyes.

Then he squeezed his lids shut, held his breath, and ran right out into traffic.

CHAPTER TEN

N ate had no intention of following Nalla out of the club. But as he'd been watching Evan get in through the velvet rope thanks to one of his uncle's thugs-in-a-three-piece—there she was, doing her own exit into the *hoi polloi*. Nate hadn't wanted to notice her, and he'd been banking on her not noticing him because camouflage came in many forms, and he'd made himself good and gone in the human sea.

Not good enough.

Her eyes had found him, and then she'd seemed to be closing in on him. He had no clue what she could want him for, and he didn't want to know so he'd backed away. And as soon as she gave up the hunt and headed for the exit, he should have let her go. What the hell business was it of his where she went? Alone. After midnight. In a section of town where the men roaming around were almost as dangerous as *lessers*—

Annnnnnnd that was how he'd found himself out on the sidewalk, playing bodyguard to a female he didn't give two shits about.

"God*damn* it."

As she strode away from Bathe, he told himself it was just until she dematerialized to wherever she was going to end up, and he was careful not to track her too closely—so when a woman wearing a postage stamp skirt and a stripe of pink sparkles across her nipples got in his path and refused to back off from him, he pushed the hard offer out of his way because he didn't want to lose sight.

"You too good for me?" came a shrill demand. "You don't want this, bitch?"

Fucking fantastic. The last thing he needed was Nalla turning around to check out the commotion—

Some stocky muscleman with a duffle bag slung on his shoulder stepped in and became Nate's human shield against the offense, picking up the ego slack with some soothing hey-baby's and probably looking to get a blow job out of his efforts. With that handled, Nate got back on the trail, hoping like hell Nalla ghosted out at the next alley so he could get the fuck on with his life.

Nah. She was in no hurry.

But she was conscientious as fuck. The female was careful to stop and check both ways at each block's intersection, whether it was an alley or a proper road crossing with a traffic light, and this was true even if there weren't cars coming or a red light halting traffic in favor of pedestrians.

Man . . . she moved nice. When she was in motion, her stride was good and long, and she kept her head down, the wind blowing around her ponytail. No perfume. She smelled like fabric softener, natural shampoo, and something that was entirely about her.

He told himself he wasn't breathing in deeply—

An intermittent vibration in his inner pocket tickled his pec four times and then cut the crap. When it immediately started up again, he knew what it was about: His father was calling about the text that the Brother had sent after Shuli had reported their little carousel ride in the Tesla to the powers that be. The cleanup was already underway, but that wasn't what Murhder wanted to talk about.

Nate let things go to voicemail a second time.

When a third round of ringing started up, he took his phone out—
Not Murhder. His adoptive mom, Sarah.

He halted, his thumb hovering over the screen. *Don't answer it.
Donotanswerit*—

"Hello," he said.

There was a silence, like she was surprised. "Ah, Nate? Hi."

His eyes shot across the street as someone shouted at somebody
else.

It was just a couple of humans yuckin' it up as they jaywalked
across Market. They were probably heading for Bathe. Like everyone
in Caldwell tonight.

He refocused. "What's up."

"I just . . . wanted to know if you're okay."

He glanced down at his body. He was bleeding under his jacket—
just a surface abrasion on his upper arm, but he could feel the wetness.
His bad right knee was bitching, but he was used to that. There was
bruising across his chest from the airbag, and the top of his head had an
impact ache from hitting the Tesla's roof when they'd rolled.

He was also hungry. For food . . . and blood.

And a little dizzy. Which could explain what he was doing out here,
trailing after that female: Concussions made people stupid.

Stupid-er.

"Yeah, I'm fine."

"Your father's looking for you."

I'll bet, he thought.

"Do you want to tell me what happened?"

"Nothing," Nate muttered. "It was nothing. Listen, I gotta go. I'm in
the field."

"You're *fighting*? After the accident?" His mom's fake-calm self-
control started to slip, a choking sound rippling through the connection.
"Nate, come in so Doc Jane can get a look at you. You weren't wearing a
seatbelt and . . ."

As his mom went down that old, familiar rabbit hole, he closed his eyes and wished like hell he had the guts to tell the woman the same thing he had Shuli. Sarah and Murhder hadn't birthed him; he was a responsibility they'd volunteered themselves for when the latter had raided the lab Nate had been imprisoned in, and the former, a human who had been working in the facility, had discovered what had been done to him.

If he kept pushing them away, sooner or later they just had to let go, if only because the law of attrition applied to emotions. Or at least . . . it should.

"I was wearing a seatbelt," he cut in. "And you can verify that with the car's computer."

"Nate," she whispered. "Please."

Please what, he thought.

"I've got to go—"

The punch on his shoulders came from out of nowhere, knocking him forward, his phone flipping from his hand and cracking on the pavement.

"How you like it, asshole? Huh? You think it's fucking okay to push women around?"

Nate turned around to the bulldog human with the duffle bag who'd deflected the temper tantrum. The knight in shining Under Armour was a gym bro looking for a squat rack, all roid muscles and not much engine between the ears, it seemed—or he wouldn't be picking this fight. With his jutting jaw and his cologne, he probably didn't have to look for dates, and given the way the woman with the sparkles across her chest was all superior at his six, he wasn't going to have to search far after this heroic confrontation.

"You think it's fucking okay, asshole? Answer me, pussy—"

The man went to punch forward with his palms again.

That was as far as he got.

Slapping a hold on both of those thick wrists, Nate pulled a pivot-and-push, pinning the guy face-first with arms behind the back against the front of a restaurant that was closed for the evening. With his fangs descending and his upper lip twitching, Nate had a thought that he was waaaaay too close to the edge. But he didn't care enough to follow through on the whoa-Nelly to his own temper.

Putting his face in close, he said in a low voice, "Do you *really* want to do this tonight."

The thick-necked human did not move. No breathing, no talking. It was as if he were frozen in time as their eyes met over that pumped-up shoulder.

Then again, Nate really did want to rip the man's throat out. Right here, on the sidewalk with so many humans around. He could practically taste the blood.

And clearly that message had been received.

"You tell him!" the woman said. "That's right!"

Like she didn't understand how the upper hand in physical conflict worked.

"What are you," the man whispered.

No doubt Nate was showing off some hard-core dental hardware. But he didn't care about that either.

"You can take the woman," he said softly, "and get the fuck out of here. Or we can do this, you and me. Your choice. Make it now."

The second he loosened the pressure, the man slipped out and took off, running across the traffic, dodging cars to the soundtrack of blaring horns, his duffle bag slapping his ass like a jockey on the final leg of a horse race.

The half-naked woman stared at the departure in disbelief.

"I'm sorry I pushed you," Nate said to her.

"Ah . . ." She glanced back to him, her brows flickering like she was trying to decide whether or not she needed to be afraid. "What did you say to him?"

"Do you really want to know."

Her head went back and forth slowly. "No, I don't think I do."

"You better get over to Bathe. You don't want to catch a cold."

"Okay. I'll . . . do that."

Nate nodded to her, and then he looked down toward Nalla. Who somehow hadn't noticed him or the humans.

Let the female go, he told himself.

Bending down, he picked up his phone and was relieved it still worked. And when he walked away, resuming his stupid trail, there was no more from the woman in pink. Maybe she even had the sense to get out of the winter chill by going home and sobering up. He doubted it. Then again, he probably should go home and start digging a hole for Mickey Trix. Instead, he was shadowing a female who was none of his business—

Baby powder.

Flaring his nostrils, he breathed in deep just to make sure his aggression wasn't translating into some kind of olfactory delusion that the enemy had shown up. But then he saw—a block away—that a figure had stepped into Nalla's path. The pair stared at each other for a moment . . . and then she backed away, into a fucking alley, out of sight.

The *lesser* followed her.

Of course it did.

Nate took off at a dead run, pounding the pavement as he went for one of his knives—no, a gun, he wanted one of his guns—beneath his leather jacket. Arriving at the curb cut, he skidded around the corner, and pointed his .357 Magnum hand cannon down the brick-faced chute.

Fuck.

The slayer was directly in front of Nalla. So any lead that went through it was going right into her.

"You don't want the female," Nate called out. "Come for me."

The *lesser's* head turned and Nate got a quick image of its profile, the lean bones of the face showing through its white skin, its white hair gleaming in the darkness, its eyes flashing with unholy white light.

And then everything went slo-mo.

For some reason, a knife flashed in an arc at the slayer's shoulder level—and then the thing went for its own throat with both hands, the blade it had been holding falling to the asphalt and bouncing away.

As the undead lurched forward into a bow, Nalla came into full view, and . . . ohhh, shit. Her face was a dead mask of composure, no fear or shock distorting her features. She might as well have been at a grocery store feeling up avocados—

The female moved so fast, she was nearly impossible to track.

She double-fisted her knife, wound up like she had a bat in her hands, and went grand slam, burying the blade in the ear of the slayer. Horrific noises geysered up as the torso jerked to the left, and she let the weapon free itself by keeping a strong hold on the hilt. Then she just took the fuck over. With a solid kick to the side of its head, she sent the undead bastard on a tumble to the ground, and as soon as it was on the pavement, she shoved the *lesser* onto its back, straddled its hips—

She stabbed both of the eyes.

Her aim was absolutely perfect, the tip of her weapon piercing the meat of the peepers in two quick down strokes. After that, she just stood over her prey and seemed to enjoy the show as black blood dripped off her dagger. When the arms and legs finally slowed down with their jerking and flopping, she dismounted and ended the show with one final penetration directly into the center of the chest.

As the bright light flashed and the *pop!* sounded out, she jumped back so she didn't get singed by the disintegration—and the way her calm face and lithe body were silhouetted against the illumination was something he was never going to forget.

Well, he wasn't going to forget *any* of it—and how fucking weird was it that, for a split second, he wondered if they weren't soul mates: They'd both opened attacks by slitting the throats of their enemies. If that wasn't compatibility, what was? Fuck toothpaste caps and sleep schedules.

As the flash of the *lesser* getting sent back to its maker faded, and there was only the smell of burnt marshmallows and dead animal, she turned to him calmly.

"Do you mind lowering your weapon? Unless you perceive me as a threat, of course. Which would be pretty ridiculous."

Nate blinked and glanced down at his Magnum. Then he cleared his throat. "Duck for me, would ya?"

"What?"

"Duck."

The female frowned and glanced behind herself. "*Fuck—!*"

As she went flat to the asphalt, he fired two bullets into the slayer who'd come out of the shadows behind her. The thing fell back like a sack of potatoes, landing with a thump, but the job wasn't done. You had to stab them though the sternum, driving a length of steel into the empty cavity where their heart had once been, if you wanted to eliminate them.

"I'm totally not threatened by you." Holstering his gun, Nate took out a blade of his own and looked at the female who was prone at his feet. "Not in the slightest—"

Pop!

Okay, that sound didn't make any sense. Who the hell was shooting?

"Nate! Shit!"

"What?"

As the female pointed at his waist, he looked down and things got real fuzzy, real fast. Sure enough, there was a strange fire in his gut, like he'd eaten a ghost pepper or two, and as he put a hand over a red smudge on his Hanes t-shirt, he felt a fresh warmth and wetness.

"Do I *always* have to get hit in the stomach?" he muttered as his knees started to go loose.

And fucking hell, the *lesser* he'd just dropped had a gun.

"Run," he croaked. "You gotta get . . . out of . . . here . . ."

CHAPTER ELEVEN

Z sadist got to the 1075 Cedar Post Road location first. Re-
forming in the darkness, he did a quick instinct check in the
glen of birches, and when nothing pinged his radar, he stepped
out of the tree line and stared across the winter meadow that rose to
meet a two-story cottage. With the fresh snow that had fallen, the acre-
age was like a vanilla sheet cake.

Up ahead, the stone structure had little old lady written all over it.
From the exterior, it looked like the kind of place where cookies were
baked in the oven every day, there were doilies under everything, and
housekeeping was done scrupulously and by hand. The fact that the
curtains were never opened because there weren't any real windows,
and there were cameras mounted on the perimeter like it was a sting
operation in full swing?

Nothing to see here. Nope. Nada.

Instead of ruining the perfect snow—because its pristine nature was
like a security camera for the ground—he dematerialized onto the back
porch. Exactly three seconds afterward, the copper lock was remotely

sprung and he opened the first of the steel-reinforced panels. The outside one had been faced with a wooden faker that, like the front entry, always had a seasonally appropriate wreath hanging on it. The other two in the short hallway beyond had no camouflage because why bother. If you got to them, you were either welcome or you were going to be killed.

Each lock released for him and then reengaged behind him as he passed through, and finally, he was in the kitchen with its rustic table and chairs, the Aga, and the deep-bellied porcelain sink. No *doggen* keeping the coffee and Danish coming because there were no civilians in the waiting room tonight—and just as well. He was rank-mooded and best left to his own devices, and the last thing anybody needed was him making the pastry chef cry because he'd turned down a cherry-filled something and a cup of java with a tone that was less than airline-stewardess pleasant.

Helping himself to a Granny Smith from a bowl of mixed varieties, he unsheathed a black dagger and started peeling things on a oner as he opened the way into the sealed corridor. This restricted-access, fireproof, bombproof hallway formed the steel-wrapped core of the structure, and there were four reinforced doors opening off of it as well as one down at the far end.

The front half of the Audience House was cut up into a jigsaw circuit of rooms and hallways that were controlled remotely by V's offsite security staff. Civilians were let in the main entry into reception on the right, where they were greeted and signed in. They were then shown farther down into one of the confidential triage offices, where Saxton's team of paralegals registered their causes of action, determined whether there was a civil or criminal issue, and assigned them a case number—or if the audience was about a mating or the blessing of a young, set into production a certificate with ribbons. When it was time, the civilians were taken back around to see "Wrath," and then the final room, out in front on the left, was the disposition of the audience, including whatever kind of follow-up was required, whether that was an official investigation or a filing receipt or some kind of collections activity—or the presentation of the finished mating or blessing certificate set with the King's seal.

Saxton had developed the process, Tohr had designed the spaces and the layout, and Vishous had wired everything up with security, monitoring, and good old-fashioned booby-traps. There were lots of doors and hallways. Lots of dedicated off-site security staff. Lots of moving civilians around the central sealed corridor. Lots of secret things that could be triggered to defend against any kind of attacker.

It was all about protecting Rahvyn as she pretended to be Wrath.

And it had been working well for the last decade since they'd relocated from the safe house they'd been using as a stopgap measure. As far as any of the civilians knew, their audiences with the King were better run, better tracked, and more efficient than they'd ever been. And not one of them knew about the explosion that had changed everything thirty years ago. The repair on Darius's former principal residence had been started immediately, the rear entry rebuilt and repainted within a day by *doggen* carpenters, a ruse that it had been a gas leak gone *boom!* fed to the humans in the neighborhood and the cops that had come to investigate.

The reality that the King had been killed was a secret that had been protected for a long time now—so long that the nights when the real Wrath had seen members of the species and mediated their disputes and conferred royal favor upon their milestones seemed like something that had been done back in the Old Country. Hell, the second generation of young didn't even know the truth. They'd all been little kids when it had happened—well, except for Bitty. But her memories had been altered because it was safer for them to all live the lie.

L.W. was the only one who knew. After all, it was one thing for the King and Queen to be formal with each other in public. When your moms was sleeping alone every night?

Rahvyn and Beth had saved the species in so many ways, all so that L.W. could take the reins. Like father like son, though. The male had no interest in the throne. All he wanted to do was fight, and every night he rolled the dice with greater recklessness. So maybe they were stuck with this lie permanently—and by permanently, until someone noticed that Wrath was two thousand years old or something, and showing no signs of the sharp decline that vampires exhibited at the end of their lives.

It was wrong, all wrong. The whole damned thing, but what could you do?

Other than kill *lessers*, of course. And hunt Lash down.

As a spike of anger nailed Z in the chest, he checked the clock on his phone and then went back to working on his apple peeling. When he was finished, he dropped the bright green spiral into a trash can and took his first cleave off the rounded swell of fruit.

Sweet and tart at the same time, with a molar crunch that was satisfying. Candy from a tree, and maybe it would bring up his blood sugar levels and cut the crankies a little.

There were a couple of stools against the unadorned wall and he took a load off to wait for the others. The fact that he was stuck with an emergency meeting of the Brotherhood—which wasn't an emergency at all because, as usual, something bad had happened and that male Nate had been involved in it—was the way the night was going. He'd been boots-on-the-ground downtown for only about ten minutes when he'd watched a very familiar iridescent white Tesla stop in the middle of the fucking four-laner, get approached by a cop-bot—and then take off after a bullet had been discharged into the law enforcement robot from a gun that had no silencer on it.

"At which point things went from crap to shit . . ." he muttered as he took another slice off the black blade with his fangs.

Courtesy of the emergency-services light show that turned the bot's patrol car into a roman candle, he'd been momentarily blinded, and then he hadn't been able to dematerialize out of Dodge even if he'd wanted to because of all the lithium lamps and traffic enforcement cameras that were triggered as part of Caldwell's Civil Protection Protocol. After that? Cue the car crash. As that idiot Shuli hit the gas to escape the disaster of his own creation, the Tesla had jumped the curb in front of a bagel place, flipped over, and gone for a carnival-ride-slide on its roof.

Naturally, Z'd had an obligation to go and make sure that Tweedle-twat and Tweedle-twit were okay—so he could bash their heads together himself. Setting out at a jog, his footfalls and repeated *fuck*s had been a steady heartbeat of the beatdown he was going to give the pair of jackholes in the Tesla—and he'd known there were two in there before any visuals had confirmed it. Shuli might be an easy-living aristocrat, but the male was not the type to pop a bot in the middle of a downtown street without provocation.

Sure enough, Nate had crawled out from the passenger side, and as Shuli had laid into the guy, even though police were streaming to the scene, there was no question whose finger had pulled that trigger.

The geniuses had taken off before Z could get to them, ducking into an alley, and no doubt ghosting out from there. Of course they'd fucked off the car. With all the money Shuli had inherited after both of his parents had died, the male could afford to leave the two-seater on the sidewalk, and yeah, there was no tracing it.

Some things changed over time. Fake New York State registration chips did not.

But that wasn't the point. You couldn't be target-practicing on law enforcement droids like that. Gone were the nights when brothers or soldiers could fix the oopsie of getting the CPD's attention with an on-scene mental scrub or two. Those fucking bots had to be dealt with by V and his team of hackers at F.T. Headquarters, and that bunch of brainiacs had enough going on already with their remote monitoring of all the places the Brotherhood owned and operated.

What Nate had done wasn't even sloppy. It had been a deliberate act of defiance against the non-involvement clause of engagement—and now the brothers all had to have a meeting about the unhinged idiot. Instead of being out and doing their real jobs. Or being in and doing their jobs here by monitoring the audiences in person: All civilian appointments had been canceled per Tohr's order, and all members of the Brotherhood told to convene here.

Nate was a brutal soldier, a real killer in the field. But when that aggression wasn't tempered by self-control? It was worse than useless. It was a complication that slowed things down, endangered peoples' lives, and created work for others—

Bing-bing.

At the cheerful chime, Z took his last slice, tossed the whittled core, and wiped his blade off on a bandana. Then he looked down the hall. Tohr was always early too—

The vault-worthy door swung wide and . . .

The hair on the back of his neck stood up straight at what was revealed.

Later, he would wonder how he knew. The scent? Some kind of molecular recognition? Or maybe . . . it was the dog.

There was just something about the way George was pressed right up close to that leather-clad thigh, as if he were steering the male who gripped his harness, instead of walking side by side.

Zsadist never fumbled with his black daggers. He had used them for too long in too many different ways.

For the first time in his life, he dropped his blade.

As the weapon hit one of his shitkickers and bounced off the steel-toed tip, he forgot all about the thing.

"Is it you," he said softly as he shifted off the stool.

Even though he knew.

"Z."

Wrath put his free hand out and Zsadist walked forward in a daze, his mind going haywire-crisscross-bonfire.

As he noticed Tohr standing behind the King—the *real* King—he knew this wasn't a dream.

So he grabbed Wrath and was grabbed in return. Somehow, the great Blind King . . .

. . . was back from the dead.

CHAPTER TWELVE

A s Nate fell to his knees, time slowed to a crawl and Nalla parallel processed everything about the alley, from where the two of them were to the burn mark on the pavement to the *lesser* who'd been shot in the chest.

And still managed to pull his own trigger.

Nate's voice was weak. "You have to go—save . . . your—"

The slayer's eyes slanted up at her from where the thing had fallen face down on the pavement, and the smile that tilted up its lips was pure hatred—as it recalibrated the gun in its hand at Nate.

Whose own sternum was a perfect target.

Nalla blinked once. And sprang forward in one, two, three strides.

With the fourth, she angled her foot to go soccer ball on the gun. Just as the *lesser* pulled that trigger again—

She missed. She fucking missed the kick.

And the bullet went directly into Nate's heart.

As he barked an exhale and fell to the side, she tripped while wrenching around, and she was never going to forget what she saw . . .

Nate focused on her and her alone as blood came out of his mouth and he landed with the bounce of a dead body on the dirty snow.

A sound came out of her like no noise she had ever made before, and she saw nothing, just a white plane of rage. Baring her teeth, she launched herself at the *lesser*, going for the hand that gripped that gun.

She was unaware of biting the wrist until she tasted something foul in her mouth, and she didn't even think about what she did next. She bent the elbow with her free hand, turned the barrel into the slayer's face, and forced her finger into the trigger guard.

The bullet entered through the bridge of the nose and the body seized on a oner, all the muscles contracting in sync, a spray of black blood and gray matter blowing out the back of the skull. No fucking around this time. With a sweeping plunge, she swung her right arm downward and stabbed him through the back.

It wasn't enough.

Oh, God, what if there were more slayers, what if there was backup, what if—

Her strength doubled, and she peeled the *lesser* off the snow by the sleeve of his jacket, rolling him over with a jerk. Even though her hunting instinct swelled until it took the place of what was normally in her veins, she didn't look into the white face of her prey.

Her eyes were on Nate.

As she stabbed the center of the slayer's torso, she was blinded by the light and momentarily stunned by a blast of bus-exhaust smoke.

But then she crawled through the dissipating heat. "Oh, God, Nate..."

His voice was just a croak. "Don't call for anyone—"

"Are you out of your mind—"

"—I just need a minute—"

"—you're bleeding to death!"

"—I'm *not* bleeding to death!"

As they both got to the finish line at the same time, Nalla was done with the arguing. Glancing up and down the alley, there didn't seem to be any other *lessers*. And what humans were around were way out on the sidewalk of Market Street. And there was no monitoring by the city's crime prevention systems in this irrelevant alley or windows for people with prying eyes and phones.

Thank fuck.

Getting out her cell, she tried not to drop it with her shaking hands—

Nate snatched the thing from her and smashed it on the pavement.

"What the hell is wrong with you!" she barked. "We need help—"

"No—gimme a minute. No . . . matter what . . . happens . . . just . . ."

He started coughing, and as blood came out of his mouth and speckled his chin, she jumped up. But where was she running to?

"What the hell is wrong with you!" she yelled again.

"Relax," he said through a choked inhale. "Minute. Maybe less. All it . . . takes."

"For you to die!"

Fuck this, she thought as she started diving into his jacket to go through his pockets.

Of course he tried to fight her—because he was an idiot. But the only good thing about the fact that he was bleeding out in two places now was that his strength didn't last long and it was a case of patty-cake-patty-cake. And she found his phone. The screen was cracked, but it came alive in her palm. He was coughing up so much blood now, she wasn't sure facial recognition was going to work—

It did.

Meanwhile, his lips were clicking, and going by the glare on his increasingly gray face, it was clear he was yelling at her as best he could. Which was frickin' insane. The last moments of your life, and you're wasting them getting all hostile with a relative stranger?

She went into his contacts, to the final entry there was. Yet even with all the urgency, her fingertip hesitated over the name: *Zsadist.*

"You need to be giving me a last message to your parents," she snapped at him as her heart rate tripled.

Call him.

Except she couldn't do it. Even though her sire was one of the best people anybody would want in a life-or-death situation . . . he was the last person she needed here. She could just imagine him losing his shit that she was out of the house, then add in the slayers?

"You should be—" Her voice cracked as tears made that name blurry. "You should tell your parents that you love them and you're sorry. For all the . . . miscommunication and distance."

"I'm . . . okay . . ."

The sound of that raspy voice made her pull shit together, and she wiped her sleeve across her face. "What about a girlfriend or a lover. Jesus Christ, stop wasting your energy being pissed off at me and stupid about yourself."

On that compassionate, totally noncritical note, she scrolled up, triggered a call, and put the phone to her ear. Then she went back to staring at Nate—as if that was going to do fuck all? Like there was anything to be done? There was no resuscitating him. She sure as hell couldn't plug the holes inside of him by doing chest compressions—

A male voice cut into her spiral. "Nate?"

"Nonoit'sNallayougottahelpmehe's—"

"Slow down," Dr. Manny Manello said. "Who is this?"

"N-n-nalla—he's been shot. In the chest and the abdomen. He's dying! We're in an alley off—"

There was a soft cursing. "Listen, take a deep breath for me—"

"You need to come now! We're off Market between—"

Right on cue, Nate went into some kind of seizure, the spasms in his torso contorting him and turning him on his side on the pavement. The blood that flowed out of his open mouth was a copper bloom in the air and a red stain on the grimy snow, and as tears waved up her vision again, she knew she had to pull it together.

"We are off of Market Street. Get our location from this call—"

"Can you get to a safe place? I want you to dematerialize if you can—"

"Fuck that! You need to come save him—"

"He's going to be all right."

The statement was so strident, so out of left field, that she took the phone from her ear and checked the Samsung to see if it was malfunctioning. Had the man decided he didn't like the M.D. after his name all of a sudden?

She put the thing back into place. "He's dying!"

"No. He's not. Look, you just leave him, and I'll send someone now—"

"I'm not leaving and good, get your ass here! Get somebody here!"

As a strangled sound vibrated up, Nalla dropped the phone, and captured Nate's face in her hands. She thought about when she'd noticed him earlier, out in front of the club. She'd give anything to get annoyed by that big-swinging-dick energy again. How were they here? Why had . . . this all happened?

It was her fault. If she hadn't come out tonight, she—

"You fucking stay with me," she choked. "Help is coming. They're on their way."

"Doesn't matter . . ."

Those blue eyes swung up and clung to her own. Then his blood-speckled lips turned gray. He had very little breath left, very little life left.

Nate softly whispered his last words: "You're so beautiful . . . that I hate looking at you."

She sucked in a bolt of shock. But there was no following that up. His eyes rolled back in their sockets, and he dragged in a deep inhale that wasn't followed by any coughing. It wasn't followed by . . . anything.

Her tears fell onto his bloody cheeks, and she now wasn't breathing either. "Nate . . . ?"

The stillness in him brought the world to a screeching halt, the lack of movement in his chest the kind of thing that stopped her heart, too.

"Nate." Like she was so powerful, she could call him back from the Fade? "I'm so sorry . . ."

Gathering him up, she shifted his heavy torso into her lap and draped herself around him. As she squeezed her eyes closed, she replayed those final words and wanted to scream. What he'd spoken was a starting place, an out-of-the-blue confession that could have changed everything.

Hatred struck a chord, deep inside of her. The war had always seemed far away, even as it had touched so much of her life.

It was breathing down the back of her neck now. Especially as she endlessly replayed the way she'd tried to kick that gun, her foot missing, always missing. She might as well have shot him herself—

"What the *fuck* is going on here."

Nalla jerked her head up. Her father stood over her, tall, strong, dressed in black leather and black blades, with an expression on his scarred face like he was prepared to kill the entire Lessening Society with one hand behind his back: Zsadist was as he had always been, and maybe because of that, and definitely because of what had just happened when she'd failed to redirect that gun, Nalla became the young she had not been for a very, very long time.

Her voice was small and soft, a child's. "He's dead, Daddy. Oh, my God, he's dead and it's my fault—"

"What are you doing out here?" Then Zsadist pointed to the asphalt with the phone he had in his hand. "Are those *lesser* ashes on the pavement? And what are you doing with *that?*"

Nalla's brain was lagging so badly, she couldn't connect his words to any coherent meaning. Although she had a feeling he might have just referred to Nate as an inanimate object.

"I don't understand—"

"Get up." Her sire grabbed her arm and tried to drag her to her feet, even though Nate was still in her lap. "I want you to dematerialize right now—"

She pulled against his hold, refusing to budge. "Nate is dead—"

"We should be so lucky."

Like a rubber band snapping back from a stretch, her mind caught up with the conversation—and so did her anger.

Nalla ripped her arm free. "What did you say."

"You heard me." Zsadist started texting on his phone. "Now get out of here, and let me handle cleanup—"

"No."

Her father froze and looked up from the screen. "Excuse me."

"I'm not leaving him." She tightened her hold on Nate's shoulders, the red stains on his white t-shirt like something she heard instead of saw: Screams woven into the cheap fabric. "I'm *not* leaving here."

Off in the distance, she heard the din of traffic, the laughter of humans out on Market Street, a car alarm going off. But none of that mattered. She could only smell the fresh blood and feel the heat of her fury in her face. And even as her sire's eyes went from the yellow they usually were to a black that seemed as evil as anything in the Lessening Society, she wasn't fazed.

"*Go home.*"

Shaking her head slowly, she said in a voice that broke, "This was why I didn't call you."

"Well, Manny was about to operate when you interrupted him with this bullshit. Now, will you be part of the solution instead of the problem, and get the *fuck* out of this alley—"

"I don't have to listen to you anymore. And I'm not leaving him."

Those evil eyes shifted to Nate and then returned to her face. "Who is he to you."

"None of your business. Just like the rest of my life is none of your business."

"You are my daughter."

There was a pause that seemed to last a lifetime.

"But all you really care about is your *shellan* and the war."

"Where'd that come from?" Zsadist nodded at Nate. "Is he putting shit in your head?"

"*What?* You don't know anything about me, do you."

Dimly, she realized this showdown had been coming for a long time. She just could never have guessed the two of them would do the knockdown-daughter/dad-drag-out over the remains of a male she barely knew.

Those black eyes narrowed. "This male isn't worth blowing your life up."

"Well, first of all, he's dead, so aren't you relieved. And secondly, you're not responsible for keeping my life together, and after this— I don't even want your opinion—"

"He's already tried to kill a buddy of his tonight, and now he's working on getting his girlfriend into a grave. You might as well be dating a goddamn grenade—are you *really* this bored."

"*Bored?*" she yelled up at him. "Maybe I'm just over being nothing but the footnote of an epic love story!"

"Is that what you think you are?" Her father glanced off to the left. And when he looked back, he was as grim as she'd ever seen him. "How long have you waited to share that little zinger."

"Years." She eased Nate's shoulders to the side, and got to her feet. Because she wanted to be as close to eye to eye as she could get. "Every night you made me stay home as a matter of fact."

Her father put his palms up, flashing that phone. "I *never* told you to do that. I never once told you you had to—"

"Your meaning was *always* clear."

"There's a fucking war going on here! Was he showing off to you? Being the big male, killing a couple of *lessers*, while he put you in danger—"

"I lured the first slayer in here. Nate was nowhere around. And I was the one who killed it and its backup. But I'm also the reason he—" Her voice cut out. "I'm the reason he's dead. Are you *really* this cruel? To fight with me with his body cooling on the pavement between us?"

Her father's mouth clapped shut, the fit of his teeth making the noise. Then he focused on the front of her parka.

"Yes, that's *lesser* blood." She wiped her mouth and chin, and showed him her palm. "I bit one, too."

"You did *not*." All of the color ran out of his face. "Nalla—"

"It sucks when the facts don't fit your pattern, right?" She nodded at his phone. "You going to finish that text asking for an ambulance? Even though it's too late? Or do you want to keep fighting with me because I'm not falling in line like one of your soldiers."

"You shouldn't be out here."

"You trained me yourself."

"That was for self-defense."

"Yeah, well, it worked." She brushed the bloody snow from her jeans. "I'm still here, aren't I."

What she wanted was to confess to him that he was right. She had made a mistake luring that *lesser* into an alley, and it had cost Nate his life.

But the last thing she needed was to feel worse, and somehow, any conversation she had with her father always ended up with anger in her veins and pain in her heart.

"You don't belong here, Nalla."

Bingo.

"But Nate does?" she ground out.

"The rules are different for him."

"Because he's a male."

"No, because for him, it's never too late—"

The gasp that exploded into the charged air between them was so unexpected, Nalla spun around, expecting to see another slayer behind her. Except the enemy hadn't made the sound.

Down on the asphalt, Nate sat up and took another deep breath as he wiped the blood from his mouth. With his legs out in front of him and his torso so stiff and vertical on his hips, he was like a puppet whose strings had been picked up by his puppeteer.

"Nate . . . ?" she said weakly.

His head swiveled in her direction and then angled so he could look at her. "I told you. Just . . . gimme a minute."

CHAPTER THIRTEEN

T he stench was *terrible*.

As Evan hesitated at the entrance to the abandoned office building, he pinched his nose and propped open the boarded-up glass door with the toe of his snow boot. Did he even have the right address? He leaned back out and looked up to confirm the number. Yes, he did. But why would the seminar be here in this run-down location?

God, the stench was like a three-day-old crime scene with someone baking sugar cookies in the back.

No wonder whoever owned the place left the front unlocked. Anyone with a functioning nose would turn around and walk out.

"Hello?" he said into the darkness.

The echo of his voice suggested that the lobby was vast and empty, and instinctively he put his hand to his brow as a sailor would, like the sun was glaring in his eyes and that was why he couldn't see the sea before him. Of course that didn't help.

A lack of light was the problem.

Easing back out, he looked around at the other twenty-story-tall buildings rising up from this spin-off from Market Street like the trees of some futuristic world. The road he'd run down seemed like a cattle chute leading to here and here alone, the sidewalk pavers laid solely to deliver him to this door, this entry: Even though none of this made sense . . . all of it struck him as inevitable. As soon as he'd sent that DM and received this address and nothing more in response, it was like he'd been locked in. Or maybe this had been set in motion with Uncle at the club. Or even earlier with Mickey in the car driving out to that cabin.

Maybe it went all the way back to the moment of his birth, a coward put upon the earth to suffer until he finally grew a set and decided to become a real man.

And yet he hesitated.

You're such a pussy.

He couldn't even remember which of his family members had told him that or whether it was specifically from tonight or another time. Perhaps it was finally his own voice in his head, the flagellation caught like the common cold from those around him and brought inward, the tide finally turned, the acceptance made.

And with it had come something he'd never felt before: Anger.

Fuck. Them.

"Hello?" he repeated into the darkness.

God, what was that *smell*—

Bing!

Across the hollow space, light bloomed as a set of elevator doors opened, the illumination revealing an empty corporate-America landscape of busted waiting area chairs and litter. As for the Otis, there was nothing inside the steel box but the remnants of mirrored panels that had been shattered by vandals, only their ragged remains retained in their frames.

With that rhyme in his head, he took a step forward, and then he had to choose whether or not to release the door and let it close behind himself.

You've come here. So get what you want, what you need.

The voice entered his head from somewhere outside of him, no memory this time, not even a conglomeration of derision.

He pictured the blond-haired man who had approached him at the gym a couple of weeks ago, so strong, so handsome, a Ken doll who lived and breathed, a personal trainer who seemed to know just what to say to a loser like Evan who wanted to be more than what he was.

The seminar here, tonight, could change Evan's whole life, give him a new outlook and community, provide him with support and a greater purpose.

So why was he hesitating? He had nothing really. No job, and Mickey had been the only one who tolerated his presence.

The personal trainer wanted him, though.

And what an opportunity. A secret group in Caldwell that worked together for their common good, defeating their enemies and forging a future where they were in charge of their own destinies.

It was what his family's organization was supposed to be.

It was all he had ever wanted . . . to belong like the others did.

Do this for yourself, the voice in his head told him. *You will not regret it. Your whole life will change, I promise.*

Evan's weight started to shift, and then it happened. He lifted his back boot and released the prop of the door, the panel closing him in with a clang that he felt in his bones—

Instantly, there was a shift of metal-on-metal, a lock being engaged. Like the trap had been set and the raccoon was caught.

Evan whipped around. Punched at the bar. Got nowhere.

Panic jumped into his throat as he jerked and rattled things, trying to get the lock to spring free. Curling up a fist, he banged on the glass that was covered by boards on the far side—

The sound of his phone ringing stopped him.

With a shaking hand, he took the cell out and answered. "Hello?"

"It's for your safety. Don't freak out."

The personal trainer's familiar voice had him sag with relief. "Where are you?"

"I'm downstairs. In the basement. Take the elevator."

The other man's confidence had an undercurrent of power to it, and as Evan exhaled, it was such a relief to turn his life over to someone who knew better.

"I'm waiting for you."

Evan's eyes shifted over to the elevator, which was standing open, just for him . . . because he was wanted here. He was important here. Here, somebody thought he mattered enough to offer him a blueprint of success, improvement.

"All right," he said.

The call was terminated on the other end and he thought about the disdain of his uncle and all those second lieutenants. He had to become the kind of guy who would have done something about his cousin's murder . . . and who was going to fucking do something about the disrespect he'd been shown at the club.

He was over being a pussy.

"A soldier, not deadweight," he said under his breath. "You are the master of your own destiny, Evan."

As he went forward toward the illumination, there was a crunching underfoot. Glass? Shards of something, certainly, maybe those mirrors that had been vandalized, and he felt a surging rush at crushing something that was more delicate than himself. The ego boost faltered a little when he realized he was following some sort of an oily trail, and he paused to pick up the sole of one of his boots. Whatever the stuff was, all kinds of footprints were in it, as if dozens of people had gone between the entrance and the steel box that led down into the basement.

It made him feel better. Clearly, there had been some success with the guru's training program. Didn't bodybuilders tan themselves really dark for showing? Maybe it was spray tanning stuff.

As soon as he stepped into the elevator, the doors closed and there was a bump and a descent. Another *bing!* announced the arrival at the lower level, and as the panels parted, he finally had better lighting. What he saw . . .

A whimpering sound came out of his lips.

Black oil, everywhere. In orange Home Depot buckets. In puddles on the vast open area's concrete floor. Splashed on the gray-washed walls. And the stink was so much more intense here, so overwhelming that it burrowed into his nose and seemed to fill him from the inside out.

As if he were a repository for whatever it was.

"I'm glad you came."

"Hello?" Evan said as he tried to see around the concrete support columns. "Is that you?"

"Of course it's me. Who else would it be. Are you coming out of there?"

The personal trainer's voice was low and soothing, and Evan thought about the first conversations he'd had with the man. Evan had had a New Year's resolution to start working out, and he'd met the guy that very first night. Lash—short for Thomas Lashelle—had been so helpful, teaching him how to do the weights safely, encouraging him to keep at it, warning him against the three-week barrier that most people who tried to turn over a new leaf couldn't get past.

And then the offer had come. A private workout group for special clients at the gym. Evan had been invited even though he hadn't signed up for one-on-one coaching because the trainer had said his follow-through had been so good: Evan had made it past the three weeks. He now had a—what had the guy called it, a habit base—*habit base* that could be built on.

He'd felt honored to be asked, and he'd met a bunch of other guys. Some had been straight-up power lifters. Some had been easygoing gym bros with thick shoulders and lunkheads. And then there had been him. But Lash had never stood for any bullying, and Evan must have proved himself yet again even if he couldn't lift much.

Because he'd been invited to come to this transformational seminar.

Except . . .

"Where's everyone else?" Evan asked.

"This is a special thing, just for you."

Lash stepped out from behind one of the columns way across the basement. Beneath the ceiling fixtures, the man's blond hair seemed white, and his workout clothes were a dense black. His handsome face was the kind of thing anyone would want to stare at in the mirror, but the effect he had on people was about so much more than those eyes and the cheekbones and the jawline.

There was a magnetism to him.

Bet no one had ever called him a pussy.

"Like I told you, Evan, I'm so glad you reached out, and you're not going to regret the commitment. You told me you wanted to be stronger, physically and mentally. I can give you that."

"What is this place?" he heard himself ask.

What he really wanted to know was what was on the floor and why everything smelled bad and where the other guys were.

"It's a way station, Evan. A place for things to begin. Are you ready to be transformed? You've told me that you want to be bigger, and stronger, and not just physically."

As those low, hypnotic words rode across the fetid air, Evan measured the breadth of the trainer's shoulders, the bulk of his arms.

"I told you I don't want to do steroids," he mumbled. "It's just not natural to have those chemicals in your body."

"And I told you this is not about doing drugs. Now, are you coming out of there? You can't very well expect me to work with you when you're standing in an elevator."

Evan looked at the control panel, the buttons for all the floors above him like other avenues he could have taken. Maybe should have.

It was just the smell, he told himself. If the basement didn't stink like this, he wouldn't be second-guessing everything.

As he extended his boot, he remembered tromping through the snowy forest with Mickey and then his cousin pushing him to the ground. Like he was nothing. A nobody. A cowardly piece of shit who'd been a momma's boy until his momma had been put in her grave, probably because she, like everybody else, just wanted to get away from him.

Pussy. Dummy. Sonofabitch wimp—

With resolve ringing in his chest, Evan's boot landed on the far side of the threshold. The second his weight transferred and he picked up his back boot, the doors closed with a snap as if they were spring-loaded— and he jumped away from them, like they were a pair of teeth—

"Shit!" he blurted as he leaped back a second time.

Somehow, the trainer had gone from being thirty feet away to right in front of him.

"How . . . did you do that?"

The smile that came back at him was reassuring. Almost gentle. "Stronger. Better. More powerful. That's what you want, right?"

Evan pictured the scorn on his uncle's face. And knew that he'd been allowed to leave the club so he'd think it was all okay, that nothing was going to be done to him. But his uncle didn't let shit go like that. He was going to have Evan killed for not protecting Mickey. Even though he'd tried to get his cousin to leave that awful snowy forest. Even though he hadn't been the one with the knife.

He was a target now.

"Yeah," he said. "I need it."

"And you're willing to work for what you want, isn't that right, Evan."

The trainer's eyes searched his face, and it was then that Evan noticed there was something not quite right. The irises were . . . black and the pupils . . . blue.

Lash's eyes had never looked like that before.

"Yes," he heard himself say anyway.

A heavy hand came to rest on Evan's shoulder. "Sacrifice is required and there's no going back. Remember how I told you that?"

No, he'd never heard that before.

"Yes, I remember," he said for reasons he didn't understand.

"What did I tell you? When we were in the gym."

"That if I want to change," he parroted with a trance-like obedience, "I have to make a commitment."

"For life." Lash's all-wrong eyes were so intense, Evan felt a flush come over him. "Say it, Evan. I want to hear what skin you're putting into the game. If I'm going to do my side of things, I need to know that you're going to do yours."

The strange pull between them intensified, making Evan feel like he was physically tied to the trainer, by ropes. By chains. And even though he started to panic, there was a bigger part of him that didn't mind the trap at all. He'd wanted a tether ever since his mom had died, and this was what he'd hoped to find with his uncle, with Mickey.

"For life," the trainer commanded. "Right? Say it."

"For life," Evan whispered—

Everything went wrong in the blink of an eye.

Lash bared his teeth, and just like with his irises, there was something wrong about his canines. And then a hissing noise came out of him, as if he were a snake about to strike.

Before Evan could jerk away, or even think about what was happening, the trainer went for the side of his throat with those extra-long incisors. There was a blaze of pain, and then arms strong as steel bands were locked on him.

As the sucking started.

Evan screamed as loud as he could. But as with the world up above . . . no one was there for him.

CHAPTER FOURTEEN

Over in the alley off Market Street, Nate stared up at the two fellow vampires who were standing over him. They were so clearly father and daughter, their facial structure the same, their eyes set in similar sockets, their stances identical as they leaned forward on their hips and focused on him.

Nalla was looking like she'd seen a ghost.

Zsadist was looking like he wanted to turn Nate back into one.

"How is this . . . possible . . ." she whispered.

Nate brushed his leather sleeve over his face again and tasted his own blood as he swallowed. "Long story."

With a grunt, he pushed his palms into the filthy slush and got his feet under him. The rise to a stand was rough going, but he was never at full strength right after he came back. Not that he did this very often anymore.

"I don't understand." Nalla swept her stare up and down him, and then locked in his chest, where the kill shot had entered his heart.

Or what should have been the kill shot.

In the tense silence, a blast of wind shot through the alley and swirled around, like it was looking for gossip. And with its current, the stink of *lesser* blood and burn residue was a sinus salad that sucked.

Meanwhile, all he could see were the stains on Nalla's parka: Black and red, the colors of the war. She had been . . . magnificent in her fury at that second slayer, and she had tried, more than anybody else had in such a long time, to save him. Why? He had no fucking idea.

He met Zsadist's pitch-black stare and kept his voice level. "This is not what it looks like. She doesn't want me, and I'm not going to try to change her mind. Nothing is started that needs finishing, and before you say it, I won't go near her. You have my word."

As he spoke, the residual pain at the wound in his chest exploded into a white-hot suffering. He told himself it was just the last bit of healing kicking in . . . because that was all he could live with. He'd fallen in love once and gotten crushed, and that had been child's play compared to what he felt like anytime he saw Nalla in a crowd.

Even if she'd have him, which she wouldn't, where would it end? He couldn't die, so he'd just roam the world in loneliness after she was gone? 'Cuz no Fade for him. Not even *Dhunhd*.

So no, he wasn't starting shit with her. He had enough of a curse to live down already, fuck him very much.

And in the silence that followed, the Brother's eyes didn't budge from his own. Then again, a Black Dagger Brother didn't back away from anything.

"Your word means nothing to me," Zsadist said grimly. "And you earned my disregard the old-fashioned way."

"I know I have. And I'm going now."

"The fuck you are. We're not done, you and me. You got shit you need to account for from tonight."

"I know that, too. But here's not the place, is it."

Nate glanced at Nalla and thought about what she'd looked like in

the club, a breath of fresh air among all those made-up attention seek-
ers. Now she was shell-shocked, bloodied . . . yet just as beautiful in a
raw, brutal way, her yellow eyes luminous from unshed tears.

He felt like he needed to say something to her. But in the end, he lost
his voice so he just gave her a nod, and turned away from them both.

Dematerializing would be a great idea, but that was not going to
happen. Shoving his fists into his jacket, he trained his senses on what
was ahead of him and got to walking—

"Nate!"

He glanced over his shoulder. Nalla ran up to him, then reached out
to touch his mouth. When she drew her hand back, her fingertips were
red with his blood.

"*Nalla,*" her sire barked.

She looked back at the Brother, and spoke the one word that was
guaranteed to make the night worse: "No."

"Fuck," Nate breathed.

Zsadist narrowed his eyes. "You are going to find out that sooner
or later, what you choose becomes what you pay for. But you're right,
Nalla. I'm not in charge of your life anymore. You're going to have to
learn that lesson on your own. And, Nate, now's your one chance to do
the right thing with me. I hope like hell you mean what you said."

On that note, the Brother dematerialized, up-and-outing from the
alley.

With a curse, Nate shook his head. "You should have left when he
told you to."

"How do I know if you're well enough to go home on your own?"

"I'm not your problem."

And Jesus, he was a big one. Not only was he in trouble for popping
that cop-bot on Market, but he was in the cross hairs of a Brother now.
Oh, and he still had a dead human in his side yard that needed a good
burial—or a fire, given the ground's frost layer.

As Nalla crossed her arms over her chest, he knew she was going
nowhere fast. "Tell me what just happened."

"Like I said, you don't have to—"

"Worry about you? That's only part of it. At some point, I am going to have to try for sleep and I really need some context for . . . this." She looked back at the puddle of his blood. "Who are you?"

"No one special."

"That"—she jabbed her finger at the place he'd "died"—"is not normal."

"It's not me."

She gave him a don't-be-an-idiot look. "So who the hell am I talking to right now."

All he could do was shake his head again. Shuli knew about his "situation," and so did his parents and the Brothers, but other than that, he kept things quiet. The shit was hard enough to live with, impossible to explain, and he wasn't interested in helping other people understand what he didn't want to talk about in the first place.

"It doesn't matter." He glanced out to the street. "But your father's right. I'm not worth blowing your life up for, and anyway, you shouldn't be angry at him for keeping you safe—from *lessers* or anyone else. That's love and you're lucky he cares."

There was a stretch of silence, and for a brief moment he felt the quiet satisfaction that comes with doing the right thing. Not an emotion he'd had for a very long time.

Then again, he hadn't done a right thing for the right reason in—

"Oh, my God, will you spare me the benevolent rescuer act."

Nate snapped to attention, all record-screech. "I'm sorry, what?"

"You know, you and my father should get along better. You've both got the same attitude." She motioned back and forth between them. "Couple of fence lines for you and me going forward. One, I'm not blowing up my life over anybody, and that includes you. I don't even know you. And two, as difficult as it may be, try to resist commenting on stuff you don't know anything about. It might make you feel superior to stand on a mountain, but the truth is, there's no victory in being patronizing. Especially when your intended target"—she pointed to herself—"doesn't care about your opinion."

Nate felt his brows pop up. Then he glanced at one of the two ash spots on the asphalt, where she'd sent a slayer for a little metaphysical ride back to Lash.

"But I am sorry I missed."

He met her eyes again. "I'm sorry, what?"

"When the *lesser*—shot you. I . . . missed. When I tried to kick the gun out of his hand."

Nate had an absurd impulse to step forward and wrap his arms around her. Instead, he could only shrug. "Weapons can't hurt me."

"I didn't know that at the time."

Before he could respond to that, she cleared her throat. "And I apologize if I sound like a bitch. But this has been a very long night. I'm tired, and you scared the shit out of me, and my father really pisses me off. So that's where I'm at."

Everything about her, from the flush on her cheeks, to the way she crossed those arms, to the scent of her and the rhythm of her words, became vividly, achingly clear to him. Then again, the fog that covered everything and everyone around him—that was so innate to him that he didn't really notice it anymore—never had applied to her.

He had always seen her clearly.

"Why's your night been so hard," he asked softly. "Apart from me playing dead back there. And the *lesser* thing. Well, things, really, 'cuz there were two. Then your dad. Actually, you're right. That's a list right there, isn't it."

Her eyes flared in surprise like people didn't ask her for personal details very often. He felt the same way. They weren't something he asked for very often. Or at all.

"I, ah, I started it with a fight with my best friend."

"Oh, yeah." He nodded. "I know what that feels like."

Not that he and Shuli had been friends for a long time. But they absolutely had had conflict in that Tesla.

"Some nights are better off not starting," he muttered.

"You're not going to tell me anything, are you?"

"There's nothing to tell."

"Your definition of 'nothing' and mine are different." She paused, as if to give him an opportunity to speak. "But there you go."

As she took a step back, he wanted to ask her to stay with him. Yeah, and then what? They were just going to stand here, shooting the shit, while he dodged her entirely reasonable questions and they were sitting ducks for *lessers*?

"I'd tell you to take care of yourself," she murmured, "but like you said, I'm guessing that isn't necessary. Anyway, thanks for having my back over there, and here's your phone."

He accepted the thing from her. "You're welcome—"

With a curt nod, she was up and out, the thin air she left behind nothing compared to her physical presence.

As he felt a letdown, he reminded himself that he had more important things to worry about than a female who was never going to be his, anyway.

Time to go get rid of that body.

◆   ◆   ◆

A couple of blocks away, in Bathe's VIP section, Bitty was hitting the proverbial wall. It wasn't that the people around her weren't fun. They were laughing and enjoying themselves, for sure. And it wasn't that she felt unsafe. She was surrounded by other vampires, many of whom had been trained by the Brotherhood to fight. And it wasn't that she minded the music or the presence of humans or the attention her dress was getting her.

Well, she was a little tired of hem maintenance.

But she was ready to leave. She didn't hate the club scene; it just wasn't her—and she had to admit that Nalla might have a point. Going out just to not be home wasn't much better than staying home to avoid going out.

A cup of coffee would have been better.

"Lyric," she said. "I think I'm going to go."

The female turned away from the guy she was talking to, her beautiful silver dress shimmering as her body moved. "But you just got here."

"It's been an hour."

"That's no time at all."

"I have to go to bed early today. I'm working a double tomorrow night."

That wasn't exactly true. She was going to volunteer for a double so that she had an excuse in case anybody asked her to do something.

"Well, I'm *so* glad you came."

Lyric threw her arms around Bitty, and the hug was so genuine, so not a social performance, that there was shy happiness in the way her presence was accepted by one of the "in-crowd." And yes, that was kinda high school–ish, but the fact was, Shuli, Rhamp, and Lyric were a trio people gravitated to and revolved around.

"You'll come again, right?" Lyric asked.

The hopeful expression was kind of inexplicable, but Bitty found herself nodding and feeling optimistic. It wasn't always the club that they all went to. The group did movie nights and pancake marathons, mountain climbing and house parties. She would like to be a part of all that. Or some of that.

Or at least have the option to go to a few things.

"I would love to."

"Great."

There was another hug, and that started a rush of embraces— except for Shuli's six-pack worth of rat pack, as he called them. Those aristocratic males hung back, even as she clinched up with everybody else. Well, almost everyone.

L.W. was where he'd been the whole time, still in that lean-back sprawl with those hooded eyes missing nothing even though he'd been drinking all along.

"You'll want to go out the rear," Lyric said, pointing to the fire door. "That alley is really quiet so you'll be able to dematerialize easily. Rhamp, take her out so she's safe."

"Yup, absolutely." The female's brother put his martini down. "Come on, Bitty, I gotchu."

Rhamp did up the button on his slick suit jacket, slipped a friendly arm around her shoulders, and walked her up the steps and around the sitting area. Just as they came to the exit, one of his boys called his name.

"Wait here a sec," he said as he started to go back.

At that moment, the music changed beat, and it was like someone in the sound booth had turned the volume up. When her stomach rolled and she felt a little dizzy, she punched the bar on the steel panel and—

"Oh, thank God," she murmured as she went out into the cold and took a deep breath.

The door slammed shut behind her and she released an exhale as if she were a smoker making rings. Her overheated skin basked in the temperature drop, and the wonky feeling dissipated, too. With her relief hitting, she was glad she'd taken a chance, on the dress and the club—

Behind her, the door reopened, the music and laughter flaring, a waft of heat warming her back like a hearth set with a fire.

"Thanks, Rhamp," she said. "I'll just head—"

The scent registered first. And then a deep voice rumbled, "Not Rhamp."

Bitty turned around slowly. L.W. was standing just outside the club, and God . . . he was huge. It wasn't just that he towered over her in height, it was the breadth of him. His expression, too. Resting bitch face? More like trained killer, who might, or might not, wait for a private corner to make his move.

His pale green eyes were so unwavering that Bitty had to look away—and as for all of January's freezing cold? Was it cold? She couldn't feel anything.

No, that wasn't exactly true . . .

"I've noticed something about you," he said.

She tugged at the hem of her dress, thinking that the damn thing seemed tighter and shorter and lower cut. "What might that be."

"You're a hugger."

It was such a non sequitur that she glanced back up at him. "I'm sorry?"

"You hug people, and when you do, you mean it."

"Oh. Thank you? I guess."

His eyes traveled down her body. "New dress. You usually wear jeans and sweaters in the winter."

"How do you know what I wear?"

"I watch you."

"Why," she whispered.

The shrug was causal. The light in his eyes was volcanic. The energy coming off his body was . . .

"You never hug me," he said.

"I'm sorry, wha—" She cleared her throat and measured his heavy shoulders. "Well, you're not . . . exactly the huggable type."

"No? Why not."

Her eyes drifted to his chest. There were weapons under his jacket, probably holstered beneath his arms and around his waist. The guns and knives weren't off-putting; her father was always armed, so she was used to all that. But the idea of getting up close to L.W.'s body, feeling it against her?

He opened his arms. "How about me."

This was why I had to come, she thought. *This moment, right here.*

And yet she was frozen by the sense that something was coming, something that was . . .

After a moment, L.W. lowered his arms. "Fair enough. But I'm staying until you've safely dematerialized."

Bitty shook herself back to attention. "You've just surprised me, that's all."

"You don't have to explain." And he didn't seem particularly offended. "Have a good night."

"I don't know if I can dematerialize."

"Why not?" He frowned. "Are you ill?"

"No."

With his hair all but shaved on the sides, and the length of it braided down the center of his head, his face was accentuated, the jaw cut but not heavy, his cheekbones high, his brows somehow always arched with disdain no matter what the bottom half of his visage was doing. Not that she had seen him smile. Ever—

The emergency exit opened abruptly, a blue glow flooding out.

And that was when it happened.

The vision that had vibrated just under the veil of her consciousness broke through into proper awareness, and she saw L.W.'s autocratic face just as it was now, with one side in shadow and the other bathed in a dark-blue illumination. And then—yes, exactly like he was doing now—he looked at whoever was peering out.

"You have a secret," she heard herself say softly.

L.W.'s head whipped back to her. "What."

"Something you cannot share . . . and it's come home tonight." She narrowed her eyes as her words came faster and faster. "You need to be careful, L.W. Your anger is your downfall, and that which you were cheated of was stolen by a thief who doesn't care about its ill-gotten gains. Unless you can forgive fate, you are going to destroy . . . all of us—"

"L.W." Mharta leaned out of the door she'd opened. "What are you doing out here."

He ignored the female. "What did you say."

Bitty shook her head and took a step back, mostly to get herself free of the trance-like state that had come over her. "I'm sorry. Nothing. It was—I don't know, I was just rambling. Forget it."

Mharta nodded and waved a pointed see-ya. "Yeah, goodnight. Great to have you—L.W., let's go back inside. It's freezing out here."

Forcing herself to calm down, Bitty closed her eyes, took a deep breath, and prayed—*prayed*—that she could focus well enough to get herself away from the alley. Unfortunately, concentration was required, and she couldn't decide what freaked her out more.

What she'd just said to L.W.

Or the fact that he'd wanted her to hug him.

CHAPTER FIFTEEN

I n the basement of the abandoned office building, Evan woke up
facedown in a warm puddle. He was making awful sounds, all wet
and bubbly ... just like the noises that had come out of Mickey right
after his throat had been cut. But at least Evan could breathe, even if he
couldn't think, and he pushed at the hard surface he was on, feeling a viscous liquid drip off his nose and his chin, and drool from his mouth—

One of his palms slipped out from under him and he slammed
back down. Turning his head so he could get some air into his lungs,
he shifted his stiff legs and moaned. His joints felt like they had nails
driven into them, and his skull was throbbing as if his brain had swollen
three times its size ...

The stench was inside him. Under his skin, inside his bones, clog-
ging up his chest and his guts. He *was* the smell—

That wasn't so bad, was it.

The trainer's mocking voice echoed in his consciousness, as it had
echoed in the barren basement, and with it came images, terrible images, that filtered through his logy confusion. The memories were hor-

rific, his blood being taken by that man who was no normal man, what was in Evan's jugular swallowed like something extracted from the earth, claimed by the one who had bitten him, taken until he was on the verge of death. And then the black oil that smelled so bad, that was in all those buckets and on the floor, had been forced down his throat, his mouth cranked open, a wrist pressed and held against his lips until his front teeth were going to snap off, the flow like a hose, pumping and plumping him up, a tire about to burst.

He had cried the whole time, his tears hot on his cheeks.

He did not cry now. He was too spent.

Pushing at the concrete floor again, he flopped over onto his back and stared at the flat panels of LED lights mounted on the basement ceiling. His eyes were soupy and he rubbed them, making the blurriness worse—

The elevator.

He needed to get in the elevator and leave. He wasn't safe here. What if that horror came back for him?

What if that ... monster ... returned.

Lifting his twelve-hundred-pound skull, Evan located the elevator's closed doors and orientated himself. It was so far away and he told himself he just needed a minute.

As he let the pressure off his neck, he looked down his naked torso. He had a vague memory of being laid out on the floor and his parka, fleece, and t-shirt getting cut off. He didn't know where they'd gone and he was too scared to care: Something had been done to his chest. In the center, at his sternum, there was bruising, the skin bright red, a dull ache thumping to the beat of his heart.

After the oil had been geysered down his throat, the trainer had ... what had happened next?

Evan tried to remember. All he got was the image of Lash's palm hovering over his heart and somehow creating a pressure that threatened to split him in half. And then—

The trainer's head had snapped up to the ceiling, as if his name had been called.

He'd cursed and punched Evan in the pecs in frustration.

Then he'd disappeared. Like an apparition.

"I gotta leave now," Evan said with a rasp. "Must . . . leave now."

Whatever had transpired between them had been interrupted. And he wasn't going to survive when that horror came back.

Getting to his feet was a struggle, but his fear drove him to the vertical. With a zombie lurch, he headed back to where it had all started. At the elevator doors, he hit the up arrow to summon things with a trembling hand, but he didn't expect anything to happen and he looked around for some kind of staircase—

Bing!

The steel panels opened.

He jumped inside and wheeled around, punching at the "L" button like his life depended on it.

As the doors closed in lazy contrast to his panic, they cut off the vision of that oil on the floor. But the shit was all over him—on his boots, on his jeans . . . on the skin of his doughy abdomen. Halfway through the achingly slow ascent, he realized he was going to freeze when he got out of the building, but he couldn't worry about that.

Did he go to the police? Yeah, and tell them what? He was the nephew of a crime boss and he'd been bitten by a . . .

He touched the side of his neck, probing the puncture wounds. *Shouldn't they hurt,* he wondered.

He couldn't worry about that either. He needed to get out of this building, and go—where . . . ? Where could he crash? Going back to his apartment wasn't an option. One of his uncle's assassins would be waiting for him there—

Mickey's hideout. He could go to Mickey's secret place, the one his cousin didn't tell nobody about, that Evan only knew because he'd found out by mistake and Mickey had thought he was too stupid to believe the lie he'd been fed.

When there was a bump to a halt, he waited. And waited some more.

With his heart pounding, he went for the seam in the panels. Shoving his hands into the crack, he tried to pry things apart—and as he got nowhere, he lost it, flailing, scratching, pounding—

Bing!

The doors opened. But he didn't move.

Splaying out his fingers, he looked at where the tips had been scrubbed raw. They were black with oil.

He told himself it was from the puddle he'd woken up in. But then he turned his palms face up.

Drip. Drip. Drip—

His blood was . . . black. He was bleeding . . . the oil . . .

Evan opened his mouth and screamed.

As the elevator doors reclosed on him.

◆   ◆   ◆

When Nalla re-formed, it wasn't anywhere near one of the entrance houses in that cul-de-sac that led down into the Wheel's subterranean sets of quarters. No, she was out in the countryside, in front of a rambling farmhouse that had a curl of smoke rising from its brick chimney, a charming wraparound porch, and a big tree in the yard. Walking up the shoveled path, she knew she should have gone home. Also knew that if she had to spend all day locked underground with her father and her *mahmen*, she was going to lose her fucking mind.

It seemed far colder out here than it had been downtown, and the treads of her running shoes squeaked on the snowpack. When she hopped up the four steps to the porch, she thought of the steps leading into the sitting pit at that club.

God, she couldn't believe she had trampled all those drinks. She could believe she'd killed those two slayers, though. Her father had insisted on training her himself, and no, it hadn't just been for self-defense. She knew about explosives, poisons, and how to sneak up behind someone and piano-wire them.

She had loved that time with him. It had always been so special because he'd carved those hours out just for her. Her father spent so much time in the field and training soldiers, and her *mahmen* always got him during the daytime when everyone was hunkered down and sleeping.

Hard to be third in line, even though she'd known he had so many responsibilities.

As soon as she stepped onto the porch, the front door opened for her, and the platinum-haired female on the other side was a vision in a gray sweater and black pants. Then again, did Rahvyn ever look bad? *No.* She was like an ethereal pool of moonlight, even as she lived and breathed.

"You are supposed to be off tonight," the female said with a smile.

"Well, I had some extra time." Nalla stomped her feet on the mat to get most of the snow out of her sneaker bottoms. "Figured I'd see if I could help out."

"You are always so giving—" Rahvyn glanced down and recoiled. "Are you all right?"

For a split second, Nalla couldn't figure out what was wrong. Then she swallowed a curse: *Lesser* blood on her parka. Nate's blood, too.

She closed her eyes. "I'm fine. I just need . . . a shower, a change of clothes, and some privacy. Only for the rest of the night."

"Of course. That is what we are here for, are we not."

Stepping over the threshold, Nalla felt like she was entering the place for the first time. Then again, she'd never come here as a resident, and as she'd explained what she'd needed and been greeted with such acceptance, she had a fresh perspective on what they did here: Luchas House had been established in memory of Uncle Qhuinn's brother, who had died decades ago. Its purpose was to provide transitional housing for young who could no longer stay at Safe Place because they were males who had gone through the change, and to give support and skills training to males and females who were seeking to live independently after trauma or parental death. Nalla had started as a volunteer, gotten her social work degree through a human university—thanks to remote learning—and then been brought on as a full-time counselor.

"Let me take that coat and clean it for you."

As Nalla let the thing get peeled off her shoulders, she glanced around the main living room. Over the last thirty years or so, the furniture had changed, and out in the back, the kitchen had been done over twice—but the vibe was always cozy, especially with the fire crackling in the hearth, and the throw blankets that were folded over the soft sofas and deep armchairs. Off to the left, a wing had been added about a decade ago, with individual counseling rooms and a group meeting space on the ground level, and another five bedroom suites built in underneath. There was also an annex with staff rooms and office space that was connected by a tunnel that ran under the lawn.

Still, no matter how big the footprint got, the place still smelled like Toll House cookies every night, and the people were kind, and though the stories were hard to hear, the work made a difference.

"What else can I do for you," Rahvyn asked as she folded up the parka.

Nalla could only shake her head. The other female, who was Lassiter's *shellan*, was their very best volunteer, clocking in as a house *mahmen* on the weekends. She saw too much, though. When those silver eyes looked into your own? You had the sense she could read your whole life's story.

"Nothing?" the female prompted.

"I don't . . . really know what to ask for," Nalla whispered.

"Then do not even try. Come on, let us get you upstairs. I will bring you some clothes and something to eat—"

"No food, please." Every time she breathed in through her nose, she smelled blood. "My stomach's off."

"Fair enough."

The next thing Nalla knew, she was up in one of the bedrooms that were no longer used by the male and female residents, but instead kept as quiet spaces for reading and meditation. The beds were still in place, though, and man, that duvet looked like heaven.

"Any particular requests for clothing?"

Glancing back at the doorway, Nalla shook her head, and then went into the bathroom, flipping the light switch by the door. Even though she didn't want to see her own face, she stood over the sink and stared at herself in the mirror. There was a speckled pattern of black dots up her neck and on her cheeks and forehead. There was also slayer blood in her hair, and Rahvyn was right about her clothes. They were a mess, and she probably stank to high heaven.

What had she been thinking, coming here like this?

"I should have gone somewhere else," she said as she looked down at her jeans. "This is a tremendous trigger for some of our residents."

"Everyone is at group right now. And I will make sure your clothes are laundered in the annex."

"I wasn't thinking straight."

"Yes, you were. You knew you needed safety."

"You're not going to ask why I didn't go home?"

"No."

Meet your client where they are, Nalla thought. *Excellent approach.*

Then she frowned. "It's not a weekend, and yet you're here?"

Unless she was wrong and had lost an entire night between when she'd left downtown to come out here? Anything seemed possible right now.

Rahvyn smiled in that way she did, so compassionately. "I am going to have more time during the week now. And like you, I want to be where I can make a difference."

With shaking hands, Nalla cranked the water and started rinsing the blood off—and as it ran into the drain, she hated to see the black mix with the red.

Flexing her fingers under the cold rush, she felt . . . too little of the chill. She was probably in shock.

As she glanced up into the mirror again and focused on Rahvyn over her shoulder, she thought back to doing the same with Bitty, when the female had been sitting on her own bed back at home. Things felt like they had changed irrevocably, and she wished lives were like clothes . . . that you could put them into a Maytag with some OxiClean and have everything come out fresh-smelling, warm, and ready to wear out of the dryer.

"You really aren't going to ask me what happened?" she said roughly.

Rahvyn shook her head and spoke in that formal way of hers. "You will tell me if and when you are ready. All I know is that you are alive, and we can work with that. I would like to know if there is anyone else who needs something, however."

Between one blink and the next, Nalla returned to that alley. "After what I saw tonight, that's another thing I'm not sure how to answer."

"Was medical support contacted?"

"Yes, but they weren't needed. As it turned out."

"Okay. I am glad whoever was with you did not need treatment."

Nalla turned the water off and reached for a hand towel that was looped, plump and fragrant, through a chrome circle.

"Yeah, that's not the half of it. But you wouldn't believe me if I told you the whole story."

"Try me." Rahvyn put her palm forward. "But no pressure."

"I saw a male get shot first in the stomach, and then in the heart—and he died in front of me." As there was a gasp, Nalla pivoted and dried things off. "Except then he sat up. Stood up. And was perfectly fine. So no, he didn't need any help, although I sure as hell need some time to try to put that into perspective."

Rahvyn stared down at the floor for a long moment. Then she rubbed her eyes like her head hurt. "Hop in the shower. I will get you what you need."

"See? I knew you wouldn't believe me. But it's the truth."

The other female glanced back over, and God, she seemed as ancient as Nalla was feeling. "Oh, I realize you speak the truth."

"So you know who I'm talking about? He obviously keeps it mostly to himself. My father knew, though. And so did Dr. Manello."

Nalla shouldn't have been surprised. The female was mated to Lassiter, who was the spiritual head of the race. She probably knew a lot of things, about a lot of people.

"Can you tell me anything about Nate?" Nalla asked. "How . . . he is what he is?"

Rahvyn seemed to blanch, and a sadness came over her. But all she did was shake her head.

"I will leave some clothes at the end of the bed while you are in the shower," the female said before stepping away. "Take your time in the hot water. Sometimes it is a balm for so much more than what ails the battered body."

As the door was closed, Nalla glanced at the faucet of the sink and thought of her hands under the cold rush. "If you can feel anything, that is."

CHAPTER SIXTEEN

U mm, hi, Uncle V. Do you have a minute?"

As Bitty hovered in the doorway of the steel and glass office, she had to talk loudly to project over the old-fashioned Post Malone, but she knew she wasn't surprising the Brother who was staring so intently at the bank of computer monitors. Vishous, son of the Bloodletter, mated of the healer Jane, was in charge of security for all the sites the Black Dagger Brotherhood maintained, and he'd known the instant she'd materialized onto the Audience House's driveway and approached the entrance to his this-is-just-an-old-barn.

F.T. Headquarters was the hub for security, and she'd had to be cleared to get through its door.

The Brother swiveled around in his chair and exhaled a stream of Turkish tobacco as he turned down the music. "What do you need. Name it."

For as long as she had known the male—and it had been decades— he'd had a goatee, tattoos at one temple, and a black glove—and always a hand-rolled cigarette with a little orange glow at the tip close by. He also had a razor-sharp stare that had taken her a while to get comfortable around. He wasn't exactly a softie under the hard shell. But his reply was his whole character: For those he considered his own, he would do anything.

"Can I talk to you?" She glanced over her shoulder, at all the people sitting in front of computers out in the open area. "I mean, I know you're busy—"

With that black leather glove, he motioned for her to come in, and as soon as she did, the frosted glass door shut by itself.

"Not too busy for you."

"Thank you."

She approached his glass desk, and as she sat down on the single chair next to it, she was grateful that she'd changed back into her normal, comfortable clothes. No hem to worry about. No cleavage showing. And she was keeping her parka on because she felt badly about disturbing the Brother.

"I won't take long," she tacked on.

"I'm good," he said briskly. "I've been cleaning up a mess, but I think it's finally taken care of."

He leaned forward and tapped the cigarette into a glass ashtray. Everything inside the office, from the shelves that displayed all kinds of Victorian medical equipment, to the lighted tiles on the floor and ceiling, to that see-through desk, was glass. With the bright illumination streaming from all angles, it was as if he and his office full of computer equipment were being projected from a monitor, the Brother becoming the very technology he spent so much time with.

"You clean up a lot of things, don't you."

He nodded to the screens. "I'm like Farmers Insurance. I know a thing or two because I've seen a thing or two."

Bitty smiled, but she couldn't manage to keep the expression going.

"Someone giving you a problem," Vishous said in a low voice.

"Oh, no. Nothing like that."

"You sure?" He put up his dagger hand, the one that was covered.

"I won't go behind your father's back, but if you need something done and don't want the person ripped apart, I can take care of things in a certain way. If you know what I mean."

She tangled her hands in her lap. Looked around at the frosted walls of the office. There were screens that could be lowered inside what she suspected were dual panes of soundproof glass, and with them currently down in place, she wondered what he'd been doing in here that even his most loyal programmers and security personnel couldn't know.

And she was glad no one could see in, even though none of his subordinates at those black desks and anti-glare monitors would be able to hear what was said. Sometimes you needed a little extra privacy because faces and body positions revealed a lot.

"You have . . . visions, don't you." When he didn't respond, she risked a glance at the Brother—and couldn't believe how direct she was being. "I've heard stories about them."

Vishous tamped out his cigarette, pushing out of the way the butts of the others he'd smoked so he could find the smooth ceramic surface of the ashtray's belly.

"What kind of stories," he prompted as a new song started playing, the beat like that of an autoloader going off.

"They say you see only death, nothing else."

"Who's they."

"People." She cleared her throat. "So I just want to know . . ."

As she searched for the right words, he shrugged. "If I did see any visions—and I'm not saying I do—I wouldn't tell them to anybody unless there was an outcome that I could positively affect. And if I didn't happen to see anything about someone or, like, their parents, that is pertinent to health or longevity, I would tell them not to worry. So don't worry, true?"

"Oh, that's good. Thank you."

"Not that I see things."

"Of course." She shifted in the hard seat—and wondered whether he'd deliberately chosen the chair because it was like sitting on cold cement. "That's not why I came, though. I, ah, I want to know . . . what do you do if you don't know why you were . . . shown something. Like, what if you were shown something that you knew was important, but you didn't know the context. Or . . . something."

There was a moment of silence. Then Vishous sat forward, his diamond eyes so intense that she felt as if she had a goose-necked interrogation lamp shining in her face. She even blinked like she was blinded.

"Bitty, do you see things?"

Flushing, she wished she hadn't come. All of a sudden her private chaos was getting an airing, and boy, she wished she'd given more thought about who she'd picked to talk to. But like she could go to anyone else?

"It's not visions exactly. Well, sometimes I see pictures in my head, but it's more like reading a history book aloud." She put her hand to her lips. "The words just come out of my mouth, but I try to keep what I'm shown to myself because I don't want people to think I'm crazy. And I'm not, honest."

Vishous reached over to a neat pile of hand-rolls, the little wrapped tubes of tobacco like cordwood stacked for a fire.

"How long's this been going on?"

"Since . . . I was a young. I used to know when my birth father was going to beat my *mahmen*." She pushed her sweaty palms up and down her thighs, the jeans catching and dragging. "I would see a snapshot, of the angle of her face, the arc of his palm. Sometimes, when there was . . . blood . . . I would see the droplets in midair. Frozen. And then the words would come out of my mouth. I would warn her, she would listen—but nothing ever changed."

The Brother put a fresh cigarette between his front teeth and talked around it.

"Fucking hell, Bitty." He flicked his thumb on the wheel of a red Bic and then talked through the exhale. "You shouldn't have grown up like that."

On a reflex, she stretched her arm out, feeling the old ache from where some of her many broken bones had reknit badly. "It was an early warning system. Or it was supposed to be, maybe. I could never save her, though."

Uncle V's upper lip twitched as if his fangs were descending and he was holding in a growl.

"It's okay," she told him.

And she would have reached out to—pat his arm? Or something? Except he was too intimidating when he was just being his sarcastic normal self. Like this? Nope. Hard nope.

He put the Bic down with exaggerated precision, making sure it stood up on its base. "Do you see yourself in the images?"

"No, never. Only others."

He nodded. "That's right. That's the same for me."

"So it is true. About you."

"Yeah." He pointed his cigarette at her. "This is not for public consumption, are we clear? This is between you and me."

"Oh, of course." She sat up a little straighter. "Yes."

"I don't need a bunch of people coming up and asking me questions they do not want the answers to."

"I understand completely." God knew she hated what she'd seen of her birth parents. "I won't say a word."

He smoked for a moment, and the scent calmed her, maybe because she could remember the times she had gotten to stay up during the day to watch her uncles V and Butch play billiards in that room full of green-felt-topped tables. It had been a very special treat, to get cozy in her PJs and curl up on the big couches with a blanket—and pretend, as her lids grew heavy, that she was just resting her eyes as she listened to the grown-ups talk and laugh.

"Bitty, I'm going to tell you a truth you're not going to believe right now, but that over time, if you're smart, you'll come to know is fact." He tapped his cigarette over the ashtray even though there were no ashes at the tip. "What you're shown is not your fault. You can't control the channel when it opens up or what it delivers, and there's nothing *you* can do to stop destiny. You also can't insert yourself too much. I've always sensed that if I get too far into it, the energy that is due to another is going to pull up in my own driveway. I give people hints and clues when there's a possibility they might be able to help the outcome, but how they handle the situation as it arises is up to them."

"And you never tell them when they can't change anything?"

As his brows dropped low, the symbols in the Old Language around his left temple distorted, although the warning remained legible—and she had to agree with what he'd said. The glimpses into the future that they were privy to meant they were walking a dangerous line. Mortals were not supposed to dabble in fate. They were only supposed to walk forward in it, the course carved by individual decisions forging a path that, if you were lucky, maybe allowed you to see a couple of feet in front of you.

The longer course of a life was to stay veiled, the unknown and unknowable . . . like death: A law of nature that stalked you, and hopefully was kind with a quick-and-easy when it finally caught up and claimed you.

In the silence that stretched out, part of her wanted to know what her uncle was remembering, so she could learn firsthand exactly what lines he'd drawn and when. Except she had enough of her own problems, and besides, she wasn't a war-hardened Brother. If Vishous, son of the Bloodletter, looked like he was revisiting traumatic events, she couldn't imagine how she would handle the trip.

"You need to tell me what you saw," he said eventually.

Bitty glanced at the computer screens, all of which had the filters that required a person to sit directly in front of them to view whatever was being projected.

"You know all kinds of private things," she said as she hesitated. "And you keep them that way."

"It's a vault up here." He tapped the side of his head, by the tattoos.

"Provided it's not illegal or goes against the stated rules and regulations of the throne. And even then, there are gray areas."

"I haven't told my father or mom about any of this. I didn't want them to think I was dangerous and send me away."

And that was another truth she hadn't wanted to even put into words: She'd always worried they'd renounce the adoption. They'd never given her any reason to doubt their love, but she was an "other" to them. What if they decided she was too much trouble or too complicating?

"You're not dangerous, sweetheart. And like I said, none of this is your doing. Now, talk to me. What did you see that brought you here."

She pictured the image of L.W.'s autocratic, arresting face, bathed in dark-blue light.

"It has to do with Little Wrath." What a stupid soubriquet. The male was "little" like a tank compared to a golf cart. "And that's why I want to be . . . careful. He's more important than other people—"

"You need to tell me *exactly* what you were shown," Vishous said in a sharp tone.

Gone was the reassuring uncle, in his place was the Black Dagger Brother who was one of the King's private guard. And she should have expected the shift.

"He has a secret," she blurted, her internal pressure releasing in a flow of words. "It's something he keeps close to his chest with his friends. And there's been some kind of theft. He doesn't know it yet. When he finds out, he's going to be very angry, and it takes him to a dark place . . ."

"What kind of a dark place."

She touched the center of her chest. "It's inside of him. A dark place in his soul, and he will endanger us all."

Vishous muttered something. "Did you talk to him about this?"

"Not really? It just kind of happened. I mumbled words to him, and I mean, I don't really know him. We grew up in parallel, you know?

Not in each other's lives. I've always thought he was kind of apart from everybody."

"Yeah, he got that from his sire," came the dry response.

"So I don't know what to do. I thought because you have experience with visions, you could tell me how I should . . . I don't know. And then, really, because it's him, this is not something I feel like I should handle myself."

Vishous tapped his hand-rolled, this time because he needed to if he didn't want to ash on his keyboard. "You did the right thing coming to me."

"I don't want him to get in trouble."

"He isn't."

Overhead, cool air drifted down from a vent, and she realized how hot the towers under the desk had to be. It must be like having space heaters blowing on your ankles, she thought as she glanced down at the Brother's shitkickers.

As everything got really quiet between them, the fact that Vishous was just sitting in his ergonomic black leather chair, not even smoking, probably wasn't a good sign.

"Does this make any sense to you?" she asked.

He opened his mouth as if to answer, but then he frowned and glanced at his monitors. Sitting forward over his keyboards, he moved a mouse around and clicked it a couple of times.

"You need to go, Bitty," he said. "I've got business to take care of."

Jumping to her feet, she nodded like a bobblehead. "I shouldn't have bothered you—"

The Brother reached out and took her hand. As those diamond eyes bored into her own with an earnest regard, she took a deep breath and tried to calm down.

"You did the right thing," he repeated. "And I'll never tell you not to talk to your parents, but outside of that? Let's keep this quiet."

"I'll do that. I promise."

"You can always come to me, anytime. About this or anything else.

You know my rules, though. Health or safety, and I have to go to your parents or even higher up the food chain."

"I understand. That's what we do at Safe Place." She focused on the glowing floor. "I need to know, though. Do you have any idea what this is about?"

The grave way he shook his head seemed like regret at the situation, rather than a denial.

"You've got to go now, sweetheart. You know where to find me."

The exit opened on its own, as if he had willed it so, and she made a mumbling, stumbling departure. As she went down the aisle between all the IT workstations, none of the males or females looked up, and she couldn't decide whether her invisibility made her feel better or totally lost—

At the opposite end of the open space, the inner entrance to the facility opened, and as Bitty got a gander at who'd arrived, she immediately hopped to the side to clear the way.

L.W.'s father, the great Blind King, stepped through the jambs with his service dog and his private guard—and the imposing male seemed to take up all of the space and air in the entire building. As a ripple of fear went through Bitty, she didn't get it. She'd been around Wrath before, going all the way back to when the Brotherhood and their families had lived together in the mansion on the mountain. Sure, she hadn't seen him much after the Brotherhood had moved off the estate and into that subterranean village in the 'burbs, but she'd been at the new Audience House from time to time and run into him there. More to the point, he'd never once been mean to her, no matter how hard his expression always was.

Bitty narrowed her eyes. Still, there was something . . . different about him now.

Then again, maybe her nerves were just plain shot. And anyway, the King wasn't even paying attention to her. He was focused straight ahead, his wraparounds trained on Vishous's office—while that Brother slowly stood up from his desk chair and came forward with an expression of shock.

Even though Bitty knew she was staring, she couldn't look away as the two stopped in the doorway of the glass office.

"About time," Vishous said roughly to the King. "What took you thirty years."

Wrath laughed in a low rumble. "Leave it to you to be unimpressed, even by a miracle."

"Is that what this is?"

"You want me to go back where I came from?"

"Nah. I think we'll keep ya."

The embrace between the males was a hard, back-thumping one, as if they had been parted by much passage of time and vast distances. Which made no sense. They saw each other every night in front of civilians—

Over the King's shoulder, Vishous's eyes shifted to Bitty, and she ducked her head and hustled out, bypassing a number of uncles who had congregated at the entrance. Her father wasn't among the other Brothers, though.

Just as well. She wasn't sure what she would tell him about tonight.

As she stepped out into the snow, she looked across at the cozy cottage where the audiences were conducted. Then she glanced back at the steel door, and felt like some kind of reset had happened, some piece that had been missing returning to its rightful place.

Except that was crazy, she told herself as she dematerialized back home.

Nothing had changed in the first place.

CHAPTER SEVENTEEN

The flames of the bonfire licked into the darkness and plumes of smoke swirled around in the cold wind. As light flickered out from the blaze, the illumination cascaded over the winter landscape, enlivening the bare-limbed trees and the pristine snow cover.

Nate stood upwind of it all. He didn't like the smell of burning flesh, not even when it was something edible on a grill, and the gasoline he'd used as an accelerant wasn't any better in his nose. He'd used the latter, though, because there was a lot to burn up. Most of it was Mickey Trix's body, but he'd also tossed in the pants he'd been wearing when he'd done the job on the guy, and the towel he'd wiped his bloody hands on when he'd had to go greet Shuli.

While he watched the combustion, images played in his mind, and none of them made him feel any better—

Fireflies. *Fireflies?*

Even though it was the wrong season, there appeared to be a colony of fireflies that had gathered on the far side of the fire. But that couldn't be right. They had to be sparks from the flames . . .

Suddenly, he knew what it was. And who.

"Mother . . . *fucker.*"

Across all the flames, just inside the ring of light, the tiny sparks coalesced into a solid figure, a female with hair like moonlight and an aura like the sun itself.

Not tonight, he thought. *I do not have the energy.*

Still, he began to walk around to her, and she did the same, until they met at the eastern mark of the compass. Rahvyn's silver hair lay on the shoulders of a red wool coat, and she had proper snow boots on, as well as gloves. As she stared up at him with wariness, he thought of another gunshot wound he'd had in the gut, all those years ago.

When the course of his life had changed forever.

"Are you not cold?" she said.

He didn't glance down at all his lack of jacket. The thing was hanging on a tree from when he'd warmed up dragging Mickey's dead weight through the snow. And she could take her concern elsewhere.

"Why are you here?" he asked.

"I wanted to make sure you were okay."

Nate held his arms out and turned in a circle. "Fine, like always. Why're you asking?"

"Do not play games with me. You know why."

Zsadist must have told her about the alley scene, he thought as he stayed quiet.

"Nate, I wish you would talk to someone. It does not have to be me." She looked in the direction of his cabin. "This is not healthy, any of it. The isolation. The anger you have. And you are not eating well—"

"Did you interview my parents before you came here, or are these all your observations?"

"People are worried about you."

"I can't do anything about that."

"Yes, you can." Her silver eyes went down him. "You can take better care of yourself, and seek some support."

He just shook his head because he didn't want to say what was really on his mind.

"That is it?" she prompted into the silence with her formal speech pattern. "You are just going to stand there and—"

"Rahvyn, you have your own shit to worry about. That's all I've got to say."

The wind changed direction and smoke came between them, obscuring her and, God, he wished she'd finish the job and just ghost the fuck out. He didn't like to be around her, and even though he hated the memory, he thought back to all those years ago, to when he'd seen her and Lassiter, out in the field behind Luchas House. Nate had brought her a bouquet of flowers. That angel had turned the entire meadow into a sea of blooms.

As she kept staring at him, he wanted to yell at her to get the fuck off his property. Instead, he went with: "Okay, you clearly have something to say to me, not the other way around. So have at it."

"What are you burning here?"

"Wood."

"What else?"

"Nothing."

"Nate." She looked away. Looked back. "You received a second chance. What are you doing with it, though. This is no life you have."

Nate glared at the female. Angel. Whatever the hell she was. "I didn't ask for your magic, and I don't owe you anything because you chose to bring me back from the dead thirty years ago. If you don't like the outcome, that's your problem, not my fault."

"Life is still a blessing, Nate. Even if you do not have to worry about death anymore. It is still precious even though your own is no longer rare."

He thought back to the last time the two of them had been alone together. The goodish note they'd left on had soured over the decades because he'd soured on everybody and everything—and that was about so much more than the crush he'd had on Rahvyn, and the way she'd ended up all happy-happy-joy-joy with Lassiter. The reality of Nate's existence was that all he had was time, and he was suffocated by the countless years ahead of him. Every night he woke up and faced the hours like a bog he had to trudge through, and every day he braced himself for the nightmares that stalked him to the point of madness.

Rinse and repeat.

Until what . . . the world exploded? Yeah, and then what? If his body was completely destroyed, he'd probably just regenerate, sprouting arms and legs and a head again, and end up floating out in space dying and being reborn for eternity.

Oh, and the shit with Nalla tonight? And what he'd put her through? There were so many reasons to stay away from that female—but the biggest one was the lesson he'd learned that was standing in front of him right now.

He'd been burned once already. He wasn't looking for a repeat that he could mourn for the rest of time.

"Immortality is not a gift, it's a curse, Rahvyn. And you never asked me whether I wanted this kind of forever. If you had, I would have said no."

The bleak shock that tightened her beautiful face nearly made him take it back on the surface, tell her he didn't mean it, that everything was fine. But he didn't lie to himself, and he wasn't going to lie to anybody else.

A silver tear traced the contour of her cheek and she captured it with her fingertips. "I am so sorry you feel that way."

He looked away, to the flames, and thought about how the decisions made by other people steered the course of destinies, for the good, and for the ill.

"Nate, there are so many people who care about you, who want to help you. They have stopped reaching out after all these years, but they are still around you, ready to try again. There is no time limit on love. Even if it is up on a shelf, it can be taken down and held again in the heart—"

"Do us both a favor and leave," he cut in with exhaustion. "You may have practiced this conversation in your head a couple of times, but it's exactly the kind of interaction I'm not interested in having. I am not responsible for managing the emotional knickknacks on other people's heart shelves—or whatever that sappy metaphor is. You've already done your best work on me once, and no offense, I'm not looking for any kind of repeat. This first go-around has been enough of a nightmare. Now, if you'll excuse me, I'm going inside."

As he was turning his back on her, she said, "I can take it away from you."

Nate stopped. Pivoted around. "Excuse me."

With the flames flickering over her face, she was at once of the winter landscape and an ethereal specter. "If you are that miserable . . . I can end things for you."

He thought of the first time he'd tested the boundaries of the whole immortal thing. He'd shot himself out in the woods, right in front of Shuli—and then he'd sat up, recovered his senses, and gotten back on his feet. The pain of dying, the suffocation, reflexive terror and sense of impending doom, were all things he'd experienced as if the result was permanent, but the regeneration had come at the end, like a computer rebooting itself after a power outage.

There had been a period in his life when he had tried to deal with the darkness inside of himself by repeating that cycle over and over again. Eventually, he'd gotten bored of it, proof that consciousness could adjust to any stressors if given enough exposure.

What the mind could not deal with was emptiness.

"You're lying," he said.

"No." Rahvyn brushed her silver tears away with both hands. "If it is what you want, I will remove the spark I put into you, and you will die. Then and there."

He took a deep breath and released the tension in his body with it. Except then he frowned. "Why is this only coming up now?"

"I had hoped you would find your way. I hoped . . . for a lot of things for you. I thought with enough time, you would come around to see the beauty and the possibility that is—"

"You can end me."

"Yes," she said roughly.

"And it's truly over."

"You will return to the state you were in when I brought you back." The female put her palms forward. "But you need to think about this seriously, Nate. Take some time. Because there is no guarantee you will end up in the Fade. I do not know what happens to you."

"Well, *Dhunhd* can't be worse than my version of Caldwell."

"I want you to make sure you know what you are asking for."

He thought of the nightmares that plagued him, the ones that put him back in that human lab, the ones he could not escape from. Then he pictured Nalla in that alley, black and red blood on her clothes, her eyes red-rimmed and wide because she blamed herself for a death that didn't matter for so many reasons.

Nate took a step toward Rahvyn. "Do it. I'm ready now—"

"You have to say your goodbyes first."

"What? Why."

"That is my condition." Rahvyn looked to the sky as if searching for stars behind the cloud cover. "I will not do it until you say goodbye to your parents. Shuli. The Brotherhood. And you will do this properly, with sincerity. I will know if otherwise."

"Now you're putting rules in? Really."

"I brought you back to save your loved ones pain, and all I see is unhappy people around you." Her head leveled and she stared at him with hard eyes. "There is no peace for your parents. There is just a different kind of suffering from the grief I tried to relieve them of. As for you, you are no better off. I already made this situation worse once, I am not doing that again by cheating your loved ones of closure. You will do this,

CHAPTER EIGHTEEN

The following evening, after Nalla had taken over the preparation of First Meal for the Luchas House residents, she put her nicely cleaned parka on and stepped out one of the kitchen's rear French doors. The night was even colder than it had been, no doubt because the sky was crystal clear, the heavens above alive with stars winking in their alignments, the Milky Way just beginning to appear in a glowing swath.

The moon was still on the rise, its perfect crescent making her think of the way Uncle Rhage had taught the young how to hold it in their palms when it was full: Back when everybody had lived together in the mansion on the mountain, once a month he'd insisted on the kids coming out with him, all those hands of different sizes extended toward the lunar face, giggles and gasps of awe rising up like offerings unto the Fade.

She'd only been four or five at the time, but she remembered so much so clearly.

And those had been such good times, she thought as she made

and then I will give you what you seek. And that is the way we will proceed."

Oddly, he pictured none of the people who technically came under the heading "Nearest and Dearest." Instead, he saw a female with the grace of a ballerina and the knife skills of someone who'd worked in a meatpacking district for decades.

Ah, the romance.

"End things in a real way, make the peace, and then you can go." Rahvyn leaned forward on her hips. "But I will know what you do, so make it count."

With that, she disappeared with that sparkle of fireflies which were not fireflies.

Nate stared at where the female had stood. Beside him, the bonfire was slowing its roll, the flames not so tall, the heat not so great, the crackling not so loud.

In another hour, it would be embers.

By dawn . . . nothing but ash.

After decades of wanting what he was being offered, you'd think he'd be relieved. Resolved. And God knew he was used to the physical pain of dying. He'd done it often enough. As for talking to his parents? He imagined they would like to hear that he was sorry about the way he'd been behaving.

All he could think of was saying goodbye to Nalla, though.

At least her father was going to be thrilled.

sure the door was closed properly behind her. Made all the more special because no one lived up there anymore.

She started off across the terrace, and then went out over the lawn
and into the snowy meadow that extended back to a far-off tree line.
The going was slow, her boots punching through the icy top layer to
find the cushion beneath the crackle.

She'd ended up staying the whole day and she was glad she had. She
hadn't been able to sleep, but the insomnia had been easier to bear in an
anonymous place where her father wasn't down the hall. She'd borrowed
a phone and texted her parents to let them know where she was, and
there was no way they'd believed her explanation that she was needed at
work. But they'd given her the space, maybe because they needed it, too.

What was Nate doing, she wondered. Probably out in the field.

Part of her day had been spent wondering if everything in that alley
had actually happened as she remembered it. The other part had been
wasted on one-sided conversations with her father.

Now she was out here, and what do you know. The fresh air wasn't
doing anything to clear her mind, and for some reason, she kept thinking about the way it had been back when the Brotherhood and its
families had all been living together at the mansion.

It had been a while since she'd thought about that palace surrounded
by *mhis*, with its entire staff of *doggen*, all the art and antiques, and the
red-carpeted, gold-leafed staircase that had descended to that mosaic
depiction of an apple tree in full bloom. Even though she'd been pretty
young, she could still remember how the place had smelled, the lemon
floor polish and the fresh bouquets, the distant whiff of silver polish,
and on the second floor, the laundry soap that she'd been told was hand-
made just as it had been in the Old Country.

She was sad that the younger kids, like Lyric and Rhamp and L.W.,
had no memories of being there.

As she pictured the mansion in her mind, she couldn't help but consider the way the adults had changed. Nothing had ever been said or
explained, but overnight, all of the Brothers, as well as the other males

and the females in the household, had become grim—and they'd stayed that way. Over the years, the gravity had been less up-front, but the shift in emotions had remained. There had been times when she'd wanted to ask her parents about it—and why they had all moved to town—but she'd always faltered over the wording of the question.

And she'd always wondered if part of whatever had happened wasn't why things had gone sour between her and her father. Then again, maybe that was just her getting older and all the separations that happened when daughters became mature females and—

A flicker off to the left caught her eye and she stopped. When nothing seemed out of place, she almost kept going, but there it was again: A flare of yellow and orange, like a small fire had been started somewhere inside the forest.

Even though it maybe wasn't the best idea, she headed in the direction of the glow. The good news, from a security point of view, was that there were trail cameras everywhere in the woods. If there was a problem or a security risk, the place would already be swarming with fighters.

As she walked into the trees, she followed the scent of smoke. With all the trunks and branches, she couldn't see that far ahead, but then as she closed in on a clearing, she slowed down . . . and halted.

In the center of the open area, there was a depression in the ground, and the earth was not just barren, as if nothing could grow there, but there was no snow in a good twenty-foot radius from the center. And yes, a small fire had been set in the middle of the sizable divot, the flames working on what looked like a stump that had been dragged over and rolled into the pit. There was also a pile of gathered branches off to the side, and a container of what she assumed was lighter fluid.

But none of that was important. The male who was standing on the far side was the thing.

Nate was dressed in black leather, his clothes fitted to his body, his jacket open in spite of the temperature so that some of his holstered weapons showed. In the restless light of the fire, his face was serious, his eyes locked on the flames, and she took a moment to look him up and down.

He was okay. Physically, that was—and going by all the gunmetal and steel under that jacket, she knew that whatever was happening here was a stopover on his way into the field.

Was that a sweatshirt in his hands?

When he didn't appear to notice her, she glanced over her shoulder, and thought that maybe she should go back to the house—

Nate's head shot up and one hand jammed under his jacket for his gun. But he stopped in the process of pulling the weapon out.

"Jesus!" he said. "You should be careful when you sneak up on someone."

She lifted a hand in greeting, like an ass. "Actually, I've been standing here for a little while. I saw the flames and was worried something was wrong."

"What are you doing out in these woods?" he asked as he reholstered the gun and hid the sweatshirt behind his back.

"I work at Luchas House." She glanced at the fire. "What's going on here?"

"Just felt like roasting some marshmallows."

"What's with the sweatshirt?"

He frowned. "Do you always ask so many questions?"

"Yes, I do. When it comes to counseling, that's kind of what you do."

Nate shook his head. "You're wasted as a social worker. You're a fighter."

She thought about the way she'd missed that kick in the alley—and everything that had happened afterward. "No, I'm no soldier. My father made sure I was nominally trained in self-defense, but—"

"You can't teach the way you handled yourself last night." His direct stare held total respect. "Your aggression, your instincts, the way you moved without fear? It's in your blood. There's no instruction that tells the student to stab the enemy in the eyes just to dominate them before you kill them. You do that because you're a warrior."

Nalla opened her mouth. Shut it. "I'm not sure what to say."

He shrugged. "Then silence works."

She searched his too-lean face and wondered about the tension in it, in his entire body. Something had happened since she'd seen him last.

Or maybe that promise he'd made to her sire was haunting him. But fuck that.

After a long moment, she asked, "So why do you want to burn that sweatshirt?"

◆   ◆   ◆

Great, Nate thought. He had not been looking for an audience—and he most certainly hadn't been interested in this particular female showing up at this particular moment.

With everything that was going on between his ears, he felt like he was naked in front of her. In the cold. With all that entailed in the shrinkage department.

And no, he didn't want to talk about the stupid fucking sweatshirt—

"I'm saying goodbye."

The second the words came out of his mouth, he wanted to take them back. But as that wasn't possible, he tossed the article of clothing into the flames, and watched as there was a greedy rush, a flare of heat and flame bursting up out of the pit where, thirty years ago, a meteor that hadn't been a meteor at all had landed here.

Rahvyn. It had been Rahvyn, coming in from wherever the hell she had been, hitting Caldwell's soil—and his fucking life—like a bomb.

He wasn't surprised that nothing had grown in the soil after her impact. Nothing had grown in him, either—until Nalla. And he really had to nip that shit in the bud, especially given his new exit strategy.

"Who are you letting go?" she whispered.

Shut up. Shut up. Shut— "Not a who. A what."

"So that sweatshirt smack-talked your mama?"

He crooked a smile. But couldn't hold it.

"I'm burning a dream." He crossed his arms over his chest, the holsters of his weapons pulling at his shoulders. "Not a person, a dream. And how stupid is that."

"That's not stupid at all."

This time, when he looked at her, it was properly. Standing just off to the side of the impact pit, she was in the parka from last night, but had a red scarf and buff-colored trail pants that were new. Her hair was pulled back in a ponytail, as usual, and her face was arresting in the firelight, her features coming alive.

But as he tested the air for her scent, he smelled a different shampoo and fabric softener.

"You didn't go home last night, did you." As she recoiled a little, he blamed himself. "Do you want me to go talk to your father again?"

"Why would I ask you to do that?"

"Did they kick you out because of me?"

Nalla's frown was a reminder that she wasn't looking to be rescued. "No, and even if they did, that's my problem to deal with, not yours."

Bingo, he thought.

"And as for the dream you're burning?" she continued. "You're not being stupid or sentimental. Dreams are even harder to give up on than any reality. What we want, what we imagine in our heads, is a fiction that lives and breathes even though it doesn't actually exist. When we recognize that it's not real and we have to let it go? We give up a tender part of ourselves along with the fantasy. It hurts."

He had to look back at the fire because he didn't want her to see into him.

But like she hadn't already?

"You trying to psychoanalyze me," he murmured.

"No, I'm just sharing an observation."

"So you've given up on some dreams, too, huh."

"Worse." When he glanced over at her, she shrugged. "I've always been too scared to have any. I'm a coward like that."

"You're no coward. No fucking way."

There was a period of silence, nothing but the crackling from the fire making noise between them. Well, that and some owl half a mile away who was talking into the cold darkness.

"Do you feel better now?" she asked.

He kept staring at the flames, thinking about all the things that could be consumed by them. And all the things that couldn't.

With a shrug, he replied, "With what I've burned? Not really. With pointing out you're a good fighter? Yes."

Nalla laughed a little. "I think you're biased for reasons I can't fathom. Whatever, though."

As she stood there, he wanted her to leave, but not because he didn't like having her with him.

"The sweatshirt was over thirty years old," he remarked. "It was in perfect condition because it's been in a drawer all this time. I used it as an excuse to go somewhere and see someone, and it's time to say good-bye to all that."

"Letting go of things can be healthy. Even if it's hard."

How am I going to say goodbye to you, he thought.

On that note, if he was starting down this path of see-ya-laters that Rahvyn was sending him on, he might as well begin with the hard ones, right? Rahvyn herself, with that stupid sweatshirt he'd left at the worksite at Luchas House—just so he could force Shuli to go back with him, just so he could maybe, hopefully, run into that female.

In burning the damn thing he was shutting the door on that ridiculous fantasy he'd created about her. So following that theme, how about he did himself a favor, now that he was warmed up with romances that went nowhere, and stage-left'd it with Nalla?

Right here.

Right now.

"Your fire is going out." Nalla nodded at the sticks he'd gathered. "Do you have other things to let go of?"

"Yeah. You."

As her eyes flipped up to his own, he cursed himself. But there was a serious no-take-back on that shit.

There was a long silence. Then she said in a low voice, "What if I don't want you to let go of me."

"Then I'd say we have a problem."

"Do we?" she countered.

He nodded his head. "But it's up to you."

Her answer was in the way she moved: With slow, deliberate steps, she came forward, stopping when she was toe to toe with his shitkickers. She was not as tall as he was, and he liked the way she had to look up at him, because it exposed her beautiful throat.

As his blood pounded, he wanted to know what she tasted like. What her naked skin felt like against his own as he pierced her vein and took her inside of him.

"Just so we're clear, I'm okay with getting burned a little." She put her hands on his jacket, right over his pecs. "I'm feeling pretty hot right now, for example."

She was looking pretty fucking hot right now, too. Especially as her lips parted like in her mind, they were already kissing.

Don't do it, Nate thought. *You're going to lose worse this time.*

Good advice.

Too bad he couldn't take it.

Reaching out, he slipped his hand around the warm nape of her neck. Then he leaned down and hovered his mouth right above Nalla's.

"Are you sure," he whispered.

As she curled up grips on his jacket, she rose onto her toes, and she was the one who closed the distance—

Oh, fuck.

Nalla tasted like fresh mint and too-good female, her lips soft under his own—and getting softer as he put more pressure into the slow exploration. God, she smelled amazing, the scent of her arousal burrowing into his brain. All kinds of plans immediately struck him: If they could go back to his place, they could get the kind of privacy that guaranteed—

Nate pulled back abruptly. "I don't want to hurt you."

"Well, you do burn me," she said in a husky voice. "But it feels so good."

Smoothing a hand over the flyaways around her face, he fucking agreed. He also needed her like she was the last female in the world.

Then again, she was the only one he wanted, so that checked out.

Except he had to think about the future. After all, he was leaving the planet soon. So starting this with her? Was beyond unfair.

"Nalla . . ."

Her brows pulled together. "Okay, there's too much regret in the way you say my name like that."

"It's not . . . a good time. For me."

For a second, she seemed like she was poised to make a joke, a forced smile tilting her mouth. But then she obviously couldn't follow through with it, and instead took a step back from him, her hands releasing the folds of black leather she'd gripped so tightly.

"Okay." She shrugged. "If I'm going to beg, it's because we're both naked and enjoying ourselves. And that's not what's happening here, is it."

"Goddamn it," he muttered.

Pacing away from her, he stalked around the dying fire—and wasn't that really a ball-twister of a commentary on things. When something hit his steel-toed boot, he cursed and bent over to pick up his lighter fluid container.

He paused to read the back label. Well, would ya look at them warnings . . .

"Stand back," he growled.

Instead of waiting for her to move, he positioned himself in front of her and then threw the fire starter into the pile.

Nalla immediately cursed. "I don't think that was a great idea—"

The explosion hit him harder than he'd expected, the blast of heat blowing him backwards so that he took Nalla with him down to the ground. As they landed in the snow, he flipped over and covered her so that she was protected from the fireball, and at least the flare was a short-timer, which was good.

Unfortunately, his clothes didn't want to leave the party, and the agony was blinding.

As his leather jacket ignited, he flopped over and started rolling in the snow. Nalla was right on it, shoveling handfuls onto him, packing him with more and more until things were extinguished and the pain backed off a little.

As the rush to put him out passed, he lay wherever the hell he'd ended up, panting, head swimming, nose full of the stink of his own burned skin.

Man, he hated barbecue. Especially when he was on the menu.

Nalla's worried face appeared above his own. "Are you okay?"

Great, he thought. *Two nights in a row.*

"I'm always okay. Just—"

"Give you a minute," she finished hoarsely. "Yeah, I've been through this before with you, remember."

With a series of shrugs, she got out of her parka—

"No, no—" He batted a lame hand. "You need to stay warm—"

"Shut up." She put her hand over his babbling mouth. "Just because you don't stay dead doesn't mean you're not suffering. I'm taking you back to the house and we're going—"

"I'm *not* going to Luchas House."

As she stared down at him, the female was looking like she was in charge. So it was not entirely surprising when she announced in a voice that could have gotten steel I-beams on their feet and marching to her orders:

"Yes, you are."

CHAPTER NINETEEN

Nalla was done with the arguing. The only thing Nate had more of than willpower was stupidity. The good news? He was too physically compromised to do much about anything. The bad news? Trying to fit him into her parka would be like stuffing a boulder into a backpack. So she put her Patagonia back on, got down beside him, and pushed her arms behind both of his knees and just below his shoulder blades—

Nate hissed in agony.

Oh, God. The leather had melded with his skin. She could feel it— and she knew enough about basic medical care to fear he had third-degree burns over a lot of his back.

This could be fatal. And what if . . . he didn't come around again.

"Brace yourself," she said as she locked her teeth.

"Wait, you can't lift me—"

Sucking in a deep breath, she punched her feet into the ground, and used all the muscles in her thighs and her ass. It was a hard graft, but she got him up off the snow.

"The hell I can't carry you," she grunted.

"I'll walk—"

As Nate started to shove himself against her hold, she glared at his flushed face. "Cut that out or I'm going to drop you on your head—God, do you *always* argue with everybody and everything?"

"No," he snapped.

"Now I know what people feel like around me," she muttered.

It was not a catwalk model-strut to be sure—although even if she'd been on a level floor and not carrying two hundred fifty pounds of loose-noodle deadweight, she doubted she could ever pull off the Mharta routine with her hips. But she made it through the woods, and what a relief to get out of all the cloying branches and underbrush. In the meadow proper, she made better time, although it was a trudge, her lungs burning and making her think of her saying she didn't mind getting burned.

Ask, and ye shall receive.

Nate, meanwhile, was not doing well. His lips were peeled off his fangs, and his raw, singed hands were clawed up in front of his chest like he was trying to limit the contact he had with anything.

It was a toss-up as to what would hurt him more: Lying in the snow, waiting for death and then the revival to come, or this trip to the house, his raw back exposed, all the jostling and bumping making things worse for him. And what if he didn't die out in the forest? He'd just be out in the elements, suffering.

What a mess—

"You ... shouldn't ... take me inside," he gritted. "Too upsetting ... for them to see ... me ..."

"I already ... thought ... of that ..."

Well. Weren't they twinsies, a little panting duo.

Halfway to goal, she had to stop and catch her breath. She wanted to put him down, but she was afraid if she did, she wouldn't have the strength to lift him again. Besides, as bad as things were on his injured back now, laying him out in the snow?

That was going to kill him for sure.

"You . . . know . . . something . . ." she said between gasping inhales. ". . . what . . ."

"I'm . . . really . . . fucking tired . . . of you . . . dying on me."

As wind whipped around them, her eyes sought the only light in her tunnel, the only light there was: The farmhouse off in the distance. Her brain told her it was just about three hundred yards away. Her body was convinced it was more like seven hundred and fifty thousand miles.

She started walking again because the only thing worse than going forward was staying put and her strength draining out completely.

Left foot. Right foot. Left foot . . .

And that was how it went. Meanwhile, the house seemed to be on some kind of rail system that drew it farther and farther away, the closer she got. Every time she stumbled or thought of pulling another pause, she stared harder at the lights and thought of how much it would hurt to be burned and in the cold, in the snow.

Nate's suffering was her motivation.

"What," he groaned.

She glanced into his pasty face. "Huh?"

Those blurry eyes sought her own, and seemed to focus the way she was on the house. "You keep . . . saying my . . . name."

Nalla shook her head. "No, I . . . don't."

"Yes, you . . . do."

"Shut up." The chuckle she got back was not right. "That is . . . not funny . . ."

Nate started laughing in earnest. "This whole . . . situation is so . . . totally fucked up. Oh, my God . . . ow, ow, ow . . . don't make . . . me . . . laugh—"

"I'm not!"

"You . . . are . . ."

"I'm . . ." She choked out a laugh. A couple of times. "Not . . . funny . . ."

She had no idea what was happening. One minute, she was on fire from exertion while getting a burn victim to a house where no one could find out he was under the roof because of the condition he was in. The next, she was laughing, too. So hard, she lost hold of him and they both fell into the snow in a tangle.

As they both howled and giggled and snorted at absolutely nothing, and everything at once, she had a thought, in the way back of her brain, that there were so many different ways to release emotion. You could curse. You could throw things. You could run until you fell down. You could trap it inside and go banked geyser 'til you lost your shit.

You could cry until your eyes swelled up and your nose plugged solid and ran at the same time.

Or . . . you could ride the magic carpet of funny-for-no-damned-reason.

With someone who was in the same shitty situation you were.

◆　　◆　　◆

When their laughter finally dimmed, Nate brushed at his face and tried to catch his breath as he glanced over at the female who was next to him in the snow. Nalla's cheeks were bright red and her hair was smudged this way and that out of her ponytail and her lips were rosy and smiling. She looked younger. Or maybe the dark humor just erased the sorrow that he hadn't noticed lurking behind her eyes until it was gone.

She was so strong, she hid her unhappiness well, but she was grieving for something.

Just like he was.

As she exhaled and clearly tried to pull it together, he reached up to her face and moved a strand of hair out of her eye.

All of a sudden, everything got serious. To the point where he didn't feel the cold anymore. Or the pain . . . outside of him—or inside.

"You're beautiful when you laugh." Now he touched her cheek even though there wasn't anything to give him an excuse to. "And you were s-s-s-saying my name. Over and over a-a-again."

"No, I wasn't."

"You're l-l-l-lying."

She took a deep breath. "Your teeth are chattering."

"Are they? I d-d-didn't notice. You kind of m-m-m-make me forget things . . . that hurt."

Nalla blinked like she was clearing tears out of those uncanny yellow eyes of hers. "Can I please get you inside?"

"I'm not d-d-d-dying."

"It doesn't matter." She put her hand in his. "Dying isn't the only measure. You ever hear about that thing called quality of life."

"Read about it s-s-somewhere. And I c-c-can walk."

She stood up, and before he could tell her no, stop, he didn't need the help—or d-d-d-d-didn't n-n-n-n-need h-h-h-h-help, as was the case—she reached down and pulled him to his unsteady feet. Throwing his arm across her shoulders, she grabbed his waist and they were off, hobbling through the snowy meadow.

As the wind swirled around them, he glanced back at how far they'd come—how far she'd carried him. "You d-d-don't give up, do you."

"No, I don't."

On that note, he concentrated on not falling over and taking her with him.

"We're going in through the garage's back door," she said as they got within range of the farmhouse. "And up the stairs by the mudroom. Group will have just started. No one will see us."

The last thing he wanted to do was go back inside that house. But what choice did he have? If he got a couple of hours of rest, he'd be healed up enough to dematerialize off the property—and just as he was coming to the conclusion that he'd cross the Arctic Circle with her if she asked, they arrived at the garage and she got them in quick by punching a code on a keypad. The rear stairs were a fucking bitch, and even though he wouldn't have admitted it if asked, there was no way he'd have made it down the hall to the bedroom she picked for him without her support.

"Here we go," she said as she closed them in together.

He let a little momentum and a lot of gravity take him over to the bed and he sprawled on the thing face-first—and that was when he scented her. Burrowing his face into the pillows, he breathed in deep and felt a primal thrill that she'd brought him to where she'd slept.

"Let me help you get your . . . um, clothes off?"

His eyebrows popped even as his puss stayed in her pillow. Then he turned his head and looked at her around his burned-ass shoulder.

"I thought you'd never ask," he said in a deep voice.

Nalla crossed her arms over her chest in that way she did, with her eyes sparkling and her chin kicking up. "And I thought you said now wasn't a good time for you."

"Considering you just carried me through the woods and that damn meadow? Looks like I've changed my mind."

The fact that it was only for tonight was something he kept to himself. But not because he was being a shithead.

The idea of never hearing that laugh of hers again depressed the ever-living shit out of him and he didn't know what the fuck to do about it.

CHAPTER TWENTY

T wenty miles to the south and west, Zsadist was back in Caldie's Financial District, stalking Market Street the same way he'd played promenade on the night before. No Tesla. No cop-bots getting shot. Nothing to fix at the moment, and no dogfight with a first-degree relative.

But what was the old saying? The night was still young. Who the fuck knew what was coming next.

As he jumped off the curb and cut across the opening of an alley, he was glad Nalla was still out at Luchas House. V had provided an update thanks to the security cameras there, and as good news went, he supposed it was better than almost everything that had been re-ported yesterday.

Well, Wrath being back had been hand of God shit. Hand of . . . Rahvyn, that was. But everything else had been shit, and as a result, he and Bella had been up all day, worried about Nalla. The text she'd sent them an hour before dawn from one of the social workers' phones hadn't helped much—and he disagreed with his *shellan*. He didn't think their daughter needed space. The three of them needed to hash things out so that she saw he was right, stopped whatever the hell she was doing with Nate, and came the fuck home—

"And no, I'm not too hard on her." A horn blared next to him and he sent the passing Volvo a glare even though the problem it was having was with someone else.

"I'm keeping her alive, goddamn it," he said to a Kia who was also hitting its brakes.

On that note, he needed to get his head in the game.

As he pushed all his domestic fucking bliss away, it was a relief to focus on the war with the Lessening Society: Courtesy of a *lesser* who had fallen into Brotherhood hands, intel had been extracted that there was a slayer induction site down here somewhere. Interesting location choice, but he could see the logic. With so many people working from home, a lot of the downtown office space was just full of computer servers, data-mining farms, or robotic manufacturing for chips and processors.

Totally different than the way it had been back in the twenty-twenties. Back then, the skyscrapers had been choked with profession-als who commuted in on the nine-to-five grind, with the only time things were quiet being on the weekends and after dark. But now, if you wanted privacy? You got it.

As he came up to the head of yet another alley, he double-checked the cross street and then randomly looked over at a building on the far side of the four-laner. The purple glow of a billboard was bathing the entire block in a grape soda kinda way, and he narrowed his eyes on the profile of a woman with long dark hair.

Resolve2Evolve was the logo, and the tagline was real groundbreaking shit: Be Alive, Do More, Be More. Then there were details about some kind of conference that was coming to town.

Knock yourself out, he thought as he kept going, approaching that club Bathe and its blue-green entrance.

Several more blocks farther, he paused at the next intersection.

Looking down the well-lit side street, he almost kept going. Some kind of echo inside of his body stopped him.

Figuring he'd scratch the itch, he sent out a ping on his location per protocol and made the turn, sticking to the right side of the brick-and-mortar valley, getting good and fucking quiet as he went about fifty yards into the flanks of some twenty-story spires and stopped. Tohr was two blocks over, Phury down one, Xcor over three. The intel hadn't included a precise address, and even though he'd wanted to chase this lead down by himself, the coordination of effort was not just more efficient, it was better to have so many of them in a concentrated area.

If he was going to lecture Nalla on staying safe, he should at least do the same for himself.

But he didn't like working with others.

When his instincts were certain there was nothing coming or going in the shadows, he started forward again. All the security lights were mounted at regular intervals, and he willed them off, the step-by-step extinguishing like the countdown of a horror movie. With a vampire in it. Who was hunting something.

"Yeah, but we're the fucking good guys," he muttered.

Up ahead, a set of plywood panels covered with graffiti was the first clue he might be in the right place. And then the wind changed directions and came from the bridge end of things . . . and the scent was unmistakable.

Baby powder and death.

Under his skin, the predator in him woke up sure as if the aggression was an "other" who lived inside of him, a separate consciousness all together. He was no shifter, though. It was just the duality of his nature, the civilized and the barbaric just a flip away, always.

In the past, there had even been a third part to him. But his Bella had healed that darkest fissure, only remnants of it remaining now—which was why he wasn't like that fucker Nate. Z had things to lose, and they were so important to him, they'd brought him back from the brink of madness and kept him in place.

Broken, instead of ruined.

And this made him think of Nate's history. That male had been raised in a human laboratory, treated like a pincushion and a petri dish for diseases, and then rescued after he'd watched his *mahmen* die. All things considered, his gruesome backstory was probably the only fact pattern on a par with Zsadist having been used and abused as a blood slave for a century by the Mistress. And on top of that torture, add in Nate's immortality? You had an interpersonal H-bomb waiting to go off.

So no, he didn't want the guy anywhere near Nalla.

Without Bella's love, Z knew damn well that shit could very easily have gone a different way for him. But his good result was a one in a million, and he didn't want his daughter rolling those odds.

Arriving at the boarded-up entry, he inhaled through his nose—and smelled fresh human blood.

"Nailed it," he said into the darkness.

Gently testing the handles, he knew he should alert the others.

But he also needed a good outlet for his rage. If there was something to fight in there, he wanted first crack at whatever it was.

He was in a mood to slaughter the enemy.

Slowly.

◆　　◆　　◆

On the other side of the plywood sheets, Evan heard the entrance rattle, and the soft sound brought his head up. He was sitting on the chipped, cold floor by the elevator, his back against the wall, his knees up, his arms around his middle. He had been in this position since dawn, and had passed the time watching a slice of daylight pinwheel across the black oily tracks on the marble.

A millimeter gap in the plywood had let the illumination in, and he had felt all the more isolated for the light—the sun's golden gleam had been a reminder that all around him, residents and visitors of Caldwell were going on about their lives, working, driving, eating, drinking, fucking, crying, laughing. The sense that he had taken a step away from all the hustle and bustle was inescapable, and if he needed a refresher, all he had to do was look at the black ooze on his torn-up fingertips.

What was now inside him did not dry. The substance had retained its viscous consistency over all the hours, even as it ceased coming out of him. And if he rolled his forearms over, he could see that his veins were darker than they had been.

He could still taste the sickly-sweet residue of it in his mouth, and if he thought too much about what had gone down his throat, he started to get sick to his stomach—

The entrance rattled again, and he tensed up.

But maybe now he would get his answers.

Evan got to his feet and brushed off the seat of his jeans. Shortly after . . . whatever had been done to him, he'd run out of the building and just kept going for as long as he could. He'd ended up in some parking garage and had stayed there for a while all crying and confused. He hadn't even wanted to go to Mickey's hideout because he couldn't face the comparisons with who he'd been before.

In the end, he had returned to the office building. He'd been . . . "made" was the word . . . with intention so he didn't think the trainer would destroy him. And he needed to understand how to undo all of this. Surely, there was a way, and he knew the trainer had to be coming back at some point—

Evan froze in place. Then looked down his body.

The strangest sensation was going through him. His skin had tightened until it felt like shrink-wrap over his muscles and bones—and underneath it, there was a vibration, like the oily substance was boiling in his veins.

Get out.

The instinct for him to run was so strong and clear, it was nearly a voice from outside of himself—and he heeded the impulse without being aware of choosing to.

Cursing, he hit the down arrow to summon the elevator. Punched it again. Punched it a third time.

A whispered prayer left his lips, and his heart pounded.

Abruptly, the mouse-soft sounds at the entry silenced, and all he could hear was the rushing in his ears—

Bing!

The sound made him jump and he quick-pivoted to the doors that opened a millimeter at a time, like they didn't want to wake up from a nap. Glancing back over his shoulder, he felt that sizzle under his skin again, and he knew that whoever it was . . . they hadn't left the entrance. It was so fucking weird. It was as if he could see the presence just outside on the sidewalk, sure as if he had X-ray vision and could visualize them through the glass, steel, and plywood.

It was a man and holy shit, they were backing away from the boarded-up entry, in a crouch.

"You're blowing the door," Evan breathed as he squeezed into the elevator. "And you are my enemy."

Even though that didn't make any sense. How would he know this?

Except it didn't matter. He just had to GTFO. He was not up for any fight at the moment. He didn't have any weapons, and he still felt dizzy. Plus he sucked at it, like he sucked at everything.

Frantically pushing the LL button, he kept his eyes locked on the barricaded entry, the sound loud as he wore out the little glowing circle, *chk, chk, chk, chkachkachka*—

"Come on, come on, close—"

Pop!

The breach was less a proper explosion, more a firecracker, but it got the job done. One side of the boarded-up doorway went loose, the panel flopping free of its hinges and falling out to the sidewalk like a dead body landing on a bounce.

"Oh, God, close, *close*—"

The elevator's doors were tentative as they emerged from their sheaths, and he planted his palms on them and tried to get them to hurry—

Over at the lobby's entrance, a figure stepped into the opening that had been created by force, tendrils of smoke swirling around its legs. The size of the entity alone would have scared Evan. The fact that his internal senses began to scream turned whoever it was into a serial killer with an axe over his shoulder.

As the doors got closer and closer, the massive male was like a spotlight in Evan's face—and he knew he would never forget what this particular enemy looked like, from the scar that ran in an S-curve down his face and distorted his mouth, to the skull trim and all the black leather.

Their eyes met, and Evan felt a sucking sensation, as if the elevator had already started for the basement: All at once, like it was a resurfaced memory rather than a conclusion he was coming to, he realized he was involved in something bigger now, something that, though he had just fallen into it, had been going on for millennia.

A war, with things that looked human, but were not.

Like he was no longer human.

Evan broke out in a cold sweat as he realized that the black blood in him carried with it information and . . . some kind of legacy.

"I'm going to kill you, *lesser*," the man in the doorway growled. "I'm gonna fucking k—"

The elevator shut with a thump, and the descent to the lower level began.

Evan backed up until the panels of broken mirrors caught him, and he splayed his arms out as if he were about to get attacked.

If that creature out there found the basement stairs?

He was going to die.

CHAPTER TWENTY-ONE

In the bedroom at Luchas House, Nalla stared into Nate's eyes as he looked at her over his shoulder. Though his pupils and irises were her focus, she saw everything about his face: From his long lashes to the curve of his skull, the line of his full lower lip to the thrust of his jaw.

And she wanted to tell him to be serious. That when she'd suggested taking off his clothes, it had been for a medical reason.

Or okay, fine, a comfort one. Immortals like him—what the hell?—didn't have medical problems.

But out at that fire, after he'd burned a sweatshirt that she knew damn well had something to do with another female, they'd crossed the line that distinguished friends from lovers.

Acquaintances from lovers, more like it.

So "naked" meant different things now . . . and she didn't believe what he'd told her about changing his mind about timing.

Yet as he stared back at her, he wasn't stepping off from what he'd said. There was no *Ha-ha, I didn't mean that like it sounded.* No *Just kidding.* No *Wow, this is awkward.*

Because he did mean it, he wasn't kidding . . . and this was awkward.

But this was also something that had been started out in that forest—and needed finishing.

"Okay, let me help you," she said in a husky voice she didn't recognize.

Except then he shook his head. "Nah, I can do it."

Like she'd called his bluff or something?

As she tried to figure out what was going on between them, Nate eased onto his side, his torso shifting stiffly, his jaw locking in pain. And now he was sitting up and gingerly peeling the burned leather and the fragments of his t-shirt from his shoulders and arms. She could only stand by and watch for so long, even though as she went to the bed, she wasn't sure how to make it easier on him. She settled for helping him get his holsters of weapons off.

Oh . . . *God.*

He had been burned on the front and the back, probably because he'd been hit by some blowback accelerant during the explosion, and then he'd rolled in the snow and spread it and the flames around while he'd been trying to get things extinguished. As a result, the damage was widespread and shocking, the ropes of muscle over his bones exposed, the latter showing through bright white against the pink and red—yet his skin wasn't so much healing as regenerating before her very eyes, his epidermis reknitting so fast she could track the change by watching his tattoos reemerge: The ink that was permanent reappeared along with the skin, the swirls of the patterns becoming visible once again as the third degree burns became second degrees, and then firsts, and then . . .

"You're . . ." she breathed.

Instead of finishing whatever the hell was going through her head, Nalla reached out and touched his shoulder. When he hissed, she jerked her hand back.

"I'm so sorry—"

"It didn't hurt me." His stare dropped to her lips. "That's not what I felt."

Abruptly, Nalla couldn't breathe. She couldn't think. Especially when he put her hand back on him: His skin was so warm and smooth, supple over the ridges of muscle and in spite of the patterns in it, which was a surprise. But like the ink would make it uneven?

"Was all this tattoo . . . did it hurt?"

"Yes, it was painful," he answered. "That's why I wanted the work done."

Her eyes shot back to his. "Why would you do that to yourself?"

"I needed to feel something."

She closed her eyes briefly. Then she glanced down to where the tattoos disappeared into the waistband of his leathers.

"Why?" she asked.

"Just where I was at the time."

"And now?"

There was a long pause. And then his lids lowered to half-mast. "Yeah . . . I need to feel something now."

So do I, she thought. But as she looked at his biceps, the cognitive whiplash was insane.

"I don't understand how . . . any of this is real," she whispered. "How you . . . are real."

In response, Nate just pushed himself back against the pillows, and put both hands behind his shaved head, his pecs and shoulders filling up half the wall it seemed, his abdominal muscles flexing in a series of ridges.

"That's a cue, by the way," she prompted.

"For what," he asked.

"For you to talk." When he still didn't answer, she shrugged and sat on the edge of the mattress. "You want to do this as charades?"

His exhale was long and slow. "Are you ruining the mood on purpose or . . . ?"

"Is there a mood?"

"Well, I wasn't going after a foot massage," he said dryly. "Unless you're volunteering or have a kink you want to explore with me. In which case, I'm down."

Nalla didn't want to laugh. And did anyway. "You're funny."

"And you're beautiful."

She reached up and touched her frazzled hair. "I'm a mess, and I smell like campfire."

Those eyes of his traveled around her face. "It has nothing to do with what you look like. And everything to do with who you are."

"I bet you say that to all the girls."

"Only the ones that go rucking, and use me as their sack."

"That sounds dirty," she said as she laughed again.

Down below, from what sounded like the living room, voices percolated up, and there was the orchestral introduction of a movie studio logo—or maybe it was HBO.

Nate looked at the bedroom door like he was hoping it was locked. Then he refocused on her.

"Do you want to kiss me again?" she asked softly. "Even if it's not good timing."

The stark hunger came back to his face and he unlatched his hands and reached out to capture one of hers. When he gave a tug, she went along with it, leaning onto his chest and feeling the contours of his strong body under her own.

"Yeah, I want to kiss you some more," he said as his eyes lingered on her lips. "But it's not a good idea."

"Are you mated?"

"God, fuck no."

"Girlfriend or partner?"

"No."

"So how about you and I stop talking about timing." Nalla shook her head. "Otherwise, I'm going to assume you're scared of my father, and using the calendar as an excuse. Which is not a good look for you."

"I don't want to get you in trouble."

"You need to mind your own business with that." She stroked his shoulder. "And I'm not looking for anything more than right now from you."

"Fair enough." His eyes shifted to her parka. "Aren't you too warm in that?"

Nalla knew that if she took her jacket off, everything else she was wearing was liable to end up on the floor.

So she sat up and unzipped the puffy black folds. As she pulled them off, she could feel him staring at her body, his eyes lingering on her breasts under the fleece and t-shirt she'd been loaned.

Lowering herself back onto his chest, she stroked his pec. "You're so hard everywhere."

There was a beat of silence. Then he cocked an eyebrow. "Now, there's a comment."

Nalla blushed. "I didn't mean it like that."

"Well," he murmured. "It's true."

◆   ◆   ◆

What the *hell* was coming out of his mouth?

As Nate was spitting lines like he was Shuli in a club, he couldn't believe what the fuck he was saying. But here was the thing. When he looked at Nalla . . . he liked what was going on inside of him. For the first time in an eternity, there was something other than the darkness and anger, and though the mating instinct was like a freight train pounding through him, it was so much better than where he usually was.

Plus she was so close, her mouth just a couple of inches from his own, her breasts cushioning against his pecs, the scent of her arousal tingling in his nose, in his blood.

He touched her hair, stroking back the flyways that were damp from them rolling around in the snow, laughing. He still couldn't believe she had lifted him up and marched across the meadow, and he was never going to forget the sight of her concentration, everything she had in her focused on getting them both back to the house: There could have been an NFL defensive line set up between her and that back door into the garage, and he was quite certain she would have plowed right through it.

Did he want to kiss her some more? Fuck, yeah, he did.

Except it had been a while since he'd done anything sexual with any-body, including himself, and anyway, he didn't think the escorts he'd paid for back in the day had prepared him for this moment, right here, right now. That had been transactional. This was . . . real.

And as with how it had been by the fire, Nalla was the one who came forward—and he wanted that. His urge to roll her over, mount her, and penetrate her was so strong, he didn't trust himself not to rip off her clothes with his fangs and—

The contact of their mouths stopped his thoughts, slamming all of his consciousness into the brick wall of sensation: More of her warmth and velvety softness. The movement of her breasts against his bare chest. All kinds of sexual stimulation shooting down his spine and going right into his cock.

Which throbbed against the button fly of his leathers.

More. Now.

Cupping her nape, he urged her into him, tilting his head so they could continue the exploration. His reward was a moan that vibrated out of her and into him, and as he swallowed it, another, different kind of urge exploded in him—

She pulled back sharply.

At first, he thought she was getting off the bed—at least one of them coming to their senses—and the disappointment sucked. But then she unzipped her blue fleece, and shifted over so she was lying on her side next to him.

His heart rate exploded as she exposed her throat and held the collar down.

"Take my vein. I can feel how much you need it."

She was right, of course. For the last decade, he'd been living off the synthetic stuff his mother had formulated in her lab. That breakthrough, which the species had needed for centuries, had made things so much easier in so many ways, but bio-identical was not the same as the real thing—especially not when the vein in question was a female like Nalla's.

Turning to face her, he ran a fingertip over her jugular, feeling the pulse, bump . . . bump . . . bump . . .

His fangs dropped and he licked his lips.

"Are you sure?" he breathed.

"I wouldn't have offered otherwise. You've got to need it after last night and just now."

In the silence that followed, all her questions about who and what he was threatened to come between them, and he found himself wanting to answer them. On the surface, it wasn't that hard: Rahvyn had resuscitated him after he died from a gunshot wound to the gut, and that was all he knew about the immortality stuff. The subject was a Pandora's box, however. Everything that was under his surface, going all the way back to his past in that human lab and what had been done to him there, was bound to come out.

And he could not deal with that.

Good thing the single most powerful drive in a vampire was front and center in his mind.

Moving slowly, in case she changed her mind, he stroked her face. Then put his mouth to hers once more. This time, the kiss was deeper, and as he entered her with his tongue, he felt her hand slip onto his lower back. Putting his leg over hers, he gradually shifted so that he was on top of her—something that was made easier when she parted her thighs for him. As they intertwined, he got an even better sense of her body. She was strong, but softer than he was, and he relished the differences in her, so much smaller, so incredibly compelling.

When he finally broke the contact of their lips, he stared down into her yellow eyes. "You're not afraid, are you."

"Of what—you? No, I'm not."

"I won't hurt you."

"I know."

He kissed her cheek, and did the same to her jaw. Then he was nipping at her ear . . . before moving over to nuzzle her neck. Extending his tongue, he licked up her vein—

"Do it," she commanded.

Closing his eyes, he was surprised as a sudden calm floated under his hunger. Deep inside of himself, he abruptly knew he could trust his self-control—but it was for a reason even more shocking than the fact that he was going to bite her.

It had everything to do with the dark spices flooding the bedroom:

He had bonded with Nalla.

And bonded males had one, and only one, prime directive: Protect their females against any threat, from any source.

Including themselves.

CHAPTER TWENTY-TWO

Downtown, in the abandoned office building, the elevator bumped to a halt in the basement, and Evan almost shot out and ran around all panicked, willy-nilly-nowhere—except at the last minute, before the doors could close and the Otis could be summoned upstairs by that killer, his brain kicked in and he jumped back inside and hit the stop button to freeze it in place. The alarm started ringing, but what did he care about that.

Stumbling out, he looked around at the buckets of black oil and red blood, got assaulted by gruesome memories, told himself to get the fuck over it.

That entity or whatever it was would not lose any time finding the stairs. What was going to save Evan, if anything did, was whether or not there was a fire door that he could barricade. If he could just secure this level, and if the trainer could come back, then—

Evan's body wheeled around on its own and started moving fast, his feet shuffling and then running properly toward a dark corner.

"Wait, wait, wait—"

His head bobbed on the top of his spine as he kept looking back over his shoulder. But as much as he commanded his legs to change direction, and take him to that door with an EXIT sign, it was as if he were on autopilot.

And then came the same popping noise from where the main entry had been breached upstairs.

Over in the opposite corner, a flare of light and then the banging sound of a door once again flattening itself on concrete announced that Evan was officially out of time.

"No!" He began to hyperventilate as his feet stayed their course into the shadows. "Oh, God, no—"

He might be in the dark, but he wouldn't be able to hide there for long. His heavy breathing was making too much noise, and—

His arm ripped forward with such strength, it spun him around, and before he could fall on his face, he threw a hand out and made contact with something that was cold.

Instantly, a keypad glowed blue at waist level.

"I see you," the thing with the explosives said from across the basement. "And I'm coming for you, *lesser*."

"My n-n-name is Evan," he called out. "I don't know you—"

His free hand went down to the keypad, and against everything that made any sense, he punched in a seven-digit code. Or maybe it was eight? He didn't know. Immediately, there was a hiss as a vapor lock released, and he found himself gripping a cool, vertical rod and leaning back with a sharp pull.

The vault-like portal was oval shaped, and it revealed a well-lit metal-walled corridor. Without missing a beat, he jumped over the lip, spun back around, and yanked the heavy weight behind him. The instant it was in place, there was a click and a whirring sound.

Tumblers falling into place.

He was breathing so hard he was wheezing, and as he contemplated a tunnel that seemed a mile long, he didn't understand how he had known it was here and had gotten access. The autopilot had saved his life, however.

It would take a ballistic missile to get through that portal.

With a shaking hand, he touched the burnished silver wall. Then he knocked on it with his knuckles. Steel? Who made an underground tunnel out of—

His feet pulled another turn-and-burn, pivoting his body around and falling into a jog. As his arms started to pump and his strides became more sure, he wondered where the hell he was going—although clearly whatever was taking over had his survival in mind.

What was a *lesser*? he wondered.

And what about this speed? He hadn't had it last night when he'd been bolting around the city in the dark. Because he'd never been athletic.

So this running, as the tunnel continued on ahead of him, shouldn't have been a thing. Yet he had no soreness in his muscles, and his heart rate and breathing slowed down as his fear lessened. It was like he had an engine inside of his body, and one that was a car, not an electric bicycle, his thighs and calves, his respiratory system, more machine than human.

And what was weird was that the harder he went, the stronger he felt—until he was sprinting, his heavy snow boots pounding down onto the steel floor, the impacts a thunder echoing around and reminding him of that freak snowstorm with the lightning.

Back when all this had started.

What the *hell* was a *lesser* . . . and who was his enemy?

He was still wondering all that when the end of the subterranean pedway finally presented itself. He must have run a mile or more and he could have gone a hundred more—he was breathing like he was sitting on a couch, and as for sweating? What sweat.

The awareness of his newfound strength was a kind of intoxicant, and he was so distracted by cataloguing his capabilities that he barely noticed as his forefinger square-danced with another keypad and another oval door was released from its locking mechanism.

Pushing things open, he peered out into . . .

A basement apartment, it looked like. And a shitty one at that.

Worn furniture and dust in the corners. Trash scattered everywhere. A dripping faucet in a kitchen sink that had probably been white, but was currently stained with mineral deposits and God only knew what else.

He was cautious as he stepped out. There were a couple of doors, one of which was open to reveal a closet with a splatter stain on the back wall and another showing a slice of a bedroom that had a dirty mattress on the floor and tapestries hanging in shreds from the ceiling.

Someone was in there.

He knew this not because he heard them moving around, but because there was a radar ping to the recognition, a like-to-like registry that was akin to seeing a reflection in a mirror: *Oh, it's me.*

There was no following up on whoever it was.

Evan's body turned to one of the doors and marched him over to it. As his hand reached out, he had a thought that he needed to close the tunnel entrance—but a quick glance back showed that it had shut and relocked itself, and talk about camouflage. There was a pretend crappy door tacked onto the front of the portal so it looked like it was just another part of what clearly was a stage set.

Turning his attention back to the knob he was gripping—

"Come on, we're late."

A woman strode out of the bedroom with all the command of a military sergeant. Short and built like a powerlifter, she had braids tight to her head, no earrings in spite of having holes that went up both lobes, and a switchblade in her hand. There were other munitions on her body, strapped and holstered on, but as she drew on a black duster coat, they were fully covered.

She stopped. "Where are your weapons and your clothes?"

He looked down at himself—and realized that all he had on were jeans and boots. Why hadn't he been cold? And as for weapons, Mickey'd never let him have any.

Before he could answer out loud, she cursed in Spanish. "You fucking new recruits are never ready."

With her coat in place, she strutted over and shoved him out of the
way. "I'm not giving you none of mine. After the meeting, we get you the
weapons."

Evan opened his mouth to—

His body just started forward after the woman, falling in line and
heading up a flight of rickety stairs. After he went through another door
that only appeared to be flimsy—but which shut with a clang like it was
made of steel—he found himself out on the street. Glancing around,
he wasn't sure of his precise location. Did he really need it, though? This
was some avenue in the teens, about ten blocks to the south of the Financial District.

"Come on. We late and I ain't a tour guide."

The woman had strides like she was in the NBA despite her short
stature. He kept up easily, however, his body resuming that strange state
of physical performance that didn't seem to require—

Hold on. Why wasn't he hungry? He hadn't eaten in an entire day.
He wasn't thirsty, either—

His hand shot out and grabbed the woman's arm, going anchor on
their forward motion. "What is going on here. You need to tell me."

As she wheeled around, she looked like she was going to slap him,
and the fact that her disdain reminded him of Mickey made him hurt
for so many reasons. But then he wasn't thinking about everything he'd
lost and how disappointed in his family he'd always been.

There was something wrong with her eyes. Her pupils were black,
but the irises were nearly white, only a little ring delineating where the
line of color was. And then there was her hair. Though it was dark, the
new growth was icy white, like she colored it often.

"Please," he said. "Help me."

There was a cascade of Spanish. Then she tilted her head. "You really don't know."

Evan shook his head. "Last night, I . . . met this personal trainer in a basement, and . . ." He shuddered and covered his mouth. "After something terrible happened, I thought maybe he'd come back and explain it all—but then this other man showed up. He called me a *lesser* and said he was going to kill me. I somehow found the tunnel and—"

"That man," she cut in. "What he look like."

Evan put his hand out at a level above his own head. "Very tall. Dressed—well, like you, actually. He had a scar—"

"Like here." She drew on her own face from the nose to the side of her mouth. Then she waved a black-gloved hand over her skull. "And the hair is no."

"That's him," Evan breathed. "He blew open the door, and—"

"Shut up." She pointed her finger into his face. "That's no man. That's our enemy. That is vampire."

At that last word, Evan's hearing took a total timeout—so when her mouth started moving again, there was a delay with her words registering. But the meanings filtered through: Ancient war. Vampires. *Lessers.* Lessening Society . . .

Undead.

"What." He pushed a hand into his thinning hair as his panic returned. "*Undead*—"

"We do no die." She punched his sternum. "They can stab in the chest and send us back, but we no die. Be careful. You get hurt bad, you stay like that until the stab—"

"It was just personal training." He swallowed an urge to scream. "I was just trying to get strong—"

"You did. You feel more of it over the next day. You have strength like you cannot know, and you will use it to kill."

The satisfaction threading through her voice revolted him. "I don't want to kill anyone."

He looked at his hands and the thought of the black blood on the floor, down his throat, coming out of his scratches . . .

Undead.

As a moan came out of his soul, he lifted his head. The woman had started walking again and was way down at the end of the alley, her duster flaring in her wake like she was the villain in a comic book.

He watched her take a left and disappear from sight.

Putting his hand to his heart, he felt a *need* to follow her. It was as if he had been summoned—and in all his confusion and terror, he had no reserves to override the tide. His feet got to walking again, and he followed once more the path that was before him, though he could not see it.

Around the corner he went, and down the next avenue he proceeded.

Others did the same.

As storm runoff hits a riverbed, so too did the street flood with a flow of men and women who were dressed in black and moving with the same purpose his body was. Falling in among their ranks, he looked around—whereas their heads never varied, their stares fixated on their destination.

Wherever that was.

Good thing his body knew the way.

He couldn't see for the tears.

CHAPTER TWENTY-THREE

As Nate nuzzled the side of her throat, Nalla was waiting for the strike. Breathlessly suspended on the sparkling charge between her and the fighter she was determined to feed, pinned down by his greater weight with his lower body resting between her open legs, she was live-wire present and floating off into a realm of sensation at the same time. And then she felt his fangs, sharp but not breaking her skin, ride up her vein. Moaning, she slipped her hands onto his back—

Instantly, her brain came awake in a bad way, the logical side of her restless and unsatisfied, even as her body was about to do what it had been made to do: There were just too many questions about Nate, and worse, no sense she was ever going to get any answers—

As she took a deep breath, dark spices filled her nose and yanked her out of that spiral.

Dear *God*, she had never smelled anything as enticing as the scent that flooded the room. His arousal was her favorite cologne.

Screw Gucci.

Arching up into him, she rolled her hips so that the hard ridge at her core stroked her in the right place, and the groan that rumbled out of him vibrated on her throat.

"Take my vein," she said again.

There was a hiss and then his body went tight against her own, as if every muscle in his body tensed at once—

Nalla cried out as she felt the penetrations, the two pinpoints of sweet pain bringing her close to orgasm. And then there was the seal of his mouth and the sucking, as well as the primordial knowledge that she was giving him what he needed to be strong, to fight, to protect. His body required her. Without what she gave him, he was half of what he could be. After all, when the Scribe Virgin had used her one act of creation to bring vampires into existence, the *mahmen* of the species had made the sharing of blood a requirement of survival.

Until now, feeding had been an inconvenient need that Nalla had serviced in herself with awkward embarrassment or by using the same synthetic stuff Nate had no doubt been taking.

But there was no substitute for the real thing.

Riding up the muscles that fanned out from his spine, she found the nape of his neck, her short nails digging in. The locking-on juiced him further, and he repositioned the seal of his mouth, drawing even harder.

She hadn't realized how dead she was until she felt this . . . alive.

And she wanted more.

Retracting her clawed hand, she pushed her arm between them, feeling the hard planes of his abdominals—before going lower still. The waistband of his leathers was a rough barricade that contrasted with the smooth skin under his belly button, and flattening her palm, she went even farther down—

The purr that rumbled through him was almost a growl, and it made her bold. Finding the hard length of his arousal, she stroked him over his leathers and imagined him inside her, filling her . . . coming as he sucked her blood and swallowed her down deep into his gut. And Nate was right with her. His hips helped her, pumping against her palm, and as the movement got faster with a tighter range, she knew if she kept this up he was going to orgasm.

She wanted that. Even if it wasn't inside of her. She wanted to know what his face looked like, she wanted the power of giving him the release, she wanted him . . . to feel good. Because she now knew why he stayed away from people. Why he was covered with tattoos. Why he thought now wasn't the time.

He suffered underneath the hard face he showed the world.

So yes, she wanted him to feel something else when he was with her—it seemed like the fairest exchange, considering he made her feel something else, too.

As Nate released his lips, she felt the quick rasp of his tongue sealing the puncture wounds. "You gotta stop—"

"Doing what?" She squeezed his length, and as he groaned and jerked against her, she drawled, "This?"

"I'm going to come—"

"Good, because I need to watch you." As he lifted his head, his glossy eyes were surprised, and she nodded. "Let me see you. Right now."

With a curse of submission, he flopped over onto his back and arched his spine, his spectacular tattooed torso carving into the duvet, pillows dropping to the floor as he pushed one arm up to grip the iron bars of the headboard.

"Take my pants down," he grunted. "These are the only ones I have to fight in."

Rising up on her knees, Nalla straddled his thighs and went to work on the button fly. She didn't watch what she was doing. She focused on him, the way his other arm went over his head, how his calloused hands held on, what happened as his pecs flexed and the veins popped under his skin . . .

How those black-and-white tattoos changed shape as his hips twisted and turned with impatience.

The full design only became visible with him as he was now, and she stilled her hands on his fly as she took it in. In the center of his chest was a skull, and snakes, vines, and tendrils that looked like clouds flowed out of the eye sockets and mouth to all over his body, even the palms of his hands and under his arms . . . even the wedge of skin she revealed as she unbuttoned the top of his fly.

It was artwork that was alive, the design shaded so that it popped out like a 3D hologram, the execution that of an absolute expert.

His heavy lidded eyes focused on her. "What?"

"Your tattoo is . . . beautiful." She put her palm on his six-pack, and swept it up over the skull. "I've never seen anything like it before."

Sure, there were other skulls, and a vine was a vine, and clouds were clouds. It was the whole thing, the way it seemed to cover all his skin, that was so arresting. Plus how many hours had it taken?

Is his . . . erection tattooed? she wondered.

Well, that was something to figure out firsthand, wasn't it. Getting back to work, she continued with those metal disks, slipping them free of their stitch-finished holes, until—

His erection exploded out at her, long, thick, and hard, extending up his lower abdomen. Dear Lord, he'd even inked his . . . shaft and head: A single vine wound its way up the arousal, rooted by the others that spooled out from his pelvis.

"It's not original," he said in a low, groggy voice.

"What?" she whispered as her eyes memorized what his sex looked like.

"I didn't care about the design."

"It's beautiful . . . it must have taken hundreds of hours."

"A human did it." His words were guttural syllables. "I agreed to be a clean canvas, they agreed to use my special ink. Salt makes everything stick, doesn't it."

Tracing one of the vines on his hip across his belly, she liked the way his muscles beneath her touch flickered, as if they were trying to touch her back through the containment of his skin.

She paused just before she got to his swollen head, her eyes seeking his. "You don't show this to people very often, do you."

"At all. I've only ever fucked with my clothes on."

Keeping her surprise to herself, she murmured, "Lucky me there was a fire tonight."

With that, Nalla gripped his shaft, wrapping a hold on it—and his powerful body arched off the mattress. As his head kicked back, his lips peeled off his fangs, the dagger points bright white against the pink of his mouth and tongue.

The idea that his canines had been in her vein made her feel like having her own release. But she didn't want to stop even if it was to get out of her own clothes or find an orgasm herself. Somewhere deep inside, she knew that what was happening between them was a fleeting thing, his self-protection only letting her in for this brief moment.

"Come for me," she said as she started to stroke him.

As if he'd been waiting for permission, Nate instantly orgasmed, and with the first ejaculation, he pulled so hard on those wrought iron bars that he bent the headboard forward.

"Nallaaaaaaaaaaaaa—"

"More," she commanded him. "Give me . . . more."

The animal sounds he made deep in his throat were something he tried to keep a lid on, and good idea on that. The bedroom wasn't insulated for that kind of noise. What a cheat, though. She wanted to hear him loud and clear, hear her name again, hear all the moans. But she made do with what she got because there was also a perverse pleasure in witnessing him try to control himself.

And Nate's tattooed body was so magnificent, from the sheer size of it, with his thicker bones and muscles, to the veins that were like ropes under his smooth skin. Sure she was a physically strong female, and he was right, she was good in a fight. But the power in him fascinated her, especially as he kicked out a knee and nearly punctured the mattress as he drove his heel into it.

Kneeling over his sex, she kept going, stroking him up and down, feeling the hot jets that came out of him slick things up, watching the ink in his skin undulate under the gloss until it looked like the tattoo was growing in size, the ivy twining, the snakes spooling, the clouds coming in like a weather front, all emanating from the skull at his sternum that was not evil, not fierce or horrific . . . but a *memento mori* that all living things die.

Or should.

And as that occurred to her, he stilled, the last of the pulses leaving his arousal and landing on his stomach.

His lids, which had been squeezed tight, lifted and he focused on her.

Taking her hand from him, Nalla put her fingers to her lips. Extending her tongue, she licked up the lengths, then slipped them into her mouth. With slow, easy penetrations, she mimicked what she knew he wanted to do with her sex, what she wanted him to do with it—

Another hoarse sound of need rippled out of him.

She glanced down at his erection. The swollen length kicked of its own volition—and she discovered that the more she fucked her own mouth, the more he came again. Without realizing what she was doing, she rocked her hips against his thigh, the one that wasn't out to the side, the seam of the pants she had on hitting her just right—

"Nate . . ." she groaned as she let her head fall back.

Her orgasm slammed into her, tackling her so hard, she had to throw out her free hand and catch herself to keep from falling on him—

In a rush, Nate sat up on his hips, righted her easily, and replaced her fingers with his tongue as he kissed her deep and hard. With a rough hand, he yanked out the tie in her hair, and the dull pain sharpened her pleasure, especially as he grabbed a fistful of the tangling waves.

More orgasms were had.

Before the stillness finally came back.

Their faces were so close together, she saw each of his lashes and the flecks of dark blue in his eyes and the beard growth that was coming in on his jaw. For no good reason, she wondered what he looked like shaving as he stood in front of his own reflection, at a bathroom sink.

Or maybe he did it in the shower, without a mirror, his practice-made-perfect such that he didn't require guidance, but knew all the angles of his face, his head?

For a moment, she lied to herself and imagined these intimate details were the promise of their future, things to discover and cherish, tendrils to entangle them in the best of ways because they were private secrets only a partner knew, vulnerability witnessed and shared as personal habits were performed.

Like his orgasms, she wanted them all—

Knock-knock-knock.

"Hey, Nalla," came a familiar female voice. "I am about to make cookies. Would you like to help?"

With a jerk, Nalla looked to the door. She hadn't locked it.

"Um, hi, Rahvyn," she said roughly. "Gimme a minute and I'll come right down."

There was a pause. "Are you okay? You sound . . . odd."

Flushing, she tried to stay cool. In spite of the fact that she had a very naked male all up close and personal. "I'm fine, just fine, yup. Two secs."

"Great, I will get everything out."

Nalla bugged her eyes and went to look at Nate—

Her silly expression instantly faded. Her lover was staring at the panels of the door like he'd seen a ghost.

Or maybe someone he couldn't forget.

CHAPTER TWENTY-FOUR

I t went in through here."

At the induction site downtown, Zsadist pounded on a steel vault door as he spoke. He'd called in his location as soon as the *lesser* had gotten in the elevator, and Phury and Xcor had come right over. But it had been too late by the time he'd blown the basement's fire exit in the far corner.

All he'd gotten was a quick look at the scrawny slayer and a name. Evan.

"The fucker entered something on the keypad," Z continued over the dim ringing of the elevator's *my-door-is-open!* alarm, "and sprung this vault. I got a quick view of the tunnel on the far side. Smart move using steel so we can't dematerialize in or out of it."

"You called V, yes?" his twin asked. "Maybe he can spring the lock electronically."

"Yeah, he's coming as soon as he can. I told him it was a numerical thing, but I don't know enough to give him any more information than that."

Z glanced around the basement again, not that anything had changed in the last five minutes. The place looked like it had been ridden hard and put up wet, all the bucking fuckets—

Fucking buckets, that was.

"I need a vacation," he muttered as he went over and checked out one of the Home Depot drywall specials.

The thing was filled with the oily black blood that coursed through Lash's veins, and Z had a feeling it was because the slayers threw up after they were turned. Always buckets at the induction scenes. There were also smudges of the nasty shit all over the floor, and articles of stained clothing lying around like dead soldiers on a nuclear battlefield.

Phury nodded to the stairwell that had been blown open. "I think we need to relocate until reinforcements come. This site is beyond not secure. For all we know, the slayer wasn't leaving, but going for backup, and we're about to get ambushed."

For a split second, Z saw his twin properly, in the way he always did when there might be a threat coming, a final snapshot in case something went badly: Phury was standing under one of the ceiling lights, and with his long, multi-colored hair pulled back in a tie and all that black leather, the similarities between the two of them were even more clear—and as the center of Z's chest got tight, the shot of fear was a reminder that having his blooded brother by his side in the field was always a double-edged sword. On the one hand, because they were twins, there was no one better to fight with. They had a sixth sense on what to do and when with each other, and that coordination, whether there were weapons involved or it was a hand-to-hand combat ground game, was deadly.

Really handy when you'd infiltrated one of Lash's lairs, tipped your hand to your presence by chasing off a *lesser*, and were rolling the dice on maybe becoming the target of a coordinated attack.

But their closeness was also a weakness. The flip side to their connection was that he and his twin were not objective when it came to each other. Not only did they have families of their own to return to, but because of their history? There was an enmeshment that didn't promote the kind of objectivity required by war.

"Well, I think we should stay," Z said. "Butch and Rhage are up on the street, monitoring the entrance, and more of us are on their way."

Except Phury was right, the street access wasn't the real problem. If the slayers pulled a reverse Uno and swarmed through the tunnel seal with their Ken-doll-looking evil master?

"Has Lash *never* heard of a mop," Xcor announced as he drew his shitkicker through the ooze on the floor.

The stocky Band of Bastards leader lifted his foot and glared at the tread on his boot, his distorted upper lip curling off his canines.

"I don't think that male's worried about any Yelp reviews," Phury tossed back. "The intel was right, though. This is a *lesser* factory—"

The scent of Turkish tobacco preceded the arrival of the resident computer genius, and as V bottomed out at the lower level through the busted fire door, the brother took a last inhale and flicked the butt off to the side like the whole building was his ashtray.

"Gentlemen," he said as he came forward. "What we got."

"You tell us," Z said as he went back over and Vanna White'd the vault door. "And fair warning, we might have company soon."

"When do we not, true? And could someone turn off that fucking elevator alarm?"

There was a ringing *pop!* as a bullet was discharged into the Otis. Then Xcor glanced over his shoulder and lowered his gun. "Fixed it for you."

"I love you, man. I mean"—V put his gloved hand over the black daggers strapped to his chest—"I *really* love you."

With that out of the way, the brother went to the keypad and took out a black box the size of his hand. As he hovered whatever the hell the device was over the square of numbers, Zsadist palmed up both his guns—and Phury and Xcor did the same, the three of them establishing a guard perimeter around Vishous while he worked. The good news:

In this corner, there were no ceiling lights, no doubt to conceal the tunnel entrance, so there was a little coverage here—assuming those stairs all the way across the induction scene were the only other way down to the basement.

Assuming a flood of slayers didn't flush out of the vault door.

"Goddamn it." Vishous straightened. "Whoever set this up knew what they were doing. I'm not getting in with the usual hacks. It's encoded that well."

Zsadist eyed the steel oval. "If I try to blast this open, I could end up bringing the entire building down. But if that's where we're at . . . that's what I'm going to do. Lash is using this tunnel to move through the city—and I wonder how many others he has."

Vishous took out a hand-rolled and nodded. "Set the charge and blow it. We can watch the show from a block away."

As the others covered him now, Z took out the rest of the C-4 he'd brought with him. Just as he was considering whether he needed to dematerialize back to the off-site garage to grab some more, he stopped. Looked around. Measured the distance to the stairwell, the elevator . . . and the contours of the tunnel's steel portal.

"I have a better idea," he said softly.

◆   ◆   ◆

Under the bridge. Of course.

As Evan stepped out of the tidal wave of men and women, he looked up at a rumbling sound overhead. A semi was going across the suspended strip of asphalt above him, and he measured the reinforced beams and pylons that held the Northway up. Then he refocused on the homeless camp that had taken over the two-block area underneath. In between the tents and the shopping trolleys full of dirty clothes and sleeping bags, there were people standing bent in half, their addled bodies drifting like seagrass in the still, stinky air. Others were wandering with restless compulsion, their withdrawals animating them even through their malnutrition and illnesses.

It was bleak. It was sad.

It was the perfect cover for an army of darkness to funnel through because nobody was paying attention to anybody else's business.

And while the soldiers wove around an obstacle course of humans they didn't acknowledge, they headed toward the row of crumbling, vacant brick buildings that had been built in the early nineteen hundreds for manufacturing businesses. The fighters seemed to make a point of keeping their paths uncoordinated and crisscrossing, and they filed into various entrances along the waterfront's collapsing facilities.

Like they were attempting to escape notice.

Evan's body wanted to go with the others, like any herd animal corralled through a gate with its kind.

He fought the pull, however, backing off until he tripped over something and landed on a rotted-out wooden pallet. As a rusty nail pierced his palm, he lifted up his hand.

That godforsaken black blood gleamed in the ambient light and he thought of the scarred man who had promised to kill him for reasons he did not understand.

"I don't want this . . ." he moaned.

As emotion overtook him, Evan endured another spin of his inner roulette wheel of humiliation: Uncle calling him a pussy. His father telling him he was a waste just before the man died. The lieutenants at Bathe rolling their eyes at him.

Mickey pushing him down in the snow when he'd just wanted to protect his cousin.

It was hard to say exactly when Evan's pain turned to anger. Later, he'd decide that the shift started as he looked at the ones who were like him, even though he hadn't chosen this transformation.

There was no going back, was there. No undoing what had been done to him.

He was stuck.

So even though there was that true-north pull in the center of his chest, the fury he felt overrode the instinct to stay with the others.

On a surge of aggression, Evan got up and stood on his own two feet. Then he pivoted around and strode against the tide. As he passed the soldiers, they looked at him. He looked back.

He almost wanted one of them to stop him—and not because he was seeking to have his mind changed.

He wanted to . . . kill something all of a sudden.

The instinct was so foreign to him, he should have been shocked. He wasn't. The urge seemed as natural as following the others.

And as he considered the disrespect his uncle had always paid him? It was going to come in really fucking handy.

Before he knew it, he was running, and he paid attention to the pounding of his boots, the resilience in his legs, the calm breath going in and out of his lungs. Emerging free of the bleak landscape under the bridge, he linked up with the alley he and that woman had come down, and he went faster and faster, until the buildings were a blur and so were the burned-out car carcasses and the decaying dumpsters he dodged around.

Without any thought at all, he found his way back to the female soldier's shitty apartment building, and he knew the way inside the walk-up's sturdy outer door. It was as if he'd been shown everything before, especially where the hidden locking mechanism was, and what code to punch in so the entry would give way. Once inside, he jumped down the stairwell to the basement instead of taking the steps, and as he landed in a crouch, he held his breath and listened. Then he jogged over to the flat's door, and started to punch in a code—

The entrance opened.

A man with white hair, white skin, and eyes the color of eggshells looked at him. "What the fuck are you doing—we're late. He hates when we're late."

The accent was British aristocrat. The vibe was sociopath. And the narrowed stare was suspicious.

The old Evan would have stuttered. New Evan's voice was level as he

caught the door and held it open. "I was told to get clothes and weapons first."

"You better be fast."

"I will be."

The other slayer took off and Evan watched him go. Then he entered the apartment. The first door revealed a bathroom that had a
dry toilet with a crack in the bowl, a tub with primordial sludge in its
stained belly, and a mirror that reminded him of what the inside of the
elevator in the office building had looked like, all frame, no reflection.

Just fragments left of what had once been whole.

He kept going.

Door number three was the winner. The size of the boots lined up
against the wall told him it was the right place. Small. A woman's—

Where was his sense of smell, he wondered as he glanced over his
shoulder. Surely this place stank like a mosh pit, but his nose was fine?

Whatever.

In the closet, he found a gun safe the size of a refrigerator, and as
he confronted the old-fashioned rotary dial, his plan threatened to fail
when no number sequence came to mind. But then he saw a key pad
and the combination appeared to him.

As he entered the digits, his hand did not shake—and he had a
thought that he should be trembling. He should be majorly freaked out
at the fact that he was about to steal weapons from someone who was
obviously a killer.

And use them against members of his own family.

But he didn't feel anything other than a focus rooted in rage.

The instant the lock tumbled, Evan yanked the handle and opened
the safe. An interior LCD light came on and the display was more guns
than he'd ever seen in one place. He didn't know which—

His hand reached forward and chose two nine millimeters. Then
it grabbed magazines. Everything went into the pockets of his stained
jeans, and before he closed the safe back up, he took two suppressors.

In the second bedroom, he found clothes that fit him, as well as holsters.

When he stepped back out, he was better prepared than he'd ever been allowed to be, and he felt strong in the way he had as he'd run over here.

He went to the camouflaged door to the tunnel.

And as he entered the steel passageway, he hoped that thing with the scarred face was still in the basement at the other end.

He was going to need to practice first, and that enemy of his was going to be a good way to learn fast. Fortunately, his body seemed to know what to do in all kinds of situations.

Killing surely was no different.

CHAPTER TWENTY-FIVE

I 'd give you my jacket, if it fit."

As Nate got off the bed, he shook his head at Nalla's offer and finished buttoning up his leathers. Then he gave the waistband a yank to get everything in place, and went across to assess the window situation. The daytime shutters had all risen, and as he threw the latch and opened the closest sash, he got a blast of cold air—and the sight of an old maple tree.

He kept his cursing soft, and glanced at the reflection of what was behind him in the panes of glass.

He should have known—or at least noticed.

This had been Rahvyn's bedroom.

There had been no cluing into it when he'd entered. For one, he hadn't been up here for thirty years, literally. Not since he'd put some furniture together with that female. And since then, all of the stuff they'd set up had been replaced, another reason he hadn't recognized things when he'd come in.

And then there had been that whole chestnuts-roasting-o'er-an-open-fire thing.

Turning back to the bed, he looked at Nalla. She was sitting up in the messy covers, her hair falling over her shoulders in waves of blond, red, and brown. Her cheeks were flushed and her fleece was disarrayed. Between one blink and the next, he pictured her underneath him, tilting her head to the side, offering him the vein he'd taken so roughly.

"I'm fine," she said as she brushed at his bite marks.

"Are you sure?"

"Yes, of course."

As he gathered up his weapons, and started putting his holsters back on, she cleared her throat. "I have a favor to ask."

"Anything." He cinched up his gun belt. "Name it."

Her eyes traced his bare chest, lingering on the forties strapped under his bare arms. "I might want to get a tattoo. Will you introduce me to your guy?"

Nate stopped for a second. Then he found himself glancing down her body—and thinking it was a crying shame they'd been interrupted. Or . . . maybe it had been for the best, actually. He was in over his head—and out of time.

Which was fucking ironic for someone who couldn't die.

Yet.

"Yeah," he said roughly. "I'll totally take you in. You'll like them."

"Tomorrow night?" she blurted.

"Ah, yeah. Sure."

"Where will I meet you? I need to get a new phone, in case you don't remember, and I don't know if I'll be keeping my number."

"I'll get a replacement for you. It was my fault."

"That's okay, Uncle Vishous will take care of it."

Nate frowned. When it was just the two of them, it was easy to forget who she was. But "Uncle" Vishous? Shit. Just what he needed—Zsadist coming after him with the whole Brotherhood as reinforcement.

"So where do we meet?" she prompted.

"Needle." He felt like kissing her goodbye. "At Twenty-first and Main. Amore is their name, and I'll set it up for midnight. They always open the shop for me after hours, but if there's a problem, I'll get word to you."

"Amore."

"Italian for love. Or so they tell me."

"You sure this isn't too much trouble?"

He thought about the promise he'd made to her sire. To stay away. "No, not at all."

Over at the foot of the bed, he picked up what remained of his combat jacket from the floor—which was just a pair of sleeves connected by the collar and a couple of streamers of hide.

At least his battered burner phone had been in the ass pocket of his leathers.

"I'll see you tomorrow," he said as he went over to the window he'd cracked.

"Yes. Okay. Thanks."

In comparison to where they'd been only a matter of minutes ago, the distance between them felt colder than the draft that had killed the actual warmth in the room. But again, he was not going into the Rahvyn thing with her. No fucking way.

"Take care of yourself," he murmured.

"That sounds like a big goodbye. Not a 'see you later.'"

"I also happen to mean it."

Closing his eyes, he had to calm himself so he could ghost out and—

Before he was aware of making the decision to go back to her, he was striding across the rug. And the next thing he knew, he was taking Nalla around the waist, and bringing her to his mouth.

The kiss returned them to where they had been, panting and straining, ready to break out of their clothes and get good and goddamned naked. When he finally eased her back down where she'd been on the bed, he liked the dreamy smile on her face so much more than the reserve that he had known was hiding hurt.

Yeah, he couldn't leave her like that.

"I'll see you tomorrow at midnight," he vowed.

"Needle."

"Amore. Go to the side entrance."

He kissed her once more, and this time, when he stood in front of the open window, he was able to close his eyes and concentrate.

Flying away from the farmhouse in a scatter of molecules, he reformed on his own property, between his log cabin and his barn. For a moment, he glanced at the red outbuilding. A wild impulse had him picturing what was in there, under its cover. But then he picked up one boot and glanced at the snowpack in his treads.

All-season tires only went so far, and besides, if you couldn't floor your horses, why bother taking your toy out at all.

Heading for the cabin's front door, he had places to go, but first a shower and another set of clothes—

As soon as he opened things up, he went for his gun and pointed it at the male across the interior. The good news was that his guest wasn't an enemy. At least . . . not in the conventional sense.

His father, Murhder, was sitting in the ratty old armchair in front of the cold hearth. The Brother's black-and-red hair was braided high on his head, like he'd come ready for some ground game aerobics, and he was dressed to be out in the field.

"We need to talk about what happened down on Market last night," the Brother said grimly. "And after that, we're going to cover why the hell you aren't answering your phone—and then, for shits and giggles, our chaser is going to be why you're half naked and holding a burned jacket in your hand."

Fucking perfect, Nate thought.

But at least he could get this goodbye out of the way. Even though it was the one he'd been planning on finishing with.

✦   ✦   ✦

At the downtown induction site, Evan exited the tunnel by jumping out and landing in a crouch with both of the guns he'd boosted front and center. With quick eyes, he scanned the well-lit parts of the basement. The elevator was still sitting open and at the ready, but there was no alarm anymore. Other than that?

Nothing out of place, no one in the space.

Leaving the shadows, he was prepared for an attack, and when he came up to the Otis box, he was surprised he wasn't shooting. Peering in, he saw that someone had discharged a bullet into the control panel.

Keeping his guns up, he went silently over to the emergency exit. Sidestepping the door that had been blown out of its hinges, he leaned around the jamb and assessed the stairwell. It was dangerous to go up it, but he was as ready as he would ever be for that scarred vampire who was after him. On the ascent, he was careful to remain as quiet as possible—but he didn't know whether that was his mind being smart, or his body making decisions for him.

He was hoping it was the latter as the autopilot thing was probably better at keeping him alive.

Or . . . less dead?

Whatever, whichever, who the fuck cared. He just kept going. At the first-floor landing, he paused and glanced at the big 1 that had been painted on the concrete wall. This fire door had had a limited breach, just the lock blown, the black blast ring localized by the bolting mechanism. Taking a deep breath, he pulled the panel hard, the hinges resisting because of the warping from the explosion, and he jumped out once again.

The lobby was still dim, and as he rounded the corner, he looked to that oily trail that led out from that fucking elevator.

His body paused, even though he told his feet to keep walking. As his head turned from side to side, he saw nothing out of place, noth-

ing lurking, nothing . . . anywhere. The only difference was that the plywood panel that had been blown off the entrance had been put back on
somehow.

The scarred killer had left. Evan could feel it.

Now he moved fast, but he still kept things as silent as he could,
putting his new high-performance boots down carefully because there
was debris and cracked mirrored glass that would be loud if he walked
on it. At the building's entry, he stopped for a moment. When nothing pinged his instincts, he used the side of the door that had stayed in
place. The last thing he needed was the other plywood sheet falling in
again.

As soon as he was out, his head jerked left. Right. And up.

Reholstering one of the guns, he fell into yet another run and re-
traced the path he'd taken the night before, shooting out onto Market,
dodging cars that honked at him, ignoring pedestrians that looked his
way. He felt nothing of the cold, and still no hunger or need to take a
piss. He had plenty of anger, though, and it seemed, like his physical abil-
ities, to be getting stronger by the moment.

Maybe it was just an effect of the toxic shit in his veins.

He didn't care.

Up ahead, the blue glow of Bathe was like a semicircular rainstorm
that misted out into the street, and he avoided the illumination by sticking to the opposite side of things, skirting the edge of the light show.
The alley on the far side of the club was what he was after, and he jaywalked at a run and shot down into its shadows.

The side entrance to the club, which led into the VIP lounge, was
smack in the middle of the building's long wall, and he continued past it.

In the rear, there was a shallow parking lot, with wedges of dirty
snow framing the beaters that were parked with all the organization of
dropped Legos. In another couple of weeks, the available spaces were
going to be taken up by even more of the plow's work, those brown-and-
black piles growing like tumors.

But not everything was out of order. There was a pair of vacant spaces set in the midst of the mess, and they had been properly cleared of ice and snow, and salted with a heavy hand, to the point where the spots' yellow lines even showed on the ground.

Evan tucked himself into a fan-shaped shadow created by one of the security lights being out. Fishing a hand into the pocket of the black coat he'd stolen, he took out one of the suppressors. Even with his eyes forward on the back lot, his hands found the end of his gun's barrel without any inefficiency, the rims of the two pieces joining as if they were something you clicked into place instead of screwed—and then, as he rotated the extension until it locked in, he heard the nearly imperceptible metal-on-metal sounds in spite of the bass that reverberated out of the club, and the whistle of the wind, and the loud *whrrrring* of the HVAC system.

No smell, still. But God, his hearing.

From his hideout, he watched a lone man stroll down the sidewalk. The guy's clothes were high-class club, but he looked out of it, like he'd scored something that hit him a little hard. And then there was a car that passed by, a junker.

Overhead, a plane came in very low, and as he glanced up, he wondered if it was about to crash into the bridges—

His head ripped around to the alley he'd come down, and every inch of his skin prickled like he'd been dragged through poison sumac.

Before his eyes could confirm what his inner radar reported, he shifted his defensive position to a dumpster at the far corner of the lot. Making sure he stayed out of sight, he was surprised by how calm he was.

Given that he'd been stalked.

Something was coming down the club's flank, and it was looking for him. He just hadn't sensed them before now—

Right as he was wondering if he needed to start shooting, a pair of headlights swung across the back of the club, and Evan went to ground to avoid the glare. After the blast of illumination passed him, the sedan he'd been waiting for parked in one of the two cleared-out spots.

As he noted the silver Mercedes S660 with its tinted windows, the surge of triumph he felt was tempered by the reality that he was being hunted.

He glanced down the alley. The—vampire?—was coming closer. Meanwhile, no one was getting out of that luxury sedan.

Tick-tock.

Which was going to win—

His stalker passed by the door to the VIP section, and in the low glow of the light above it, the identity was confirmed, the scar on that face as obvious as the gun that was pointed in Evan's direction, like the entity could see him.

Right on cue, just at the tipping point when Evan was going to be forced to pull his own trigger, three men got out of the long Mercedes.

It was his uncle's lieutenants—the ones who had disrespected Evan last night. And Uncle had to be in that car, in the rear on the opposite side—

Incandescent rage overtook him, and before he could stop himself, he pointed his gun and shot in that direction.

With the suppressor on, there was just a *whiff!* sound, and then the driver of the car, his second cousin once removed, grabbed for his shoulder and looked confused.

Juiced with triumph, Evan started shooting repeatedly, hitting the men and the car, busting out safety glass, sparking the pavement, nailing the quarter panel and even one of the chromed-out mud flaps.

He didn't care whether he actually got his uncle. He wanted chaos and fear for the whole organization.

And then he could come for Uncle.

As the lieutenants scrambled back into the car, and the Mercedes was thrown into reverse, those icy-white headlights slapped the back of the club as it spun its tires on the salt, got purchase, and wheeled around.

Just before it shot forward out of the lot, the vampire was spotlit like the felon he was, his gun down by his side, his face a mask of deadly composure as he measured the sedan and then looked in Evan's direction.

Haul ass, Evan told himself. *Fucking haul ass.*

He took off from the club, linking up with the cross street behind the lot and sticking to the shadows. He made sure that his boots fell as quietly as he could make them, and avoided cans that would be noisy if they were kicked, and jumped over paper bags and frozen spray paint cans. The wind in his ears roared, but once again, his heart remained steady Freddie.

It wasn't until he'd gone a good ten blocks that he slowed down and checked if there was anything in his wake.

There was not.

Wherever the vampire was, it wasn't with him.

CHAPTER TWENTY-SIX

The cookies turned out perfectly.

Then again, when chocolate chips and melting were involved, and your base was made out of butter and sugar, how badly could you go wrong? Nalla stayed all through the cleanup, too, working side by side with Rahvyn at the sink, the other female on washing, her on drying.

"Just in time for group to get out," Rahvyn said as she turned the water off and flicked her hands before reaching for a dishtowel. "Thank you for the help."

"Anytime." Nalla hung the damp one she'd been using on the oven's pull rod. "And we have taste-tested 'em properly. You know, for manufacturing defects."

"Exactly."

As Rahvyn turned around and leaned back against the sink rim, she took her time with the drying off.

"I think you have something you want to ask me," the female murmured.

Annnnd cue the putting away, Nalla thought as she grabbed the mixing bowl and walked across to the lower cupboard it belonged in.

"Not at all." She went back and sifted through the mixing utensils she'd dried. "It's time for me to get back to work, you know. Two nights off in a row is a weekend."

What the hell was she saying?

"And maybe we should have waited on the washing thing." She went to the glass jars next to the stove and returned the whisks and spatulas to their places. "Until after the dishwasher was finished running from First Meal, you know? I think it saves water versus hand doing it."

She made busywork reordering all the utensils and then she pulled the flat drawer underneath out just to double-check the sharps were good to go. Man, she wished she had a house with this setup. The kitchen had been done over just a couple of years ago, the new solar-powered appliances paired up with hand-paneled cherry cabinets and beautiful red-and-brown granite counters and gray slate floors that had red area rugs on them. The long table that ran down the meadow-view side of things was already set for Last Meal, and for a split second, the twenty places reminded her of the mansion.

No sterling, porcelain, or damask napkins, but stainless steel, pottery, and gingham squares. But many seats, for a community of people.

She rubbed the ache in the center of her chest, and knew she had to go face the music at home. Even though the last thing she wanted to do was get into a fight about . . .

"What about him?"

Nalla shook herself to attention and glanced over her shoulder. "I'm sorry? What?"

Rahvyn was still at the sink, her silver hair down over the bright-red sweater she was wearing, the combo candy-cane bright, yet her beauty such that it wasn't overpowered.

"Nate."

Shit. She must have spoken his name out loud. "Ah, nothing."

There was a long pause, and Nalla filled it fiddling with the knives some more. Which even to her was an admission of guilt, not that she'd been accused of anything—

"It is not any of my business, but I know he was upstairs with you."

As Nalla's head snapped back around, Rahvyn put her hand up. "It is fine. You are a guest here, and he is not a resident, so there is no conflict of interest. And before you ask, no, that was not why I went up there. I really did want you to make cookies with me. I was worried about you last night."

Nalla shut the drawer and eased back against it, mirroring the other female's pose. "I'm surprised you're here again this evening." She winced. "That sounds bad. I didn't mean—"

"Like I said, my life has changed." The female ran a hand through her silver hair. "Time is precious, so I like to use it where I can make a difference."

As their eyes met, Nalla knew she really had to go. But then she thought of what had been interrupted on the second floor. "Nate is just . . . a friend of mine."

"I am glad to hear that. He needs a friend right now. More than ever."

Nalla frowned. "Why's that?"

"He has got a lot on his mind." Rahvyn shrugged with what seemed like sad resignation. "But it is really not my place to say, you know?"

"Oh, I'm not prying." *Bullshit. Bulllllshitttttt.* "Really, I'm not."

"I hope you give him a chance. He needs . . . a friend."

"I wish I knew why."

Nah, she wasn't prying. She was just dying to know anything about his past and what kind of pain he'd treated with those tattoos . . . hell, how about the sweatshirt? For fuck's sake, she'd take a DL on the XXL.

"He's very different . . . from other people," Nalla prompted.

Rahvyn nodded gravely. "Yes, he is, and that alienates him. But everybody needs support and—"

A soft chiming sound brought both their heads around to the monitoring screen mounted by the microwave.

"Looks like we have company," Rahvyn said with a sudden smile. "Your *mahmen*, how great."

As the female headed out to open the front door and do the greeting thing, Nalla closed her eyes and let her head fall back.

But come on, she couldn't avoid her parents forever.

◆   ◆   ◆

Out at his crappy log cabin, Nate closed the door and leaned against the rough planks, his arms crossed over his chest. As he opened his mouth to speak—

He didn't have a chance to say anything.

"You've got to cut the shit downtown." Murhder's eyes were as direct as a slap in the face. "You can't be pulling the crap you do, expecting other people to clean up after . . ."

As his father continued speaking from that worn-out armchair by the dead fireplace, Nate knew that responses from him weren't required. Then again, it was all things that had been said before, none of the condemnations wrong, all of the conclusions correct, each sentence punctuated with the same frustration with which it was received.

He *had* gone off the chain with the shit he'd pulled on Market. He *had* been an asshole the last decade or three. And . . . ?

"So what do you have to say for yourself?"

You fucking asshole, Nate tacked on for his father.

And well, he was surprised that there wasn't anything about Nalla and the slayer in that alley.

"Nothing? That's what I figured." Murhder shook his head and got to his feet. "So I'll stop wasting my time. You're off rotation—"

"Oh, fuck that." Nate uncoiled himself as well. "That's—"

"The only responsible thing to do."

"—ridiculous. There are *lessers* all over the city. The Brotherhood is stretched thin. You can't spare me."

"We can't *afford* you. Do you have any idea how many hours Vishous and his team wasted last night, striking footage from those municipal cameras on Market? But worse, did you not consider, for even a second, the danger you put Shuli in?"

Nate started pacing around, making a circle of the mostly vacant room. Certainly the old sofa and that one armchair didn't get in his way much, and in his current mood, it was a good thing all his stuff was on the lower level. He was feeling like throwing things, mostly because he knew the Brothers were right to remove him from the schedule.

He was out of control.

"Okay, fine," he said as he forced himself to calm the fuck down and face his father. "When do I get back on."

Murhder's upper lip twitched like his fangs were descending. "You don't."

With brows popping, he leaned forward on his hips. "Excuse me?"

"You're out."

"You can't be fucking serious. Over one car accident."

"That's not the first time you've done something stupid, and you know it—"

"I want to talk to Tohr."

"He's not interested in talking to you. And the only reason this termination hasn't happened sooner is because I went to bat for you in the past. I'm not doing it anymore. I'm done."

As his father headed for the door, Nate stepped into his path. "Hold up, we need to talk about this—"

"Oh, *now* you want to talk." Murhder narrowed his eyes. "You didn't have the decency to return my calls before. But with consequences falling on your head you're looking for conversation? Fuck you, Nate. It's too late."

"Fine, I won't pull a gun on a cop-bot again—"

"Not even close to a solution."

Nate threw his hands up. "I wasn't even on duty last night. When I'm fighting, I'm tight—"

"I'm not going to argue with you about this. The decision is final." Murhder looked away. Looked back. "I know you went through some horrible things in your past. How you survived in that lab, I do not know, and nobody expects you to just put all that behind you and move along like none of it happened. But even with your past, you are responsible for your actions, and the consequences are hitting now."

"What does Mom say?"

The darkness that came across that face was the protection of a bonded male for his mate. "You've broken her fucking heart. And I'm leaving it at that because the only thing that will hurt her more is me with your blood on my hands. Immortal or not, I want to tear you the fuck up for making her cry like she has the last twenty-four hours. After years of the same. Do yourself a favor and drop that subject right now."

Nate closed his eyes. And to avoid feeling like an absolute asshole, he distracted himself by trying to imagine his life without the fighting.

"I can't just sit here and do nothing," he said.

"We're well aware of your work on the human side," came the dry response.

As his surprise obviously showed, Murhder cocked a brow. "Did you think we didn't know? And you can play in that cesspool until it blows up in your face if you want, I don't care—and neither does the Brotherhood."

"I thought we weren't supposed to be involved with humans," Nate shot back.

"You're not one of us anymore. So your business is your own."

Murhder went over to the door and opened the way out, and Nate reminded himself that this was one of the goodbyes he'd been dreading most—so yeah, it was good to get it behind him. Hell, arguably it covered his adoptive mother as well.

God . . . he hated that he'd hurt her so badly.

Just as the door was shutting, he said roughly, "What do I have to do to get back in?"

Murhder looked over his shoulder, his red-and-black hair shifting across his strong back, the leather of his jacket creaking.

"Start caring about someone other than yourself and then maybe we'll talk. Until then, you have what you've wanted. We're all leaving you alone."

CHAPTER TWENTY-SEVEN

R esolve to evolve. Be your own reason for change. Anything that is given to you by someone else—motivation, purpose, esteem, well-being—can be taken away from you . . .

As Bitty sat at her desk at Safe Place, she was processing intake forms, updating patient files in the database, and typing in her own session notes—and the strong female voice piping into her ear was nearly as familiar as her own after the last month.

But the message was hitting different tonight.

Well-being is like territory in a battle. You must fortify and surround it with high walls of self-regard. You must protect it with your army of healthy habits . . .

Usually, she just sucked the words in and held them tight in her consciousness, repeating them, applying them to her own life, trying to go as deep as she could with whatever the message was.

Tonight, there was a parallel processing thing going on. As she typed on her keyboard, and double-checked the words she was using, and took pulls off her insulated Starbucks traveler, her brain was sifting through the content and probing for bullshit. She'd watched the videos so much that as the presentation(s) rolled out, she could picture the woman on her trademark red and purple stage, striding up and down, being the end result she was promising, everything that she wore and all that she looked like proof that her program of reinvention, self-determination, and empowerment worked.

Bitty reached up and readjusted the pod in her left ear. Then she flipped the page on the legal pad next to her.

God, she had bad handwriting.

And good job she was just transcribing. There were only so many things her brain could do at once.

As an ad interrupted the flow, she glanced at her phone screen and waited for the five secs to pass so she could hit skip. The little break provided her with an opportunity to take her own internal temperature on the merits of the material.

Her conclusion? After three hours of listening with a critical mindset instead of an acolyte's one?

Nalla was just wrong. All parts of the message tracked: If a person wanted to change, they could. Change required discipline and the ability to withstand being uncomfortable. Evolution was always the goal if you wanted to be better in any part of your life. Anything that you didn't directly control, whether it was thoughts about yourself, your goals and ambitions, your finances, your house, your decisions, was subject to a third-party tax that could wipe you out if they collected on their due.

Yes, it was on social media. Sure, there was a glitzy side to it, an aspirational oh-so-shiny of beauty and success. But none of it was wrong, and all of it was better than hiding at home and pretending you were being forced to be a shut-in.

Skip.

The woman resumed her talk, Bitty resumed her typing, and when she came to the last of her notes, she checked on how much longer she had to go on the video. A good twenty minutes. She was getting ready for a proper break—and as she stretched in her office chair and felt her back crack in a dozen places, she grimaced.

Not that kind of break.

Putting the video on pause, she got to her feet, took out her pods, and had to turn around in the tight spot between her desk and the back wall. She loved her micro-sized space. The old broom closet was on the second floor of Safe Place, just down from her mother, Mary's, office—and she'd been allowed to decorate it any way she wanted because nobody else would claim the nook. But come on, it had a window with a view out the side of the house.

And okay, fine, she'd gone a little girlie with things—and by "girlie," she had antique patterned wallpaper made up of pink roses, and pretty cream and yellow drapes on that one little window. The carpet was a needlepoint project she'd stitched herself from a Victorian design, and the sketches on the walls were Dior fashion prints from the nineteen fifties with ladies in perched hats and teacup skirts. There was barely enough room to roll her chair around, and if she wanted to meet with someone, she needed to do it elsewhere. But it was a cozy nest that she enjoyed coming to when it was time to be quietly productive.

Or . . . when she was engaging in a heated, one-sided argument with a friend who she was not really speaking to anymore—

A wink of red light caught her eye and she glanced to the window.

Down below, in the cheerful illumination from the living room, a dark figure was standing underneath her office and pointing a little laser up at her.

Frowning, she peered out her open door—but like the hall could help her?—and then she scooted around her office chair and bent over the sash. When she got nowhere with the lifting, she realized she'd forgotten to flip the lock.

The cold air curled in, and she shivered as she . . . leaned . . . out. "Are you—ah, are you looking for me?"

Down on the ground, L.W. nodded. "You got a minute."

"Um, yes. Sure. Hold on."

She tripped over her chair on the way to the door—then doubled back to shut the window and hit the rollers again. As she spilled out into the second-story corridor, she pulled her sweater down and her jeans up and fluffed her hair. Then on the way down the stairs, she found herself tiptoeing and told herself to get over it and lose the fluster while she was at it. She wasn't a prisoner, and even though males weren't allowed in the house, it was perfectly fine to meet one on the lawn.

Her adoptive sire did that a lot when he came by to see his Mary.

Down at the base of the stairs, she smoothed her sweater again and patted at her hair—and told herself that she wasn't doing it for any particular reason—

"Oh, Bitty!" someone called out from the back of the house. "Hey, can you—"

"I'llberightbackjustgimmeaminute—"

"What about your—"

Bitty waved to the other social worker over her shoulder, and refused to look too closely at why she didn't want anyone to know who she was meeting. She was also absolutely not going to go into how excited she was. Or how fast she moved as she blasted out onto the porch, all but skipped down the steps and then skidded around the corner of the—

"Hi," she said breathlessly as she halted in the snow.

God . . . he was huge. And as L.W. tromped down toward her, his long strides and heavy shitkickers making quick, crushing work of the distance, he got even bigger.

As Bitty measured the breadth of his shoulders under the black leather that covered them, she realized she'd never seen him in "civilian" clothes. Never blue jeans or a sweatshirt. Absolutely never a jacket and tie.

"Are you cold?" he said as his jade green eyes narrowed.

Wow. His eyelashes were as jet-black as his hair, and just as thick. Like usual, he had a thick braid running along the center of his head, the long tail disappearing down his back, and the sides had had a fresh shave. He'd also put in a pair of black earrings. Black diamonds? Set in black metal?

Would it kill him to wear a color—

"Bitty? I asked you, are you cold?"

As if she'd stroked out from the zero-degree temperatures or something.

"Oh, no. I'm fine." She crossed her arms and rubbed her upper arms. "I was getting stale at my desk, so your timing is great. What's up?"

For a moment, that hard stare circled around the yard behind her, even though he had to know nobody got onto the property without clearance. Which was how she'd been sure it was okay to open the window and look out. The Brotherhood's monitoring never failed.

And when he was finished casing the place, he just looked at her— so it was her turn to focus off to the side, on the ring of trees. Dimly, she noted the wind coming through the hibernating maples, the straggler-leaves that had refused to fall back in October like shrunken flags, rattling instead of waving on their stems.

I should have guessed, she thought as she figured out why he'd come.

"I'm not going to be able to tell you much more," she said roughly.

"How do you know I have a secret?"

Bitty shook her head, aware of a biting disappointment. "I don't know how I know so I can't help you with that. If I can't answer that question for myself, I certainly can't answer it for you."

"Do you know what it is? What I'm hiding?"

Her eyes swung back to him. And she opened her mouth to tell him no—

The strange, off-the-planet pall that always preceded a revelation came over her, dulling her senses and slowing down her body and mind. Blink . . . blink . . . *blink* . . .

"You're back," she heard herself say. Then she frowned as the message began to warp. "After you've been gone for so long . . . you have returned . . . and yet you were here all along. There are two halves to the whole, which must not be separated . . ."

When nothing else came, she floated in space for a moment. Then, kicking herself out of the trance, she tried to fake-laugh and couldn't hold the smile. "I don't know what I'm—"

"You know exactly what you're saying." L.W.'s shoulders shifted, his arms coming up. "Wait, hold on."

"What?"

The next thing she knew, he was taking off his jacket and draping the heavy, warm weight on her narrow shoulders. Instinctively, she grabbed on to the lapels so it didn't drop to the snow, and—oh, wow. It smelled like him, and it was *so* heavy.

Twenty pounds? Thirty?

As he was just wearing a black muscle shirt now, she couldn't help but look at his upper arms. They were so cut, they cast shadows, and she loved the ink in his skin. Not many males had as much as he did. Nate did . . . and that was about it.

Not that she checked out males very much.

"Bitty?" He waved a hand in front of her face. "You there?"

"Sorry." She cleared her throat and tried to pull herself to attention. "Don't worry, I won't tell anyone. About . . . whatever it is."

"Nobody knows. So, yeah, please keep quiet. No offense."

The wind swirled around again, and she huddled into his jacket. Good thing he hadn't tried to get her arms into the sleeves. They'd never find them again.

"You better go inside," he told her. "And I'm sorry, I shouldn't have come."

"I don't mind. And I wish I could tell you more."

"I just want to know what I'm angry about." His eyes moved up and over her head. "I don't know what it is. That's a problem."

Bitty tilted her head and studied the hard cut of his jaw. "You don't know?"

"No. But it comes out sometimes."

"When," she said grimly. Even though she could guess. "It's when you're killing *lessers*, isn't it . . . at the end, right before you stab them back to Lash."

His brows popped and he recoiled a little.

"It's okay. You can tell me about it." When he stayed quiet, she reached out and put her hand on his forearm. "I'm not afraid of what you do, no matter how ugly it gets. Violence for protection's sake does not scare me."

His eyes searched her face. "You keep surprising me. I don't get surprised."

A flush went through her. "It's just because you think you know me and you don't. If you knew . . . where I come from, you would know that I've survived so much worse than the truth you live in and what you do to keep us all safe."

Those eyebrows sank down low, making him look positively evil. "Who hurt you."

Not a question. And she had the very clear thought that if her birth sire were still alive, L.W. would have hunted the male down and hurt him. Very badly.

"He's dead." She kicked her chin up. "My father killed him."

"Good."

"You don't mean that," she chided.

L.W. seemed surprised again. Then he laughed in a low rumble. "Are you always so honest?"

"Only when people try to hide. And you are too strong a male to have to take cover behind falsities."

"Even if they're for someone else's benefit?"

"Not mine," she countered. "You don't have to buffer any kind of truth for me. I will say it again. I am not afraid of you."

L.W. crossed his arms over his chest, his pecs flexing underneath his skintight muscle shirt. As the hollows under his cheekbones undulated, it was clear he was grinding his molars.

"You're right," he said after a moment. "I wish whoever hurt you was still alive."

"So you could take him to his grave yourself."

"Yeah." He reached out and stroked back a streamer of hair from her face. "People like you shouldn't be hurt."

Dearest Lassiter, he was so close, and the proximity made her feel like she was seeing him for the first time. He was as his father was, as her adoptive sire was, as the members of the Black Dagger Brotherhood had always been: A killer. A predator.

Under the veil of what civilized him to some degree was an animal.

"No one should be hurt," she intoned gravely.

His lips flattened in disagreement. "That's a dangerous lie, Bitty. And if you know what I'm like and what I do, you know I'm right—"

All at once, her body stiffened, and her vision went dark as her eyes rolled back. The last thing she was aware of was her own voice, speaking in the Old Language:

"Be of care with thine anger, Little Wrath. Your wrath shall be the death of us all."

CHAPTER TWENTY-EIGHT

I thought I'd check on you."

As Nalla's *mahmen* spoke up, Rahvyn backed off into the living room. And the female must have gone down to the basement because there was a clicking sound as a door was shut.

"Fresh cookies?" Bella asked as she hovered in the archway. "How nice. May I have one?"

Oddly, Nalla noticed the wool coat first. It was red and black, the colors alternating in big squares that shouldn't have worked, but really did, especially with the red scarf around her neck and her black slacks. Her hair, which was a rich chestnut, was shiny and bouncy, cut in a long bob that no doubt would be left to grow out so that come spring it would be down between her shoulder blades and ready to be pulled back for the summer's heat.

The female was tired. There were shadows under those blue eyes, and sadness in them, too.

Coming to attention, Nalla cleared her throat and pushed the plate forward on the counter. "Of course. There's plenty."

"They smell so good."

Bella came forward and peeled off her coat. Laying the folds on the back of one of the chairs at the long table, she rubbed her bare hands together and seemed to force a smile.

"It's cold tonight," she said as she inspected the plate. "My cheeks are windburned and I wasn't out on the porch for long at all."

When her *mahmen* was done choosing, Nalla took a cookie for herself. So her fingers had something to futz with. "Winter's gotten serious."

"Sure has." Bella broke her Toll House in half and took a test bite. "Oh, perfection—"

"I'm okay," Nalla cut in, more brusquely than she'd intended. "They just need me to chip in here a little bit. It's busy."

Bella nodded. "Someone's on maternity leave, right? I heard Mary talking about it the other night."

"That's it, yup." When Nalla tried hers, all she tasted was cardboard. "Short-staffed, you know how it is—"

"Your father is really worried about you."

As those blue eyes became direct, Nalla stopped chewing. Then she rubbed the center of her chest. "Is he."

"We both are."

"But you came because of him, right." She cleared the corner of her mouth with the tip of her tongue. "You're worried about him."

"Of course I am."

"Right. Of course."

Bella frowned. "Is it so bad that we both care about your safety?"

Don't do it, Nalla thought. Now, not the time, here, not the place, and all that jazz.

And there was another reason to just let it go. People had conversations with others in the hopes of improving things . . . communication, connection, situations. But she knew that nothing was going to change. There was no combination of words, backed up with whatever expressions were necessary to convey proper meaning, that could get her what she wanted from her *mahmen*.

Part of it was the sheer selfishness of how she felt: It was a two-year-old's temper tantrum in a grown-ass adult, and that was not only unappealing, it was embarrassing to some degree. Except have fun negotiating with your emotions.

Once, just once, she wanted to be the number one priority to Bella.

For Nalla's entire life, their household had been all about her father: Was he eating? Had he slept well. How were the sessions with Mary going? Who was his partner in the field tonight. When was he coming home? Did he need anything. Did he want anything? Was he injured, who was treating him . . .

And then the big one, even bigger somehow than the mortal threat he faced every night in the field: Had he been triggered by something, a hole poked in his shield against his inner demons, one of them escaping and having to be contained before it hurt him even worse.

There had been good times, sure. But the darkness inside that male had defined their lives, and everything had been second fiddle to it.

"Do you care about me, really?" Nalla said softly.

Bella recoiled as if she'd been struck. "How can you ask me that?"

And there it was. Honest surprise.

"Sorry, I don't know what I'm saying." Nalla tried to wave away everything with her cookie. "Anyway, how's things at home—"

"What's gotten into you?" Bella indicated the kitchen. But clearly meant so much more than the room they were in. Or even the house. "You've never done this before."

"I work here. I've absolutely done 'this' before."

Sick of pretending she wanted the frickin' cookie, Nalla went over and chucked it into the garbage disposal. Then she ran some water and hit the switch on the wall. The whirring was loud and she wished she could just keep the thing on to drown out the conversation. She really didn't want to fight with either of her parents.

Maybe that was a sign she'd finally given up.

"You've never not come home at day," Bella pointed out as the InSinkErator was silenced.

"I texted you. Both."

God, why had she and Rahvyn done all the dishes? There was nothing else to put away, either.

"Nalla, you can tell me what's wrong."

Lowering her head, she braced her hands on the lip of the sink, splaying her fingers out, looking at the short nails she had clipped just days before. Funny, when she'd been doing that snip-snip stuff, she could never have guessed where her life would go in a mere forty-eight-hour period.

Bitty. Her father. Now . . . this.

"I love you, Nalla. I want to fix whatever's wrong between us." There was a choked sound. "We used to be close, you and I. I don't understand what's happened."

Memories of when she'd been a young at that grand mansion came back to her, and she relived those nights of getting jacked into party dresses, and having her hair brushed, and of bows and nail polish, of Mary Janes and short white socks. There had been dolls, too. And tea parties.

Her *mahmen* had been there for all of that. It had only been after the great divide, as Nalla had always thought of it, when they'd all left the mountaintop and the grown-ups had gotten grim, that things had begun to shift. Or maybe it was more like she'd started to get older and had recognized all the autopilot that was going on, time that was precious to her not being as significant to Bella because of all the other things the female was more concerned about.

"Were we ever really close?" Nalla said dully. "Or was it because you were in charge of keeping me alive and fed and clothed?"

"Nalla . . ." Those blue eyes welled up. "Of course we were, and I want to bring us back to where we used to be—"

"You want to fix what never was." Tears came to her own eyes and she slashed them away. "And I do think you love me, although only because there's a piece of him in me. It's never been about me. It's always about—"

"That is not true! I can't believe you're saying this—"

"I know what was done to him when he was a blood slave." That shut her *mahmen* up, Bella's face going pale. "You think I don't know what those bands are on his neck and wrists? I know what he was."

Bella put her hand out in what looked like a blind way, locking a grip on the back of one of the table's spindle chairs as if her balance was off.

"We've never kept that from you."

Nalla shrugged. "You never talked about it, either."

There was a pause. And then in a hoarse voice, her *mahmen* said, "Some things you are not going to want to hear about firsthand. And I've always worried about you, too—"

Nalla pointed to the archway her *mahmen* had come through. "You walked in here, supposedly to check on me, but the first words out of your mouth are that *he's* worried about me. It's the story of my life. 'Let's not upset your father—'"

"I've *never* said that."

"You don't have to. The subtext is there—and please don't deny it. We both know what's been going on."

"But you never talk about your life. I don't know anything about—"

Nalla yanked her fleece down, exposing the still-raw bite mark on the side of her throat. "I fed a male of worth tonight and I do not regret it. I'm not going to apologize for it, either. And if you think I'm in a big hurry to talk to you two about what happened, you're out of your mind. Father already hates him, and I know that you're going to back your *hellren*—and I'm not interested in having this male threatened by a member of the Black Dagger Brotherhood."

And no, she didn't care that Nate had promised not to see her. This was her business, and her father needed to back the fuck off.

"Nalla, we want you to go out and live your life."

"Maybe, but on your terms." She threw up her hands. "Do you want to know what happened to me last night? A bunch of males at a club bet who could get me. They think it's a game, proving who can bag the Brother Zsadist's daughter—and live to tell about it because my father is so fucking scary."

"That is terrible." Bella shook her head. "There's no excuse for that kind of behavior. But we can't control what others do, you have to know that."

"Yeah, well, it's just one more way him being who he is affects my life. I have spent so many festivals sidelining things because no guy wanted to ask me to dance in front of him, so many nights alone, no future except work—"

"Again, I'm really sorry, but your father didn't have anything to do with that—"

"Yes, he did. He threatened four males I know about, and God only knows how many I don't—oh, he didn't tell you?" As her *mahmen* continued to look surprised, Nalla nodded forcefully. "I always heard about it afterward, when I was hoping for a second date or even a first one, and the guy went hands-off because your *hellren* decided to 'set them straight.'"

Bella rubbed her eyes like her head hurt. "He is protective of you, but that's crossing a line."

"You think? He was going to throw one of them off the bridge downtown if they treated me wrong. And before he tries to excuse it by saying he's just watching out for me, those males didn't even take a chance on me. They just up and left. I never had an opportunity to even try to find a relationship—and finally, I just gave up. I sat alone in my room . . ." Or with Bitty, who was naturally shyer. ". . . and didn't live because it was easier than dealing with him."

Bella dropped her hands as if in defeat. "You have to understand where your father is coming from."

"At some point, that doesn't matter anymore."

"He really wants to support you. I'm not saying he's doing it in the right way, but he loves you and he wants the best for you. If you brought home a male you—"

"Oh, I'm not bringing the one I'm with home. Like I said, Father already hates him. He made that amply clear last night. The good news is the guy I like doesn't give a shit."

Well, at least she could assume he didn't based on how they'd ended up in that bed upstairs—

"Nate." Bella almost kept the wince to herself. "I heard."

"Spare me the lecture. You don't know him like I do."

"What I'm worried about is that you don't know the real him, either." Her *mahmen* put her palm up. "But I'm not going to argue with you about your feelings—"

"Of course not. Because, as always, it's about my father for you. Not me."

Bella's eyes narrowed and got hard. "I did *not* raise you to speak to me like that." When Nalla opened her mouth to argue, that voice got downright stern. "And fine, you want to talk about your father? Okay, let's talk. Do you know where he is right now?"

"Working."

"*Fighting.* In the war." Her *mahmen* pointed to the nearest window. "He's out there, in the night, where things that aren't alive want to kill him. He's not sitting behind a desk. He's not on vacation. He's using guns and daggers to protect our species—and half of his mind is on you right now. Where you are. Whether you're okay. What's wrong. How to fix it. That kind of distraction could kill him—and he was my true love before he ever was your father. So you're goddamn right I came over here to check on you, and I will not apologize for worrying about him while he's in the field. You may think it's the height of insensitivity, but I'd like my *hellren* to come home in one piece at the end of the night—instead of on a slab. And P.S., you're my daughter, so part of *me* is in *you*, too, so yes, I'm equally as worried about you. I'm having a great time, thank you very much, panicked about the both of you."

Nalla closed her eyes. And took a deep breath that she released on a defeated exhale. "I don't want to distract him and make things even more dangerous."

"Just so that we are clear, his life and mine are over if anything happens to you. *Over.*" Bella picked up her coat and pulled it back on. "You may be angry about things that we didn't do or things that we did, but please don't ever forget what you mean to us. Rest assured, we do not."

Nalla's *mahmen* walked to the archway and looked over her shoulder. "I brought you a backpack with a change of clothes and the shampoo and conditioner you like. And before you accuse me of going through your room, it was all stuff I found in the dryer or bought on the way. Oh, and there's a new cell phone in there, too. Your number remains the same."

On that note, the female walked out to the front of the house. A moment later, the heavy door opened and closed.

There was a little delay before the draft made it down to the kitchen, but Nalla felt the cold.

All the way into her bones.

CHAPTER TWENTY-NINE

The Riverdale Social Club was not anywhere near the river. It wasn't a club, either, in the squash or the smash sense, and as for the hoity-toity "dale" tail, the shit was about as pretentious as a butcher's shop ca. 1940: The place was nothing but a flat-roofed, concrete box on the fringes of downtown, with two tiny windows that were blacked out and caged with iron bars, and grime drooling down its whitewashed, unremarkable exterior.

It was the urban equivalent of Nate's crappy log cabin, a tomfool that hid what was really in there.

As he re-formed across the street, he stayed in the lee of a darkened Tex-Mex restaurant. Everything else in the neighborhood was also asleep for the night—and likewise the "club" appeared to be vacant, from the outside.

Which was bullshit.

When he walked across the street, there was no traffic to watch out for, but he checked both ways anyway, as Rhage always said. No pedestrians. No cars—except those two that were parked half a block down, and might well be federal or local agents.

The alley to the left of the barred entrance had no security lights, and as he came to the head of it and looked down, the narrow lane was far from empty—Uncle's Mercedes was parked right beside the fire exit and blocking the way.

The first clue something was off was the smell of gunpowder and blood. The next was the hushed conversation bubbling up from the silver sedan's back bumper.

All the chatter stopped as his presence registered, and he walked over to the three men who were clustered around the bullet holes in the car's driver's side.

"Not a good night for interruptions," the stubby one said.

Nate nodded in greeting. "Do we know who ordered the hit."

It rankled to use "we" as it applied to a bunch of humans. But his true tribe had voted him off the proverbial island.

"Not yet," Stubby replied.

"Come back later," another cut in as he lit a cigarette, his cupped hand around the flame kicking the flicker back to his pockmarked face.

"Who got hurt," Nate asked.

"Jimmie Gimp, Big Toms, and Smilie," the third answered.

"I want to see Uncle."

"He don't want to see nobody—"

The door opened and Jimmie Gimp, Uncle's right-hand man, leaned out. He had his suit jacket off, and his button-down untucked and tie-less. There was a bloodstain on his shoulder and another on his side, the red spots a brilliant contrast to the white of his shirt.

"In," was all he said.

Nate passed through the guards, and as he squeezed by Jimmie Gimp's beer gut, he wondered who the hell would be so brazen.

Looked like he was going to get a couple of jobs out of this. Good thing his schedule was fucking free.

The inside of the building was stark and cheap, nothing on the walls, the tables and chairs low-rent restaurant versions draped with simple cloths, the floor bare brick-colored tile. The only thing with any intrinsic value was the stock in the bar in the corner. The help-your-self expanse was impressive, with every spirit known to man, and some even a vampire didn't recognize, but it was strictly self-serve-and-be-neat-about-it because shit didn't get bussed until the morning.

"Wait," Jimmie ordered.

The older man limped off to one of two doors, and knocked on the entry that wasn't the loo with a couple of short raps. After a pause, he opened the way up, had a word—and turned back to motion at Nate.

Uncle's inner sanctum was just like the outer space except smaller and with only one table without a cloth on the top. The man himself was sitting with his back to the wall, and he had a squat glass of some-thing brown on the rocks next to a gun that no doubt had the safety off. His double-breasted jacket was still on, but it was open down the front, the pinstriped folds parting to expose a red-and-gold tie with a diamond pin halfway down. Between the fit of the suit and the middle-aged paunch, he gave a good impression of being a big guy. The true impact of him wasn't physical, however. It was those direct eyes.

He was a lawless killer who strangled businesses for money, dealt in drugs and women, took the cash of broke gambling addicts, and de-manded loyalty out of fear, not devotion.

But at least you knew what you were dealing with.

And there were no bloodstains on him. So Nate had a feeling that whatever had gone down had been done by an amateur who hadn't waited for the target to get out of that Mercedes.

As Nate entered with Jimmie, the man smiled coldly. "Helluva night, Natty boy."

"Glad you made it."

That stare narrowed into slits. "They fucked up my car. I love that fucking car."

Behind him, Jimmie shut the door, then went to stand next to Blue Bill, who was a looming mountain of tough guy in the corner. The two humans were identical in their dark suits with their dark hair and narrowed pale eyes. Then again, like everyone, they were related and went to the same tailor.

Uncle picked up his glass of whiskey and indicated the chair across from him, his gold cuff links flashing. "You just gonna stand there all night."

With a shrug, Nate sat down, spreading himself into a comfortable lean that the balloon-backed little chair couldn't really handle. "We have something to talk about."

"Yeah, we do, and it takes guts for you to come here." Uncle took a pull off the lip of his glass. "What if we don't let you go, huh?"

"I'm not worried about that."

For a split second, Uncle went very still. Then he smiled, like a cobra. "You got bigger balls than me sometimes."

As Nate shifted to put his hand into his second-best leather jacket—because the one he really liked had been burned to hell and gone, fuck him very much—he looked at Jimmie Gimp and Blue Bill.

"I'm not taking out a weapon. Relax."

Everybody waited until Uncle nodded and g'headed the movement. At which point, Nate finished retrieving the USB that had cost a man his life the night before.

Actually, that death had been more about Mickey's arrogance and stupidity.

Nate put the black slip in the center of the round table.

"Your nephew came to my place intending to kill me and plant this. He wanted to make it look like I was stealing from you and he took care of the problem." Nate leaned onto the four-top and felt the tips of his fangs tingle with aggression. God, he fucking hoped Uncle or one of his cousins did something stupid. "I don't give a fuck who you are, you don't show up on my property and try to pull that shit. He got what he deserved."

Uncle stared forward for a couple of beats. Then he glanced over his shoulder at Jimmie Gimp and Blue Bill. "This guy. Can you believe it. Comes in here talking ill of our dead."

"You know I'm right." Nate kept his voice level. Not that it was hard. "Mickey was always trying to get up on it, but he never could function any higher than where he was. That's why you never promoted him."

Uncle shook his head. "You kill one of us, you know what the punishment is."

"So try to drill a hole in my head right now," Nate said in a bored tone. "Please, fucking do it. 'Cuz then I'll be totally justified when I kill the three of you where you are, and walk out of here with a smile on my face."

Uncle's brows flickered. Then he laughed in an honest way and tossed back everything that was in his glass.

The ice clinked as he set the empty down with a smack. "You are the craziest motherfucker I ever met."

"That is a correct statement."

"But that doesn't mean I believe a fucking word you—"

Nate was beyond done dealing with everything, so to cut the conversation short, he burrowed into the boss's mind—and implanted what he'd learned when he'd popped the top off of Mickey's consciousness and peered inside.

Uncle hissed and winced, rubbing at his temple. And then when that meaty paw lowered, he looked across the table with banked surprise . . . like he was trying to comprehend how the math equation, which he understood with total clarity, had gotten into his head.

"Mickey got what he deserved," Nate repeated. "He made the choice, he ate the consequences. You know I got problems with no one. I just do what I do. In ten years, I haven't fucked with anybody in your family. I let them make all the money, take all the women, and do all the things. I've been loyal to you, I've executed the assignments you've given me with no questions, and you and me, we've never had any trouble. Let's not fucking start now. You won't like what happens next, and I'll be out of a good job."

There was a stretch of silence. Then Uncle looked at the other two men and indicated the door with a sharp nod.

Jimmie Gimp huffed. "That ain't smart—"

"Leave," Uncle said. "*Now.*"

Nate focused on the blank wall straight ahead of him as the pair of organized crime felons played four-year-old-getting-kicked-out-of-the-birthday-party. When the door finally closed behind them, he looked at Uncle.

"Mickey was who he was. I'm sorry for your loss."

Uncle lifted his glass to the ceiling and murmured something. Then he took a sip of melted ice cube. "Rest in peace."

After that, it was just a question of waiting. Uncle liked to take his time as an exercise of control.

"Where's the body," he said eventually.

"There's nothing left of it."

That stare got good and icy as the man shook his head on a jerk. "His mother needs something to bury."

Nate shrugged. "So give me someone to kill. I'll give you a body."

◆   ◆   ◆

Bitty woke up on the couch in Safe Place's living room, her eyes opening slowly on a flutter. As the ceiling came into focus and she recognized the nice landscape oil painting over the fireplace, she went to sit—

"Whoa, whoa," Mary said. "Take it easy."

As Bitty allowed herself to get urged back down, she tried to stitch together what had happened. She'd been at her desk in her office, and something had caught her attention—

All at once, she saw L.W. leaning into her, draping her with his heavy leather jacket . . . the one that smelled like him and was warm from his own body. Then he was staring into her eyes, and asking her—

"Where is he," she blurted.

"Do you want to tell me what happened?" her mom asked.

Focusing on the female, Bitty had an urge to tear up and she tried to beat that back. Mary was already worried, that familiar face tight with concern, the short cap of brown hair tousled as if she'd been pulling her hands through it.

"I'm sorry," Bitty mumbled. "I didn't mean to worry you."

Mary shook her head and reached out with a soothing touch. "No, no. You don't have to apologize. I'm just concerned because you fainted in the cold."

"I went outside . . ." L.W. must have called for help after she'd collapsed. ". . . to see a friend. And I just got dizzy."

"Doc Jane is going to come check you out, okay?"

"Of course." Because, hey, all the tests were going to come back fine. The fainting thing hadn't been physical. More like a soul seizure. "I'm all right. I just forgot to eat at First Meal."

Mary frowned. "You've been doing that a lot lately."

"I have?" When her mom nodded, Bitty rubbed her eyes. "You know, I think you're right."

"And you've complained about headaches over the last month."

"I did?"

"Mm-hmm." Mary stroked Bitty's arm again. "Honey, I think it might be coming."

Bitty lifted her brows. "What might be coming? If you're talking about spring, it's a long way off—"

"Your needing."

Cue the record squealing. Cars screeching to a halt. A crashing sound. "My nee—no, no." She shoved herself up into a sitting position. "It's waaay too early. I just had it a couple of years ago—"

"It'll be ten years in February."

A cold pall came over Bitty, like she was back out on the side lawn without a coat. "It . . . can't be."

"I'm afraid so. I've wanted to broach the subject, but I wasn't sure how."

Bitty closed her eyes and let her head fall back until her nape pinched like it was in a vise. Jesus . . . Christ. Not again.

A female vampire's fertile time was a torture. The cravings to be serviced by a male were so overpowering and debilitating that unless you were prepared to be with one for a good twenty-four hours straight—and run the risk of pregnancy and the birthing bed's high death rates—your only option was to get sedated and stay secluded until the whole two or three nights passed and your hormones reregulated.

"It seems like it just happened." Bitty stared at the area rug under the coffee table without seeing much of the braid of muted colors. "Then again, it always feels that way."

"I'll be there for you. So will Doc Jane."

"Thank you, Mom."

As Bitty looked up with worry, Mary wrapped her in a hug, and after the female pulled back, she smiled a little.

"So . . . there's someone waiting outside for you. He wants to make sure you're okay, and I have a feeling he's not going to be satisfied until he sets his own eyes on you."

"Oh." Bitty ran her hands over her hair. "Really?"

"Really. But I can also tell him to come back after Doc Jane assesses you. She's finishing up a consult at Havers's and then she'll be here."

"I'm fine. Honest."

And she really didn't want to have the doctor tell her what she and her mom had just guessed. That was not an argument she was going to win, though.

Mary got up from the edge of the couch and stared down with her hands at her hips, just the way she'd done when Bitty was younger and she'd been sick.

"You sure you feel well enough to go out there?" came the demand.

Taking a deep breath, Bitty felt a flutter in her chest as she nodded—maybe a little too enthusiastically. With a shift of her legs, she planted her feet on the carpet, and was slow in getting up just in case her balance was bad. When she reached her full height, she gave it a moment—

"Yup, good to go." She smiled at her mom. "I'll just, you know . . . I'll see him by myself. If that's okay."

"Sure thing. I'm right here if you need me. And your running shoes are over there."

As Bitty put on her Brooks, she ducked her head—so her big, giant, tomato-red blush didn't put her mom under a damn heat lamp—and then she tried to not look like she was straightening all her clothes, down to her frickin' knickers.

"I won't be long," she said.

"I'll wait here—you two take your time."

Bitty hesitated.

"You don't have to be embarrassed," came the gentle reassurance. "And you don't have to explain anything. You're an adult now and you're allowed your privacy."

"So you aren't going to tell . . . Father?"

Mary covered her heart. "Girls unite. I won't say a thing."

"Thanks, Mom."

Technically, there wasn't anything to tell, she reminded herself. L.W. had given her a coat, not an engagement ring. Still, it all felt live-wire fresh, fraught with peril, super exciting. And there was something about sharing a romance with her mother that seemed natural, but admitting it to her father felt . . .

Well, she just got a case of the sheeps about that kind of conversation.

Pulling a pivot, she tried to be calm about the whole walking out to the front entry. When she came to the door, she hesitated before she opened it, her hand gripping the copper latch and staying put, her breath getting tight in her lungs, that flutter thing turning her heart into a strobe light in the center of her chest.

It was like leaping into a lake on a hot summer night. At some point, you just had to leave the dock planks and fly.

Or you were never going to know the joy of the plunge.

Closing her eyes to make the leap, Bitty yanked open the door, and the way the cold air hit her made her gasp. And then she was extending her running shoe over the threshold, and thinking of the Resolve2Evolve tagline: *Be Alive, Do More, Be More.*

Boy, had that message been received, and she did feel more alive, and she was going to be more, with L.W.—and oh, God, she just wanted to feel that warmth again. Not from his jacket, though.

From his body—

All the way down at the end of the walkway, standing in the snow by the lantern, the male who was waiting for her turned around and looked up to the porch.

Not black hair, braided down the top of the skull. No harsh brows and stark looks. No tattooed neck or black diamond earrings.

Blond hair. Brilliant, Bahamas-blue eyes. And a worried, hesitant expression.

"There she is," Rhage said tenderly. "My girl."

The disappointment was . . . crushing. And to cover it up, from her father, from herself, Bitty rushed forward, skipping down the little set of stairs and racing down the shoveled walk. Before she was really in range, she leapt into the air, throwing herself forward, knowing that she would be caught and held, captured by her father and kept safe from gravity's pull and the hard, unforgiving ground.

Rhage did not let her down. He never did.

Those big, strong arms were as they always had been, lifting her up, but holding her carefully, too. And as she looked over his huge shoulder, she pretended that she wasn't searching the lawn for another male.

A different one.

CHAPTER THIRTY

As dawn arrived and bathed Caldwell in the kind of light that grew and nourished so many living things—but was a straight-up death sentence to a vampire—Wrath transported himself off the planet entirely. Good thing his body didn't need to leave home to do it. His consciousness—or maybe it was his soul, he didn't know—went up, up, and away, to a place far from the ground, and yet not in the clouds, either.

Not in the conventional sense, at least.

And given that the Sanctuary didn't really exist in a physical manner, he'd always wondered how he knew the second he was there. When he'd had his eyesight, that hadn't been a thing, but now—he just *knew*. Even before he scented anything, before he felt the strange, bathwater-like air, before he sensed beneath his shitkickers the springy grass . . . he just knew he was no longer on Earth.

Taking a long draw in through his nose, he smelled the place and saw it in his mind's eye: The tulips. The went-on-forever lawn. The crystal-clear water of the bathing pool and the fountain in what had been the Scribe Virgin's private quarters. Even the milky sky overhead and the ring of trees that, if you were to walk into it, just spit you out on the opposite side from which you'd entered.

As his mind puzzle-pieced all of it together, he had to remind himself that everything had color now. Gone were the shades of white and gray. Phury, as the last of the Primales, had Pantone'd the landscape, so that the flowers were pastel and the grass was vibrant and those bathing pools shimmered with blue.

Fucking hell . . . he was suddenly exhausted. In the way you felt after you'd come home from a long vacation that had been hectic rather than restful.

"Years," he murmured to himself. "It's been . . . decades, hasn't it."

Moving his head from side to side, as if he could see, he didn't understand why he felt the time that he'd lost so acutely here. Down below, what he'd missed had been just a blink, and only as the change of circumstance and landscape had become apparent had the decades measured at all. Up here in the Sanctuary, though, he felt the calendars like he'd lived all those days and all those nights.

So, yeah, it was as though he'd been long and wearily traveled, his shoulders and spine aching, his head thumping to a dull, irregular beat.

Stress was a bitch, wasn't it—

He stiffened. Then said, without turning around, "You didn't keep me waiting."

Lassiter chuckled in that good-natured way of his. "Yup, I've turned over a new leaf since you've been gone."

Wrath looked over his shoulder even though it was a why-bother when it came to his eyeballs. "Oh really?"

"You bet your bippy, King of mine. Thirty years later, and I'm a peach. People love me. I'm hardly ever annoying, even to V. And I've taken up needlepoint."

Shaking his head, Wrath had to smile. "You're such an ass."

"Of course I am. Especially to V—and really, that's a public service. He needs the exercise."

"Personally, I think self-improvement is overrated."

Lassiter's laugh cracked like lightning. "Well, I gave it a shot. You have no idea how many books I've read since I saw you last. And videos I've watched. And seminars I've attended. I'm not sure you're aware of this, but making yourself better is a whole industry."

"I'm surprised you haven't taken up that pulpit."

"Don't think I haven't considered it seriously. I'd be a hit, plus zebra print was overdue for a comeback way before you took your little vacation."

"You sure about that? And if I was on a vacation, I'll pass on R & R for the rest of my mortal existence, thanks."

"Oh, you'll get over that. Everyone needs a break sometime, a change of scenery. Like, I've heard Disney cruises aren't half bad."

"From who—someone who wanted to get rid of you? And make sure you suffer while you're gone?"

"Now that I think about it—I do believe V was the one who suggested I try a five-day."

"That checks out."

All at once, they both fell silent, the pleasantries over and done with, the reconnection established . . . the real reason for the visit taking the proverbial wheel.

"Let's walk," Lassiter said gravely.

Wrath nodded and orientated himself by the soft rustling of the grass next to him. There was nothing to worry about in terms of trip-and-falls. The ground of the Sanctuary was a perfect undulation, no gopher holes, nothing uneven, no rocks.

And he did trust Lassiter not to run him into anything. Which was a vote of confidence in favor of the angel that surprised him. Then again, the Scribe Virgin hadn't been completely out of her mind when she'd turned the job over to the guy.

"Tell me about the war," Wrath said in a low voice. "How bad's it gotten."

"I'm surprised you're not asking Tohr."

"He takes things personally. It would eat him alive to report on losses suffered by our civilians. I'm not putting him through that."

There was some silence, which was answer enough in and of itself. And then Lassiter said, "They've taken excellent care of Beth, you know. Her and L.W. Your *shellan* and your son were well watched over, every night, all day long, by everyone."

Wrath felt his chest expand with pride. "That's my brothers. And my fighters."

"They're devoted to her."

He thought back to the very beginning, when he'd had Beth at Darius's mansion in town, and he'd walked in to find the Brotherhood down on one knee around her, their black daggers buried in the floorboards, their heads lowered in devotion. Even Zsadist's.

"She's worth being devoted to," he said.

And when he thought about all the pain she'd endured over the last three decades? He wanted to feel Lash's blood flow, warm and thick, over his bare hands.

"Now tell me about the war," he growled.

"We've been holding the line."

"Bullshit. I'm hearing about the inductions. They found a site earlier tonight—and it's been used a lot."

"Lash is efficient." The angel's bitterness was clear. "I'll give the bastard that."

"What about the demon? No one's talking about Devina."

"I haven't seen her around for years. Something happened between them, I don't know what."

"So one thing broke our way. We don't need the pair of them working together."

"Aw, come on, I thought they were just *darling*."

"Bonnie and Clyde, the undead version."

"And I was never on their Christmas card list. Such a disappointment."

Wrath stopped. "How many have we lost. Civilians, that is. I already know all the brothers and fighters made it."

Lassiter kept going, but his wander was in a slow circle, like he was tethered to the patch of ground Wrath stood on. He couldn't totally picture the angel. He'd had Beth describe the male as he currently was, so there was a cobbled-together vision of something tall, covered in gold chains and piercings, with blond hair on the top half of his head and black on the bottom. Edit in some hot pink and zebra print, and maybe a halo? A set of iridescent wings?

It was like if David Lee Roth got canonized.

Eventually, the angel reported with sadness, "We've lost too many—and I'm not saying that because even one death at the hands of those slayers is too much. It's been hundreds. The brothers and the fighters do their very best, and they've eradicated a lot of *lessers*. But Lash is faster than his father with the inductions, and he's using women now."

Wrath had a sudden, nearly overpowering urge to go downtown and fight, and the drive brought back the past. In a series of flashbacks from his time in the field, he saw his throwing stars shimmering through the darkness, finding targets, cutting down the enemy so that he could get out his daggers and send them back to their unholy maker, the Omega.

Flexing his hands, he could still feel the metal, cold at first, when he took them out of their slide on his waist, warmer after he'd held them.

Abruptly, he thought about last night and the hours he'd spent in the new Audience House, meeting with his subjects, as if nothing had interrupted him.

"I saw a lot of males and females of worth, yesterday," he said. "I proclaimed two young, blessed a mating. Released a property."

"I know you did. Felt good, right?"

Well, except for at the end when he and the Brotherhood had

decided to give Nate the fucking boot. And of course everything would have felt fucking great if he could just get out and fight.

He frowned. "I owe your *shellan* a lot, for filling in for me in my absence. She did an amazing thing for the species."

"She's an amazing female. That's why I mated her—plus she puts up with me."

"So we know she's a saint." Wrath shook his head. "Can you explain something to me?"

"I'll give it a shot."

"Why can I feel the time up here so clearly? The decades that have passed?"

There was a pause, and Wrath imagined the angel looking around. "This is the absolute timeline, the universal one, established by the Creator. Down there, everything is relative and subject to manipulation to some extent. Think about all the different lives, the different perspectives, the whole of it a fruit salad of personal destinies colliding in good ways and bad. It's a fucking mess. Up here, there is clarity because of the absolute nature of moments—and that means that those thirty years are very real. Fudging isn't allowed in the Sanctuary."

Wrath put his hand over his heart. "It's fucking weird, but I miss my mate with an ache up here, like I didn't see her in forever. Down there, it felt like just a matter of hours."

"You can bring her up with you, you know. This place isn't just for you and me."

"This is not a conversation I wanted my *leelan* to hear."

"She's heard it before. My Rahvyn was the face of you, but Beth was in charge, all along."

As a fresh wave of aggression hit him, Wrath cursed under his breath and got to the point.

"I need you to give me my eyesight back." When there was no reply—because clearly Lassiter was choosing words carefully—he slapped a grip on the angel's forearm. "Don't give me that non-interference bullshit.

You've helped before and I need your help now. You've *got* to give me my eyes so I can go out and fight."

The angel broke away, and the sound of him pacing around again in the grass that was always the same cropped height, always with the perfect blades, was soft as a brush of cloth over skin.

"I need my eyes, angel, and you can give them to me. You have to do this for me. I'm the King, goddamn it. I command you—"

"You remember how the Omega got access to all the vases?" Lassiter cut in. "The evil got a nice juice right at the end so it could keep fighting. You know why he got the location to the Tomb and those shelves with all those hearts? It happened because my predecessor got over-involved and was punished. We're *not* rolling those dice with the Creator again. Fuck knows what Lash would be granted. And besides, you can't go out and fight, Wrath."

"The fuck I can't—"

"We just plugged a thirty-year absence with my mate. I'm not doing that again to Rahvyn—and besides, there's no way we're winning the lottery twice in a row and saving your ass by hiding you in time like that. It was a one in a million—"

"Rahvyn resurrected Nate. If I get into trouble, she can do the same to me—"

"Never again with that." Lassiter's voice got very low. "My *shellan* is out of that line of work. That male is out of control *because* of what Rahvyn did to save him. It's eaten her alive, the way he turned out, so no, she's not going to ruin anybody else's life by saving them. That card is no longer available to you or anyone else."

Wrath grit his molars. "You have the power to help me and you know how high the stakes are—"

"I already *have* helped you, asshole. You know that dog you love so much? You want to ask yourself why he's still alive thirty years later? How about all the humans in the lives of your fighters? You think I'm not already walking the line by making sure they don't age?"

Wrath cursed again. "Fine, I'll just go out and fight blind—"

Suddenly, Lassiter's voice was right in front of him. "No, you won't. You're not doing that shit. You're going to be what we need you to be, on that throne—"

Wrath shoved the angel away. "I need to fight!"

"Then do it from where you sit! Do you think you're not out there with the Brotherhood already? They fight *for* you, for your family, for the species you are in charge of. You are their ruler, you are more important than combat."

"For three decades, they needed me and I wasn't there. They were hurt, and I wasn't there. They killed our enemy, and I wasn't there. And now I'm back and I'm still sitting on the sidelines—"

"You're doing what you need to do. We have fighters, we have soldiers. We *need* a leader—and fuck you, dickhead, you're it. Show a little self-control, would you? There's only room for one half-cocked idiot between the pair of us, and I'm *not* giving up my day job being a douchebag. So that leaves you being the reasonable adult in the room, you're welcome."

Before Wrath could respond, Lassiter continued intently, "You were born to lead. Not because of who your sire was." There was a subtle poke on Wrath's chest, right where the star scar of the Black Dagger Brotherhood had been punched into his left pec. "You're a leader because of *who* you are. Be that male for us. Don't let the anger get away from you. I'm telling you right now, your wrath will be the death of us all."

CHAPTER THIRTY-ONE

The key ring was the key, and thank God he hadn't left it anywhere, but had taken Mickey's open-sesame with him when he'd stolen his change of clothes.

As Evan limped down the street, he wasn't sure which one he was on. He was orientating himself with peephole views of the bridges, and knew that if he kept going, sooner or later the triangulation would occur.

And it did.

The walk-up he'd been searching for was sandwiched between Needle, a tattoo and piercing parlor, and a rare book dealer, and like the rest of the mixed-use neighborhood, the apartment building wasn't much to look at from the outside. It was well-maintained, however, with no windows broken, the steps shoveled, and nothing crumbling at the roofline or on the corners. As he took out the key to the vestibule, he remembered when Mickey had first rented the place secretly. His cousin had been so proud, and Evan had been impressed because that's what had been expected of him. The truth was, he'd thought it was nothing to brag about.

Then again, Mickey had always been about the moving-up thing.

All his life, the guy had had a knack for amplifying shit. Like, this apartment was a penthouse, even though it was only on the top floor of a run-down place and just the same as all the other units. Like, even though they were only trusted with baggies, he made it seem that bricks were what they were dealing. Like, even though Uncle had despised them both, Mickey was the guy's favorite out of the two of them.

Like, even though that outsider enforcer was getting the real wet work, Uncle was saving Mickey for something special . . .

Coming back to the present, Evan pushed the key in and turned it, thinking that this really was an old place with all this analog entrance shit instead of facial recognition. As the dead bolt released, there was a clunking sound, and then he was in the shallow space where the mailboxes were. The steps up to the second door were perma-dirty, wedges of grime in the right angles at each level, the foot traffic scuffs indelible now.

The tide of people had been too pervasive for too long, filthy toes in worn-out soles, over and over again on the same path.

Kinda like the route to that elevator.

Evan used the key once more, and then he was at the bottom of the stairs. The balustrade was rickety on the way up, but he had to use it because of the gunshot wound in his thigh. There was no knowing when he'd gotten nailed. Probably a stray fly-away, a ricochet, an off-target out-the-way.

At the top, he went to the left, to the second of the two apartments on that side.

As the key went into the lock, he paused. He missed Mickey, even though his cousin had never been nice. It was kind of like how if you lived in a crappy house, you still got homesick when you were away from the dripping faucets and the chipped floors and the creaky doors. Home was where the familiar was—

Evan froze as he opened the way in.

The first thing he noticed was the smell. Old urine, sharp and lemony.

Frowning, he stepped inside and closed things behind him. As his weight transferred, the floorboards creaked and he hesitated.

What was that other sound?

The apartment had a short hallway that opened into the living room, and he put his back to the wall and eased his way down, the gun with the suppressor in his hand. As the corridor yielded to the open space, he stopped again.

Across the bare floor, in front of the puffy leather sofa . . . tipped over on her side . . . a woman was tied to one of Mickey's crappy kitchen chairs. There was a gag in her mouth, and duct tape had been used to keep her hands restrained in front of her, while nylon was doing the job locking her forearms and ankles to the chair's structure.

The woman began flailing around, her red-rimmed eyes bugging, her frazzled dark hair tangling even more, her buckled shoes clapping—

Evan put his forefinger to his lips. "Shhhh."

She stilled the big movements. The little stuff, like her panting and the way her mouth worked against the gag, kept on going.

The whimpering sound reminded him of a dog left behind.

Evan left her where she was and scouted the rest of the apartment, even going through the closets. Mickey had been a messy person, and seeing the laundry on the floor, the bed with its wrinkled wedge of a comforter, and the hodgepodge of shoes and boots all over the place, was a reminder of how the guy had always been moving. The only time his kinetic energy had decreased was when he'd been high or passed out drunk.

Evan had always wondered why his cousin had never channeled all that into cleaning. But he'd certainly never shared that opinion.

A quick catalogue of assets was necessary, and Evan took the top mattress off the box spring, and was rewarded for the effort. Two more handguns. A couple of magazines. In the bedside table, some handcuffs— no key, though. The closet yielded a rifle, for which there didn't seem to be any bullets, and two boxes of nine millimeter ammo. Also a baseball bat. And a duffle, which was handy to pack shit up.

In the bathroom, he went to the medicine cabinet and—

Evan froze when he saw his reflection in the mirror. "Oh . . . God."

Leaning into the glass, he pulled down his lower eyelids, one after the other. The whites of his eyes were now . . . gray.

"Fuck," he breathed as he dropped the bag and gripped the edge of the sink with both hands.

He was still going bald and his face was the same, but he was looking at a stranger—even though he couldn't define exactly what had changed. Maybe it was the flat quality of his skin, like he was a wax figure of himself.

Lowering his head, he tried to keep the tears back and lost the battle. The weeping racked his body, and he felt dull aches and pains from all the sawing breaths. But he couldn't stop the explosion of emotion, his eyes squeezing shut, his lungs burning—

Hard to know exactly when he saw the black smudges on the floor. But when they registered, he lifted his head . . . and knew what he was going to see before he focused.

He was crying black tears, his pasty cheeks scored with mascara-like riverways.

Throwing out a hand, he expected there to be a towel hanging on a rod, but there wasn't one. He ended up scrubbing off his face with the limp shower curtain.

When he could focus a little better, he ran some water, and he didn't wait for it to get warm before he splashed it into his eyes—the cold felt good, but it was a distilled sensation, like through a filter of numbness. Turning back to the shower, he avoided the black stain he'd left and wiped things dry in another place.

He was pivoting away when he saw the toilet.

Putting a shaking hand down to the front of the pants he'd stolen, he couldn't remember the last time he'd taken a leak.

Back at the medicine cabinet, he opened the thing all the way so there was no chance of seeing himself.

Tylenol. A couple of joints. Half a bottle of penicillin for that tooth Mickey had broken.

He picked up the duffle and went back out to the living room.

The woman was like a mouse in a trap, re-reacting to his presence, flailing once again as if he was the plug for her wire.

Putting the duffle down, he went to the kitchen and started opening drawers. He found a serrated knife in the third one down, and he took it over to the woman. For a moment, he watched her cry, marveling at the crystal-clear tears that dripped off the bridge of her nose. Then he knelt next to her.

When the knife got close to her face, she started screaming, the sound trapped by the gag—

"I'm really sorry," he said roughly. "But I need this place. I got nowhere else to go. I need . . . to think . . ."

He started crying with her, and the weapon shook in his hand.

Especially as he realized the noises coming up from the woman were something like *n-n-n-n-nnnnnnn-ooooo*—

Hold up, he thought. The knife was going to make a mess. What if her blood seeped through the floor and onto the ceiling of the apartment below?

There had been a lot of the stuff when Mickey's throat had been cut.

Evan put the blade aside, and the woman shuddered like she'd been given a reprieve.

"Shhhh . . ." he repeated.

Standing back up, he went into Mickey's bedroom. There were a couple of pillows crammed into the seam between the mattress and the wall, and he picked them out of the tight squeeze, testing them for firmness.

He chose the softest one, even though it was fucked up. When he was suffocating her, was she really going to care that he'd picked something for her comfort? That was like getting ribbed condoms for a prostitute.

Back in the living room, he glanced over to the windows. Mickey had already pulled the drapes before leaving the other night—and good thing.

He should have checked that before. He was going to have to get better at not being distracted.

Over by the woman, Evan lowered himself down once more. When he wiped his tears, the black smudge on his fingertips was what came out of his veins, what was on the floor of that office building, what he'd been forced to swallow . . . the worst kind of Kool-Aid there was.

"Hold your breath," he said in a voice that cracked. "It will be over sooner that way."

Bringing the pillow to her face, he—

He had to stop again. It wasn't going to work with her head to the side. She needed to be face up.

As he got frustrated with himself, her crying also got on his nerves. He was upset with this turn of events, too. Fucking hell, like she thought he wanted to do this?

With his newfound strength, he easily cranked the chair a quarter turn, so that it was as if it had fallen straight back.

"You gotta give me a break," he muttered as she started screaming again. "I've never done this before, okay?"

She was totally hyperventilating now, and her bound hands were like a snare drum on her lap, the beat as she tried to get her arms free so fast he could hardly track it. Once more with the pillow, and as he put it just above her face, her eyes stretched so wide, if she'd been a cartoon, they would have popped out.

"It's not going to be long," he said roughly as he got sad again. "I promise—"

He surged forward and pinned the pillow to the floor on either side of her head, right by her ears. The soft one proved to be a good choice. The seal was easy and immediate.

As she struggled, he got too busy tracking her movements against the binds to keep with his crying thing. He was worried that they were making too much noise. The apartments in the building were occupied with people who could call the police to investigate strange thumping sounds.

It felt like a year and a half before the woman finally fell still, and the concentration and effort required to kill her right reminded him of having sex, what with the way he had to work at it and pay attention to what was happening with his partner.

He stayed in place for a full five minutes afterward.

Then Evan slowly lifted the pillow, and the way he peeked under it reminded him of his mother cooking, the way she would always lean to the side as she lifted the lids to pots or the dishtowels over rising dough or the seal on leftovers.

"There you go," he said with an exhale.

The woman's eyes were wide and pointed at the ceiling, her mouth open farther than the gag required, her face dry of tears, the pillow dotted with wet spots.

Just like sex.

As Evan fell back on his ass and set the pillow on his lap, he stared at the still woman and noted that he wasn't crying anymore. And this was good. This was . . . what was expected of him.

Uncle and the others didn't get upset when they killed people. He'd heard them talk about it.

Mickey had killed three people—well, two had been on account of that car accident when he'd been drunk driving. But he hadn't cried over any of them.

And he wouldn't have cried if he'd been able to get uphill of that enforcer, Nathaniel.

And that enforcer hadn't cried over Mickey.

Putting his elbows on his knees, Evan became as still as the woman, his inner awareness settling down, becoming a reflecting pool instead of a rushing river.

Calm. Focused.

"I am changing . . ." he whispered, no longer as horrified at what was in his veins.

CHAPTER THIRTY-TWO

At midnight the following evening, Nalla stepped out of Luchas House, closed the front door, and went down the porch steps. On the walkway, she leaned back and checked out the dense cloud cover. A storm was brewing, weather-wise.

When it came to her life, the blizzard had already hit.

She hadn't slept all day. Had just lain upstairs in that messy bed, the shutters down to keep out the sunlight, her brain playing solo tennis against the backboard of her regrets, alternating between the fight she'd had with her *mahmen* downstairs and the argument she'd had with her sire in that alley the night before.

And, there had been one other thing on her mind.

From time to time, she'd rolled over to the side of the mattress and stared down at the pillow that was still on the floor right by the bed. She'd refused to pick it up. What had happened between her and Nate had been mind-bendingly vivid when they'd been together. But in a weird distortion, the very fact it had been so good made her question whether she'd blown the hookup out of proportion.

So the pillow they'd knocked off was staying where it was.

Proof she hadn't made anything up.

Closing her eyes, it was a while before she could calm herself enough to dematerialize, and when she was finally able to spirit away in a scatter of molecules, she knew she had to get her head right before she got to the tattoo parlor.

After all, the problems with her parents would be waiting for her following this . . . date? Was that what this was? At any rate, she didn't want to waste what time she had with Nate.

Re-forming on the roof of a restaurant that was closed for the evening, she walked over to the lip and looked down.

Needle was across the street, and with its darkened windows and sign, she wasn't sure whether the artist had come to re-open things yet. She hadn't heard from Nate, but she hadn't expected to—okay, fine. Maybe she'd thought he might get a message to her at Luchas House somehow.

He didn't know she had a working phone again. Or her number. But he sure knew where she was—

"Shut *up*," she said into the cold air.

It was beyond time to pull herself together. After the day she'd spent with her racing mind, she was so over going around in circles in her head about whether Nate was still coming, if they were still on, if he still wanted to hook up with her. The good news? At this point, only she was aware of the OCD Olympic track her thoughts were running relays on, and she was damn well going to keep it that way.

There was a fire escape off to the side of the building, and as her nerves were too raw, even after her shut-up pep talk, she went down the rungs hand over hand, jumping free off the six-foot drop at the bottom, her boots landing with a slam on the grimy snowpack.

Heading out to the main street, her strides were more confident than she was feeling, and she told herself to get a grip all over again. The fact that she was losing her mind after talking to that male a couple of times and hooking up a little with him probably meant Bitty was right all along: She needed to get out more.

Although feeding Nate had been more than just a hookup. At least on her side.

Crossing Market Street, she sized up the shop as well as the area in general as she went along. Everything was closed for the night, and there were no pedestrians or cars around, but she felt safe enough. The neighborhood was not fancy, yet it wasn't nasty, either.

Stopping in front of Needle, she looked up at the darkened neon sign that was just block letters, no glow. The plate glass windows of the front were also blacked out, velvet drapes pulled across them on the inside, no glow from the interior seeping through the folds and breaks in the heavy fabric.

Was she supposed to knock? she wondered as she eyed the many-times-painted front door. There wasn't a doorbell to ring.

As a crushing, sinking feeling hollowed out her chest, she wrapped her arms around herself and glanced back at the roof of the restaurant across the street. The idea of retracing her steps to Luchas House, and making some excuse as to why she was going to work even though it was a Saturday and she was always off Saturdays, made her cringe. But she still wasn't ready to go back home yet, and like Bathe was an option?

She'd already met her once-a-year club quota.

Besides, she might be banned for hopping up on that table and playing soccer with all those glasses—

"Nalla? You Nalla?" The resonant, deep voice rippled out to her, and as she jumped and looked around, it ordered, "Over here."

Glancing to the right, she zeroed in on the thin seam between the tattoo parlor and the apartment building next to it.

"Hello?" she said.

"I'm holding the door open, you gotta come to me."

With caution—and a heart that was suddenly tap-dancing a little with hope—she headed over to the six-foot-wide breezeway. About twenty feet down, a pool of light spilled out . . . along with a figure who was tall as a basketball player, thin as a model, and tattooed everywhere. With neon pink hair peaked like the top of a lemon meringue pie, a micro-mini, and thigh-high, pencil-heeled boots the same color as the hair, the person was—

"Well," they snapped. "Are we just standing here, honey, or are we doing something? I have *not* got time for this."

"Sorry, yes, sorry."

Nalla scrambled forward, and she couldn't help but stare as the person stepped out and motioned her into a long hall that was painted black from floor to ceiling.

Wow. Just . . . wow.

The tattoos that covered their pale skin were all black-and-white portraits of movie stars from waaaaay back set against a background of the Louis Vuitton logo. Meanwhile, their face, which was professional-level made up, was easily beautiful enough to be on a magazine cover, the hollows under the cheeks, the plump lips, and the luminescent eyes the kind of thing that might have been bought and paid for as part of another canvas to make art with, but really, the end result was so striking, it had clearly been an investment worth making.

"Are we going to have a problem." That voice, which was both bass and soprano together, was sharp as a knife. "Because Amore don't beg for anything, honey, and I am *not* starting with you tonight."

"I'm sorry." Nalla glanced down to those boots again. Then went back up, way up. "You're just . . . too dazzling to look at. Like Marilyn Monroe and *Vogue* magazine had a love child."

Amore arched their perfect brows. Then they fussed at their hair with their neon pink nails. "Girl, I *knew* we were going to get along. From the moment I saw you. Now, tell me more about how fabulous I am."

The next thing Nalla knew, she was draped by a tattooed arm and escorted like she was royalty down into a scrupulously clean workroom that was all black and pink and gold. The focal point was the table in the center of the space and the chandelier of bright lights over it, but there were also an upright, padded chair, various rolling tables, and a couple of silk armchairs. The rest of the square footage was taken up by equipment, including autoclaves, an entire twenty-foot bank of ink colors in squeeze bottles, and all kinds of glass-fronted cabinets filled with needles, tattooing guns, and supplies.

The best part? The walls were covered with photographs of Amore with famous people, as well as countless awards and diplomas.

Nalla wandered over to look at one of the shelves full of trophies. "Are these all yours?"

"You bet your ass, honey."

"This is incredibly impressive." She looked over her shoulder. "I mean, *whoa*."

Amore leaned back against a stretch of countertop. "I've been at it for a while, what can I say."

"You're also very good at what you do."

"I am one of the best." Amore cocked a brow. "So what are we doing for you? What do you want."

Nalla inspected a framed picture of what clearly was the old-fashioned model Naomi Campbell standing with a very young Amore. "I'm not really sure. I just know that I've wanted a tattoo for years, but didn't know where to get it done or what it might look like. I love . . . Nate's, by the way."

"Oh, that little thing." Amore gave a *pshaw*. Then got really serious. "We worked forever on that. I'm proud of what we did."

"It's a masterpiece."

"It took him forever to get the design right—the artwork was all his idea. We did so many planning sessions, I didn't know when I was finally going to be able to ink him."

Nalla frowned. "He did the image?"

"All his idea." Amore shook their head. "He told me he'd seen something like it on someone he knew, and then he noodled with the skull as the core until it was right. The snakes and the vines and the clouds were all him. After he got the chest piece done, he had a buddy come in for something not dissimilar. Now, that was a male specimen, right there. Too bad he was straight."

L.W.? she thought. Had to be.

"Nate won't let me put him in any publications," they said. "I mean, you've clearly seen his, shall we say, hidden talents. He should model—what's wrong?"

Nalla shook herself back to attention. "Oh, it's just . . . Nate told me that his tattoo was—well, never mind." She smiled. Or tried to. "And yes, he is . . . um . . . attractive."

"Look at you, blushing." Amore came over and took Nalla's arm. "Come here, let me show you some things."

Nalla let herself be led through a door and out into the reception area—and talk about your library of images.

"Holy . . . crap."

"I have to give my clients ideas, right?"

The entire front part of the shop was a waiting area that was wall-papered with sketches and stacked with books of tattoos, everything organized by type, from flowers, and fish, and birds, to the hard-core horror stuff, to the old school, Gothic-lettered designs. There was also a lineup of chairs, a desk with a computer, and a coffee bar. And of course, everything was pink, black, and gold.

"I am totally . . . overwhelmed," Nalla said.

"Take your time and look around. I'll be right back."

Nalla moved slowly down the wall, her eyes bouncing from abstract swirls and a whole panel of roses . . . to tribal designs and famous quotes in various fonts.

As the door behind her opened again, she wished Nate were here, and was worried he wasn't going to show up after all.

"I just don't know." She exhaled. "There's so much to consider . . . and it's permanent."

For vampires, if the ink was going to stick, there had to be salt in it—so no lasering the design off if you thought better of it.

Then again, if Nate didn't come, she didn't have to worry about the permanent thing, did she—

"Take your time—"

Nalla spun around with a smile. "You're here."

Nate was standing where Amore had been, and, dear God, he was good to see. For some stupid reason—considering she had been thinking about him all day long—she felt the need to re-catalog everything about him. Yes, he was still a fighter first and foremost, and dressed in black leather, with what was clearly another jacket. And yes, he was still powerful, all coiled aggression and reserved confidence. And yes, his eyes were still hooded and intense as he looked down at her.

But somehow, she felt like she was seeing him for the first time all over again.

Although on that note, she closed her eyes briefly, and pictured him as he'd been on that bed, no shirt, his leathers open—

"Are you okay?" he asked.

Pulling herself together, she stared into those blue eyes of his and nodded. "I am now."

The smile that tilted his mouth up on one side was like a secret shared between them, something only for her, only given to . . . her. And she wasn't sure who took the first step forward. Maybe it was him. Maybe her.

Did it matter?

Nope, sure didn't.

They met halfway, in the middle of the waiting room, and for Nalla, putting her arms around his waist and pulling herself against his hard body was as natural as breathing—and so was tilting her head back and offering her mouth.

Nate didn't wait even a heartbeat to bend down and kiss her deep. And as she smelled those dark spices, she had a crazy thought. An absolutely insane one.

Had he bonded with her? Was that even possible?

Considering that promise he'd made to her father . . . it could explain why he kept breaking his word.

When they finally came up for air, she was ready to fuck off the tattoo stuff and go back to Luchas House. Or get a hotel. Or hey, there were chairs over there—the desk, maybe? She was willing to bet Amore would give them a little privacy.

"I'm sorry I was late." Nate reached into the pocket of his leather jacket and held up a small container. "I had to get your ink."

"You're here now." She put her hand up to his face. "You're forgiven for everything."

A darkness filtered through his face, but he covered it up quick. "So I guess you met Amore—"

"She's in love with me, honey." The artist sailed into the waiting area like they were riding a magic carpet, all smooth stride and fabulousness. "You're just coming up short. But really, can you blame her?"

Nate tucked Nalla against his side. "Nope, not at all."

"Ahh, see, that's why you're my favorite client. You're not just decorative, you have half a brain."

"Are you ready for this?" Nate asked her.

Nalla smiled. "I have no idea what I'm doing, but I gotta give that a hell yeah. Let's get some ink done on me."

CHAPTER THIRTY-THREE

Y ou did great, honey."

About two hours later, Nate was hovering over Amore's table and watching as the human made a last pass over Nalla's shoulder blade with a rinse and a wipe-down.

His favorite female vampire turned her head and angled a stare at him. "How's it look?"

The depiction was of an apple tree in full bloom, the branches extending out from the core in a graceful arch, each flower perfectly drawn, as if it were ink on paper, not ink on skin put there by a needle.

He knew exactly what had inspired the design.

It was the mosaic floor from the Brotherhood mansion's grand foyer. He'd visited a couple of times with his parents, back when the First Family had lived there. He'd never felt particularly comfortable in the palace, but he knew it had been Nalla's home for a time.

"Beautiful," he said as he rubbed his thumb on the pad of her hand. "You miss that house, don't you."

A flicker of sadness darkened her yellow eyes. "Things seemed . . . easier there. Then again, maybe that was only because I was little."

God, he hated the fact that he was coming between her and her father. And he could not blame the Brother.

"It's with you forever, now." He reached out and brushed a strand of hair back from her face. "It's a tangible memory."

"That's why I picked it."

Nate thought of his own ink. He'd done the same, but what was in his skin was his nightmare. Stupid, really. To think putting some ink on him would draw the torture out of his soul somehow. But at least the discomfort of the needle had distracted him from the real pain, at least for the hours he'd been on the table.

"I'm glad . . ."

As his voice drifted, she prompted, "About?"

For a moment, he was sucked into his own past, once again back in that bright white and stainless steel lab, trapped inside a cage with wire walls, staring out as his *mahmen*, withered and exhausted and bruised, was laid out on the exam table and strapped down even though she had been all but dead from the experiments. He had been crying, but he had not begged. The humans in the lab coats never responded to words, like he was just an animal yelping.

He hadn't known what they injected into her. Just like he'd never known what they put in him. Viruses, diseases, poisons . . . a flood pushing into him and taking over his body, the symptoms that bloomed a toxic garden cultivated by his captors.

Nate cleared his throat as the old, familiar agony of recollection ached in his very bones, sure as if his consciousness had been in a devastating car accident, and though he could still walk, his mental limbs were permanently fractured.

"I'm glad that what you've chosen is a happy memory," he said roughly. "That you have some from when you were young. And the tattoo is seriously well done."

"Of course it is," Amore cut in as they gave the floor a push with their heels and rolled over to a bank of cabinets on their stool. "And if you ever want anything else done, I'm yours anytime. You don't have to bring tall, dark, and broody with you. Although I always enjoy the view."

Nalla laughed and then those sunshine-yellow eyes grew hooded. "You know what? I like looking at him, too."

"I knew we had similar taste, soon as you started glossing me." Amore rolled back over with a stretch of Saran Wrap and some surgical tape. "And you got my number, girl. You call Amore when you need your ink."

Nate glanced down at the other planning sketch the two had worked out together, using pictures from Nalla's phone. It was the grand facade of the Black Dagger Brotherhood mansion, with the fountain centered just in front of the ornate entry and those massive doors. Even though the artwork was just a conceptual, it had everything, the little circles at the roofline representing the gargoyles, the windows all aligned, the three-story wings extending off to the sides.

"You also grew up in that house, Nate?" Amore asked as they laid the clear sheet over their work. "Pretty fucking fancy."

"No, I was just a visitor."

"And my family doesn't live there anymore." Nalla's eyes also went to the drawing. "I haven't been back to that house for years. Too busy with work . . . and stuff."

"Adulting sucks," Amore announced.

"It sure does." She pinned a smile on her face and picked up the hand mirror again, angling it to see what had been done through the protective barrier as Amore taped things in place. "Boy, that is perfect. And I'm glad it's on my back. I couldn't look at it all the time. Too sad."

"Honey, we've all got those parts to us." Amore patted her arm gently. "And we gotta do what we can to keep 'em. I'll meet you in front and we can settle up, 'kay?"

"Thanks, Amore."

"You got it."

The tattooist gave Nate a nod, and then extended up to their full height on those tall heels. After they left, Nate handed over Nalla's black bra and turtleneck.

"I'll go talk with Amore, and let you get dressed," he said.

It was supposed to be a statement. Like, of course he was going to give her some privacy while she put the top half of her clothes on again. In a semi-private setting. When she had to be sore, not just on her back, but in the muscles she'd tensed up while that high-pitched, vibrating Sharpie had been going in and out of her skin at a hundred miles a second.

Instead . . . there was a question weaving in and out of his words.

And what do you know, Nalla's eyes lifted to his own—and yup, there it was. Fire. Pure elemental fire, the kind of thing that made the world disappear as his attention locked on her and her alone. Plus he had the sense that it was the same for her: Sexual need was in the way her lips parted, as if she were remembering what it was like to kiss him, and how she shifted her lower body on the padded worktable . . . as if she were reliving what it was like for him to be between her thighs.

"You don't have to go," she said in a low voice.

"And I didn't want to."

With a sinuous movement, she slipped her legs off the edge and sat up, one arm covering her breasts. She'd worn her hair free and loose tonight, but had tucked it down for the work. Now the lengths released again, and under the chandelier, the multi-colored waves gleamed in invitation for him to thread with greedy fingers.

That were going to go a lot of places on her body. In her body.

As she extended her hand to him, he wanted to grab it and yank her to him. Instead, he gave her the bra.

And then watched the show.

With her eyes locked on his, she lowered that arm—and holy fucking shit. Her breasts were tipped with pink nipples that tightened under his gaze, their weights perfectly balanced to her upper body, the image of her naked in front of him searing into his mind.

"Jesus, Nalla . . ." he breathed.

She took it nice and slow with the bra, threading the cups under everything he couldn't stop looking at, arching her back as she did the clasp under her shoulder blades—which was an offer if he'd ever seen one. And then she flipped the cotton triangles up and put her arms through the straps one by one, things swaying—and then getting squeezed by the supports, the top halves of her swelling out.

"Help me?" she said as she leaned forward. "I didn't have it on exactly right."

Nate licked his lips. And then glanced at the door Amore had put to use. But the tattooist wasn't stupid. They weren't coming back in here, even if Nate and Nalla didn't resurface for an hour.

"My pleasure," he murmured.

Reaching forward, he ran his fingertips over the top rims of the cups, where the cotton fabric cut into her fine, soft skin. When she moaned, he glanced up at her face. She had let her head fall back, and he liked the way her grip was cutting into the padding of the table.

Lowering his mouth, he brushed a kiss to the swell.

Then he hooked a finger on the cup and pulled it back down. With the straps still on her arms instead of her shoulders, the tension pushed her nipple up toward him.

"Look at me, Nalla," he said in a guttural voice. "Watch me . . ."

Extending his tongue, he made sure he tilted his head so she got a good, clear visual of him licking her tip. Once. Twice. Then he flicked the nub back and forth.

She moaned and grabbed on to the back of his neck, trying to bring him closer, but that was a nope for two reasons. One, the sharper the anticipation, the sweeter the release. And two?

If he got much further with this shit, he was going to fuck her right on the damn tattooing table, under the bright glare of that chandelier, surrounded by Amore's equipment—something he was certain wouldn't be a first. He just didn't want it to be *their* first.

"You like that?" he murmured as he closed his lips and rubbed them back and forth on her nipple.

The noise he got back made no damned sense and how perfect was that.

Moving to the other side, he did the same thing, forcing the cup down so the breast was offered up at him, then teasing her with his tongue. But he had to stop tempting them both. As his cock pounded in his combat pants, he sat back and looked at his feast.

"Do you want to know what I want?" he growled.

"Mmmm . . . yes."

He put both hands under her breasts and moved the weights together, thumbing her nipples. "I want to come all over this."

The groan that rippled out of Nalla's parted lips was just too good.

"And then I'm going to lick you clean."

She was panting now, and that was what he wanted. He wanted her out of control and under him, nothing else on her mind but what he was doing to her and how he made her feel. He wanted her sex wet and swollen, and he wanted to do a little watching too as he penetrated her.

"Spread your knees, let me in," he said.

As she opened herself, he went in with his hand, curling up a fist and putting his row of knuckles on the seam of her jeans. Rubbing her right where it counted, he was rewarded with her tilting her pelvis so he had greater access—and then she worked herself against him, her breasts bouncing to the rhythm of thrusts and pressure . . . until she had to clap a palm over her mouth as if she knew she wasn't going to be able to control the sounds she was making.

"That's it," he said in a deep voice. "Come for me . . ."

It didn't take her long, and as she reared back, he nearly made a mess in his own fucking pants—and wasn't that amazing.

The whole thing was amazing.

She was . . . amazing.

When she slumped, he stepped into her, holding her up with his body, his strength. As he stared over her shoulder, he had a ripple of emotion he couldn't afford to look too closely at, and needing to concentrate on something, he focused on the tattoo she'd gotten.

He thought about that house and the people who had once lived in it.

And what he had told Rahvyn he was going to do.

Goodbyes, to one and all.

CHAPTER THIRTY-FOUR

O ut in the countryside, next to the Audience House, Zsadist entered Four Toys HQ, making sure to clomp his shitkickers on the mat: V was not only a taskmaster, he was a nasty neat. Everything had to be surgical-unit clean, and it was well known that the brother's team wasn't especially fond of the edict. If they wanted something to snack on or drink, or even have a coffee to perk up? They were relegated to the break room.

Which was not exactly a death sentence, and at least as it related to liquids, was something that made sense given the number of keyboards in the place. But you could imagine how the commute, even if it was a short one, was an inconvenience when you were pulling close to twenty-four-hour shifts.

Also, word had it that you could only heat liquids in the microwave. Apparently, someone had gotten their Orville Redenbacher on and burned the stuff, and there had been no going back after that olfactory debacle.

As Z strode down the aisle between the workstations, he was amazed at how quiet it was. Then again, V hated the sound of clicking of keys and had designed the equipment himself.

Nobody spared a glance away from their screens. Not a surprise. The V-team, as they were called, weren't a laugh riot and no doubt had little appreciation for social graces—something that Zsadist could totally get. The males and females were super-serious IT brain trusts ambulated by scrawny, left-behind bodies—because when you were that smart, and your job making sure the vampire race stayed secret was that important, you didn't have a lot of time to Planet Fitness yourself.

Out the far end, he came up to V's glass box, and paused before he knocked. Inside, a tall young male with a shock of black hair and a lanky frame was staring over the brother's shoulder. The two were talking about something neither of them was happy about, their identical frowns the kind of thing you might see in a movie that spanned an entire lifetime, one the boy, the other the man.

Vishous glanced over and motioned for entrance.

"Another night in paradise," the brother said as Z came through the door.

"Always." Z waved at Allhan who, as usual, appeared surprised that there was someone else with them. The kid always looked surprised. "What's good, Al."

Vishous's protégé stammered something, then went back to looking at the four screens that were obstructed by a privacy filter. The flush that hit that lean face was another as-usual. His social anxiety was so crippling, it was a wonder he could acknowledge anyone.

"Whatta we got about the Bathe parking lot shooting? Anything?" Z asked.

V shook his head. "I sent a representative down there as soon as they opened tonight. Management said there was no footage, that the system's 'malfunctioning.'" The air quotes were mimed with a dry look. "When the human's brain was investigated, it was a lie—big surprise. But the club hadn't followed up with the CPD and there's nothing in the papers or the news. I'm guessing that rear entrance sees a lot of illegal activities and they don't want any trouble."

"And no bodies showing up anywhere."

"Nope. And no mention of a Mercedes full of bullet holes in the CPD impound, or at any of the major tow services. Right, Al?"

The kid stuttered a response that was in the general range of affirmative.

"Okay, good." Z stepped in behind so he could see what was on the monitors. "Can I watch the tunnel footage from that office building?"

"You got it." V leaned forward and tapped on one of his keyboards at lightning speed. "Here it is—Al, you can go."

Allhan nodded like a bobblehead on the dashboard of a car, and disappeared out the glass door.

"*Lessers* freak him out." V sat back as the screens changed what they were showing. "So we avoid exposing him when we can."

"He still living with you?"

Those diamond eyes swung up and around. "Why wouldn't he be?"

Z put his palms out. "Just making conversation."

"Luchas House is too noisy. He doesn't sleep well there."

"You're really good to take him in."

V frowned. "He's just staying with us. His utility here is invaluable, and without a stable environment, he's not able to function at a high level."

"So it's just about work, riiiiight."

Those diamond eyes narrowed. "It's *just* about work. Don't complicate a critical member of the team's efforts with sentimentality."

Even though it wasn't in Z's nature to submit to anything, he put up his palms, all don't-shoot-me. 'Cuz the shit was fucking amusing.

"I wouldn't *dream* of doing such a thing."

As the brother went back to the monitors with a determination that bordered on a temper tantrum, Z had to smile a little. But he knew better than to keep ribbing the guy, even though, as Lassiter always said, Vishous could use the exercise.

And then it was time to focus on the screens and the various images of the induction site with all those buckets.

"Infrared . . . a thing of beauty," Z murmured.

"You had a great idea. Those micro-cameras are highly effective, and we got really good angles."

"I want in that tunnel."

"You're getting no argument from me on that." V sat back in his chair and stroked his goatee with his gloved hand. "But you're gonna have to talk to Tohr about it—and it's gonna be an uphill climb. You know how much he hates unfamiliar tunnels. Hard to control egress and ingress, no coverage, it gets him antsy—"

"We need a drone."

V's brows popped. Then he sported a that's-not-actually-ridiculous expression. "Except we can't hide that as well. Something flying around in there? The *lessers* are just going to use it as batting practice."

"You're going to get us through that combination lock somehow. And then we use a nano-drone. Just slip it in and let it go to town."

"That's what she said," V muttered with distraction as he stared at the screens.

"Have our cameras picked up anything?" Z asked.

"One *lesser* came through, looking twitchy. He checked out the elevator, headed up the stairs. No Lash, though. No inductions. Al set up a screening program for the feeds, but went through all the footage himself anyway." There was a lift of pride in that deep voice. "He trusts, but verifies, especially when a brother is waiting on something."

"He's a good kid."

V grunted and changed the subject. "The encryption on that vault's locking system is impressive. Haven't seen much like it."

Zsadist glanced out through the glass walls. Al's desk was set away from the others, in the corner, facing the wall. As always, the kid's dark head was lowered, his thin fingers flying over his keyboard.

"I'll bet Al could get through it."

Vishous immediately shook his head. "I am not putting him in that basement."

"I'd protect him."

"No."

"I'd have backup."

"No."

"You could be there."

"*Fuck no.*" Those eyes glared over. "And you can stop asking. That is *never* going to happen."

Zsadist popped a brow. "But if he's just an employment asset, what do you care. Even if he's a good one, there will always be other boy geniuses—"

"Don't take this the wrong way, but fuck you, true? For real."

Z gave it a minute. Then, even though he told himself that it was none of his business, and they really had no reason to get tangled in personal shit, he had to go there. Maybe because what was wrong in his own life was an echo of what V was facing while refusing to acknowledge it.

"You and Jane are going to see him through the change, aren't you. That's the real reason he's with you guys after hours."

V didn't even look shocked at what should have been a non sequitur. Which told a guy how much the male was thinking about what was coming for Allhan.

Worrying about it.

There was a long silence. Then V put his head in his hands. "We did a blood draw on him a couple of nights ago. The transition is a freight train heading straight for him."

"He couldn't be in better hands. Who're you using for a vein?"

"The Chosen Sahsa."

Z whistled under his breath. "Can't get much more pure than that. He's getting his best chance."

"He's just an employee." V dropped his palms and fumbled for his stack of hand-rolls. "I mean, he's not my responsibility. He just happens to have a knack for computers, and no family."

"Mm-hmm."

After V lit up, the brother all but poked Zsadist in the eye with his cigarette as he emphasized, "Okay, see, *this* is why I don't tutor. You go to Luchas House, because Rhage's *shellan* asks you to, and no one says no to fucking Mary, and the next thing you know, you've got some kid sleeping down the hall from you and your mate, and you're all like worried about his scrawny ass and the fact that he doesn't talk about where his parents are or what happened to them—oh, and you're not asking him about that bullshit because you want him reunited with them." V pinwheeled with that lit tip of his. "Nooooo, you're asking because you're terrified that they'll show up and it won't be like Ruhn and Bitty and Rhage and Mary, no, you're shitting yourself because what if the parents take him home— wherever the fuck that might be—and if that happens, you're going to have to pick your *shellan* up off the ground because she'll be fucking heartbroken, over *something you told her you two shouldn't do in the first place.*"

The last part was said with emphasis on every syllable, that handrolled going aerobic with the jabs. And then V kept going.

"My Jane is going to get *fucked* in the head if that kid leaves us, or dies during his transition, or"—furious eyes pegged Z in the face— "some asshole like *you* gets a bright idea about taking him out into the field. Which is *never* happening, got it? I'll try that lock a thousand times over before I let him get slaughtered in that fucking nasty-ass basement full of *lesser* blood."

The brother paused for a deep breath, then took a drag that was so long and deep, it was a wonder smoke didn't start coming out of his ass.

"And fuck you, Z, with your perfect family, okay. Just because it worked out for you, doesn't mean anybody else is going to be so lucky with their young. Not that he's mine. *Fuck.*"

Zsadist glanced over his shoulder again at Allhan. Then he sat down in the vacant chair next to the desk. "Nalla isn't speaking to me, I think she's moved out of our house, and she's dating Nate."

Cue the whiplash.

Then V leaned forward. "Say . . . *what?*"

"Don't make me repeat it. You heard the shit right the first time, and it was hard enough to get through once."

"Jesus."

"My point is, don't romanticize anybody else. And I get how much it drives you crazy when you think something is wrong with them or about to happen to them. Or when they seem farther away than the Old Country when they're still physically in the same zip code as you."

"Nate?"

"Kill me now."

Vishous sat back in his chair. Then picked up the little porcelain dish of fresh hand-rolls and extended it forward.

"No, thanks."

"You sure?" The brother put the thing back. "It's easier than homicide and at least vampires don't get cancer."

Zsadist rubbed his tired eyes. "I haven't slept for two days, and no matter how much I run the conversation through in my head, I'm not coming up with any great ways to patch things up. I still think that male is a total loser, and she is always going to believe that I hate everyone she's going to be with."

"Well . . . don't you?"

"Of course I hate them. But she doesn't need to know that."

V tapped his cig over his ashtray. "It is entirely possible, my brother, that you overplayed your hand with protecting her against males."

"Yeah, if that was your daughter, would you want her to date someone like us?"

"Fuck no."

Z motioned a there-ya-go. "And here's the only thing I've learned about being a parent: It's too late for us."

"Well, that's encouraging," came the dry response. "Please tell me more."

"The instant they come into your life, whether they're born to you, or adopted by you, or somehow their paths cross yours, it's too late. No going back. A piece of your fucking heart is out in the world running into things, getting run over, falling off heights, getting sick, falling in love with the wrong person. And you can't stop them from living. So I guess you just have to suck it up, I don't know. I really don't."

Vishous stared off into space. "Can I ask you something? While we're talking about this subject—which, P.S., we will never talk about again. Ever."

"Hit me." Shit knew he couldn't feel worse.

"Was it true that you threatened to castrate Bronwyn the Younger's kid at the Winter Festival eight years ago because he was going to ask Nalla to dance."

Z ground his molars. "Absolutely not." When V cocked a brow, he shook his head. "No."

Silence. Except for smoking.

But fuck knew that raised eyebrow was talking at him.

"I was just going to break his leg, okay?" Z went all *hello?* "Broken bones heal. It's not like slicing off a nut sac."

"Oh, yeah." V leveled a stare. "Totally different."

"It is! That other shit is permanent."

Vishous's eyes narrowed. Then he glanced pointedly at his own crotch. "No, really. Tell me more."

Crossing his arms over his chest, Zsadist looked away. "Sorry."

"Why did you come here again?"

"I have no idea." Something about work. But who the fuck cared. "Anyway, I hope Al makes it through the change. I can't imagine what it would be like to lose ... whatever. I shouldn't have brought up the subject."

After a moment, V stabbed his cigarette out. "And I hope you and Nalla work your shit out. You love her so much. She's gotta know that."

"I hope so. I've made mistakes, but I've done my best." Z laughed a little. "Look at us. Who'da thought you and me would ever be talking about our kids, huh."

"Allhan is not my young."

As Z shot the brother a little brow action of his own, V rolled his eyes. "Fuck."

"That just about covers it."

"Yeah." There was another stretch of silence. "But Nate really is an asshole. No daughter of mine would be allowed to date something like that, true?"

Zsadist nodded gravely. "True. Too bad I can't kill the motherfucker. Just my luck, the one male on the planet I can't put in a grave also happens to be the off-the-chain idiot she falls for." He wiped away his words with his dagger hand. "Not that I would do that."

"Of course you wouldn't. Nah. Not at all."

Zsadist frowned and lowered his voice. "I'll tell you this, though. If he breaks her heart? I will find a way to destroy him. I don't care what it takes."

Vishous stared across his desk. Then he nodded. "And the rest of us'll help you. She's our baby girl, too."

Z inclined his head once, and almost felt sorry for the cocky sonofabitch. Almost.

It was good to have ride-or-die brothers, wasn't it.

They came in handy in all kinds of situations.

CHAPTER THIRTY-FIVE

All Nalla had to do was follow the signal of her own blood in Nate. And as she flew in a scatter of molecules through the night, she was aware of a tingling anticipation that threatened to make her lose her concentration and go solid in mid-flight. Which was not the kind of outcome she was looking for, so she battled back the sexual charge and kept herself going.

When she sensed that he had landed, she re-formed in front of a . . .

Okay, so where he lived was no castle. She hadn't expected it to be. But she was a little surprised at how run-down the log cabin was. The one-room hunter's crib looked like a stiff wind could knock it into pick-up-sticks condition, and as she checked out the barn off to the side, she wondered why he didn't live in the other structure. At least that seemed to be a little sturdier.

"This way," he murmured as he held out his hand.

Oh, who the hell cared about real estate anyway?

Taking what he offered, she practically floated over the snow as he drew her under the shallow entry and opened things up.

It was just as cold inside as outside, but as he spun her around and drew her against his body, like she needed any extra heat? She could have been in an ice pack and felt just frickin' fine.

"I'm about to fucking lose it," he growled before he kissed her.

The feel of his lips against hers was an explosion of raw sexual sensation, and she was no more gentle than he was as she grabbed on to his shoulders and dragged him to her. As her breasts rubbed against his chest, she curved into him, and felt the hard length at the front of his hips. And when his tongue entered her, all she could think of was what he'd done with it before—where it had been on her, how it had felt to be licked by him on her nipples.

What else he'd been looking to lick up.

As she moaned and didn't have to hide the sound, he started walking her backwards. She hadn't had much impression of the cabin's interior as they'd come inside—she hadn't seen a bed, but like she cared? He could fuck her on the bare floor if he wanted to.

Or maybe . . . standing up, her backed into a corner, her legs around his waist—

Nate broke the seal of their mouths, and leaned to the side. To a keypad of some kind.

There was a series of soft beeps, and then a mechanical shifting.

Light pooled in the floor, illuminating a set of stairs that went down into the earth. And they were nice stairs, carpeted in a neutral, with a handrail.

"After you," he said.

Nalla took the descent slowly, not because she was worried at all about what she was going to find, but because she wanted to savor the experience of seeing his personal space for the first time.

And now, she wasn't disappointed.

It was just an open area, like the cabin above, but his sleeping quarters were clean and warm, and they smelled like fabric softener, as if he'd recently put something through the stackable washer and dryer set up in the corner. The bed was on the far wall, and though it didn't have a head- or footboard, it was perfectly made up, with white sheets and a cream comforter and an extra roll of something soft and blue at the base.

For a kitchen, there was a small stretch of countertop with a hot plate next to an inset bar sink and a little dorm refrigerator with a microwave on top. A short stack of bookshelves was where he kept his food and the single plate, glass, and set of steel utensils—and the safe beside it, which was the largest thing in the place outside of the bed, had to be where he stowed his weapons.

As a whirring registered overhead, she glanced up. The panel that had rolled back was easing into place once more, locking them in. Safe.

Locking the world out. Entirely.

"The bathroom's through there," he said as he pointed to a closed door. "'Scuse my clothes."

She turned in that direction.

Before she could say anything, he shrugged. "It's not much, but it's mine."

Nalla smiled and started to draw off her coat. "I think it's just perfect."

The tension in his shoulders seemed to ease. "You're lying."

Laying her parka on the seat of a padded armchair, she immediately started to tug her turtleneck free from the waistband of her jeans.

"The kind of privacy we have here," she murmured as she pulled the black folds over her head, "makes this a palace."

Nate purred in the back of his throat, the sound reaching her like a caress all across her whole body at once. "Does it now."

"Do you want to help me with this?" she asked while she tickled the edges of her bra with her fingertips. "I think you'll do a better job than I will."

Pivoting, she made a show of drawing her hair together and holding it up high on her head.

She sensed, rather than heard, him approach, and as he caressed her shoulders and then followed her spine down to her hips, she bit her lower lip.

"Bend down for me, will you," he said.

Nalla was more than happy to do just that—and good job that chair was close. Balancing her weight on the seat by putting her arms out straight and bracing herself, she looked over her shoulder.

Nate was staring at what she was blatantly offering him, and his palms were light as they discovered her ass, skimming over the contours. He didn't make her wait for what she wanted: He stepped into her, and pushed the front of his hips in tight—

Squeezing her eyes shut, she moaned and nearly fell face-first into the chair—and thank God the thing was right up against the wall. She would have pushed it across the room.

His erection was even better than his knuckles, the pressure stroking her as he rolled himself into her. And when all of a sudden her breasts were hanging free, she was surprised because she'd forgotten about the dumbass bra.

What she really wanted off now was her frickin' pants.

The idea that the two of them were going to get naked and nothing was going to stop them made her heart soar. This whole thing with Nate seemed both inevitable and a total impossibility. Had she really gone from being frustrated at Bitty for calling her out about the whole shut-in thing to *this*?

Whatever, she wasn't going to question anything. She was going to enjoy it all—

The sound of a phone going off was like getting hit with an ice bath, and she jerked her head up. With her hair in her face, she couldn't see Nate. She heard him loud and clear, however.

"Mother*fucker*."

He stopped in the process of cupping her breasts and rearing over her. And as he grew still, she could have sworn she felt his heartbeat in his arousal through where they were in contact so intimately.

The muffled ringing continued. From inside the jacket he'd tossed on the floor.

When things finally went silent, he said, "I'm sorry."

"It's okay."

Closing her eyes, she tried to reconnect with where they'd been. But something had changed for him, too.

Especially when the phone started going off again.

✦   ✦   ✦

Nate wanted to stomp the fucking cell into silence. Instead, he straightened from the position he very much wanted to continue to be in, and grabbed his leather jacket off the carpet. Shoving a hand into the folds, he came out with the burner, and muted the thing without checking who was calling.

He knew damn well who it was and he was not dealing with Uncle right now.

As he put the cell back in his jacket, he looked over at Nalla. She, too, had stood up out of the glorious bend she'd been in, and she was covering her breasts with her hands.

Her face was falsely composed, like she was trying to be all I-don't-care—and he didn't want that for her. For them.

"It's nothing," he said. "It's just a side hustle in the human world that I do to remain financially independent of Murhder and Sarah. This place is really mine. The land, the cabin—the barn and what's in it. I earned the money and I've saved some, too. I don't want to have to rely on anybody."

The change in her was instant and absolute, the tension leaving her, the mask dissolving so that her real energy once again shone through her features.

"I really do mean it that I like it here." She smiled a little. "And not just because of the privacy."

"Good."

"And I'm sorry if I'm awkward." She gave him a sheepish look. "I don't have a lot of experience with—whatever this is."

"That makes two of us." He stepped in close to her. "So how about we figure it out, together."

As her head tilted back so she could keep meeting his eyes, he had a thought that he wanted to remember the way she was looking at him right now for the rest of his life. There was just a really special expression on that beautiful face of hers.

"I want to keep kissing you."

"What a coincidence," she murmured. "That's what I'm thinking, too."

They came together, their mouths fusing again, and he kissed her and walked her backward, all the way to the edge of the bed. As she let herself fall onto the mattress, she was laughing, and he made his way in between her legs, content—for a moment—just to enjoy the sight of her as she let her arms fall loose, her breasts exposed to him once again.

"Let's lose your shirt, shall we," she murmured.

He was more than happy to oblige, pulling the tails of his button-down out of his combats, and peeling it up and over along with the muscle shirt under it.

Down on the bed, she made a little noise that was the sexiest thing he'd ever heard—then again, everything she did was the sexiest anything ever.

"You're beautiful," she whispered.

He wasn't sure about that at all, but like he was arguing with her? Nope. He had other things to do with her—and to get them on track again, he joined her on the bed, the two of them shimmying up to where the pillows were.

Nalla turned her face into one of them and inhaled. "Fresh laundry."

He felt himself flush. "I washed the sheets and cases and put them back on before I left." He put both palms forward. "I was *not* taking for granted that we'd be . . . where we are. I just thought if maybe—*maybe*—we, you know, ended up here, you'd appreciate clean everything."

She snuggled in close and ran her hand up his arm. As her touch registered, his muscles contracted one by one, like they were responding on their own.

"That was really thoughtful of you."

"Not skeevy, right? 'Cuz honestly . . . I wasn't taking anything for granted."

"Me, too. But I thought about you all day long."

"You did?"

"Mm-hmm. I wasn't sure, either. I hoped, though."

"Me, too."

For a split second, he couldn't remember for the life of him why he had ever thought he was cursed. Right now? He felt like he'd won the lottery every night for the last decade . . .

The conversation dried up at that point, replaced by a furnace blast of heat. And as he kissed her again, slipping his tongue into her, he told himself to take it slow—

That went right out the window as her hands snuck around his waist and she pulled him on top of her. At first, his torso was all that shifted over, but his hips were not going to be denied that kind of opportunity— and she made room for him. Oh, did she ever. They fell into a rhythm almost immediately, the rocking motion making him squeeze his eyes shut and pray for enough self-control that he didn't come before he was inside of her.

Fuck, if that was the goal, he needed to move things along—

Like she was reading his mind, her hands went between them and he felt tugging at the front of his pelvis, then a glorious release of confinement . . . followed by a soft grip that was achingly familiar thanks to what they'd done last night.

"I want in you," he grunted.

"Then come . . . in me."

She took over dealing with her jeans, and he ran into a colossal frustration with his boots—fucking laces. But then his shitkickers were off, and his combat pants were off, and then—

Nalla was naked, and lying back in his bed like a total goddess, her hair on his pillow, her breasts so firm and tight, her graceful stomach going into the cleft of her sex, her knees together and off to the side.

"Let me see you," he said.

She moved in a sensual wave, pivoting her hips flat, bringing her thighs up to her body. Then she parted them, letting her legs fall wide.

He growled so loud, it was a wonder he didn't wake his neighbors—two miles away.

Gripping himself, he angled the tip of his erection into the core of her, and it was just as he wanted, as he needed, hot and wet, slick and tight, the penetration smooth and in slow motion. When they were joined, he lifted his head and stared into her eyes. Then he kissed her.

After that, he was moving, up and back, up and back. She echoed him once again, finding that rocking motion that kept in rhythm to his hips.

She was perfect. In every way—

Faster now. Faster still.

No more kissing.

Even faster.

At some point, his body took over for the both of them, driving into her harder and harder, until the metal bedframe under the box spring started bumping the wall and she just grabbed on to him, held on to him.

Something scratched his back, and the licks of pain tightened his balls. He knew he was close, but suddenly he was closer and—

Nalla came first, her core fisting at him in a series of contractions, and oh, man, did that ever work for him. In response, he threw his head back as his entire body stiffened.

And then came the ejaculations.

With the pleasure cresting, he thought he was done, but he should have known better. He just kept coming, especially as she wrapped her legs around his hips and milked him like she didn't want to lose a drop of what he was giving her.

It wasn't the single greatest sexual experience of his life.

It was the single greatest experience of his life.

Period.

CHAPTER THIRTY-SIX

E van ended up spending the entire day sitting with his new friend, and it was probably a sad commentary on his life that a dead body finally provided him with the kind of supportive ear he needed.

Except she was just so nice. She didn't say much, but her eyes were always on him, and her listening skills were unparalleled.

He told her things he'd never told anyone else. And she never judged him.

Now it was nighttime—after midnight, actually—and it was time to break up.

"I'm going to miss you," he said.

It was a while longer that he sat with her on the floor, his back propped against Mickey's couch, his mind sharp but unfocused, all kinds of things hitting his radar at once and pinging away, golf balls driven into blank walls.

And always, underneath the conscious chaos, there was that driving need to go to the bridge, and hang a right, and find his way into one of those doors with the others, like a homing pigeon called back to a roost—and every time he tuned in to that summoning, his anger redoubled.

He did not blame the trainer. He blamed all of the others who had worn him down over the years, making him desperate for the kind of strength he shouldn't have needed in the first place inside his own family.

"I have to go now," he heard himself whisper.

Evan shifted his feet under his butt, and as he pushed his weight upright, he braced himself for stiffness. There was none. He might as well have been doing yoga for the last twelve hours instead of sitting in the same position on the hard floor.

Standing over the woman and her chair, he focused on her wedding ring. It was simple and gold, a symbol of the life she had had before. He wondered again if she had ID on her. He hadn't looked. That seemed like an invasion of her privacy, although now that he thought about it, he felt an obligation to let her people know.

Goddamn Mickey, putting him in this position.

He glanced over to the duffle bag full of weapons. No way she was going to fit in that, not without him butchering her, and that was a no-go for so many reasons. Messy, for one, plus he didn't want to see her without her clothes on.

Protecting the dignity of his dead was important.

"I can't keep you." He shook his head. "You're going to . . ."

Well, the whole rot thing seemed an indelicate subject to bring up to her.

The car, he thought. *Start by getting the car.*

With a sense of sad resolution, he pushed his hand into the front pocket of his stolen pants and took out Mickey's keys. Three nights ago—God, had it really only been seventy-two hours? It felt like twelve years—he'd driven back from that property in the sticks and parked on Market to go tell Uncle what the enforcer had done to Mickey.

He wasn't sure whether the shitty beater was even going to be where he'd left it, and if it wasn't?

Guess he was going to have another thing to work through.

"I'll be back in a little bit."

He almost blew her a kiss. But that gold band was a reminder she wasn't his to do that kind of goodbye for.

At best, she was nothing more than an office wife to him, someone whose connection to him was work-based—and yeah, sure, the mind might wander from time to time into other areas, but ultimately, the boundaries of their relationship were established and immutable.

As he slipped out of the apartment, he congratulated himself on his mental maturity. Mickey couldn't have defined such lines, much less stuck to them. His cousin would have fucked a tree if he could have found a knothole.

Descending the building's common stairwell, he actually smelled the remnants of some people's dinners, and the fact that the vague aromas didn't stimulate his stomach in any way was a reminder of how long it had been since he'd used the bathroom. The stuff going on with his body wasn't natural, it wasn't normal.

Just like carrying on a one-sided conversation with a stiff and thinking they were a candidate for best friends with benefits.

But this was his life now, wasn't it.

Down on the street, he looked both ways, and tried to remember where he needed to go. Oh, right. Market.

God, he hoped the car was where he'd left it.

Out of habit, he burrowed into the coat that concealed the weapons he'd hid at his waistband and under one arm, thanks to the female soldier's holster collection. But the cold didn't register on his skin, and as he passed a lamppost, he imagined himself just like the metal stalk of the fixture, impervious to freeze or fire.

He wanted to go find Uncle right now, and he started fashioning an if-this-then-that series of choices for murdering the man. He'd been a little sloppy the night before, popping shots at that car all crazy and off his rocker. He'd have done better to wait until Uncle had gotten out and started walking toward that side door.

Except the vampire had been coming at him, and that—

Ping!

That was the closest thing he could approximate to the sensation that struck him in the chest: It was similar to what had driven him to the bridges the night before, a sudden registry on an air traffic controller's radar screen.

Stopping on the sidewalk, his head cranked to the right.

His body was next, following the direction of his eyes, a missile directed by a target in its sights.

There was no question, no choice.

Evan changed directions and just had to go with it.

✦   ✦   ✦

Technically, Shuli was out of a job.

So, yeah, he probably shouldn't have been in the field.

But come on, people walked the streets of Caldwell after dark for a whole host of reasons. They were going somewhere, like a club— or maybe home after having been out. They were leaving somewhere, like a date that hadn't ended well, or a hookup that had. They had a broken-down car, a lost dog, a kid who was rebelling.

And he wasn't in combat dress or anything.

Okay, fine. His hard-core footwear didn't exactly go with his silk suit or his Alexander McQueen full-length coat—the one that he and the Brother Butch had each sprung for during their last buying trip to Manhattan. There also *might* have been some click-click-bang-bang accessories that were judiciously hidden because, hey, there was no reason to cause alarm to civilians of either the vampire or the human variety. Plus, he was allowed to protect himself!

The streets were dangerous, after all—

"What the fuck are you doing?"

Shuli stopped. Closed his eyes. Reflected on how, out of all the voices in the world, there was only one other he'd rather not hear as much. But unlike him, Nate had been permanently suspended instead of only out for a week, so it was not his former best friend.

But naturally, because fate was a fucker who liked to knee him in the balls, that meant that—

"L.W." He turned around. "Fancy meeting you here."

The heir apparent was standing in the middle of the side street like his shitkickers were the canine equivalent of a piss stream: *This Is Mine.* And you had to give the big, nasty fucker his due. The impact of his physical presence was enough to make anybody think to themselves that an about-face and some Nike action were a great idea.

"You're suspended."

"You know," Shuli said, "it's always *so* great to see you. A real kick in the pants. You're just a mood lifter, vibe shifter, in a good-wood kinda way."

L.W. started closing the distance, those size sixteens of his crushing through the ice pack that hadn't given way under Shuli's weight. Then again, if your bones were made of tungsten and your blood of lead, the ground yielded.

Everything yielded.

Up close, that hard, perfectly proportioned face reminded you of the father. Big Wrath had the same cruel cast to what would otherwise be seen as standard *glymera*-handsome fare, and the young one, whose eyes you could see, had a green gaze that was cold as stone. With lips that were a slash of aggression, and a jaw that was an invitation to fuck-around-and-find-out, really, most people wanted to leave the guy alone.

Kinda like you would if a T. rex gave you the option to run.

"Get outta here," L.W. said.

"I'm just out for a walk." Shuli skipped in place. "Fresh air does wonders for a person's disposition. You should try it sometime—you never know, you could turn over a new leaf and try smiling for once."

"Why do you even do this."

"Attempt to help you improve your attitude? I mean, I don't know. I guess I'm a glutton for punishment."

"You are a total waste of training and resources."

"No." Shuli held up his forefinger. "I'm annoying you deliberately, and you hate that it works. I don't mind being called an asshole, but let's be accurate about the reason why, shall we—"

In perfect coordination, they both spun to the left, outed their guns, and squeezed off two bullets apiece.

Their next move was equally in sync. With a twist and jump back, they took cover in an inset doorway.

"—and not hide behind petty defensive insults," Shuli finished as he sniffed the air.

Going by the stink, the *lesser* was about thirty feet away, hiding in the shadows of a cut-through between a rooming house and an abandoned nail parlor—

A head popped around the corner. It was a female, with her hair in rows of braids and a couple of piercings in her face.

"Dematerialize," L.W. hissed. "Just get out of here, will ya?"

Shuli glared back at the guy. "No."

"*Yes.*"

Making a show of being dizzy, Shuli went limp and leaned back into the panels behind them. "I can't possibly. I'm too scared and distracted to—"

The rotted panel splintered under his weight and he fell back into darkness. As a hard landing ricocheted through his skull and rendered him legitimately struck stupid, all he heard was a litany of swearing.

Then there was another brief exchange of fire, bullets pinging around, sparks like stars in the sky—or in Shuli's suddenly not-so-hot vision.

Fucking . . . wonderful.

And he'd thought wrecking his car was the worst thing that could happen this week.

CHAPTER THIRTY-SEVEN

S o *this is pillow talk,* Nalla thought.

As she and Nate lay side by side in his bed under the covers, their faces were nose to nose, eye to eye. She wasn't sure how long they'd been like this, and she didn't really care. Time felt like forever, and in the back of her mind, she told herself to soak this in. When they parted, she had a feeling that it was going to seem like only a minute or two.

And maybe she'd once again question whether it had happened at all.

She needed a pillow-on-the-floor equivalent—and guessed it was going to be all the delicious places she was aching.

"I can make you some food," he offered in a drowsy voice. "If you're hungry."

"Sounds great." Then again, he could have volunteered to give her a chemical peel or a dental exam and she would have awesome'd either one. "I can help, though."

"We'll do it together."

And then they didn't move.

"Thanks for putting me in touch with Amore. I've wanted a tattoo for ages." She'd already told him this. Why was she babbling? "I already told you that."

Well, she was babbling because it felt safer than telling him what was really on her mind: She was wondering when she would be back here with him—and she hadn't even left yet. Which made her a stalker, didn't it.

Okay, fine, a stalker-in-training.

"That's okay, you can tell me anything all over again." Nate's smile was lazy and relaxed, even though his eyes were intense. "Or maybe I can ask you something."

"Absolutely. Let me have it." She propped her head on her hand. "Just not math. I suck at math, and that's what they make calculators for."

"Are you staying at Luchas House permanently?"

Nalla was aware of her heart skipping a beat. In a casual tone, she said, "Why do you ask that?"

What she wanted to say was—Are you looking for a roommate?

Except that was insane.

"Just wondering," he hedged.

As she felt a minor letdown, she knew that was ridiculous. She wasn't living in some kind of romantic comedy where the hero asked the heroine to move in because she had nowhere else to go—and they ended up pulling a happily-ever-after following a series of zany adventures.

Yeah, that was a movie, not anything that happened in real life. And besides, if you were a vampire in Caldwell, New York, the zany adventures were likely to kill you.

She pushed her hair out of the way. "I'm just crashing in that room for a little while. I pull a lot of hours so it's a convenience."

Unlike her two-second, dematerializing commute. Phew, what a time-saver.

When he didn't say anything, the silence made her feel like they were on two boats, floating off in opposite directions, and as she guessed what it was all about, she wondered when—fucking *when*—her father would cease to be a shadow over her life.

"Okay, fine," she muttered. "I don't want to be around my parents right now. I'm taking a break from them."

Was this his opening to address the black dagger in the room? Namely that promise he'd made to her sire, which he'd clearly remembered and come to the very reasonable conclusion that it put a target on his chest?

After all, even if Nate was immortal, he could still feel physical pain. She'd seen more than enough proof of that.

"The relocation has nothing to do with you," she lied.

Although that wasn't exactly false. She and her parents had plenty of other problems. Nate was just one of a number of them.

"I'm not sure I believe that," he said. But then he shrugged. "I'm not getting along with my own very well, either."

"No?"

He shook his head. "So I can understand how a little distance might help. But unlike with your situation, I'm the asshole in the crowd. Always have been. Honestly, Murhder and Sarah are good people, and I've just been . . ."

"Tell me." She smoothed a hand over his tattooed chest. "Please. You're like a ghost sometimes, even as I can feel you next to me."

Nate's expression got dark, real dark. "The two of them took me in when I had nothing and nobody in this world. And to pay them back, I haven't treated them well. I've pushed them away, pushed everybody the fuck away—including the Brotherhood. I've just been pissed off at the world, and taking that shit out on anybody who crossed my path."

She thought back to seeing him in the middle of the street, outside of Bathe, that glower, that aggression. "You're not like that at the moment."

"Yeah, well, I think you're good for me." He nodded as if he were talking to himself. "For the first time in a long time, the future has . . . something in it for me. And that changes things. When the past is ugly, and there's nothing but time in front of you, the present means nothing, gives you . . . nothing. The nights are a void, the days are full of bad dreams, and you just trudge through it all, lashing out because you can't stand yourself."

He turned his head to her and focused properly. "But when I'm with you, I don't feel like that. You change me."

"I do?" she whispered.

"Yeah, you do."

The strangest thing happened. Inside of her, she felt as though she had been filled with something warm and sustaining, sure as if she had taken his vein. It was such a transformative sensation that all she could do was just breathe and feel it.

"You've changed me, too," she whispered.

"Not possible. You were already perfect."

As her eyes threatened to tear up, she distracted herself by tracing one of the vines as it wound around his biceps—and she was amazed at how touching him felt so natural now.

"What are you thinking about?" he asked her softly.

"I, ah, I want to pretend that I'm sophisticated with you. That this"—she motioned between them—"is something that happens all the time for me. Or at least, every once in a while. Maybe because I want to fake it so I can make it. But the truth is, this has never happened to me before. Ever."

"Well, you're the first female I've had here," he said. "If that makes you feel more comfortable."

"Really?"

"Well, other than my adoptive mother."

"I'm honored." She smiled and tried not to dwell on how happy she was becoming—as if the buzzy rush was a bubble that might burst if she focused on it too much. "And by the way, I really do like it here."

"I like you here."

"Aren't we a matched set."

"We are." He brushed her nose. Touched her mouth with his thumb. "Nalla, I didn't expect this."

"Neither did I." She kissed his fingertips one by one. "And man, I'm glad I went to the club instead of stayed home that night."

"I hadn't seen you out in a long time. Not that I'm a Shuli type."

She thought about her love life. "Yeah, I'm not a big partier—or dater. I've only had two lovers, and neither lasted long. The first one I tried to like, I really did. But you can't fake what you feel, even if you're trying to put yourself out there."

"Is it okay if I hate him," came the growl.

Nalla chuckled. "He can't compete with you. No way."

"Okay, that's what I want to hear. And in another twenty minutes, I'll make sure you remember why." Nate kissed her mouth. "What about the second one? And FYI, no matter what you say about him, I'm going to hate him also."

"Duly noted, and that one . . . I think I'm going to let you hate him. He was just doing it on a bet, as it turned out."

Nate's brows got good and low. "A bet?"

"You must have heard it before. Like at Bathe the other night? A bunch of males trying to one-up themselves playing chicken with my father—and using me as the bait."

That heavy jaw worked like Nate was trying to turn his molars into powder. "I shoulda shut that down instead of just not playing that stupid game."

"Those males asked you to join in the fun, huh."

Nate nodded, his face going downright nasty. "Just so we're clear, that's not right. You don't deserve to be some fucked-up trophy."

"I agree, and when it comes to number two, I was also the goal line. He scored, and then never called me again. I thought it was because I was a bad lay." Even though the sex she'd just had with the very naked, very tattooed fighter next to her proved that was not the case—as long as she had the right partner. "But the next time I saw him, he was looking ashamed of himself as his buddies all high-fived him and tried to pretend they weren't. I knew what had gone down then."

"What's his name."

At the nasty rush of words, she shook her head. "I think it's best for everybody that I keep that to myself. He was young and stupid, so was I. But I learned my lesson and there's been no one since then—until you."

Nate ran his forefinger up and down her collarbone. "Yeah, probably better I don't know who it is."

"It's not anybody in Shuli's group, don't worry. How about you? Have you ever been in love?"

The mask he sometimes wore came down quick as a blink. "No, I haven't."

That's it? she thought as he didn't say anything else.

"And as for sex, it's been a long time for me, too," he tacked on. "I don't connect with people real well."

She had to smile. "You've done just fine with me."

"You're . . . different."

As she looked at his face, and the dark shadow of hair that was coming in over his head . . . then let her eyes go down, to the skull with its vines and snakes and clouds flowing outward . . . and lower still, to his heavy, tattooed sex that lay on his thigh, another clarity came to her, and this time, she ached from it in a profound way.

They were starting something here, in this bed, in their hearts, in their lives. There was much ahead, much to meld, but he was right, there was a future to be had for them both, and she wanted it. She wanted to make her own family.

But she couldn't escape one ringing truth that was going to destroy her in a way.

Loving Nate . . . was going to cost her her father.

Forever.

✦   ✦   ✦

Lying in his bed with Nalla cozied up to his chest, Nate still kept thinking he was going to wake up. The idea that this female was here, with him, in between his Target sheets, under his God-only-knew-from-where blankets, was the kind of thing he was convinced he'd cooked up behind closed lids.

And yet . . . she was here.

He could do without her questions, though. Not because he was hiding anything—okay, fine. He was hiding shit. But he didn't know what to say about Rahvyn, on so many levels, especially because there was no way he could talk about that female and not come clean about his plan for leaving the planet.

Which suddenly wasn't looking like the get-outta-jail card he'd been thinking it was.

Nalla made him want to stick around: Now he knew exactly what his father had been saying about not wanting to talk again until Nate started to care about someone other than himself.

It was early with this female, but yes, he cared about her, a lot, and yes, it made everything different: Time wasn't a burden, thanks to her. It was an opportunity. And he wanted to hoard it because even though he might live forever . . . Nalla wouldn't.

Oh, God, he already didn't want to think like that. And he also didn't want to freak her out with the fact that he'd made a deal to end this immortality bullcrap . . . but she was making him reconsider that whole thing.

Too soon to admit she might very well be saving his life? You bet your ass it was.

"I don't need you to be sophisticated," he murmured as he skipped the question that was hanging in the air between them.

Had he ever been in love before? He might have said yes, up until recently. After Nalla, though, he was starting to think it was a no.

What was that old line . . . that the reason they called it a crush was because the shit hurt?

Drawn by the feel of Nalla's warmth and her smooth skin, he brushed a hand over her shoulder . . . went back onto her collarbone . . . and up to the side of her neck where his bite mark had fully healed, thank God.

"Good, because I'm not," she said quietly. "Sophisticated, that is."

There was a pause, and the banked expectancy on her face told him she was looking for some information on his dating past—and considering all the things he didn't want her to know about him, he figured his sex life was the least of a bunch of bad reports.

"I haven't had any lovers."

Her eyes bugged. "I—ah, you're a virgin? I mean, were a—"

"No." He cleared his throat. "I had some . . . professional interludes."

"Like a training class on making love—" She stopped the joking as she connected the dots correctly. "Oh. Like . . . oh. Well . . . that's—"

"I wasn't a good bet for a relationship." Okay, that was still true. "Back then, I was looking for extreme experiences in everything. Like, my time in the field, the tattooing . . . other things. And for a while, I found a couple of females who shared my interests, as you might call it. But when I realized I was the same person before and after, and considering that was precisely what I was hoping to get away from, I stopped with all that. Turns out you can't remake yourself with distractions, no matter how hard you try."

She seemed to get lost in her own thoughts. "People can try to change. But you have to be careful how and who you're taking your cues from. I have a friend who's into this social media guru—and I just don't think it's going to end well."

"Sometimes it's hard to know what's a way to your destination and what's just a distraction." What he was clear on was that he wanted to be different for Nalla—and that was generalizing into other areas of his life in a good way. "And I guess, sometimes doing shit for the sake of doing it is an excuse to avoid the truth. But what do I know. I'm hardly qualified to comment on anything that has to do with self-improvement."

"I don't know, it sounds like you're turning over a new leaf. And I'm glad I'm here with you as you do."

Staring into her eyes, he felt like he was falling—and he didn't mind the rush at all. "Me too."

Abruptly, she took a deep breath. "Mmmm, I love the way you smell. Dark spices . . ."

As her voice drifted off, he felt his eyes widen—and hers did the same. Like they both came to the same conclusion at the same time.

"Sorry," he said softly. "I can't help it."

"Is that . . . what I think it is? I mean, I've kind of wondered."

Nate nodded. "I'm pretty sure I've bonded with you. I've heard it can happen fast, but I never believed it."

There was a long pause, and her eyes seemed to darken with a sadness he didn't understand. But then she was smiling widely, so widely that he could see her fangs—and imagined, with a kind of greed he'd never felt before, that they were buried deep in his vein, and she was drinking from him.

Taking the nourishment she needed . . . from him, and him alone.

"Bonded males are a pain in the ass," he said roughly. "We're a little nuts when it comes to protecting our females. So can I just do a blanket apology if I run across those assholes from Bathe again? I didn't go far enough the first time."

As she laughed and threw her arms around him, she shook her head. "Just let it go. I don't care about the stupid parlor games. Besides, I'm off the market."

Nate felt this weird glow inside his chest, like he'd been breathing in sunrays. "Well . . . if that isn't the best news I've ever heard. And it's been twenty minutes, female. Give me your mouth again."

CHAPTER THIRTY-EIGHT

Run, run, quick like a bunny. Fast, faster, fastest, you can do it, honey.

As Evan's brain tagged along with his body's explosive sprint, the refrain from his childhood stuck with him, the syllables landing in his head like his boots on the ground. Meanwhile, the wind was whistling in his ears, and he was vaguely aware of the streets that he crossed—two, or was it three?—and the alleys he ducked down—two, for sure.

Just as he started to wonder if he was just going to work out for the rest of the night, he heard the shooting.

A last right-hand turn, and he arrived on scene.

It was the short woman with the braids, whose apartment the tunnel bottomed out at. She was down in a crouch, both hands holding a pair of autoloaders in front of her—and like she sensed him, she looked over her shoulder.

As a bullet ricocheted off a brick wall and shot right by his temple, she glared at him. "You fucking sonofabitch—you took my shit, didn't you. My—oh, fuck you," she spat as she refocused ahead of herself and went back to shooting. "Will you fucking help me you fucking asshole!"

Evan's first instinct was to run away and protect himself. He had a body disposal job to do, and this was not his fight—

His own body took over, his palms finding the guns that, yup, he had stolen from her, as his legs took him right beside her. While she knelt, he stayed standing, and he started shooting before trying to see what the hell was firing back at—

There was a sudden pause in the exchange of bullets, and he peeked around the corner. Across a narrow break in the abandoned buildings' lineup, an inset doorway appeared to be where the shooter was taking cover. He couldn't see anything more than that—and as everything stayed silent, he squinted his eyes.

They must have taken off, he thought. *Into the building—*

"You fucking asshole!"

The punch to the balls was a left hook from outta nowhere, and as he grunted and doubled over, the woman went for the guns in his grips—

It happened so fast. One minute, he was gasping from the pain and she was pulling at the weapons. The next, he had her in a choke hold with the barrel of what was in his right hand pushed into her temple.

In a voice he had never heard before, he said, "Don't ever come at me again. I will stab you back to the maker. Are we clear?"

"Fuck you—"

He pulled the trigger.

As the gun went off, he was so shocked at what he'd done, he recoiled and dropped his hold so he could jump back.

The woman landed facedown in a heap, her arms out like she was trying for something just beyond her reach.

"What the fuck am I doing," he said under his breath as he stood over his second dead body. "I'm a fucking feminist."

Before he could—well, he didn't fucking know what he was going to do—there was movement. The woman dragged her arms back. Gathered her torso. Slowly raised from the dead.

Her head cranked around to him, and the black blood that oozed out of the alarming exit wound gleamed. "What *fuck.*"

Um . . . yeah, he thought. That about covered it.

"Why the hell you do that."

"I'm sorry," he mumbled. Like he'd scraped her car or maybe insulted her hair. "But you punched me in the balls."

"You think this"—she motioned to the bullet wound in her brain— "equal to slap in sac?"

"To be fair, you don't have them, so you wouldn't know."

She spit off to the side, more annoyed than anything else. "I got knuckled in the boob once. It was not that big a deal."

"You weren't going to stop at the sac," he said grimly. "Don't front."

She was silent. Then she cursed in Spanish, and against everything that made any kind of sense, she stood up—and because she had both of her weapons back in her hands, he pointed his at her. Or . . . hers at her.

"We don't need to do this." He stared at her eyes, stared into her. "And I will make it all up to you."

"How."

"I'll give you what you want. I'll give you something worth killing."

He didn't know what the hell he was saying. What he was clear on was that he didn't want *that* happening on half of his skull.

"You make good on your promise," she said as she narrowed her eyes, "and you keep the guns. But no steal from me again."

Evan thought of the additional weapons he had at Mickey's. "Done."

The woman turned back to the corner they were taking cover behind. As her matched pair of autoloaders pointed back in the direction of the doorway, he felt compelled to acknowledge her little boo-boo.

"What are you doing?" he asked.

She glared at him over her shoulder. "My fucking job. What *you* doing."

"But your . . ." He motioned around his own head. "What about—"

"You think I'm go to a doc in box? The ER? Fuck you." Then she frowned. "Fine, we call for reinforcements. Then we go finish this job."

Shoving one of the guns under her armpit, she took out a cell phone, and fumbled with her thumbs. Just as he was going to ask her if she needed help, she hissed at him and sent out something via text.

"Now we go get those two vampires," she told him.

◆   ◆   ◆

Across the way from where the slayers were, Shuli was still flat on his back. But at least his case of the stunned-stupids was dissipating, so he was able to see more clearly.

And what a view.

Looming over him, like a pissed-off Paul Bunyan who'd gone hard-ass and gotten himself a bunch of tattoos and some militia training, L.W. was doing that leg-plant thing he did, all but straddling Shuli cowboy-style.

"Must you," Shuli muttered.

"Can you walk?"

"Do I have to." But he was already sitting up. "Gimme a hand."

The only thing good about L.W. was that when it counted, the male was a doer, not a stew-er, and he pulled Shuli up to the vertical with a yank. They didn't have much time. The lag in bullets-trading wasn't going to last, and it was going to resume right up close: The slayers had to be reloading before they were going to close in.

Unfortunately, Shuli did more tap-dancing than true walking— at least until L.W. hitched up a hold and carried him under one arm like a cardboard cutout. Thanks to the excellent eyesight of vampires, the contours of the back hall they were going down were nominally visible. There were office chairs on their sides, paper bags and fast-food wrappers, a couple of what looked like sleeping bags—

Something was off about this, Shuli thought as he looked around. He just didn't know quite what was wrong with the corridor.

L.W. clearly felt the same. But as the slayers entered the hall and the scent of death and old-fashioned talcum powder drifted down, the two of them had to go even faster.

When they came up to a door, L.W. fired a bullet into the knob without even testing whether it was locked—and there was no giving him shit for the noisy decision. Then again, Shuli was essentially an armchair quarterback deadweight.

Commentary might just get him dropped.

The open area on the far side was an old office facility of some kind, but it had been a while since the desks and chairs had been used. Musty/dusty, mold, and crud—the stink was nearly as bad as the *lesser* shit. There was also no good cover to be had, and no clues where an exit was—although it was a good bet they'd gone through some kind of fire door, so maybe if they—

"Head that way," Shuli said as L.W. already started off. "Toward the front."

The place had been stripped of whatever cubicles there had been, but given the patterns of wear and tear on the carpet, he could just imagine it being some kind of call center, back before AI had completely taken over that job.

Not that he wasted much time on that kind of origin story.

Because they had problems.

When they came up to the main entrance, it was not just locked, it was made of . . . steel plates?

And meanwhile, the scent of *lessers* was getting stronger, so clearly the slayers were tracking them through the building.

"Stand here," L.W. said as he pushed Shuli against the wall.

The male took out a cell phone—then cursed. "You gotta be kidding me."

"What." Shuli looked up at the ceiling. "Wait a minute . . ."

There was a subtle gleam up above—and all around them.

"I got no signal—"

"Oh, *shit*," Shuli breathed. "This was a data security firm. It's steel . . . we're surrounded by steel and lead."

So no dematerializing.

"Fucking hell," L.W. muttered.

Shuli looked back toward the fire door they'd come out of. Then he glanced at the other male. "Tell me you have a charge on you."

Zsadist, who had trained them both, had always maintained that every fighter needed an explosive with him, just in case.

This was just in case.

"There has to be a way out," L.W. groused like he hadn't heard what Shuli'd said.

"There is. It's blasting through this steel door." Shuli started checking his own magazines. "Get yourself out. I'll hold the enemy for as long as I can—"

"Wait, what the fuck are you doing?"

Shuli started limping back for where they came. "I'm going to be a distraction—"

L.W. grabbed hold of Shuli's arm. "The fuck you are—"

"You're the future King. I'm—well, I'm rich and I'm good looking." He searched that hard, cruel face, and thought about all the Wraths who had lead the species. "But there are plenty of me's. There's only one of you—shut up. You know I'm right so quit arguing. Set the charge, get the fuck out. I'll do what I can to give you the time you need."

"Shuli—"

"You *know* I'm right. And I don't mind going out like this. It's better than a lot of alternatives—do not let me down, though. You get yourself out of here, and when your own time to die comes, don't blink at it. I'm not."

The future king seemed speechless. "Fuck, man."

Shuli looked down because he couldn't bear the surprising pain in those pale green eyes. "Damn shame to waste this coat, though. It fits like a fucking glove—and it does not make my ass look big."

Jerking his arm out of L.W.'s hold, Shuli stared hard at the male. "Don't waste this chance I'm giving you, okay?"

With that, he started off for that hallway.

Like the future of all vampires depended on him.

CHAPTER THIRTY-NINE

Z sadist heard the explosion first.

The unmistakable *whoosh!* sound fired off about four blocks away from where he was staking out the induction site with the tunnel access in its basement. And almost before the blast echo faded, he got a Mayday text so he immediately pulled an up-and-out from his position behind a picked-clean car.

He wasn't the only fighter who arrived on scene to a short building that was nothing but a windowless block of concrete: Phury, Xcor, and Tohr were right behind him, zeroing in on the smoking aperture that had been blown in the front facade.

No one was coming out, though.

Forming a stack by the breach, he was glad they didn't have to worry about any municipal surveillance cameras on this rundown block. They did not need cop-bots getting in the way right now.

Following established entry protocol, the four of them moved in sequence into the interior and spread out to clear the space. He had a vague impression of office furniture litter, staleness, and rot, but the baby powder and fresh blood under the stink was what he was worried about. And then he was in front as they closed in on a fire door—

The gunfire in its back hall was rapid, and he rushed forward.

In the corridor beyond, smoke made visibility low, but the hulking shadow that was backing toward them, while shooting and carrying something, was too fucking huge to miss.

And he knew who it was.

Zsadist jumped ahead of L.W.—was that Shuli he was lugging? *Fuck.*

There was no time to worry about injuries. Z took control, double-palming his weapons in front of himself as he back-flatted, pushed forward, and just kept discharging bullets into the swirling smoke. When there was a sharp series of signal whistles from his twin, he changed tactics. No more offense, now it was an extraction.

He began backing up—

A sudden flare of pain in his side was nothing compared to what was going on with his shoulder. But that was another thing he couldn't worry about. When he was out of bullets, he swapped magazines with practiced moves, and then he was continuing on the retreat, until he'd backed out of the fire door.

"On your left," Phury said.

"Roger."

Working in tandem, they kept the square footage controlled, and when he could smell fresh air from the blown entry, he felt a secondary, almost-outta-jail adrenaline rush.

That lasted until they made it out on the street.

And were ambushed.

There was an entire flank of *lessers* advancing from down at the river, and the slayers immediately started shooting.

It was clusterfuck time—and Shuli and L.W. were both injured and in the middle of it.

Shoving his hands into his jacket, Z whistled high and sharp. And then he started pulling out the pins of grenades and throwing them like he was in the World Series, real wind-up-and-follow-through time.

The first of the explosions lit up the narrow street like daylight, and gave excellent visualization: Half a dozen slayers, who'd been rushing forward without much coordination, pulled a spin and retreat—that wasn't going to last.

The second blew one of them up, fragments of flesh flying in chunks, the black splatter washing the windowless building next to it. The third drove the others back farther, but was again a reminder that the withdrawal was only temporary. He had one more and then he was going to have to yield his position. He could only pray that his brothers had evac'd the injured and there had been no casualties—

Flashing blue lights.

And headlights.

The Caldwell Police. Of course.

The only good thing was that the slayers scattered like the rats without tails they'd been before Lash had turned them: The Lessening Society didn't want law enforcement complications any more than the brothers did.

Zsadist turned around and assessed his options. He could head back into the building, but if there were other *lessers* in there? No way he could dematerialize. He was off-the-chain activated. No chance of calming down—

Abruptly, he was spotlit like a billboard as one of the two patrol cars came at him like it was going to run him right over.

As he went to jump out of the way, the CPD bot slammed on its brakes and skidded into a swing, its vehicle's rear coming around so that it stopped with the driver's side right by Z.

The window went down and—

"What the fuck," Z breathed.

Butch smiled from behind the wheel. "Hop in. I gotchu."

Even though it was the middle of a skirmish, Zsadist looked around. "How in the hell did you do this?"

"Hey, I used to work homicide for them, remember?" The cop nod-ded to the empty seat next to him. "I broke into the impound, got two, and L.W. and Shuli are being put into the other. But we gotta blow right now."

Zsadist shook his head. "You got it, Detective."

◆   ◆   ◆

Shuli knew he was losing blood, but he was still with it enough to know that he was somehow, inexplicably . . . in the back of a Caldwell Police Department patrol car. The blue lights were a dead giveaway. Well, that and it had showed up at the worst possible time.

The confusing part? For some reason, on the far side of the mesh that separated them from the front seat of the vehicle . . . it seemed like Rhage was behind the wheel.

But he couldn't worry about all that.

Summoning his flagging energy, he forced his head out of its awk-ward lean against the door that had been shut on him. Next to him on the bench seat, L.W. was crammed into the space that barely fit Shuli. The male had his knees up around his earlobes, and he was breathing too hard for how much he wasn't moving.

"What the *hell* is wrong with you!" Shuli hollered at the guy.

Up front, Rhage looked into the rear view mirror with a start. "Every-thing okay back there, boys?"

"No!" Shuli punched L.W.'s upper arm—okay, it was more like a pat with his knuckles, but whatever. "You weren't supposed to come back for me!"

L.W. looked over with half-mast eyes. "Can we not do this right now?"

"I am *so* pissed off—"

"You wouldn't be alive right now without me, so relax—"

"I was supposed to save you!" Shuli tried to lower his voice as his heart rate got erratic against his ribs. "Jesus Christ, you are such a hard-headed asshole—"

"I wasn't leaving you to die—"

"—that you can't listen to someone else—"

"—and right now, I am seriously—"

"—and take care of yourself."

"—rethinking that decision."

As their argument came to a pause for respiration, the patrol car blew through a red light, and Shuli glared out the window, watching the blue flashes strobe the buildings. As they went by Bathe, he shook his head.

What was next, he blew up his own house?

The soft chuckle from up front brought his head back around—which was a mistake as the pounding between his ears flared to an eye-bulging degree.

"You two," Rhage murmured with a sentimental smile. "You remind me of good times."

Shuli glanced at L.W. Who popped a brow.

The Brother continued. "And I'm glad you both got out okay. I've gotten caught in a tight crack like that before." Those brilliant blue eyes focused on Shuli. "And of course he was going back for you."

"No offense, but that makes no sense." Shuli pushed himself up a little higher on the seat. "Plus he doesn't even like me."

"This is true," L.W. piped in.

Shuli nodded at the guy. "Right? I mean, shit, if you're going to risk your own life, at least do it for someone who matters to you."

Rhage shook his head and hit the gas as the light turned green. "It's in his DNA. He's not going to leave anybody behind. You did the right thing, though, Shuli. Protecting the King or the heir apparent above all else is the correct impulse."

L.W. laughed a little and motioned at Shuli. "This guy. He runs right into the line of fire—down that corridor. Did you see that hall?"

Rhage shook his head. "Not yet. Payne and I are going back to deconstruct the scene."

"Fucking nuts. Steel-lined, nowhere to go, funneling right out into what was an ambush. It was suicidal."

Holding up his forefinger, Shuli countered, "I'm *not* interested in killing myself. Just to be clear."

"You could have stayed and defended our position right beside me."

"And tell me, how would that have worked for us as a stream of *lessers* entered that open area? You think they were just going to take a load off while you breached the door?"

"It didn't take me long!"

"It could have. We didn't know what was going to happen—"

"Because *you* decided to be a hero."

"Oh, so *that's* why you came after me?" Shuli rolled his eyes. "A crown isn't enough, you need a Superman cape, too?"

"Are you *really* still arguing with me?"

"Well, someone's gotta stand up to your ass. Everybody else thinks you shit rainbows—"

The crack of laughter from the front shut down the second wave of bitey-face, and what do you know. As Shuli glanced at L.W. with annoyance, the heir to the throne looked back at him with a similar set of pursed lips.

But neither of them was going to tell the Brother to quit it with the giggles.

After all, Shuli might have been willing to run headfirst into a legion of *lessers*, but he was not interested in getting eaten alive by Rhage's dragon. At least with the former, he had a chance at making it out alive.

"You guys are awesome together," Rhage said with approval. "A real matched pair."

Shuli and L.W. looked at each other again.

"We are not."

"We are not."

CHAPTER FORTY

C haos.

Unmitigated chaos.

As Evan tore out of the scene, he ran harder and faster than he ever had in all of his life, and he had no idea, until he was a good seven or eight blocks away from the melee, that he had in fact made it out alive.

Or intact, was more like it.

Slowing his pace, he cut around a corner, put his back against the exterior wall of a brick building, and just stood still. Which was easy to do because he wasn't breathing hard even with all the exertion. Putting his hand to his heart, he wished he could feel the pounding and the suffocation, the lethargy in his legs, the sting in his cheeks. Instead, he had more in common with what he was leaning on.

He had to keep moving. And he knew where to go.

The next thing he knew, he was under the bridges, heading for the doors he had seen the others go through before. When he came up to one, he tried the knob—

It opened.

Stepping through, he looked down at the stone floor. A black oil trail headed off to the left and he followed it, his boots tracking through the fresh blood. Not that it was blood.

Oh, God, what had he done.

What had been done *to* him.

When he arrived at a set of stairs that led downward, he breathed in, and knew he should have been smelling the dank and musky. And his legs should have been tired. And his feet should have hurt. And he knew he'd been hit with another bullet in the upper arm and in the calf and that should have slowed him down or made him dizzy.

At the bottom, there was a door half off its hinges and he pushed it aside.

There were lit candles in random places, and buckets, so many buckets. But the sound of sucking . . . that was what drew his attention to the far corner.

In the dim flicker, the trainer was bending over something on the floor, a black leather duster pooling around whatever was happening.

"What did you do to me," Evan asked in a low tone.

That blond head came up from the body on the floor, and as it swiveled in Evan's direction, there was red blood dripping from an open mouth with fangs.

The smile was as cold as the dead. "I've been looking for you."

"*What did you do to me.*"

The monster with the fangs rose to its feet. "I gave you what you wanted. You wanted to be strong, you are. You wanted power, you have it. You wanted—"

Evan pounded his chest with his fist. "I didn't want this!"

"You see one fight, and you're running away? I give you everything you need to succeed and you fucking *run?*"

Evan took out both his guns. "I'm done talking. I want you to reverse whatever you did." He nodded in the direction of the body that was lying in an oil slick, red blood pumping out of a neck wound. "Or I'm going to kill you."

"Really."

The villain walked forward, all stealth stride with that duster flaring out around him, and even though Evan was the one with the weapons, he backed up until he was, once again, against a brick wall. Except he wasn't running anymore. He was fucking done with that.

"You make this right," he said as his voice trembled with anger.

"Do you want to know why I was looking for you?" The nightmare stopped when they were only two feet away from each other. "It's because I didn't finish."

With a casual hand, Lash pushed away the muzzles and put his palm on the center of Evan's chest. "You have something that you no longer need."

A searing pain lit off behind Evan's sternum, and as he started to scream, the entity's other hand clapped onto his mouth—

Cracking sounds, like dry sticks snapped in half over a knee, sounded loud in his ears, and then there was a messy, wet series of flaps. The agony was so bad, he thought he'd surely lose consciousness, but he didn't.

He was utterly aware as a hand pushed into his heart's cavity, and the organ that had kept him alive was taken out of its seat in his rib cage.

It was still beating as the trainer held the cardiac muscle up so Evan could get a good, clear look at the nasty black wedge.

"We were interrupted before," Lash said. "But now we'll be thick as thieves."

Flashing white fangs, the mouth that had sucked him dry opened wide and took a bite of his heart.

Evan was pushed away, and as he fell on the floor, he tried to scream again, but had no air in his lungs: The gaping hole at his pecs was ragged as a bomb crater, and the black stains on his skin were like the blast zone around the detonation.

"You will listen to me when I call you," came the command, "and you will go out there and do what you are programmed to do."

"I did not ask for this," Evan said on a rasp.

"Yes, you did. With every pathetic attempt at the weights in that gym, and each frustration you expressed about your family, and all the mediocrity you were in. You have a fucking future now. *Go live it.*"

Evan stared up at the horror before him, his brain refusing to process it all. "I want out—"

"Too late," Lash said with that trademark arctic smile. "Now, get to work."

The thing turned its back and headed over to the corner again. To finish its meal.

With a shaking hand, Evan lifted one of the guns—and pulled the trigger—

It happened so fast, he couldn't track it. The monster was going back over to his prey—and then Lash was spinning around and snapping something out of the air. Sticking his fist out, he released what he'd caught—and the bullet hit the concrete with a chiming bounce.

Then he cast his arm in a sweep that somehow translated to where Evan was, his body caught in an explosive current that carried him end over end, as if he were a newspaper page in the wind.

He hit something so hard he was stunned into immobility.

Maybe he would die. But he feared that was a wish he would not be granted.

Lying just outside the glow of the candles, he stared into darkness . . . as the sucking sounds resumed.

CHAPTER FORTY-ONE

Hours later, Nalla came awake, and for a split second, she had no idea what had woken her up. She knew where she was, though. She was in Nate's bed, and he was—

A tortured sound rippled up next to her, and she rolled over with a flop. In the dim light thrown from the bathroom, he was asleep and facing her, and it was like he was contorted in pain: One hand was curled up under his chin in a claw, his chest was pumping up and down, and he was gripping the mattress with his other—

"No . . . please, no . . . not again . . ."

The voice that came out of him was a total distortion from how he normally sounded, the words strangled and vulnerable. Higher in pitch. As if he were a young.

"Nate?"

His face turned toward her, but he didn't open his eyes. "Can you help me?"

Fishing through the covers, she took the hand that was under his chin. "Nate, you need to wake up—"

"Please take me with you . . ."

"Shh, it's okay—"

"Can you get me out of here . . ." His head flipped back and forth on the pillow. "If you can take the needle out, you can . . ."

"Nate. You've got to wake—"

"I can't stay anymore. She's dead . . . *mahmen* escaped, but she's dead . . . can you help me . . . take me . . . with you . . ."

He started crying in his sleep, the tears squeezing out of his locked-down lids. "They hurt me . . . my stomach this time . . . help me . . . the humans won't stop . . ."

As horror dawned on her and squeezed the air out of her lungs, Nalla tried to soothe him with touch. "You need to wake up, Nate, you're safe—"

"Not . . . safe . . . humans won't let us go . . . the men in white coats are going to kill me."

All at once, his halting words melded with stories she had heard, of vampires taken by humans into labs and experimented on, viruses and diseases like cancer and Ebola and polio injected into them, their organs removed or dissected, their bodies violated in too many ways to contemplate.

There was no way someone dreamed of this randomly.

No way.

Trying to sharpen her voice, she said, "Nate, you're not in the lab. You're in your basement, under the cabin, on your property. You're safe and you're with me, Nalla." She stroked his muscled forearm desperately. "Can you wake up for me? Nate, please . . . just wake up . . ."

With an abrupt spasm, he threw his head back like he was straining at a set of bars, and on his torso, the skull undulated with the movement, the ivy, and the snakes, and the—not clouds, she thought with terror. Gas. She'd gotten it all wrong. The elements of the design that she'd thought emanated to all other parts of him . . . they weren't flowing from the skull—oh, God, they represented things forcing their way *into* the eyes and mouth, flooding, choking . . . bringing pain and suffering.

As he thrashed and kicked, she couldn't stand it anymore. "I'll take you with me," she said in a rush. "I'll take you out. Here, come with me . . ."

Her voice broke as she stifled a sob. But at least he stilled.

"You won't let them hurt me?"

It was a little boy's voice coming out of a grown male, someone who was powerless begging for mercy.

"No," she said hoarsely as she blinked away tears, "I won't let them hurt you. You're safe, with me. Come away . . . with me."

Giving up the fight, Nate curled into her, and she felt him trembling, his huge body shaking so badly, the mattress vibrated.

"Help me . . ." he whispered. "It hurts . . ."

Leaning over him, she rubbed his back, her eyes locking on the far wall. Then she looked around the room. She had thought it was neat before; now she saw the space for what it really was: Barren. No pictures or knickknacks, no mementos of vacations taken or fun nights out. Nothing personal, at all.

Because there was nothing personal in his own life.

She pictured him standing apart at the club—and standing apart at festivals and celebrations. If he came to them at all.

How did someone who had seen what he had of cruelty and calculation ever relate to anybody? He must always be jumping a divide when he was interacting with other people, ever on the far side, looking in . . . because the torture he'd been subjected to had broken something precious within him: His belief that there was kindness in the world that would safeguard a young when they could not safeguard themselves.

Instead, he'd been surrounded by humans who had tortured his *mahmen* and hurt him, over and over again.

Running her hand over the top of his head, feeling the new growth of his dark hair, she whispered, "Now I understand why you don't want to talk about yourself—"

With no warning, Nate shoved himself away from her, his arms punching out, his eyes wide open and terrified as they looked at her, and yet didn't seem to see her at all. And then he pushed himself all the way off the bed and crab-walked backwards into the far corner, keeping that vacant stare on her as if he expected to be flayed alive at any moment.

Her heart pounded and fear struck her in the center of her chest. What if she couldn't get him to wake up?

"Nate, it's me. Nalla."

He was shaking again, his teeth rattling, and he drew his knees up to his chest, wrapping his arms around them and holding himself. The way he lowered his head so that most of his face disappeared behind the fortification he'd created with form, only his wide, wary eyes showing, was a young's way of hunkering down.

He had done this before, she thought. Tried to disappear, while knowing he couldn't hide from his captors.

"What you must have been through," she said softly.

And she needed to help him snap out of it, but she had no idea how to get through to him—

From out of the recesses of her mind, the answer came, and it was not an exotic one.

Sitting up straight, she put her palms together, sharp and loud, twice.

Clap.

Clap.

All at once, Nate came awake, that blank stare filling with confusion, his brows dropping as he looked down at his arms as if he couldn't figure out why they were locked on his bent legs—

With slow recognition, he released the grip on himself, his fighter's hard body both uncoiling and tensing, all at the same time. Now, as he looked across at her, he seemed to know exactly who she was, but he was wary—like he wasn't sure what she'd seen. How much had been revealed. How . . . bad it had been.

"It's okay," she said in a steady, calm voice. Which was not even remotely how she was feeling. "You're all right."

Inside, she was an absolute mess, but she knew what he'd be concerned about: This was what he hid from everybody, and he was worried she'd judge him in some way. Which was not going to happen.

And she did not blame him for keeping this all to himself. Troubles were shared. Tragedies were different. The former was a conversation, the latter was a stripping raw of someone who had been raw too much and too often.

Silence could be the only armor you had, sometimes. Because if you got talking? Your voice unlocked the dungeon, and the demons in your mind jumped you and you were never quite sure you'd be able to get free of them—

With an exhale, he looked away, staring across at the stretch of countertop where the sink was. "I . . ."

As he let things just hang there, she had a feeling he was trying to construct some kind of only-a-nightmare lie.

Nalla shook her head. "I'm not going to say anything to anybody. And I understand why you don't talk about it."

After a moment, he extended his legs out in front of himself and crossed his arms again, now over his lap. "It's been a long time."

"Since you've had a dream like that?"

Nate shrugged and didn't look at her. "One that vivid, at any rate."

There were so many questions to ask, but she was not going to pressure him—

"It's just a nightmare," he said. "Everybody gets them, you know. You probably have them, too, right?"

Yes, she thought. But not because she was reliving being an animal in a lab.

"I do." She cleared her throat. "From time to time."

"What are yours about?"

Struggling to focus, she tried to get her brain to plug into her own life. "Wasps. I dream of—wasps."

"Oh, good one." His voice became a little lighter, like he was trying to embrace normalcy, fuse it to his own experience. "Do you come up on a nest or something?"

"I, ah . . ." What the hell was she saying? "No, it's not like that. I'm not in the woods or anything. The wasps are in my bed . . . under my pillow, actually. I roll over and flush them. I always wake up just as they start to sting me."

"It happens when you're stressed, right."

"Yes. When I'm stressed."

"I don't like cramped places." He shook his head. Then ran his palm over his skull, his biceps bunching up. "Claustrophobia does it to me every time. Common thing to worry about, like wasps in your bed, right?"

"Yes," she said again, softly.

He nodded, but it was in an absent way, and he still wasn't looking at her. When he finally got up in silence, then said something about taking a quick shower, she wasn't surprised. She told herself it was fine, that he was still sorting through what was real and what wasn't, and a rinse off would help that.

But as he shut the door firmly, she knew it was more than just the bathroom getting closed off.

See, this was why you couldn't get too invested in the rosy start of a relationship, she thought.

There were always layers to people—and some of them went so deep, they created fault lines that couldn't be repaired.

◆   ◆   ◆

Twenty minutes of hot water drilling on his skull later, Nate stepped out onto his bath mat and toweled himself off. Leaning over his sink, he cleaned the condensation off the mirror with a swipe and stared at himself. He looked like shit, his face pale, the whites of his eyes bloodshot, his lips pursed.

A ghost haunting himself. Oh, wait, his past was the specter stalking him.

He should have known that he'd have one of his really bad nightmares again. He'd never had a female he'd cared about in his bed before, he'd been kicked out of the Brotherhood's fighting protocol, and the best friend he hadn't had for thirty years had broken things off with him. Oh, and then there were his parents, and the fact that he was coming to understand what an absolute shithead he'd been to them. And Rahvyn.

And everything else.

Jesus, why couldn't he just dream about wasps under his pillow? And why did he have to fall asleep in the first place—

"Because you didn't sleep all day," he muttered as he looped the towel around his hips. "You were too busy thinking about her."

Over at the door, he braced himself. Nalla had to have questions, and all the answers he didn't want to give her were going to be a wedge between them. She deserved some kind of explanation, but he knew, by the look in her eyes, the conclusions she'd come to were the accurate ones, even if she didn't have all the details.

So did he really need to get personal about things . . . ?

Yes, he fucking did. Because he cared about her more than he cared about himself, and his father was right. That transformed a person . . . and was the kind of self-improvement that made all the difference.

But God, he just couldn't find the words.

Opening the door, he stepped out into the much cooler and drier open space, and looked to the bed.

She wasn't in the messy sheets—

How could he have missed the smell of bacon, he wondered as his head snapped over toward his hot plate.

Nalla was standing with her back to him, the Oscar Mayer package open on the counter, along with the eggs and the loaf of bread that had yet to be called into service. She was in her turtleneck and jeans, but her feet were still bare and her hair was still loose down her back.

But she hadn't left him. Yet.

Glancing toward the steps up to the cabin, he told himself not to dwell on the fact that she'd hung her parka off of the end of the railing, and positioned her snow boots right under all that Patagonia.

He went over and took out a fresh pair of jeans from his dresser. After pulling them on, he grabbed a t-shirt to cover up his torso.

"Can you set out plates?" she asked without looking back at him.

"Sure." He rubbed his palms on his thighs and headed for his shelf. "Thanks for cooking."

Shit, he only had the one place setting. And no table to set any places on. He always just ate standing up at the stove when he was here.

"How do you like your eggs?" she asked.

"Any way you make 'em."

"Scrambled it is."

They didn't talk again until she was passing him a plateful. Or trying to.

"You keep that, I'm eating out of the pan." He nodded across the way. "And you can have my chair and the fork. I'll use the spoon."

"I'll accept the fork, but I'll trade you the chair. I'm used to eating at the counter at Luchas House."

Fine, he'd take the chair.

As they assumed their positions and ate in silence, he realized how the clinking of forks and spoons (or rather, fork and spoon) on plates (or rather, plate and pan) was lonely when there was someone else with you. When it was just yourself? Well, you were watching something stupid on your phone, or it was like the sound of your own breathing— the kind of thing you didn't notice.

When they were finished, he got up first and took her plate to the sink. At least he'd thought to get groceries. Like the clean sheets, he'd wanted to be prepared without taking for granted.

"It's getting closer to dawn," he said as he started to run water over the plate and pan.

"I'll go."

"I'm not rushing you off."

"Okay."

He cut the water and turned around.

Fuck. She was all the way over at the stairs. Ten feet up those steps and with an opening of that hatch—and he was suddenly worried he would never see her again.

"I'm sorry," he said.

Nalla finally looked at him, really looked at him, and her yellow eyes weren't mad. They had a vivid kind of grief in them. And he didn't want that for her. Even though there was the temptation to get frustrated over the fact that he'd fallen asleep, to think that maybe if he'd stayed awake, he could have spared her, he needed to get real. Sooner or later, that shit from the lab was going to come out.

"You have nothing to apologize for," she said.

"I don't know what to say about my past."

Oh, shit, was he really going there—

Fuck it, yes he was.

"I don't talk about it because when I do, those memories take over everything—and I don't want you to look like you do right now, like you're in mourning or something. I'm still here. I'm still alive."

"I know you are." She put her hand over her heart. "I just had no idea what you've been through. I am so sorry, Nate. So . . . sorry."

Something about the compassion she offered cracked him right open, and before he could stop himself, his mouth was going, the speed of his words increasing until they were a blur.

"What happened in that lab is the kind of thing that gets away from me. Even now, all these years later. Like, I get into an elevator at a scene down in the field or my arm gets caught in a coat sleeve? Suddenly, I'm locked in a cage and I can't get out and I know they're coming for me again. Or maybe it's that antiseptic smell, you know, the one in clinics?" He snapped his fingers, the sound loud as a slap in the tense silence between them. "I'm back there, in the lab, and they're cleaning up after I've vomited because they're trying to give me lung cancer, and they can't figure out why I'm not getting it, so they've pumped me full of human cells and my body's rejecting them. If I bleed? Because I'm injured? I just remember coming around on the table because the anesthesia they gave me didn't work and I could feel them cutting open my stomach so they could look at my liver firsthand. And here's the bitch about it. It takes *nothing* to pop the top off that jar, and hours or nights to get it all stuffed back down again."

He glanced down at her feet. Looked at his own. Had some kind of absurd, magical thinking that surely, because they were both not wearing shoes or socks, that meant that she wasn't going to bolt out of his crappy little home and never come back again . . .

. . . because his shit was too heavy for even a compassionate, professionally trained social worker like herself.

"So yeah," he finished hoarsely, "I just don't know what to say without going into the swamp of it all—and really, who needs that."

"I don't blame you for wanting to keep it private. But I'm glad you've told me."

"I would have preferred to keep it to myself."

Their back-and-forth was stilted, and like she recognized that, too, she said, "Look, I'm not going to feed you some kind of line that talking about what happened to you will make it all better. But I'm not scared of your past. I hate it, and I hate what it does to you, but I'm not running, just so we're clear."

"Thanks."

Those were, of course, the right words. But her composure was almost professional-grade. So maybe she saw him as a client now, instead of a male, a project to work on, instead of a partner.

Just what he wanted.

As the silence grew even heavier, he wanted to break it, but as God was his witness—or Lassiter, as it were—he could not think of what to say. His mind was a total blank. Well, empty of words. Like an engine trying to turn over, images from the lab kept flickering into his consciousness and replacing the world around him.

So that he couldn't see her through them.

Eventually, she said, "It's about four a.m. I, ah, I think I'm going to take off."

"Yeah. Okay." Utter exhaustion sucked him down, but it wasn't the kind that was cured with sleep. "Can I give you my number?"

"Oh, yes, please."

How they had gone from where they'd been in his bed before they'd fallen asleep to these one-syllable answers, he had no clue.

Oh, wait. He knew why.

She got her phone out of her parka and held it up. "New one, same number."

"Vishous is good like that."

"He's had to replace a lot of broken cells for sure." As he read the number of his burner phone out to her, she entered it. "Got it."

"Okay."

As she started to put on her jacket, he wanted to tell her to stop. That she should stay. That maybe he'd find his voice later. Shame and shock and sorrow kept him locked in, though—another cage that existed only in his mind, but worked just fine to pen him in—and the harder he tried to pull something coherent out of his ass, the worse the paralysis got.

Her boots went on too quickly. "So, I guess I'll be going."

"Thanks. For coming here."

"Thanks again for Amore."

"Anytime."

And then he was giving her some lame-ass wave, and she was turning away to the steps. He found that he couldn't even move so he could go over and open the hatch for her, but she knew what to do. Then again, it wasn't brain surgery.

After she stepped out, the sound of the hatch locking back into place was like the top of a coffin, and as he glanced around, the fact that he was underground made sense. This place was like a grave, and though he was going to live forever, it felt like he was dead.

Without Nalla, he supposed he was. Bonded males were like that.

Fucking hell. Those goddamn humans in that lab had now robbed him not only of one of his two *mahmen* . . . but of the other most important female in his life.

His true love.

CHAPTER FORTY-TWO

E ven though the Brothers had relocated their living quarters off the mountain, the Brotherhood's clinic was still up there, a main anchor of the subterranean training center that was still used regularly for all its components. The medical facility, with its OR and examination rooms, was just too expensive and hard to move.

Plus, from what Bitty had heard, Uncle Vishous had built the clinic as an engagement present for Doc Jane. And just like you didn't toss out a diamond ring because you bought a watch, a surgeon like that Brother's *shellan* wasn't walking away from a couple million dollars of state-of-the-art equipment and supplies.

As Bitty re-formed in a forest of pines, she was instantly racked with disorientation—and it was always like this. On the rare occasions she came back onto the property, the *mhis* that buffered the landscape and made it impossible for trespassers to find their way always made her wobbly. Which was how it worked.

But she had the right coordinates, so she knew where she was.

The structure she had come for was just off to the left, and as she closed in, she had to smile. An outhouse, faithfully re-created to look old, even sporting a half-moon in the door. "The shitter," as Uncle Butch called the thing. It wasn't until you tried to open it up that you realized what looked rickety was solid as a frickin' rock, all the off-kilter as carefully made as a stage set for a movie.

And needless to say, you didn't get in unless you were allowed.

As she put her gloved hand on the pull, she looked up to the slit in the door where the tiny camera was. Not more than three seconds later, the locking mechanism was sprung and she was able to step in. The panel, which was wooden on the outside, and steel on the inside, closed on its own and relocked. Then the floor started a descent.

She was always surprised, given how cooped up she was in the tight space, that they'd made the thing this small. But the Brothers didn't use this remote entry.

No way her father could get in here, that was for sure.

There was a bump as things bottomed out, and she knew she had to wait. The door would only open when it was ready.

"Thank you," she said to the security person as she stepped out.

The windowless, doorless steel room she now found herself in was bombproof, or so she'd been told, and the whirring sound was a HEPA-filtered, self-contained, negative airflow system in the event of a chemical attack. She'd never been able to find the cameras, but they were somewhere—and she could never really locate the door until it opened, either—

Oh. Right in front of her.

"Thanks again," she called out.

On the far side, the training center's parking area was multi-leveled and largely empty, just a couple of blacked-out vans angled butt-first in their spaces—oh, and a blacked-out school bus that looked like it was delivering pupils to an academy for pool sharks and loan enforcers. As she walked over to the reinforced entrance into the training center proper, her footfalls echoed around in a way that would have creeped her out if she hadn't been in a Brotherhood's facility.

But she was super safe here. Nobody got this far unless they were allowed.

At the fortified steel door, she had to wait again, and then she was permitted to pass into the concrete corridor that ran the length of the training center.

Now the nerves hit, and to distract herself, she got walking and glanced into the classrooms that were dormant. Waves of trainees had gone through the Brothers' program and received all kinds of instruction, but the classes were staggered, sometimes by whole calendar years, and she didn't know when the next one started. There would be a new crew coming in at some point, though.

The war with the Lessening Society demanded it.

The clinic was about halfway down, right before the weight and locker rooms, and as she reached the series of closed doors, she wasn't sure what to do.

Or really even why she was here.

Well, she'd overheard her father talking about how much fun he'd had posing as a cop downtown—and then he'd mentioned his "precious cargo" as he'd called it.

So now she was here—

"Hey, stranger. Twice in one week, what're the chances."

Swinging around, she smiled. "Hi, Shuli—oh, wow."

The guy was in a set of red silk PJs and coordinating silk robe, a pair of monogrammed velvet slippers peeking out under the hemmed bottoms. He also had a medical supply cane braced against the floor, and as he came closer, his limp was such that he probably shouldn't have been out of whatever bed he'd been assigned. His hair, which was usually styled with a swoop, had been combed back wet, straight from his aristocratic face, as if he was fresh out of the shower.

He certainly smelled that way, some kind of expensive cologne or shaving cream wafting toward her.

"Like my hospital duds?" He went to do a little turn, but then winced and seemed to rethink the effort. "My *doggen* brought them in."

"Very spiffy."

His handsome face tightened. "You're not here to see me, are you."

"Oh, of course I am. I heard my father—"

"Got me and L.W. out of the field."

"Yes, that's right."

Shuli took a deep breath. "He's right in there. The door you're standing in front of."

Before Bitty could say anything to make it look less like she'd come uninvited to see a male she really had no business visiting, Shuli smiled.

"I'm going to get back in bed. The break room's enticements are not as enticing as I thought they'd be. Fucking Percocet. Always messes my stomach up."

The fighter continued muttering about how he'd prefer a bottle of bourbon as he headed into the patient room next door.

And then she was by herself.

Before anybody else came along—although it wasn't like this whole thing wasn't being recorded anyway—she knocked on the door.

"Yeah?" came the deep voice on the other side.

"It's . . . um, me. Bitty?"

There was a pause, and yup, it was entirely possible L.W. was going to send her packing. Except then she heard something that sounded a lot like—

"So I can come in?" she asked.

"Yeah. I'm waiting."

Pushing inside, she had a quick visual of the hospital bed he was on, the vitals monitor he was plugged into, and the IV bag that was tubed into his arm. And then it was all about the male who was lying back on those pale blue and white sheets: L.W. had no top on, his tattoos and his muscles out of place on the pristine bedding, not because he was dirty, but because he was the kind of thing that looked like it would sleep on a bed of nails.

There were a lot of bandages. On his shoulder. On his side.

And his eyes were not as focused as they usually were. They were still that beautiful pale green, though, and they were, as usual, on her.

"I just wanted to make sure you were okay?" She hesitated. "I don't mean to intrude or anything."

L.W. shook his head and shrugged with his hands. "You're not. What'm I doing here. Just marking time until all this is fixed."

"You're not stitched up?"

"Not yet. Manny says I need surgery. My liver's leaking or something. I didn't pay a lot of attention to it. He'll take care of me soon enough."

His sentences were short, likely because even with the drugs, he was in pain. Other than that ever so subtle shift in speech, though, you'd never know he was so badly injured.

"You're so brave about being cut open." She winced. "Okay, that was a stupid thing to say. I mean, if I were facing surgery, I'd be terrified—"

Shut up, Bitty.

The smile that hit L.W.'s face was . . . transformative, making him look closer to his actual age. As opposed to something that was ancient and tired of the world.

"It's all right," he said. "I've gone under. The knife a lot of times. With Manny. He's amazing. I'm really not. Worried about it."

As she smiled back at him, she . . .

Ran the hell out of things to say. Damn it, she really could have used a game plan for this. All of that Resolve2Evolve stuff, about expressing her truth (she was so glad he was okay), claiming her space (she was not going to be embarrassed for coming to see him), and being confident (she was staring at his bare, tattooed chest, and that was not the kind of confidence that seemed appropriate in this situation), did not appear to be helping her much.

What she really needed was practical advice. Like how not to say something stupid about being scared of surgery to a patient with a hole in their liver.

Or whatever was wrong with him.

God, why did she and Nalla have to fall out? Nalla always gave great advice—

"You could sit down," L.W. said as he pointed to the comfy chair in the corner. "And keep me company. Until they come to get me. If you want. Won't be much longer. Only about twenty minutes or so."

Bitty started to smile. Maybe she wasn't doing as badly as she thought she was.

"I'll do that," she murmured as she went over and sat down. "I'm happy to help take your mind off things."

Those eyes grew hooded as he stared across at her. "Oh, you do that. Always."

◆   ◆   ◆

As Nalla stepped out of Nate's log cabin, she glanced around at the snow-covered landscape. There was a set of tire tracks into the property and then back out again, and footprints around the entry, but other than that, nothing was disturbed, and she scented nothing.

Well, nothing that smelled like baby powder and sweaty death. She did catch a whiff of burned something or another. Not a chimney, but something else bonfire-ish. Which wasn't dangerous.

Just the kind of thing that made her nose wrinkle.

Walking forward, she made like she had somewhere to go. And she did. Kind of.

"Fuck," she muttered as she stopped and looked up at the sky.

There were no stars out, the sky dense with clouds. More snow? Sure, why not—

Holy hell, the center of her chest hurt, and those eggs had been a really bad idea. Putting her hand on her stomach, she wondered whether she was going to throw up now or wait until she was off his land. Spoiled for choice on that one.

Closing her eyes, she told herself to get a grip. She wasn't getting a divorce, for fuck's sake. She had been on two dates—not even, really— with a male she was powerfully attracted to, who had a very bad past, through no fault of his own, and who had his mind scrambled at the moment. If she couldn't keep herself together just because they hadn't parted with a declaration of eternal love? Then she needed counseling.

Except maybe she should have stayed? But he'd seemed so stiff and uncomfortable. And there wasn't another room to go into, other than the bath.

She glanced over her shoulder. Should she go back and try to talk to him?

If she could just find the right words . . .

Crap, maybe Bitty was right, and she really did need to work on herself. What had that tagline been? Resolve2Evolve? She could use a little evolution at the moment, thank you very much.

As she pictured herself going back to Luchas House and pretending Everything Was Just Great with the staff, she really wished that she could text her best friend to meet up at their real home. After two pints of ice cream and some ancient *The Office* reruns together, probably she wouldn't feel like her life was over.

She missed Bitty. A lot. And the fact that she couldn't call the female and ask for advice about Nate really made Nalla feel like a shithead. Why had she thought she'd had all the answers? Who cared about some kind of social media program? Here Nalla herself was, standing in the snow out in the cold, while portions of a conversation she was never going to have with a male she really cared about were circling like vultures over the dead bodies of her previous sense of optimism and excitement.

Like she had any better answers for life's problems than that guru . . . ?

The sound of the cabin's door opening behind her was a surprise, and as she turned around—

Nate was standing barefoot on the cabin's stoop, and before she could say anything, he started striding toward her, through the snow.

"Oh, my God, your feet, you'll get frostbite—"

"I'm sorry," he said as he walked right up and put his arms around her.

There wasn't even a hesitation on Nalla's part. She grabbed on to his shoulders and held on tight.

"You don't have to explain," she said roughly. "This . . . is all I need right now."

Closing her eyes, she turned her head so that her ear was over his heart. And as she listened to the steady beat, tears came, but she kept them to herself. Mostly.

Nate pulled back and cupped her face in his broad palms. "I want to see you again. Whenever you're up for it. Nothing's changed on my end."

As his thumbs brushed her cheeks, she knew she was going to remember how he looked in this moment for the rest of her life, so vital, so beautiful in the darkness . . . a mystery she didn't have to solve to accept. To love.

"Me, too," she vowed. "This is a start, not an end."

"I'm gonna be honest, I really have no idea what I'm doing."

She laughed. "I'm in the woods, too. So we can be lost together, okay?"

"Together."

The smile that came over his face made her feel like the sky was full of twinkling stars, and all of them were shining just for the pair of them— and that was true, on the other side of the dampening cloud cover.

Which, just like an awkward moment between two people at the start of a relationship, would pass.

And then Nate grew serious. "I'm promising you, right now, that I won't let anything come between us. Not even myself, okay? I haven't wanted to confront my shit, because I haven't needed to—but my past is not going to cost us a future. Deal?"

"Deal." She lifted her lips. "As long as we can kiss on it."

It was a request she did not have to make twice, and when they finally came up for air, she touched the side of his face and thought about how much she really didn't want to leave.

"You could stay a little longer," he murmured. "Plus . . . oh, my God, I have cold feet—and not in a relationship way. So I really might need some help getting back inside."

"Well, what do you know . . . there's no place I'd rather be. And no one I'd rather be with."

On that note, she tucked herself under one of his arms and hitched a hold around his waist. As they started back for the cabin, he kissed the top of her head.

"At least it's only a couple of yards and you don't have to carry me all the way this time."

She glanced up at him. "But I could if I had to."

"And I'd do the same for you."

CHAPTER FORTY-THREE

The following evening, after the sun went down and it was safe to go outside, Nate walked Nalla to the front door of his cabin. This time, they were both wearing appropriate footwear, and they stepped out together, him letting her go first, her waiting for him on the other side. As he shut things behind them, he was sporting the kind of half smile a male did when he'd thoroughly satisfied his female.

"You sure you want me back again tonight?" she said to him.

Hell yeah, he thought.

"Never surer. And the sooner the better."

"Then I'm going to go home and get some clothes."

"Perfect."

Unable to resist, Nate pulled her into him and kissed her properly. And then, before he couldn't let her leave without getting some more time with her in his bed, he stepped back—and reminded his sex drive that she wouldn't be gone long.

"I'll be here." Probably waiting for her on the porch like a dog. "And there's no rush."

"I'll be back."

"Okay, Terminator."

He watched her close her eyes to concentrate, and just as she disappeared, he whispered, "I love you."

When he turned away, it was a lot easier going back underground, knowing that he wasn't going to be alone for long—and when he hit the lower level and he heard his burner phone start ringing, he imagined it was the Brotherhood calling to tell him it was okay, he could go back out into the field.

Except of course that wasn't it. For one, they didn't officially have that number and the phone they had given him hadn't been charged in how long? For another, he might be making all kinds of changes personally, but damned if they knew about it.

Grabbing the burner from his jacket, he hovered his finger over the screen, and debated letting things go to voicemail. But Uncle had already left him two messages he'd ignored, and considering the organized crime shit was the only job he had now?

"Yeah," he answered. And he already knew what it was about.

He'd promised to give the guy a body so that Mickey's mom could have something to bury. Too bad he didn't feel like killing anyone right now.

See? He was totally improving his self.

There was a series of beeps as the encrypted line bounced all over the world. Then a tone came across the connection that made it impossible to record the voice on the other end of the line. After the Mission Impossible crap was done cycling through, Uncle was in a characteristically cheerful and easygoing mood.

j/k.

"Where the *fuck* have you been," the man said.

"Nowhere."

"So why didn't you answer my calls."

"Because I'm not your fucking relative." Nate switched to his other ear, and pinned the cell in place with his shoulder. Like he was going to need both his hands to strangle the guy. "Do you have an assignment for me. Or not."

The silence was supposed to be threatening. But when Nate didn't press for an answer, Uncle started talking again.

"We're sending you pictures from Bathe's security footage."

"Name and address."

"Don't have it. He's weird-looking, though, and my boys say they've seen him downtown on the streets."

"You don't have any kind of name at all?"

"You'll find him—"

"Hold up. You want me to do a job and you're giving me nothing but images to go on? What do you think Caldwell is, a small town?"

"That's not my problem. You murdered my nephew—"

"Who was a deadweight you hated and came to kill me on my own property."

"—in cold blood. You owe me this. You're gonna find the bastard I send you and put him to sleep, and then we're even. You pass this up or fail? I'm gonna settle our score the way my family takes care of things like this."

The connection went dead.

"Well, aren't you a fucking tough guy," Nate muttered as he put the damn phone down on the counter.

Instead of doing the dishes from his and Nalla's second round of eggs and bacon, he went over to his gun safe, leaned down for the retina scan, and opened up the fireproof interior. It was always a good idea to check your weapons, especially when one of Caldwell's black market kingpins was getting his panties in a wad, and you had a guest you really, truly cared about on your property. Nate had never been paranoid-private about where he lived, and now he regretted that.

If Mickey had been able to find him, Uncle would, too.

As a tingling in his upper jaw signaled his fangs descending, a sound he'd never heard before vibrated up his chest and out of his mouth.

The growl was a reminder that bonded males were next-level un-hinged, when it came to protecting their females—

Bing!

As that stupid fucking burner phone went off with a text, he would have used it for target practice, except for the fact that it was the way he was going to stay connected with Nalla when they weren't together.

With absolutely no interest at all, he opened the message from Uncle's encrypted number—

It was an image, a black-and-white still that, given its graininess, had indeed been taken off video footage.

"Oh . . . fuck."

With another grim curse, he expanded the close-up, even though he didn't need to.

He knew who the person was, recognized instantly the scarred face of the target Uncle wanted him to kill to make things right between them.

Zsadist . . . Nalla's father.

◆   ◆   ◆

Back at the Brotherhood's underground residences, Nalla was hesitating at the door to her family's quarters, her hand hovering over the latch. Even with all the tension lately, there was something unnatural about not sharing what was going on in her life. Except Nate was a complicated subject.

If the word "complicated" could be used in a bad-as-an-H-bomb kind of way.

Bracing herself, she opened things—and was stupidly shocked that there was nothing out of place in the living room. But like all their inter-personal chaos translated to couches and chairs?

After a long moment, she found herself going over to her father's baby grand Steinway. There was a guitar on a stand in the corner be-hind it, as well as a violin set in a wall mount, and some harmonicas sitting on a shelf. Sheet music was stacked on a side table, but her sire never really used it. His mind, he always said, "saw" the music without the notes.

And he truly did have the voice of an angel.

As she remembered the times he had sung her to sleep as a young, her eyes flooded with tears. Of all the divides she had ever expected to come to, choosing a male over her family was not something she had anticipated.

Except if she doubted her painful choice—and she didn't—this place here no longer felt like home. Nate's basement did. And that was less about what was in a given space, and everything about who was with you when you were in it.

Taking a deep breath, she caught a whiff of bread baking and had to smile. Clandestine, contraband sourdough. Her *mahmen* had taught herself how to bake bread for no particular reason, and Bella liked to practice from time to time—but she had to be careful. Fritz felt like any cooking efforts beyond toasting an English muffin were a referendum on the job he was doing for the Brotherhood, so the female had to time her forays into the gluten when she knew that the butler would be otherwise occupied.

She also tended to bake when she was upset.

Walking over to the doorway into the kitchen, Nalla studied her *mahmen*, who was at the counter by the sink. Bella was uncovering a bowl and investigating the rising that was going on, so distracted that she was unaware she was not alone anymore. Her mahogany hair was pulled back, and she was wearing jeans and an Irish knit sweater that Cormia had made her the previous year. Her earrings were the long, dangly silver ones that Nalla had given her for her birthday.

Just as Nalla was going to announce herself, her *mahmen* scooped the dough out onto the floured cutting board. Then she dipped her hands into the Gold Medal bag, and clapped them to make sure she had the right amount of—

Clap.

Clap.

The instant the sounds were made, those the palms meeting sharply, Nalla was back with Nate, watching him struggle with what was real and what was in his mind.

And then her *mahmen* came into focus so sharply, Nalla's eyes teared up.

At the same time, Bella glanced over her shoulder and jumped. "Oh! Oh. Ah, hi. You're home—I mean, here. Hi."

Years filtered through in a matter of moments, times when Nalla had seen her parents together, her *mahmen's* worried eyes passing over her father's face . . . over the black band that was tattooed around his neck. She remembered her *mahmen's* hands, gently soothing, always under the table or behind his back, so there was no attention drawn. There had also been the abrupt departures from the dining table in the communal space here, that were covered up with a smile and a comment from Bella, Zsadist going first, her lingering so that it didn't look like what it was, him having to leave because he couldn't handle something.

Nalla recalled the times, during the day, when everything had been silent and still, and she'd seen the light on under their door and heard low, serious murmurings.

And then at her work, whether at Luchas House or when she'd first started training at Safe Place, she remembered Bella reaching out to Mary, and Mary pulling out of meetings to take a phone call from her dear friend.

Always about Nalla's father, who suffered with dignity, and battled demons that were not of his own creation.

"Nalla? Are you okay?"

As she tried to respond, her eyes clung to her *mahmen's* face, and she saw what was familiar: Concern, worry. Stress. About someone the female loved with all her heart . . . who she didn't know how to help.

With a choked sob, Nalla rushed across the kitchen, disturbing the chairs tucked into the four-top table they ate at when they were just being together as a family.

The three of them. Sharing a meal.

She threw her arms around Bella and ducked her head as she'd done as a young, and there was no hesitation. She was instantly embraced in return, her hair smoothed by her *mahmen*'s hand.

"It's okay," Bella said. "Oh, sweetheart, it's okay, whatever it is, I'm here."

"I'm so sorry." Nalla took a shuddering breath. "Oh, I've been an—"

"Can you tell me what's wrong?"

Nalla pulled back. "I'm so sorry you had to watch him suffer all these years. I had no idea . . . what you've been through."

The shock that came over those familiar features was a terrible commentary on the selfishness of a young. It was as if Bella had never expected the understanding she offered to so many to be returned.

"And I . . ." Nalla's voice cracked. "I know you were there for me, too. I just had no comprehension about what it's like to see someone you love go to a place you can't pull them out of. A place where they were hurt when they were young. A place . . . that haunts them everywhere they go. I am so sorry, *mahmen*."

Putting her palm over her mouth, she couldn't believe the things she'd said to Bella at Luchas House.

"It's all right." Bella took her over to the table and sat her down, keeping their hands clasped. "You don't have to apologize—"

"I do. I was wrong. I didn't get it because I've never known anything different than you being there for Father and me feeling like my problems were never as important—but compared to his, they *weren't* that big. Jesus, I'm such an ass—"

"Hey, stop that." Bella took a napkin out of the holder and passed it over. "We all are doing the best we can. And I did try to support you, too, I really did—"

As a fresh wave of tears came, it was nice timing on the mop-up. "I know."

She lost it then, really lost it. Pressing the napkin into her eyes, she just let go because she didn't have a choice—and when the wave passed, and she finally lowered her hands from her face, her *mahmen* was right there. Still.

Always.

"Can you tell me what brought this on?" came the gentle prompt.

Nalla got herself another blotter. "I . . . spent the day with Nate, and he woke up from a dream—a nightmare, but he was still in it. He looked at me and didn't see me. He was back . . . in a lab somewhere. They were hurting him—and his voice was that of a young. Oh, *mahmen*, it was awful."

Bella's eyes closed and she shook her head. "I had heard about his rescue. Murhder and Sarah got him out of there. It was right before his transition. If they hadn't gotten there in time, he most certainly would have died."

"He said that his *mahmen* was killed there?"

"Well, as I understand, she escaped and died much later of complications. But the humans killed her for sure. Nate and his adoptive parents have kept it all kind of private—and I know he's struggled. I can't say I'm surprised his sleep is disturbed."

"I was trying to wake him, but I couldn't get through to him. And then he ended up cowering in a corner . . . he didn't recognize me. At all." She glanced over at the bread dough. "You helped, though."

"I did?"

"I remembered when I'd wake up, in the middle of the day to hear Father shouting in his sleep. And then I'd hear you clap, twice."

Bella nodded gravely. "Yes, that's what's worked for me. If I want to get him out of it. Must be something about the sound forcing the brain to focus on the present."

"You really, truly helped me."

"Good, I'm glad. And I'm glad you were there for Nate." Bella looked around the kitchen, as if she were picturing people in it, her eyes lingering in different places. But given her grave expression, she wasn't actually seeing anything of the tidy white cupboards and the butcher-block counters. "As for your father and me, when it comes to his past, we really didn't want you to see behind his curtain, as he calls it. He's worked so hard on himself, and now, for a lot of nights and days, what was done to him is really not forefront in his mind. Others, though? It comes back. When I think about where he and I started? He's a different male. But it's always going to be there, lurking."

Nalla nodded. "Yes."

"And he never wanted you to see him as anything other than your father. He didn't want you to feel like you had to take care of him, or worry that he couldn't protect us."

"I never thought that."

"Good. Because he's always there for the people he loves, his Brothers . . . the King and Beth and L.W. Your father is a male of worth, and I try not to get in the middle of you two, but he loves you, he really does. And this distance is just killing him."

Well, didn't that bring a fresh wave of the weepies on, so there was some more sniffing and patting on Nalla's part, her eyes burning, her throat raw. Yet there was an easiness between her and her *mahmen* that had never existed before.

Then again, they had something in common. They both loved survivors, which was a special kind of bond with someone else.

The mutual respect was also something that happened when you started to see a parent as a person, with a life that started before you, and would continue after you left the house to make your own home. When they were only your *mahmen*, they owed you everything. When they were more than that, you recognized you were an important part of a larger whole for them.

"So you must be pretty serious with Nate?" Bella asked.

"It's happening fast. And yet it feels so right."

"Bonding can be like that. And you know, from personal experience, I can tell you that love makes a difference in people like your father and Nate. Be careful, though. Sometimes the damage does go too deep—

and I'm not saying this out of disapproval or judgment. It's just because I love you. With your father and me, it worked out. I wasn't consumed by his pain, even though you're right, it is a big part of my life and always will be. You have to also take care of yourself, though. Sometimes, what is damaged is ruined, and there's no going back from that."

Even a night ago, the tender words would have been a red cape to rush at.

Not anymore.

Nalla nodded again. "I understand."

"Do you love him?"

She had to smile. "Are we doing *Moonstruck* here?"

Bella cracked a laugh. "I think so. But I'm not going to tell you it's too bad if you do."

"Good. Because I think I do love him."

"I'm really happy for you."

The two of them held hands for a long moment. Except then both their smiles faded.

"I don't think so," Bella said . . . because she'd read Nalla's mind. "Nate's given your father and the Brotherhood a run for the money these last few decades, and with everything else that's going on with the war, that's hard to forgive, harder to forget."

"But maybe if he gets to know Nate? Maybe he can see what I do. Nate isn't just what he's done in the past, and God, if anyone should be given a second chance, it's him, considering what was done to him by those humans. Father's *got* to see that, got to believe that."

"I don't doubt anything you're saying. But again, it's been three decades of Nate being a liability—" Bella held her palm up like she expected an argument. "I'm just talking about his actions. I'm not maligning him as a male."

Nalla exhaled slowly. "I don't know what he did, but I'm not going to dispute facts."

Bella smiled a little. "You have turned a corner."

"I have. And so has Nate. And I really don't want to have to choose between the male I love and the father who raised me, whose blood is in my veins."

Bella's look got serious. "I also hope that's not what it comes down to."

When there was a long silence, Nalla said, "But . . ."

Yeah, except where could she go with any arguments on that front? If her father wasn't going to listen or even give Nate an opportunity to prove he was pulling his act together, there was no hope.

"I know my *hellren*, unfortunately." Bella shook her head. "And you may not like the way he loves you, and he may not be perfect, but when it comes to his daughter, he's not going to compromise, even if that means losing you."

Tears blurred Nalla's vision. "I don't want that. I don't want to choose."

Her *mahmen* closed her eyes like she was bracing herself for a cold wind. "I don't want you to, either. And I'll do whatever I can to support you and Nate—as long as that male really does gather his own reins and turn his attitude and actions around. He needs to prove himself to me, too, but at least I'm willing to give him a chance."

"Thank you. I feel like it's more than I deserve."

Bella smiled. "You deserve every happiness in life, Nalla. I love you so much that I can't put it into words. And I truly am glad you and Nate found each other."

Yes, there was an asterisk in that statement, but Nalla had meant what she'd said. She wasn't going to argue and she was done with the pushing. Besides, what was that saying? The proof was going to be in the pudding.

"You know what . . ." she murmured. "I think I've grown up a hundred years since I left the house the other night. And it was way overdue."

Resolve2Evolve.

Not a bad tagline, after all.

Now, if she could just get her father to not want to kill the male she was in love with. Maybe they'd start and build from there—

Oh, fucking hell, who was she kidding. Her father had made up his mind.

And no matter what Nate did or didn't do, it was going to take an act of Lassiter to change it.

CHAPTER FORTY-FOUR

M iles away, in the Brotherhood's training center, Shuli made another trip to the break room. As he pushed open the door and eyed the array of vending machines, he didn't go over to the chips and bullshit. He also looked past the hot fare buffet, which was shut down, and the bowls of fresh fruit, which he would rather die than eat—because fuck vitamin C and fiber—and instead focused on the male who was sitting in one of the armchairs under the muted TV.

L.W. was looking like the cushion under his ass was full of cut glass, his limbs at odd angles, his torso shifted to one side, his lips tight as a line drawing. He was wearing a pair of surgical scrubs bottoms, his tattooed chest on display, the bandage at his side suggesting that his interior had gotten the help it needed.

"Should you be out of bed?" Shuli headed over to one of the machines after all and decided a Snickers really would satisfy. "Weren't you just on the operating table."

As the candy bar thunked into the well, the future King said, "Why are you looking all Hugh Hefner up in here."

"I have standards."

"Yeah, and they're fucked up."

"Just because you choose needles and ink and I like silk doesn't mean we can't agree on something."

"What's that."

Shuli nodded at the television and then walked across to sit in the chair next to the male. "Homer Simpson is comfort food for the brain."

L.W. looked up at the TV, too. Then nodded.

And this was no doubt the only thing they'd have a consensus on.

Unwrapping the Snickers, Shuli wondered whether he was going to wade into waters he had no business swimming in. Then he thought . . . *fuck it.*

"So you had a visitor for a while there, huh." When there was no reply, Shuli paused with the chewing. "Listen, I'm not trying to tell you your business—"

"Great, so shut the hell up—"

"—but Bitty's a female of worth."

Brows crashed down over those pale green eyes, and for a moment, Shuli measured the distance to the exit—and wondered if he could outrun the guy. Probably.

Maybe.

Okay, fine, he was going to have to punch that surgical wound first and then pray to Lassiter that his velvet slippers had more tread on them than he remembered.

"I'm not in competition with you." He put his palm forward. "So relax, tiger. I just—she's not like Mharta. She's not the type who's going to ride one night and walk off the next."

"I'm *not* having this conversation."

"Yeah, we are. And I don't care if you kick my ass. Some things need to be said—and I'm not the only one who'll come after you if you behave like an ass. Nalla will fuck you up."

Those brows got even lower. "How is she involved."

Shuli laughed. "You don't want to mess with that one. The apple does not fall far from the Z tree. I thought she was going to put a cap in the asses of my idiot buddies at Bathe. She will protect her friend, and although I don't particularly care for you or about you, I feel duty bound to warn you about that."

L.W. glanced back up to Homer and his donuts. "There's nothing going on between me and Bitty."

Yeah, right. "Okay, sure."

"Don't you have to go do your hair?"

"Yup." Shuli got to his feet. "As always, it's been soooo good talking to you. I can't tell you how *much* I enjoy these little interludes—"

The door into the break room opened, and when they saw who it was, they both cursed under their breath: The great Blind King was the first to enter, his service dog at his side—and the entire Black Dagger Brotherhood was with him. One by one, the huge males filled the space, the whole training center, with the force of their presences.

"Man, if I'm getting permanently fired," Shuli muttered, "do they all have to witness the pink slip?"

"If a vote's required," L.W. said with equal quiet, "I'm a yes."

"Good, I'm glad you're keeping me—"

"Fucking never. I'm a no."

"So you don't want to fire me. Great—"

"That's not what I mean—*fuck* you—"

"Fuck *you.*"

When the King stopped, they quit the bickering and Shuli bowed low even though the male couldn't see him—and he stayed down as he waited to be addressed: Sure, he was an asshole, but he had been raised right in the *glymera.*

He wasn't a savage.

"My Lord," he said.

"Stop staring at your loafers," the King said with characteristic impatience. Then those wraparounds shifted over to L.W.'s direction. "How you feeling, son."

"Fine."

When there was only silence, Shuli tennis-matched the two, bathing in all the father/son bonding. Not. But then the focus was on him again, and he got himself good and braced.

"And you, Shuli?"

"Good, yup." He took a deep breath. "Listen, I can clean out my locker down here and get my shit—"

"Why would you do that?"

"I—ah." He glanced at all the serious faces and wondered why he had to say it out loud: Clearly, his suspension had just become permanent, because he'd violated his time-out in the field. "Well, I'm figuring you all didn't come here just to see if I was up on my feet."

"You're right about that." Wrath's voice lowered as he switched into the Old Language. "*You have honored your bloodline by protecting mine own, your act of courage deeming you worthy of reward and the restitution of your position within our fighting ranks.*"

Shuli looked down at L.W. Who looked back.

Blink. Blink. Fucking blink.

As Homer started running around in circles—kind of like Shuli's brain—the King continued, "*Further, in recognition of your bravery, and your willingness to sacrifice yourself upon the field of combat for the benefit of mine own blooded son, I hereby confer unto you the role of* ahstrux nohtrum, *in favor of him*—"

"Wait, what?" L.W. burst up from his chair—or tried to. He wobbled and grabbed his side. "*Fuck*—"

Before Shuli could think better of it, he lunged across and caught the male.

"Will you get off me—"

"Jesus Christ, I'm just trying to keep you from face-planting—"

"I don't need the help—"

"Well, I didn't want to give it to you anyway—"

"Then what the *fuck* are you doing holding my arm!"

The collective laughter that broke out reminded Shuli of what Rhage had sounded like the night before in the cop car. Only this time, the ripple was in stereo, every one of the Brothers chiming in with a yuck-yuck'ing.

"*The honor of this position is conferred upon you by mine hand, and shall be marked in the appropriate manner.*" Abruptly, Wrath switched back to English. "You saved my son last night. I am personally in your debt."

L.W. shook his head. "You got it wrong. I saved *him*."

Wrath looked over at his son. "Yeah, you did. And if his sire were still alive, he'd feel the way I do right now. Grateful."

"So send Shuli a fucking fruit basket. You do *not* need to saddle me with him for the rest of my life."

"It's done. This is how I want it."

The expression on the younger Wrath's face was a clear warning to anybody who could see it. But Shuli had a feeling that even if the King's eyes had been working, he wouldn't have given a shit.

Immovable object, meet unstoppable force.

Well, wasn't Last Meal going to be just *great* at their house, Shuli thought.

Except then the implications hit him.

With dawning horror, he looked over at the male next to him. Oh . . . shit. Was he going to have to live with L.W.?

And get a tattoo on his *face*?

◆   ◆   ◆

Wrath really didn't care that his son had a hair across his ass.

When his brothers had reported what Shuli had done, he'd asked them to repeat the name of the fighter who had run into all those *less-ers* to make sure L.W. got out alive. And then he'd needed a second try at the whole story.

Except it was undeniable: Shuli had proven himself in the old-school way. Lip service was all well and good, but when you were willing to put your own blood down at the foot of the enemy, to protect another? Well, that was the interview for a job Wrath hadn't even realized he wanted to fill.

The fact that the two couldn't stand each other? That hadn't made a difference the previous night, and it wasn't going to change anything going forward.

And L.W. had gone back for the aristocrat, too.

"I can take care of myself," his son snapped.

"I didn't say you couldn't."

The reality was, after Wrath had gone up to the Sanctuary, the thirty years he'd lost was in his blood, sure as if his body had gone through the time that had passed all at once. And the breadth of what his *shellan* and his brothers had been through, what Rahvyn and Lassiter had done, was hanging heavy on him—and he was going to do everything he could to avoid that kind of shit in the future.

If something happened to his son? His and Beth's lives were over. And by extension, so were everybody else's. Again.

So, yes, he was going to pair up this aristocrat with his heir. There were better soldiers, certainly. But technical skills weren't the only thing that mattered when you were in the field. Having that heart, that kind of grit, was nothing you could teach. It was the kind of thing a fighter just had.

The fact that it was in an aristocrat was a surprise, although that was the way life was. Revelations came, for the good and the bad. How you reacted was a measure of your character—and he loved his son enough to give him what Wrath knew in his marrow was the right kind of bodyguard.

"Vishous, you'll follow up with the inking." Not a request. "Have a good evening, you two."

Before he left, he wanted to hug his son. But he was learning that L.W. wasn't about the clinches. That was fine. They'd had that one embrace up in the study of the mansion when Wrath had come back to the planet. That was enough for now.

It was going to have to be enough.

On his command, George led him back through the break room, the golden brushing against his thigh to take him around furniture and other objects. Behind him, the shitkickers of the Brotherhood were a quiet chant of strength, the powerful bodies in his wake falling into line out of both devotion and duty.

As someone jumped ahead and opened the door for him, Wrath turned to the right out of muscle memory. Except they didn't live in the mansion anymore, so there was no need to hit the tunnel.

He stopped and pivoted to face his private guard. As he flared his nostrils, he separated the individual scents, filing them in his mind, picturing what he knew his brothers looked like.

He thought of his time with Lassiter up above. And the message that as much as a King might want to go into the field and go hands-on with the enemy, the throne needed to be filled—and it was. By the right male for the job.

He'd never expected that angel to be an asset. But yeah, he definitely thought the Scribe Virgin had chosen her successor well. The holder of that position was supposed to be the counselor to the King—and who knew the angel had common sense after all?

"You okay?" Tohr asked quietly.

All at once, the conviction that things were falling into place after a long period of painful discord made him take a deep, easy breath.

"It's good to be back," Wrath said.

There was a short silence. And then a rumbling vibration that moved the air.

The Black Dagger Brotherhood's war cry exploded in the corridor, the voices of the males around him swearing, once again, their loyalty to the King they loved and the species they served.

United, as one.

Fearless, as always.

Behind the Wrath who stood before them . . . forevermore.

CHAPTER FORTY-FIVE

Evan used the tunnel a little before midnight.

And his strides had purpose in them as they'd taken him away from the office building.

He was in the same clothes he'd been wearing during the melee—and then afterward, when the trainer had taken the last part of who he had once been from him. The shirt showed the damage that had been done, but his skin had reknitted. And as for any bullet wounds? They were all healed, the punctures closed as if they had never been.

He guessed that the lead slugs were still in him. He didn't know where and didn't think about it anymore as he walked forward through the steel-encased chute.

After Lash had left him in that other basement, he'd dragged himself out and found the car, then gone back to Mickey's apartment to take care of the dead woman on the chair. After releasing her from her binds, he'd wrapped her in his cousin's comforter and cradled her in his arms like she was just really sick and needed a doctor.

Except there had been no explanation to nosy humans required. The back stairs had been empty and he'd sat the body up in the front seat of Mickey's beater, belting her in. With grim resolve, he'd driven out to the sticks and dumped her in the old quarry.

As the splash resounded and her bloated body floated to the surface, she had stared up at him as he'd stood on the lip of the thirty-foot drop.

She'd called him stupid for not weighing her down.

"I want you to be found," he'd shouted at her. "Your husband's gotta know."

It had been as he'd turned around and walked back into the forest—once again heading out to the car he'd parked on the side of a country road—that the pieces had started to fall together. And the fight last night was the key to everything coming together.

Uncle's favorite enforcer was a vampire.

Nathaniel was the enemy.

The signs had been there all along, Evan just hadn't noticed them, because who screened members of Uncle's inner circle for being another fucking species? Especially when you didn't even know there was one threaded throughout the shadows of the human world.

But the clues were so obvious now: The enforcer had never been seen during the daytime—not unusual, given his line of work, but he'd even failed to show at a couple of the family's funerals. Stupid move, if he wanted to advance. He'd also rarely left Caldwell—and if he did, it was only to NYC or Boston—something that suggested he had other business in the zip code . . . or couldn't be exposed to daylight during travel. He was capable of things no one else had ever gotten away with. A one hundred percent success rate over a decade? Never a police investigation, never in the news, not one complication with a human?

No girlfriends or wives. No associates. Never hung out with the others.

No ambition, either. He just wanted to kill.

On balance, what were the chances a human acted like that? None. There were a hundred people in the organization and nobody was like that bastard.

But now that he knew for sure vampires existed, and he'd seen them in action . . . what were the chances one had infiltrated Uncle's ranks and was just looking for targets like he was practicing at a range—

Evan stopped, and looked around.

What was that buzzing sound . . . ?

"Just a fly," he muttered as he kept going.

When he got to the end of the tunnel, he entered the code that he still didn't consciously know on the pad, and emerged into the shitty apartment.

He was greeted by a gun in his face.

Man, that woman was looking rough. The head wound he'd given her was still festering, but there were other holes in her now, including one at the side of her neck that seemed like it should be fatal. If she were alive in the first place.

"Where the fuck you go," she snapped.

There was black oil all over the floor, hers—and from the bedroom behind, two other females appeared. Both were sporting injuries, too, just not as dire, and he recognized the one on the left from the night before. He'd seen her in the middle of all the fighting.

"I'm here to deliver on my promise," he said.

Those strangely colored eyes narrowed on him and before the woman he'd stolen from could speak, he glanced at the pair in the doorway.

"I have a vampire for you." And he didn't care who killed it. "No one knows where he lives but me. He's been in the human world, that's how I ran into him, and I didn't guess what he was back then. I'm sure now, though. I can deliver a kill to you that will get the master's attention— and that's what you want, right. When you go to those meetings and you stand in the crowd, you picture yourself more important than you are now. And how does that happen? You prove yourself."

It was the Mickey syndrome. They were all just like his cousin—and he certainly wasn't going to bring up how Mickey had ended up.

Not that he cared what happened to these three. As long as he could bring Nathaniel's body to Uncle—and then kill that old bastard himself, that was all that mattered.

That gun slowly lowered. "Tell me more," the woman growled.

CHAPTER FORTY-SIX

Nalla felt lighter as she re-formed next to Nate's log cabin, her corporeal body floating like snow falling when the flakes were big and happy and there was no wind, just spin, spin, spin. In fact, she all but skipped to the front door—and there her male was, opening things up, holding his arms out.

She squealed as she jumped into him and was caught, and oh yeah, he was solid as a mountain—and the way his mouth found hers? It was like they'd been separated for thirty years instead of three hours.

But time was relative, wasn't it.

They kissed their way backwards through the door and all the way down the stairs, and as they flopped on the bed, the over-day bag she'd brought with her got tossed aside in favor of all kinds of clothes disappearing. And then she was naked and stretched out, and he was naked and poised over her.

Except he didn't mount her.

"Look at you," he said as the scent of his bonding flooded her senses. "You know something . . ."

"What?" she said.

"A female like you needs to be worshipped."

Nate backed up, and pulled her down with him so that her lower legs were hanging off the end of the bed. When he knelt before her, she knew what was coming, and thankfully, she was already flat on her back.

Because the thought of where he was going with that mouth of his? Her legs went weak.

"I want to taste you," he murmured as he parted her thighs.

As she moaned, his lips were a soft brushing on the inside of her knee, and the higher the butterfly kisses went, the more antsy and desperate she got, and the more she wanted him to keep her in this aching anticipation. She was writhing as he finally sealed his mouth on her sex, and the explosion of sensation as hot and wet met hot and wet was so intense, she orgasmed right against his lips.

Which going by his growl of satisfaction was clearly what he'd intended.

With his hands reaching up and capturing her breasts, he stayed where he was, penetrating her with his tongue, making her feel so good that she forgot where she was—while she knew exactly who she was with.

When he finally eased back, he wiped his hand across his chin and mouth, then licked up his own palm. After that, it was on. Still holding her thighs wide, he went into her sex with his erection, spearing her in a powerful thrust that made her cry out.

The rhythm was relentless, his face tight with harsh lines of need as he rode her. To keep from being pushed down the bed, she wrapped her legs around him and linked her ankles behind his ass. All she could do was hold on, her hands fisting the covers, a slapping sound rising up from where he pumped into her core. Looming over her, in a magnificent display, she watched his full-body tattoo move over his muscles as they flexed and released to the beat of his wild movements.

The vines and the snakes and the clouds were alive.

For a moment, what she knew about the tattoo—its origins and purpose—threatened to pull her out of the moment. But his past was going to be with them always, and she'd meant what she'd said. She hated it, yet she wasn't afraid of it.

And she was sticking with her male.

Squeezing her eyes shut, Nalla reconnected with her body and felt another release coming for her. She didn't fight it. She let the pulses go through her and grip his shaft and head—which was when he started coming, his arousal kicking, deep inside her pelvis.

For all the times they'd made love, this was different.

Maybe it was the way she knew she felt. Maybe it was something she sensed on his side. It didn't matter. Whatever it was . . . was right.

Suddenly, he was pulling out and breaking free of the cage of her legs. For a split second, she was confused—

Nate fisted his shaft and pumped himself hard, his ejaculations angled right at her core. As the hot jets hit her sensitive flesh, she arched up and started to orgasm again—and he didn't stop. With a punishing grip, he kept working himself until she was dripping, and then he went up her stomach and even marked her breasts, too.

As those dark spices of his flooded his private quarters, and her body was claimed in the most ancient and primal of ways, she felt whole as she never had before.

Satisfied as she'd never imagined.

Happy . . . as she'd never dreamed.

But then love will do that to a person—and, God, she was so glad she took a chance and went out to that club that night.

Bitty had been right, after all.

✦   ✦   ✦

This time when a beam of red light came through Bitty's office window at Safe Place, she knew exactly what it was. Jumping up from her chair, she all but fell out of her window as she threw open the sash.

Except she didn't need to worry. There was someone down there to catch her.

"Hi," she said breathlessly.

L.W. looked up at her, and once again, the glow from the house bathed him in soft yellow light, as if his whole body had a halo. Tonight he wasn't wearing black leather or weapons, and she had a thought that he had come to her first, just as he had gotten out of the clinic.

"I made it through," he said. "The surgery."

She put her hand at the base of her throat. "Thank you for letting me know."

"See? I told you it was going to be fine. Manny's a genius with a steak knife."

Shooting him a look, she continued, "I'm sure that wasn't what he used. Stay there, I'm coming down."

She didn't give him a chance to "yeah, sure, fine" it. Grabbing her coat, she ripped out of her office and tore down the stairs. Someone called to her to check about all the noise, but she waved them off with some scramble of syllables.

Out on the lawn, she shoved her arms into her coat as she skated and slipped in the snow. Somehow, she managed to stay on her feet, but there was no making like she wasn't an out-of-control race car.

It was as she shot around the corner of the house that she realized she'd made a mistake, bringing her own outerwear with her: No excuse for him to give her his jacket, damn it—

L.W. turned toward her. He had scrubs on his lower body, no shirt or fleece on his chest, and a puffy white ski jacket that made his black hair in its braid and his tattoos even more obvious: because casual wear on a deadly fighter wasn't something you saw every night.

"You really are okay," she said. Like a lameass.

For a moment, they just stood face to face, her looking up, him looking down, the winter air crisp and cold in contrast to how warm she felt in her heart, her body.

You are my future, she thought. *You are the reason I went out that night, and you are the person I want to stay in with.*

One of Resolve2Evolve's main tenets came back to her: *Be open to new possibilities, for new roads present themselves first as breaks in the trees, then as paths and trails . . . until finally, the highway runs out to the horizon, taking you to places you never dreamed.*

"So you're working tonight, huh," he said.

"Yes. I'm—yes, I am." What the hell was she babbling about. "We're down a person."

"I'm surprised Nalla isn't here. Heard she works all the time."

"I don't think she's coming here anytime soon." As he arched a brow, she shrugged sadly. "Well, for one, she's assigned to Luchas House. But more to the point, she's not going to want to be around me."

L.W. tilted his head to the side. "Why? I thought you guys were best friends."

Flushing—because who knew he'd tracked anything about her life—Bitty glanced up at her office window and thought about the time Nalla had corralled the other staff and filled the little space with bio-degradable "packing poopoos," as she'd called the cardboard peanuts.

They'd filmed Bitty's reaction as she'd opened the door and the Saran Wrap seal they'd created had broken. The whole thing had gone on loop for the holiday party that year, and God knew she'd never laughed so hard in her life. But now it hurt to think about.

Just like the female's words had hurt.

"That's more a used-to-be kind of thing," she said in a rough voice.

"Since when?"

"Oh, a couple of nights. It doesn't matter." She cleared her throat. "People go their separate ways."

"And sometimes people meet, don't they." As L.W.'s eyes became hooded, he focused on her mouth. But then he seemed to pull himself back. "Nalla's still your friend, though."

"How would you know?" Bitty put her hand out, but hesitated before touching even the sleeve of his parka. "And I don't mean to sound defensive. It's an honest question because I really don't know what to do about it all."

"Nah, it's good." L.W.'s eyes scanned the area like he was looking for targets. Then brought his stare back to her as if he'd found none. "Shuli told me she laid down the law with his buddies about you when we were all at Bathe."

Bitty frowned. "The law?"

"Those assholes were fucking idiots to her. Making bets they could bag her, being rude—they're a bunch of pricks, getting drunk and feeling like they own the world because they can pay for anything they want. When you got there, she told them if they tried the shit they did to her with you, she'd wear their balls for earrings." He shook himself. "'Scuse my French. I mean . . . issue an existential correction."

Bitty popped her brows. "She did that? Really?"

"I don't know what happened between you two, but she's still looking out for you. For real."

Glancing down, Bitty closed her eyes. "So that was why she rushed over that table at them."

"Pretty much, I'm guessing. I've never seen her do that before—not that I know shit. I don't hang out, usually."

"Neither do I." She looked at him again. "But I don't know, I might be willing to turn over a new leaf."

"Oh, yeah?" That one dark brow lifted again, and he looked so much like his father, it was impossible not to make the connection to the King. "Tell me more."

"I don't know, I think work-life balance is important." She pictured that social media star, parading around a purple stage. "And I get off tonight at two a.m. Lot of hours before dawn comes at that time."

L.W.'s smile was slow and a little cocky, but why wouldn't he be arrogant? He was a powerful force for the species in the field, and one day, the throne was going to be his.

Except then memories of the vision came back to her—and brought with them a chill that had nothing to do with the air temperature.

"Are you asking me out on a date?" he drawled.

She snapped back to attention, and kicked her chin up. "Maybe. And with the way you're smiling, I'm thinking you'll say yes."

The future King gave her a slow nod. Then those eyes went up and down her body. "FYI, I'm always going to say yes to you."

She had to laugh. "Even if I tell you to paint this house?"

L.W. glanced up the side of Safe Place. Shrugging again, he had a quarter smile and a whole lot of heat in that stare of his as he looked back at her.

"Charity work's important. And if it makes you happy, Sherwin-Williams, here I come." He nodded at her and took a step back in the snow. "See you at two a.m., Bitty. I'll pick you up . . . and we'll see where we go."

With that, he dematerialized.

In the wake of his departure, she stared at the empty space he'd taken up, threw her head back—and giggled like she'd lost her damned mind.

CHAPTER FORTY-SEVEN

Down in his quarters, Nate held his Nalla against him and drew his fingers up and down her spine. A pleasant exhaustion had overcome them both and he gave in to it, allowing himself to drift in a way he didn't think he ever had before.

Funny how "safe" was a state of mind, not just a well-defended position.

Except it wasn't going to last. Fucking Uncle—although the solution to that problem was at least clear and easy.

"Nalla?" he said as he stared at the ceiling overhead like it was a movie screen, his mind picturing all kinds of dead bodies on it.

"Mmm?"

"It was Rahvyn. Who gave me immortality."

As her head lifted from the crook of his arm, he met her shocked eyes and nodded. "Thirty years ago, I got shot in the stomach in front of her. She got me help, but I ended up dying. My parents . . . were there at the bedside, the Brotherhood, too, and I guess everyone was crying—and Rahvyn came into the hospital room. I don't know exactly what happened . . . but she brought me back over the divide between the living and the dead—and I was different after that."

"She was the one," Nalla breathed.

"I thought I was in love with her." He shook his head. "Even before she did what she did to me, I had all these feelings for her, and they got stronger afterward. I guess maybe I felt like the gift—which has been more of a curse really—meant she felt something in return. But she was always meant for Lassiter."

His eyes sought and held his female's. "Just like I am meant for you."

As Nalla smiled, the shy pleasure that bled through her beautiful features fed him at a fundamental level.

"Shortly after everything went down," he continued, "I saw her with Lassiter, and eventually, I just asshole'd out. I behaved like a total shit, and the immortality thing became a toy I tried to break. I tested a lot of lines in the beginning because I was angry. Attempting to kill myself became like a fuck-you to her, which was stupid. But the thing was, the more times I came back? The more it dawned on me that I was trapped in time. All I *had* was time, and nightmares about the lab, and nothing to live for. That was when the numbness set in and I got dangerous. But like I said . . . now you've come around." He brushed her face gently. "And I might have been immortal for a while . . . but I've only just started living. Thanks to you."

"I feel the same way," she whispered. "About you."

"I didn't want to talk to you about Rahvyn because for one, I know she volunteers at Luchas House and I didn't want things to be weird for you. But two, none of the way I've behaved toward her is any kind of good story about me, you know?" He played with a strand of Nalla's multi-colored hair. "And to answer your question about the sweatshirt I burned? It was one I used to give me an excuse to see her at that house. Not that there was anything real between us. Ever. I was just out of my transition and rootless and scrambling. It was what it was—and I'm over that now. I do owe her an apology, though, and I am going to make it to her."

He thought of the quest the female had sent him on. Kind of ironic, how it all turned out. Yes, he was going to go to her, and to Shuli, and to his parents, and the Brotherhood, to make the peace. But not as a goodbye.

Because he was going to stay around.

"Thank you for telling me," she murmured.

"I'm not hiding anything from you. Ever."

As he thought about what he'd demanded of Rahvyn and the exit strategy he'd set in motion, he wanted to throw up. Thank God he hadn't started on all that a week ago . . .

Nate closed his eyes and shivered just under his skin. "Timing is everything, isn't it. And I mean it. I'm always going to be totally honest with you. Anything that you want to know, I'll tell you. I may not be good at words, but I'm holding nothing back."

"Oh, Nate . . ." She leaned into him. "I love you."

For a moment, his heart stopped. Then it started to pound.

"Now, those are words," he whispered against her mouth, "that I want to hear for an eternity. I love you, too . . . my beloved."

As her eyes grew luminous with tears, they turned into spring sunlight, something that he had only ever seen on TV—

Nate frowned. "Wait, why are you crying? Those aren't happy tears."

When she couldn't seem to speak, he suddenly knew what she was thinking about, and he pulled her into him, cradling her to his chest. "Maybe your father will come around."

After a long silence, Nalla eased back, and as she looked him in the eyes, he'd never seen her so grave.

"It doesn't matter whether he does or he doesn't. You're my future— and if he chooses to only be a part of my past, then he'll lose me forever. I can't control that, though. Those are his decisions. But if he can't accept you, then I'm letting him go."

Picturing the Black Dagger Brother Zsadist, with that scar and those eyes that could flash black, Nate knew that this was a lose/lose for her. But what could he do? Other than start living right and being right, that was—and hoping like hell it caught up to him in the same way the consequences of his being a fucking dickhead had bitten him on the ass.

And, hey, Uncle had given him an opportunity to prove his allegiance, right?

That human wanted a body for his family to bury—no fucking problem. Nate was happy to do the job on the man himself—to save his father-in-law's life.

"Your sire's not wrong about who I've been," Nate said. "But I'm going to be different, now and in the future."

She nodded "My *mahmen* said that broken can mean ruined. But you're not ruined, Nate, and I'm going to be with you to help you. Now and forever."

"And it's a two-way street." He stroked her hair. "I'm here for you as well. It's us, together."

"Us, together."

As their lips met, he recognized the bittersweet feelings that were in her heart. He had them, too. Why couldn't life be simpler—

A subtle beeping sounded out next to the bed, and he instantly went on the alert. Instincts firing, he grabbed for the gun he kept tucked between the mattress and the box spring. Picking up his burner phone from the side table, he accessed his trail cameras.

For a split second, he closed his eyes. *Lessers.* He knew them by the white hair—except how in the hell had they found him? Not that it mattered.

"Get dressed," he barked. "Right now."

"What's wrong? What's happening?"

Even as she was asking the questions, Nalla was on her feet and going for her jeans—which was a testament to the fact that she'd been raised by a Brother. But there was no time to answer her. Jumping up as well, he yanked his leathers on, and went under the bed. As he pulled out a tray of the weapons he'd checked before, he was grateful that his paranoia about infiltration had taken him where it had.

And rank pissed off he'd been right.

"Take this." He held the mattress gun out to her. "It's fully loaded and the safety's off. You need to go out my tunnel and dematerialize from my barn."

At least there was only one flank of the enemy that his cameras picked up on—although fuck knew how long that was going to last.

"What kind of visitors?" she said, even though going by her hard tone, she knew.

But again, Nalla just accepted the weapon he gave her, grabbed her parka, and came with him, into the bathroom. Triggering a panel release, he flipped a light switch that illuminated a narrow crawl space that opened up to a passageway lined with steel mesh.

"This goes out to my barn," he repeated as he kissed her quick. "Follow it, and dematerialize from there. Go."

"Nate, I can help fight—"

"Not a chance. I can't die, remember? I'll be okay, but I need to know you're safe. That's the most important thing in the world to me. That's all that matters."

+   +   +

Nalla's heart was pounding and she wanted to drag Nate with her into the escape tunnel. He was right, though. Between the two of them, he was vastly more likely to come out of some kind of conflict alive.

And yet if he fell into enemy hands? They could literally torture him . . . for centuries, his nightmare turning into reality with no chance of him waking up and being saved.

"Nate, you need to come with me. I have a bad feeling about this."

How many other times had those words been spoken, she thought with a panic. Between two people right before the plan went wrong.

And death came knocking.

"The longer you wait here," he said, "the closer they come. Go."

As their eyes met, stark terror choked her, but there was no negotiating with him so she stepped into the tunnel.

"I love you," she shouted as he shut the steel door on her.

She could barely hear his deep voice echo those three words before they were cut off.

For a split second, she was frozen by fear. Then she was like, *fuck this, fuck them, fuck the war.* She didn't run. She was the daughter of a fucking Brother, her mate was going into danger, and she was going to stay and fight.

With quick efficiency, she ran a check of the gun, assessing its weight and sight, confirming its full magazine. Which of course was just as Nate told her it was.

Riding a wave of aggression, she reached for the latch.

It was locked. And there was no keypad. Not that she could have guessed a password for him.

"*Shit.*"

Pounding on the steel mesh didn't get her anywhere, but like Nate was wasting time in his bathroom, staring at the hatch? Hell no. He was arming himself and about to go out and face the enemy. Alone.

Fine, she'd help him from the other end.

Shuffling along the cramped tunnel, bent over, breathing hard, fear sharpening her instincts and making the sounds of her boots and the rustle of her clothes seem super sharp and very loud, she just told herself she needed to get to the other side, and then she could engage the slayers.

Assuming Nate hadn't lied to her and completely locked her in here for safety.

When she got to the far end—after what seemed like a week of pushing forward—there was a latching mechanism, and she swore she was going to punch him in the dick if the thing didn't budge. Taking a deep breath, she—

—sprang the lever, and there was a vapor lock release.

"Thank fuck," she muttered as she led with the weapon.

Emerging at a short stack set of stairs, she went up the narrow steps and waited at a wooden door at the top.

No sounds. No scents.

Taking two quick, deep breaths, she—

Threw open the panel, and had to blink as motion-activated lights came on. Then she focused and cleared what was in front of her, swinging the gun muzzle left and right.

The barn interior was not a barn space at all, but a neat-and-tidy suburban garage, with tools and equipment tacked up on the concrete walls, and some kind of hulking vehicle draped in a tarp in the center of everything.

Whatever was under there was big as a mountain, and it appeared to be parked ass in so it could be driven straight out of the double doors.

When nothing moved or came at her, and she didn't smell the sickly-sweet scent of the enemy—yet—she went over to some windows that she knew, based on what she'd seen from an exterior view, were coated in a reflective, one-way film.

So she could look out and stay undetected—

Across the way, coming through the trees toward the cabin, she saw the attack closing in . . . and she couldn't believe it.

There were so many of them.

A dozen . . . or more, the *lessers'* bodies moving in a freaky kind of unison, as if they had a hive brain that coordinated their positions and strides. Not all of them had the white hair and skin that showed up over time as the pigment in their coloring leached out. But the newly inducted were dangerous, even if they didn't have the experience that the older slayers did. As soon as a human was turned, they had an increase in strength and stamina that she'd been told her whole life she had to be careful of.

Sudden terror closed her throat, but she needed to get past that right now. Was Nate calling the Brotherhood? He'd mentioned over day that he'd been kicked out, though. And he'd have no need for backup— in his mind, he was invincible.

She glanced around and saw nothing that was going to help her.

It wasn't like there was an armored tank under that fucking tarp. She wasn't that lucky.

As she negotiated with all kinds of bad outcomes, and time funneled out the sink of this shitty situation . . . there was one, and only one, solution that came to her.

Taking out her cell phone, her hands were shaking so badly that she had to thank Lassiter for facial recognition because punching in her pass code was going to be next to impossible. And then as she went into her contacts, she almost couldn't move through the short list for the same reason.

As she stopped on the one entry she needed more than the others—on some level, had always needed more than anybody else—tears came to her eyes:

Father Mine.

CHAPTER FORTY-EIGHT

When Zsadist's phone started to vibrate with a call, he was back at Four Toys HQ, and leaning over V's shoulder to check out the footage they'd managed to get from inside that Lessening Society tunnel.

He pointed at the monitor as he took the cell out of his jacket's inside pocket. "That nano-drone is a thing of beauty. This is exactly what I wanted."

"The size of flies, I'm telling you. As soon as that *lesser* came out of there, Allhan sent the unit in and none of those bastards knew a damn thing—"

Z frowned as he glanced at the phone screen. For a second, he thought surely this must be wrong because his daughter was not speaking to him. And after the latest Nate/Nalla update from his *shellan*, things were progressing in ways that made him want to start digging the fighter's grave.

So no, she was not returning any call of his.

"Hold on, it's Nalla."

Swiping left, he braced himself for the female to tell him she and that out-of-control rage machine were eloping. "Hello—"

"I need you." Her voice was direct, but also thin as a reed. "Oh, God, they're everywhere—"

"*What's everywhere.*" Even though he knew. Fucking hell, he was going to kill that male. "Where are you—"

"I'm at Nate's—they're surrounding his cabin and he's about to go out there. I'm in the barn, and I have a nine millimeter. The slayers don't know I'm here yet, but—"

"We're on our way. You stay where you are. *Do not engage the enemy.*"

"There's twelve to fifteen of them in the woods."

As a shaft of true terror nailed him in the nads, he looked at V and nodded sharply. While the brother palmed up his own phone and sent out an alarm, Z said, "Can you dematerialize?"

Except he already knew the answer to that one, and reported to V, "She's in the barn at Nate's. Okay, Nalla, I'm coming, we're all coming."

V started sending out the location, and Z didn't wait. He busted out of the glass office, blew down the aisle between all the desks, and flew out into the open air.

It took him way too long to dematerialize. Waaaay too fucking long.

But when he finally did re-form, it was in the forest behind the rural property's barn and with a pair of fully loaded forties up and ready. Sending out his instincts, he could sense the *lessers* even before he started to pick up their movements in and among the leafless birches and maples and fluffy pines.

When he shifted his position, he used the trees just as the enemy was, taking cover when he could, moving fast when he couldn't. He told himself that it was good news that the log cabin was the target, but that wasn't going to last. Sooner or later, they would infiltrate the barn, either because they needed to for a defensive tactic, or they wanted to because they were raiding the property after they won.

But he was not alone.

Like wraiths in the night, his brothers and fellow fighters arrived on scene, Phury, V, and Rhage right next to him, Xcor, Qhuinn, and Blay off to the left, Payne and Tohr flanking right. Everyone else had followed protocol and stayed back to protect Wrath.

"We'll draw their firepower," Phury said in a hard, low voice. "You take care of Nalla."

"Roger that."

His twin grabbed his arm in a stiff grip. "We got this. Okay? You worry about her. That's your only priority."

Their eyes met. And Zsadist nodded once. "Kill them, kill them all."

Just as he said the words, Nate burst out of the front door of the cabin. For a split second, Z had to give the male a little respect. The fury on that face was epic, and that huge body was strung with so many weapons, the fucker was like a walking armory.

Gone was the laconic resister who was fucking with shit because he was bored and unconnected and hateful: The vengeance that was clearly threading through every molecule in that body . . . was exactly what was going through Z's own veins—and it wasn't because the guy was protecting two buildings and his rights as a fucking landowner.

Not even close. He was protecting his female.

Zsadist glanced at the barn he knew his daughter was in.

Indeed, something had changed inside of that fighter, something fundamental, and it had woken Nate up to the world. And wasn't that a path Z himself had walked once, a lifetime ago—

With a war cry, Nate threw himself from his porch, pumping off rounds not in a willy-nilly, but like he was picking cans from a fence rail, not a single bullet wasted as he seemed to be able to shoot in both directions and hit targets at the same time.

The *lesser* response was exactly what it always was. Swift and coordinated.

Even as slayers were hit, they returned fire, and Nate was struck, his torso jerking back, not that it slowed him down.

But the kid didn't have to fight alone.

The brothers and fighters advanced out of the tree line immediately, and they focused on pressing outward from the barn to give Z some time to get Nalla off the property.

Prepared to act fast, he turned to the—

The roar that started up was so loud, he wondered what the hell it was. And then came a screeching sound that rattled the roof of the out-building.

After that, there was a tremendous explosion out in front, and Zsa-dist ducked for cover—

Only to see a gigantic truck with tires the size of boulders blast through the double doors.

"*Fuck!*" He fucking knew who was behind that wheel. "Nalla! You're going to get yourself killed!"

Sure enough, instead of heading out for the country road and try-ing to get away to safety—not that that fucking thing was going to fit on anything narrower than a soccer stadium—she bore down on the fight-ing, bullets pinging off the front panels and the windshield.

Nalla mowed down those *lessers* like she was bowling for bitches, and as she came back around for another pass, kicking up snow and throwing up slayer bodies like confetti, he caught a very clear visual of her fury behind the wheel.

"Mother*fucker*," he yelled. "What are you doing!"

But come on, she got that shit from him.

And Zsadist's only response, like hers, was the reason he'd been born: He got his black daggers out and ran to join the fight.

He engaged with the first *lesser* he came to, a female who already had a horrible head wound. She still had the strength of ten human men, and the pair of them traded gunshots—hers—and stabs—his. Which was a deadly dance being repeated all around the landscape—

The bullet went through his side, spinning him around.

Goddamn it, he hadn't controlled the barrel of her weapon—

A sudden uncontrollable loginess overtook him, and the next thing he knew, the *lesser* had him flat on his back—and his own black dagger in her hand. Looking up, he told his arms and legs to move.

They didn't listen all that well—and it was as he tried to lift his left hand that he saw the problem was not the bullet wound in his side.

He'd somehow been stabbed in the forearm.

And he'd sustained a critical venous puncture.

Red blood was flowing out of him at an alarming rate.

At which point he saw that the *lesser* had knives in both her hands. So she'd pulled out a second one from somewhere, the silver blade marking it as hers.

The expression on her face was rapt, her eyes wide with an aggression that bordered on absolute mania.

She put her own blade away.

And double-fisted his black dagger, lifting it over her head.

◆ ◆ ◆

Nate had started the fight as he meant to go on with it: As soon as Nalla had gone into his escape tunnel, he'd strapped on his weapons and gone up his set of stairs. He'd been standing on his own threshold as the *lessers* started coming out of the fucking trees, and he'd had a moment of pause only because he hadn't been sure that Nalla was off the property yet.

Being unsure of her whereabouts had made him antsy.

But then he couldn't hold himself back any longer. Busting out of his front door, he started picking off the enemy with bullets, dropping them like flies in the forest—except as a strange sense tingled at the nape of his neck, he glanced back.

He immediately shit himself because surely it was more *lessers*.

Except no, it was not the enemy.

It was the Brotherhood. And they had come to fight.

Nalla must have called her sire—and Z must have not let her down. Like the good father he was.

As Nate continued to engage, he totally did not hate the backup. Before he'd been with Nalla, he would have gotten his dick in a crack, but with her on his land? He was grateful for the help, especially because he knew, going by the pain in his shoulder and his side, that he'd been plugged at least twice—

A *lesser* jumped out in his path and started rushing for him—and all he could think was: *You want to dance? Let's fucking dance.*

Meeting the undead chest to chest, he shoved his barrel into its face, and discharged a pair of bullets to blow the back of the skull out. Then he let the slayer drop to the snow. The thing wouldn't be dead until someone stabbed it back to Lash, but there'd be time for that later.

On to the next one. And the next.

As he worked, he smelled his own blood mixing with the stink of the enemy, felt the sweat from his body's efforts, knew the strength that came from doing what he was best at as he controlled his guns and heard the *pop!*s not just of his own weapon, but those around him. The fighting was dangerous. It required a level head. It consumed all of his attention, except for that wedge of his consciousness that would always be with Nalla now.

But in a weird, fucked-up way, he was reminded of how much he loved his job with the Brothers—

Except then everything changed.

When there was an explosion at his barn.

Jerking to face the loud, unexpected sound, Nate stopped dead in mid-stride . . . because he couldn't believe what he was looking at.

His monster fucking truck, the one that he hadn't fired up since the fall, that had sat in an unheated shed, that should have been drained of oil and gas and all fluids—and why the fuck hadn't he done that!—was blasting out of the barn, the doors splintering apart.

There was only one person who could be behind the wheel.

Nalla was all fury and pedal-to-the-metal as she plowed into the ground game. How she managed to only go bowling for *lessers*, he didn't know. But somehow, she didn't target the Brothers. Only the white, soulless killers who had come on the attack—

"Fuck!" he hollered as he was struck by a bullet.

Turning to the *lesser* with the point-blank aim, he ducked into a roll, and came up shooting on bended knee. The slayer wasn't prepared, that pasty-ass face registering all kinds of what-the-*fuck!* as twelve pounds of lead was pumped into him.

As Nate jumped back to his feet, he intended to go after Nalla—yeah, and do what? flag her down and issue her a self-preservation ticket?—when he saw something out of the corner of his eye:

A black dagger in the hand of a female slayer.

And as she lifted it over her head, the incapacitated fighter she was about to kill came into sharp focus.

"Noooooooooooooo!" Nate screamed.

Throwing all his strength into his legs, he surged forward, racing through the hail of bullets, zeroing in on that blade to the point where he didn't see Nalla's father on the ground or the hatred in the slayer's face. Just the blade.

Just that one blade . . . that seemed to hold everything that was important to him in balance.

Nate leapt into the air a good ten feet away because if he kept running, he wasn't going to get there in time. But fuck, his superpower was immortality, not being able to fly.

He wasn't fast enough to grab the blade.

But he sure as hell got under it.

Just as the black steel point reached terminal velocity, he somehow managed to slide his body in between the weapon and Zsadist's chest so that his back was what got stabbed.

And then shit was fucking on.

In spite of the blazing pain, Nate rolled over and took control while on top of the Brother. Swinging his fist, he punched the slayer in the head, where a raw wound was showing parts of her brain. Then he incapacitated her instantly by pushing his fingers into a gaping hole in her throat.

Just as he grabbed a silver blade from her belt.

"That's my fucking father-in-law, bitch!"

With a single, vicious movement, he plunged the knife into that empty-ass chest cavity.

The *pop!* was loud, the blast of light was bright, and the smell was a sting in the nose that he relished.

But he was also crushing the injured male beneath him.

Pitching himself off of Zsadist, Nate was breathing hard and bleeding badly, but adrenaline was a great thing, it really was.

"Holy . . . fuck," the Brother wheezed. "That was some kinda timing."

"Are you okay?"

"Yeah."

No, not at all, Nate thought as he measured the male's wounds.

The one in that arm was bleeding so badly, it had turned the white ground into a fucking cherry sno-cone.

As gunshots rang out, and his fucking truck—why couldn't he have just owned a Kia, *why?!*—made wide swaths through the middle of the fighting, he knew if he was going to get Nalla's father to safety, he had to move fast.

Shoving his arms under the Brother, he picked Zsadist up and started running across the field of combat. Dodging both friendly fire and *lesser* bullets, jumping over downed slayers—and staying out of the path of the monster truck that the love of his life insisted on weaponizing—Nate got Z into the cabin, over to the set of stairs, and down into the earth.

There was no time to lock things up.

He needed to get a tourniquet on that arm immediately. Putting the Brother on the bed, he turned away and grabbed his first aid kit from a shelf—

"Can I have my dagger back?"

Nate froze. Then looked over his shoulder. "I'm sorry, what?"

Zsadist's half-mast eyes were yellow as he crooked his finger. "C'mere. No, don't turn around, just lean back."

As Nate did what he'd been told, there was a blaze of pain in his upper shoulder, and when he pivoted around again, the Brother had a black dagger in his palm.

"These things can't be wasted. V gets cranky if you lose 'em."

And then the male passed out.

"*Fuck.*" Nate ignored his own pain and started riffling through the white box with the red cross on the top. "Where is—*got it.*"

His hands were shaking, but he got the thing in place over the sleeve of the leather jacket because there was no time to strip the outerwear off: The red tide streaming out of the stab wound was like a garden hose running into a fucking flower bed.

As he cinched the tourniquet so tight it nearly amputated his own fingers, he knew it was a miracle the Brother was even still alive.

With shaking hands, he took out his phone and started making a call.

The answer was quick, thank Lassiter. "This is Manny—"

"It's Nate on a burner. I'm here with Zsadist, out at my place. You need to get Bella here as soon as the fighting's over. He's lost a lot of blood."

"Nate?"

"Yeah, it's me." He glanced over to the stairs and wished he'd closed them all the way down. "I'm going to give him synthetic units until she can get here, but let her know that she needs to be ready to come quick."

"Okay, okay, all right. Good move—and I'll send Jane out—"

"No, it's too hot right now. And I'm not going to let him die. Tourniquet's in place, just like he taught me."

Hanging up, he reached under the bed and pulled out a sealed plastic bag of the synthetic stuff. Puncturing the top, he pushed the self-pack straw into the container, and put the business end to the male's pale lips.

"Wake up, Z. *Drink.* You gotta drink. You can't die on me, I'm in love with your daughter, and even though you hate me, she needs you, now more than ever—"

The sense that someone had come down the steps brought his head up, and at first, what he saw made no sense.

"*Evan?*" he blurted.

CHAPTER FORTY-NINE

As soon as Evan bottomed out at the stairwell, he had the satisfaction of being right. Across the way, the enforcer he'd come for was putting a straw into the mouth of an enormous vampire who had a tourniquet on one arm and a puddle of blood underneath him on the bed.

And what do you know, he recognized the injured male. It was the one with the facial scar he'd first seen in that office building, who'd later tracked him the other night to Bathe.

And then the enforcer looked up and did a double take. "Evan?"

Evan could understand the surprise. He'd felt it, too, when he'd put everything together.

"You're one of the enemy," he said to the enforcer. "I never suspected. Then again, until now, I had no idea vampires and *lessers* were real."

"What the fuck, Evan." The vampire straightened slowly. "What happened to you?"

I don't know, he answered to himself.

"I have to kill you." He shook his head. "It's just where we are, where you and I ended up. Kinda strange, huh."

And funny, this was so much less climactic than he'd thought it would be.

Then again, maybe it was because this male had known him from before—and he was suddenly thinking about his mother, instead of killing his uncle.

"This isn't you," the vampire said. "You've never been like this."

"I'm not like myself anymore, though." Tears came to his eyes. "I didn't mean for all this to happen, but I went to the trainer and he . . . wasn't a trainer after all."

"Lash."

"You know him? But I guess that's stupid. Of course you do. He . . . bit me and forced this vile shit down my throat and ever since then, I've been . . . evolving."

The vampire shook his own head. "I know you, Evan. You're not a killer."

He thought of the woman tied to the chair at Mickey's, saw her eyes bugging as he covered her face with that pillow, heard the splash as her body landed in the quarry's cold waters.

"Yes, I am. I've killed now."

"Oh, Evan. You need to get out of this. You're in so deep, you don't even know it."

"How—" He put his gun back up, having missed the fact that it had lowered itself. "Don't do anything stupid."

"Can you live with what you're doing? Ask yourself that."

"How about yourself. How many murders have you committed?"

"But your kind are killing innocents. Who should be allowed to live their lives in peace. You're hunting those who would otherwise leave you alone because your master is a sociopath who's using you."

After a moment, Evan said forlornly, "He lied to me."

"Of course he did. That's what he does to get people like you lined up. And when you find out you're trapped, and you can't get out—"

"I know it's too late for me—that's what they've told me."

"I can help you, though. It's not too late—"

All of a sudden, the vampire's eyes shifted up and to the left, and though that expression barely changed, Evan looked back over his shoulder.

A female with multi-colored hair stopped in mid-descent on the steps.

"Evan, don't look at her. Look at me." Nathaniel was talking fast now. "I'm the one you want. I'm the one you came for—right? You were out here with Mickey that night, that's how you knew where to find me now. You're the only one in the Lessening Society who knew where I lived."

Refocusing on the enforcer, Evan felt a lancing pain in his chest. "I did bring them here."

"Listen to me, you need to ask yourself if you can live with what you're doing. You still have a conscience and you were cheated by your master—and I can end your suffering. You're lying to yourself if you think you can handle what the future is going to be like for you. You're not built for this and you know it. You're not like Mickey, you're not like Uncle. You are *not* your family and they shit all over you because of it."

That was exactly the truth as Evan had lived it, but somehow, spelled out as it was by someone else, he felt a vital part of him collapse.

"How can you help me?" he whispered.

"I can end the suffering for you."

"That's not possible."

Except then he remembered the warning that female *lesser* had given him . . . about steel blades and chest cavities.

"You're better than this life, Evan. You're better than all those assholes who've disrespected you. This is *not* who you are."

Evan wasn't sure precisely when he made the decision to lower the gun. But like so many of his actions since that night he had taken the elevator down into that black-oily basement, his movements were not conscious.

Only this time, it was another, sepaate part of him, not some group-think that came from what had been done to him, that took control.

He nodded. "You're right."

And that was when the enforcer moved.

The vampire reached down and took a dagger with a black blade from out of the lax hand of the injured male. Then he stepped around the foot of the bed and came forward.

"I wanted them to be proud of me," Evan said in a haunted voice. "That's all I ever wanted."

The enforcer's voice was curiously gentle: "It's better to be true to you and proud of yourself. Some evolutions aren't worth the cost of pleasing others, and in the end, only your conscience, which truly knows right from wrong, can save you."

As if he were putting down a heavy load, Evan exhaled long and slow. "Is this going to hurt?"

"Not any more than the pain you're already in."

Evan closed his eyes and leaned back on his hips, dropping the gun to the floor. The thump of impact was loud in his ears, and he was aware that he was starting to pant in preparation for what was coming.

Yet there was a peace, too. Whereas he hadn't chosen how this fucked-up path had started because of a lie that had been fed to him . . . he was getting to choose when it all ended.

"Thank you," he breathed.

"You're doing the right thing."

The next thing Evan felt was a piercing pain in his chest—

And then he was consumed by heat and light.

CHAPTER FIFTY

I t tasted like Yoo-hoo.

That was what Zsadist thought when a blast of light woke his sorry ass up and his eyes popped open. He didn't need any reorientation, he knew exactly where the fuck he was.

And who he was with.

As a billow of smoke curled up in front of Nate, and the stink of *lesser* both flared and dissipated, Z had the blurry visual of his daughter leaping into the male's arms, the two embracing at the foot of a short stack stairway. When they finally parted a little, he watched them exchange words, and even though he was groggy, he could dub them in.

After all, he and his Bella had said similar things at various times in their lives, when near misses had saved two people from catastrophe . . . the reunion all the sweeter for the almost-didn't-happen.

Funny, he thought as he continued to suck on the straw that was in his mouth, how he went back to a specific moment in his own life as Nalla and Nate turned to him and warily approached the bed.

I am the luckiest male.

Those were the words that had gone through his mind when Bella had come back to him even though he hadn't deserved any kind of second chance, and told him she was pregnant with their beloved daughter . . . and he had been able to write three words in bad penmanship to show her that he had changed.

"Father?" his Nalla said in a voice that cracked.

"I'm okay." It was hard to talk around the straw, but as his brain came back online, he realized what the not-Yoo-hoo was about and why he had to keep drinking the synthetic blood. "You . . . okay?"

"Yes," she whispered as she held on to the hand of the male who stood beside her, tall and strong—and covered in the blood of the enemy.

"I have something I have to say to you, sir," Nate intoned gravely. "I don't know if now's the time, though."

Was this fucker was going to ask for her hand in mating right here? Z wondered. Over what might have been his deathbed if . . . well, if the male hadn't acted so quickly with the first aid.

Or if Nate hadn't jumped in between Zsadist and a stabbing that would have killed him instantly out on the lawn.

Talk about taking one for the team.

"Shut up," Z said harshly. "I don't want to hear it."

The way his daughter's face fell told him everything. And yet he had to ask, "Do you love him, Nalla?"

"Yes, Father. I do." She looked up at Nate. "I love him with everything I am."

"And you?" He mostly kept the warning out of his voice as he addressed Nate. "Do you love her."

Even though he knew the male did. There was no forgetting the expression on Nate's face as he'd come out of that cabin, a bonded fighter, ready to defend the female who was his whole world.

Nate nodded and looked down. "I love her." Then the male glanced back to the bed. "But that's not what I have to tell you."

Zsadist frowned as the guy brought out his cell phone. After he futzed around with things for a moment, he put the screen out.

"That's a picture of me," Z mumbled.

Nate nodded. "One of the black market kingpins downtown thinks he's hired me to kill you. I wanted you to know this right now, so in case you're out in the field, you're extra careful. I'm going to take care of it, though, don't worry. Uncle's not going to live another twenty-four hours."

The shooting in the parking lot, Z thought. *Behind that club Bathe.*

It hadn't been him with the trigger pulling at those organized crime types, but someone had decided it was.

As Nalla gasped, Zsadist stared into the eyes of the other male. "Much appreciated."

"Consider it the first of a lifelong series of apologies." Nate nodded at Nalla. "Everything is different to me now."

"We'll see about that."

"You can bet your life on it."

Fuck that, Z thought. It looked like he was betting his *daughter's* life on it.

Then he focused on his Nalla.

Clearing his throat, Z felt like he was jumping off into an abyss. But he knew, if he was going to keep his daughter in his life . . . he was going to have to set her free.

And you know, he didn't think she was blowing up her life over a bad male, after all.

"You two have my blessing," he said with authority. "For whatever future you choose to make together."

Nalla let out a strangled sound, and then, just like she had when she was little, when he'd come home at the end of the night and he'd been the only one she wanted to see . . .

She was careful about getting on the bed next to him. Because reasons.

But as much as she could, she launched herself at him.

"I love you . . . father mine," she choked out through her tears. "Forever."

"I love you, too," he vowed. "Always."

And as he held the smart, beautiful, headstrong, amazing thing that he and his one true love had made together, Zsadist looked over her shoulder.

Nate was right there, all flushed and possibly having to blink quick. Not that the male was going to show it.

As he sensed the attention on him, Nate straightened like a soldier addressing a corporal. "Oh, here, I better give this back to you. Again."

Nate leaned forward, and placed the black dagger he'd clearly used on the *lesser* who had just *poofed!* the fuck out on the bed. Right where Z could reach it with the grip that was still working.

When he went to step back, Z spoke sharply. "You better take care of her. She's my girl."

The fighter hitched a breath. "Yes, sir. I promise."

"Because I'll *fucking* kill you. Somehow, I will f—"

"*Dad*," Nalla cut in. "Really."

"What?" Z rolled his eyes. "Fine. Just don't fuck this up, Nate. You got one chance with me."

Nate put both of his palms high, like he was at a stickup. "I swear. I won't waste the opportunity. And thank you."

"Okay then." Z left the weapon where it was and extended his dagger hand. "Welcome to my family, Nate."

There was a pause that seemed to last forever.

"I will love her and cherish her, always," Nate whispered. In a way that was a vow that was going to last the guy's entire, immortal life.

When the two of them clasped palms . . . they held on longer than you would if you were just being polite. Then again, they were going to be spending a lot of time together.

In the future.

EPILOGUE

Three nights later . . .

A s Nate arrived at the Audience House, he re-formed around back. The evening was crystal clear, and out here in the sticks, the stars were brilliant overhead, twinkling in their spin around the earth. Standing with his shitkickers in the snow, feeling the brisk air on his face, looking forward to what was coming after this, the heavens didn't look cold and distant. They seemed full of possibilities, a whirl of infinite beauty.

After a moment, the fireflies he'd been expecting swirled in beside him, the sparks coalescing into a shimmer before going solid. Rahvyn was smiling as she faced him, her silver hair caught by the wind to come alive around her ethereal face.

"Hi," she said.

What a simple greeting, Nate thought. And yet in the word, there was so much. Acceptance. Forgiveness. The love that came with community.

"Hi." It was easy to smile back at her, and he cleared his throat. "Thanks for coming out here."

"Thank you for calling me."

Glancing off to the side, he measured the barn that was no barn at all, but a high-tech monitoring facility to rival anything any government had ever built and staffed. Even though he hadn't done the math on all the monitoring on the premises, he was glad he was doing this with an audience.

Accountability for one's actions was good.

"I just wanted to say I'm sorry to you," he said. "For the way I've been all these years. I'm not going to explain the whys. They don't matter."

"Nate, you do not have—"

He put his hand up and stopped her. "You told me to make peace with everyone. I'm going to do that, but I want to stay. Here, in Caldwell. With my mate."

That radiant smile returned and it was like getting hit with a bolt of sunlight. "I am so happy for you both."

"Thanks. And lucky for me, I've got all the time in the world. I have a lot to make up for." He closed his eyes. "When I think about what I did to my parents. The Brotherhood. Shuli—"

"You are going to find that forgiveness is another word for love, Nate."

He lifted his lids. "I'm going to prove myself. To everyone."

"I know you are. And I am glad you are not leaving us."

As he looked at the female now, he could recognize her beauty and appreciate it, but there was no confusion for him about who his true love was. Even when he remembered standing on the edge of that meadow, Lassiter's carpet of blooms an acre-sized bouquet he couldn't compete with, he knew that Nalla was who he'd really been waiting for.

"I have no right to ask you for anything," he said roughly. "But when my Nalla—"

"Yes, I will come to you when it is her time. And you will be reunited in the Fade. Lassiter and I will make sure of it."

He released the breath he'd been holding for nights now. "Thank you. The idea of living without her is . . ."

"I know. You do not have to say it."

"And thank you for bringing me back that night, thirty years ago. Life is a gift. I just forgot that for a very long time."

"You had your reasons. And you are very welcome."

The hug they shared was that of family, and when they stepped back, he looked to the cottage's rear door.

"Making the peace," he murmured. "It's my new side hustle."

"You do it well. I know I feel much better."

Nate thought of his parents, whose home he'd just left after he and Nalla had enjoyed a great First Meal with them. Murhder and Sarah were even better than blood to him because they'd chosen him as their son, had picked him up out of an untenable situation and stuck with him, ever since. Again, when he thought about the things he'd said and done? Shame spoiled his stomach.

But he was going to keep proving that he had changed.

And God, they loved Nalla so much. They'd accepted her instantly, and the feeling he'd had, as he'd pulled out his mate's chair at the table, while his father had done the same for his mother, had made him feel a full-circle kind of satisfaction.

He'd been lost. Now he really was found and claimed.

"You're right," he said hoarsely. "About the forgiveness thing and what it means."

Why they still loved him, he couldn't understand. But as his father had told him, and his mother had underscored, he was a part of them, of the love they had for each other, of their home. Of their past, present . . . and future. When he'd pressed them on it all, on how they could possibly look past his shutting them out, they had just smiled and promised, if he had young of his own, he would understand.

Man, he hoped that would happen for him and Nalla sometime, in some way. He really wanted to adopt at least one young.

He turned to the cottage. "Time to face the music with Wrath and the Brotherhood. I'm meeting Shuli after this. And then I think I've crossed off everyone on my list."

As if she could sense his tension, Rahvyn reached out and gave his hand a squeeze. "You are on a roll. Keep it going."

"My father said he'd help me."

"Good."

With a wave, he took his leave of her, tromping through the snow to the glow by the back door. In his head, he tried to recite the speech he'd written out over day, once more going through the words that he'd worn out from practice. You'd think the number of times he'd reviewed the thing would have made it better. Instead, the sentences were a mash, an over-tossed salad that had been profound on its first iteration, but was now just a sappy hack job.

Ah, hell, maybe it had always been that, but the emotions he had been feeling had turned the prosaic into prose, and then he guessed the treadmill of repetition had given him the clarity that those fighters and the great Blind King were going to have the second he opened his pie hole.

Whatever, he thought as he waited to be cleared at the back entrance. It was all he had, and at least his father had offered to take him into his audience with the—

The first of the three portals was sprung, and Nate stepped inside a cubicle-like space.

Sweaty palms. Pounding heart. Shaking hands.

The second clearance was granted, the heavy steel door releasing so that he could take another couple of steps and wait for another review. Looking up, he noted the tiny holes in the steel ceiling. Mounted as they were, they were not unlike the stars in the sky, so small compared to the expanse they were on. But they were nothing to wish on. If you were a trespasser dumb enough to make it this far? You were going to get hit with enough nerve gas to get turned into an inanimate object.

He was passed forward again, and as he confronted the final checkpoint, he just pictured his father standing tall and true in the homey kitchen on the far side, Murhder's red-and-black hair and leathers a comfort—

The seal let go, he pushed the way in . . . and stopped as soon as he stepped forward.

Across the way, it was Zsadist by the Aga, not his father.

Behind Nate, the steel door shut itself and relocked, and abruptly, the details of the kitchen got a little blurry, while the scents in the air got sharp: Scones. Coffee. OJ.

"Ah, hi," he said.

"Hey, son."

"I—um, listen, I really appreciate that the Brotherhood is giving me the opportunity to apologize," Nate heard himself blather in a rush. "And I don't expect to be put back on the field schedule. I'm ready to work at anything I'm offered. If you guys want me to clean something, train the young, data entry . . . I don't care—and if it's nothing, I understand."

Those yellow eyes, so like Nalla's, narrowed, and he couldn't blame the guy. Yeah, sure, everything was good between the two of them, but there were levels, so many levels.

"So, you expected your father here, yeah?"

Nate nodded his head. "Yes, but I'm prepared to go in and face the Brotherhood and my King on my own. It's my past, no one else's."

Zsadist came forward, and now the two were eye to eye. For a split second, Nate's gaze dropped to the black slave band that had been tattooed around the Brother's throat, and he thought of his own ink. He'd gotten his because he'd needed a physical expression of his pain. Now, he saw Amore's work as evidence that he was a survivor.

And he wondered if Z didn't feel the same about his own.

"You know," Nate murmured, "I'm done running from what . . . happened to me in the past."

Zsadist inclined his head. "That's exactly why I wanted to catch you. If you ever need to talk . . . I know what it's like. Trying to play normal when your head is a tornado. Mary is super helpful as a resource and my daughter, I mean, she's trained in counseling, and she loves you more than anything. Sometimes, though, it's good to know you aren't alone. Even the people you're closest to can't really relate—and aren't you and I glad that they don't carry around what we do."

Nate blinked a couple of times. And found it was hard to breathe.

"I'm going to take you up on this offer."

Z nodded again. "Good. I was hoping that was going to be your response." Then the Brother smiled, flashing his fangs. "Now let's get this shit over with so we can go to your party."

◆　　◆　　◆

Who'da thought that the sound of packing tape screeching across the bottom of a moving box would be a happy thing.

As Nalla made another 3D out of a 2D, and flipped the cardboard cube upright, she measured how much more she had to go. Dismantling her room in her parents' quarters had gone quickly. Then again, all she had were clothes, the photographs on the walls, and the stuff in her bathroom. The latter had taken up the most time, and she had culled that herd of two-year-old mascaras and eye pencils that had turned into tiny I-beams with a fresh-start rush that had made her dizzy.

Heading over to her bureau's bottom drawer, she took out the pairs of flannel PJ bottoms, and the last of her sweatshirts . . .

Then she slowly straightened and looked around.

"Am I done?" she said to herself.

Glancing back at the open doors of her closet, she got an eyeful of two empty wire hangers on the rod, a lone pair of strappy heels in a shoebox on the floor, and a single silica gel satchel that had fallen out of something. Across the way, there was the stripped mattress, the bedside table that only had a lamp on it, and her cell phone that was charging on its pad. Other than the rug needing a quick vacuum and the overflowing wastepaper basket in the bathroom, it looked like she was . . . done.

The wave of sadness that came didn't make sense. She was super excited about moving and setting up a household with Nate. It didn't matter to her that his place out there in the woods was small and modest, and Vishous had had to add a layer of *mhis* to make sure they were safe from the enemy.

Finally, she was making her own home. With the male she loved.

Which was what you did. Young didn't stay young forever. Growing up was as inexorable a process as dying, and if you were lucky, you made it to maturity in one piece. Or semi-one piece.

The question was what you did when you were there. And who out of your family of origin was still by your side: At some point, after the dependency of childhood dissipated, blooded relations had to be chosen like friends—or should be.

Turning to the moving boxes that had been filled, taped shut, and stacked by the exit, she regarded each one as an adult version of a child's building blocks set, everything balanced on the base row, the tops ascending like a set of stairs, one box, two box, three box, four . . . and then she was out the door.

She would be back, of course. But it would be as a welcomed guest, not as a resident, and that divide was a valley that would not be crossed, ever again.

Blinking back tears, she measured all the hooks that she needed to remove from the walls. There was only one photograph left to take down, and she went over to the image of a beach scene with the sun hovering at the horizon.

In this room that was being broken down, it looked like a sunset. As she pictured the thing hanging on the wall at Nate's? The image became a sunrise.

If that wasn't a commentary on how perspective changed everything, she didn't know what was.

Reaching up, she took the picture off its mount and held it to her heart. Funny, she couldn't remember exactly when she'd put it up. But she was never going to forget taking it down—

"Hi."

Nalla looked over her shoulder. In the doorway, Bitty was standing with her hands in the pockets of her parka, her sneakers pressed together tight and her shoulders tensed up. Her pink-highlighted hair was down and curling up at the ends, and with the windburn on her cheeks, she'd clearly just come from the outside world.

"Hi," Nalla said. Then she held up her finger in a wait-a-minute. "I found one of your sweatshirts."

She propped the photograph against the wall with the others, and went over to her bureau. The orange Syracuse hoodie she'd set aside was another thing that held a lot of memories.

"Here." She brought it over. "I should have given it back a year ago, but you know, once it gets in a drawer . . ."

Bitty's hands shook ever so slightly. "Thank you."

"You're welcome." Nalla stepped back and motioned around. "As you can see, I'm—"

"I'm really sorry. About what I said that night we fought. I didn't mean it. I don't know what was wrong with me—"

Nalla held her palm up. "Please. I was being ridiculous and defensive. You were right about everything, including the fact that those photographs . . ." She bent down and turned the sunrise/sunset back around so the image showed. "These pictures are of places I will never go."

"But they're also windows into the world up above and you love them. I had no right to attack what you like to look at."

"Well, at the time?" She smiled. "I was tearing down your guru for no good reason. Fair's fair."

"She's not my guru, I swear. I just . . ." Bitty's eyes lingered on the building-block boxes. "I'd like to move on with my life someday, too. I'm really happy for you and Nate."

"Thanks, Bitty. That means a lot."

"I also came here to thank you."

Nalla frowned. "For what?"

"L.W. told me what you did that night I went to Bathe. With those guys."

"Assholes, I'm telling you."

"And totally not my type, as it turns out. But thanks for watching out for me."

"I always have your back. That's what true friends are for."

There was a long pause. And then Nalla blurted, "I miss you—"

"I really miss you—"

They both laughed, and the hugging was as natural as their friendship had always been, something that just happened. When they stepped back, there were sniffles, there were tears—and underneath the emotion, there was the sense that the world was back on track, that which had been out of sync now fully realigned.

Funny, how a person could be your sister even if you two weren't related—

"Are you guys ready?" As Bella appeared in the doorway, her smile was easy, and she leaned against the jamb and shook her head. "Wow. This is the end of an era. And the start of a new one."

"I'm just a phone call away." Nalla's throat grew tight again. "And I will always answer."

The special smile that was sent her way was marked with watery eyes. "The same is true for us. Now come on, you don't want to be late to your own farewell party, right?" Abruptly, things got serious. "Fritz has been cooking all day long, and if we don't start eating soon, we're going to be up to our elbows in leftovers. Although . . . I guess that's not the worst thing that could happen."

Nalla laughed and looked at Bitty. "You're coming, right?"

The female grinned, her eyes crinkling at both corners. "I wouldn't miss it for the world."

They laughed and started to talk fast again—but then Nalla glanced at her *mahmen*. Bella had stepped into the empty room and was making a slow turn.

Bitty lowered her voice. "I'll meet you there, okay?"

"Yes, thanks."

After the female left, Nalla walked forward and took her *mahmen*'s hand. "Don't be sad. I really am only a phone call away, and Nate and I have family Last Meal on the calendar, every Sunday. We'll see you all the time."

Bella turned and smiled, even though her eyes were tearing up. "Oh, I'm not sad. This has all worked out better than I could have imagined. Right?"

"Well, Father no longer wants to murder the male I love," Nalla said with a dry grin. "So yes, I have to agree."

After they laughed, her *mahmen* reached up to touch her cheek. "If I'm somber, it's because an era of my life has to end . . . in order for the rest of yours to begin. And it's really wonderful because that's how it's supposed to work. Young move along and they move out and they make their own way, and if you're lucky—and oh, sweetheart, we're *so* lucky, we really are—when that time comes, they take you with them. Here." Bella touched Nalla's head. "And here." She touched Nalla's sternum. "It's the immortality we get with the love, the family, and the traditions we pass on to the next generation."

Nalla sniffled. "Oh, *mahmen*, I love you."

"And I love you, my daughter. You're everything I'd hoped for, and you and Nate are going to have a wonderful future together." Bella took a bracing inhale. "Okay, let's go. Let's go to your party. Maybe if we're lucky, your father will sing for us all."

Linking arms, they stepped out of Nalla's bedroom together.

"He's gonna pick a song that makes everybody cry," Nalla muttered. "He always does that."

"Fritz will make sure there's Kleenex. That *doggen* always comes prepared."

◆   ◆   ◆

Two hours later, Fritz Perlmutter was fretting over the buffet.

The gathering had proceeded most satisfactorily, with his master, the First Family, and the Black Dagger Brotherhood arriving at the prescribed time, along with the other fighters and members of the inner circle, who brought their mates and young as appropriate, the lot of them all filling out the circular room with a critical mass that guaranteed a convivial and cheerful atmosphere.

But verily, he wished they were all back in the mansion.

It was not that he objected to the simple, modern furnishings, although of course, one wished to provide a bit of splash to things, and CorningWare was not Royal Crown Derby.

The problem was that the guests stayed within the confines of the room. For the entire duration.

Back up at the mansion, following the dessert course, all and sundry would proceed into the billiards room. That vast expanse of green felt tables, leather sofas, and the TV—which Fritz really didn't approve of, honestly, as the flashing lights of it were garish and the content was mostly absurd, especially when the sire Lassiter had upon his palm the remote—as well as the serve-yourself bar—of which he also did not really approve, but one needed to bear up—provided not only the square footage but also the amusements, for the household and guests to be well occupied.

Such that the food could be cleared before it wilted, the plates, sterling, and glassware cleaned, and the staff then freed up to attend to other duties.

Here? The guests all stayed put.

Casting his eyes across the males and females, he caught the worried gaze of his two best maids. They had leaned around the doorway into the commercial kitchen that was off to the left. All he could do was shake his head: *Not yet.*

Their stares flared with the same kind of worry that consumed his own heart, but there was naught to do. As much as he hated inefficiency, he had no choice, for the only thing more intolerable than a decaying buffet was servers clearing platters and punch bowls through a party.

He needed to wait.

Tugging his jacket sleeves down, he clasped his hands behind his back and regarded his master's guests.

It would have been difficult for him to determine exactly when he began to notice their faces, but soon he did. The younger generation had cloistered together around the couple of the hour, Nalla and Nate, whose collective radiance was like a hearth that moved about the gathering, pausing to warm all whom they sought out.

'Twas lovely to see them so in love, not only for their sakes, but because surely this meant that there would soon be cause for a proper mating ceremony, something that they had not had for ages. If he was lucky, the King would order him to open the big house upon the mountain once again, and that would require weeks and weeks of cleaning and preparation before one even considered the necessaries of the occasion itself.

'Lo, he was atwitter just upon the contemplation of such efforts. And as he thought about such happy future endeavors, he searched out his master—and there Wrath was, with his dog at his side and his *shellan* under his arm.

For a moment, Fritz found himself, once again, back at the door he had opened that had changed everything, the one that had ruined decades.

Though the outcome of it all had been a miracle, the blame was still with him. And it would stay with him. For thirty years, there had been no matings, because of him. No en masse celebrations of the calendar or festival observances. No true happiness or joy. Just a funeral in the Tomb, where those who should not have been in such a sacred place had been welcomed by the Brotherhood because they had all lost their—

Wrath's head turned sharply, those black wraparound sunglasses pointing in Fritz's direction.

As if the great Blind King could read into his loyal servant's mind and see the torment that had bubbled to the fore.

That regal head shook back and forth—sternly—a command that was nonverbal, but that nonetheless traveled through the laughter and the conversation, through the bodies as they moved through the space . . . through the time that had been lost.

Fritz took a deep breath. And let it go.

For who was he to disregard an order from his beloved master?

Just as he released the exhale, the subtle chords of a guitar started to emanate throughout the room, and people, drawn to the sound, quieted and turned to the source.

Zsadist had sat down in a chair, and was strumming an instrument that was the color of honey, his skull-trimmed head bowed, his dagger hand plucking the strings.

And then he started singing, "Would you know my name . . ."

Oh, that voice. Like that of an angel, and the words that were sung, set to that simple melody, wove their way through the crowd . . . and brought the *doggen* out from the back, Fritz's staff in their uniforms lining themselves up.

". . . time can break your heart . . ."

And though Fritz attempted to remain professional, he was seduced into the moment as well, and he looked at them all with great warmth and affection. From the original Brothers whom he had served for so long, to his Queen, whom he had watched over when her father could not, and her human friend, Butch, whom he'd been sure would end up bloodying the carpet . . . to Bella and John Matthew and Xhex, Rehvenge and Ehlena . . . to Qhuinn and Blaylock, Payne and Dr. Manello, Saxton and Ruhn, and the whole of the Band of Bastards—and all of the others who had come unto the group, funneling into the household through destiny's hand, congregating here out of common purpose and loyalty, living their lives, together.

It was such a privilege to serve them all, and as he regarded them, he thought, too, of the ones they had lost along the way.

". . . no more tears . . . in heaven . . ."

The human words touched him and he prayed they were true. He needed to believe that the afterlife was just like this party the now.

All of them together.

For an eternity.

ACKNOWLEDGMENTS

With so many thanks to the readers of the Black Dagger Brotherhood books! This has been a long, marvelous, exciting journey, and I can't wait to see what happens next in this world we all love. I'd also like to thank Meg Ruley, Rebecca Scherer and everyone at JRA, and Hannah Braaten, Jamie Selzer, Sarah Schlick, Jennifer Bergstrom, Carrie Feron, Jennifer Long, and the entire family at Gallery Books and Simon & Schuster.

To Team Waud, I love you all. Truly. And as always, everything I do is with love to and adoration for both my family of origin and of adoption.

Oh, and thank you to Naamah, my Writer Dog II, and Obie, Writer Dog-in-Training, and Bar-bar, all of whom work as hard as I do on my books!